THE
NIGHT
CHASERS

Also by Jamey Cohen

DMITRI

THE NIGHT CHASERS

JAMEY COHEN

Seaview Books
New York

This is a work of fiction. The people and events described or depicted in this novel are fictitious, and any resemblance to actual incidents or individuals is unintended and coincidental.

Manufactured in the United States of America.

FIRST EDITION.

Seaview Books/A Division of PEI Books, Inc.

Library of Congress Cataloging in Publication Data

Cohen, Jamey.
      The night chasers.

      I. Title.
PS3553.O4243N5   813'.54   80-54518
ISBN 0-87223-685-4   AACR2

Designed by Tere LoPrete

The author and publisher gratefully acknowledge permission to reprint lyrics from:

STRANGERS IN THE NIGHT
Words by Charles Singleton and Eddie Snyder.
Music by Bert Kaempfert.
© Copyright 1966 by Champion Music Corporation and Screen Gems–
    Columbia Music, Inc., N.Y., N.Y.
USED BY PERMISSION. ALL RIGHTS RESERVED.

To Cassy

Simia quam similis turpissima bestia nobis.
　　　　　　　　—Ennius (239–169 B.C.)

"Hungry, huh? What do you want to eat?"

"Want candy."

"No. Candy is for later."

"Want candy."

"I said later. How about a tomato?"

"Rotten stink." He grabbed hold of his nose and shook his head.

"All right. One piece of candy, that's all."

"Damn me good." He sucked the candy and smacked his lips.

"Well, that's all you're going to get. Eat your tomato."

"Nut nut!" He threw the tomato on the floor. It landed with a splat.

"Joey!"

"Sorry sorry throw wrong."

"You bet it was. Damn, where did I put those paper towels?"

"There." He pointed to a cupboard where the paper towels lay partly concealed behind a stuffed bear.

"You rascal. Did you hide them there?"

"Joey good."

"Tell the truth."

"Fran hide."

"Oh, really? Fran can't reach that high. Tell the truth."

"Joey hide bad," he admitted.

"That *was* bad. Now clean up your mess."

He wiped the floor.

"Mess gone Joey love Abbie."

"Abbie loves Joey, too."

"You fine you."

She smiled. "You're fine, too."

"Good," he signed, his fingers and thumb meeting in the quick, delicate embraces of the American Sign Language. "Me fine animal gorilla."

A nasty beast the Simian: How dreadfully is he like to man.

—Ennius (239–169 B.C.)

I

Abbie Guisbourne became a celebrity on June 19 at 6:42 A.M., Eastern Standard Time, the moment that week's *Time* magazine hit the stands. Her passage into the public domain was uneventful. Sparks didn't fly. Champagne didn't flow. She didn't even know the article had appeared until ten days later, when her copy of the magazine arrived. The mail service to Burundi, the small Central African nation that had been her home for five years, was notoriously slow.

The story under the picture ran two columns. It tersely described the Burundi Primate Research Center and the work Abbie did there, teaching gorillas to converse in Amesal, the American Sign Language used by more than half a million deaf people in North America. The article characterized her more lavishly: "Guisbourne," it read, "resembles a latter-day Annie Sullivan, brandishing all the fiery perseverance indigenous to that Irish miracle worker."

Abbie cringed while reading the line. A latter-day Annie Sullivan? Did that mean her gorillas resembled Sullivan's famous pupil, Helen Keller? She thought not.

Granted, similarities existed in the two teachers' approaches. The most apparent: each woman's dogged determination to have complete control over her charge. It was why Annie Sullivan had separated Helen from her family. And it was why Abbie Guisbourne, at the age when most of her friends were immersed in the cultivation of family roots, was deep in the African interior, "talking" with apes.

The photograph accompanying the article was quite flattering—to her, at least. Joey, the youngest of her three gorillas, was shown picking his nose. Abbie's other two apes, Winston and Fran, weren't in the picture. The photographer had been so visibly unnerved by Joey, who in a typically brazen move had begun chewing the man's tripod, that Abbie hadn't suggested including them. She regretted that now. "The apes," continued the story, "are remarkably gentle, and often display the same—"

A loud grunt sounded from the far corner of the courtyard. Abbie stopped reading. She looked over the top of the magazine and rose to her feet in disgust.

"Stop it, Joey," she signed to the male gorilla sitting no more than fifteen feet from her chair. Her fingers moved in a complementary rhythm to her spoken words. "Now, play good."

She tossed the *Time* to the ground and walked to where Fran had tumbled. The female gorilla's coat was covered with dirt.

"Fran, you're too goddamn trusting." Abbie brushed the rich, black fur of the ape. The resulting cloud of dust tickled her nostrils. "I'd move on to a different game if I were you."

The gorilla placidly scratched her nose.

Joey got off his haunches and sidled to where the rope with which they'd been playing had landed. He grasped one frayed end, the product of innumerable tug-of-wars, and dragged it to Fran.

"Fran play," Joey signed, extending the rope toward her.

Fran made no move for the rope.

"Joey tug," he signed, shaking the rope slightly so that a free end dangled in front of Fran's face.

Fram sat motionless, seemingly uninterested.

"That's it, Fran," said Abbie. "Don't let him bully you into it."

Joey dropped the rope by his side.

"Please tug," he signed, moving his right palm in a flat circle over his chest.

The female gorilla scratched her nose once more and put out her hand.

"Good tug," she signed.

"God, Fran, you're so gullible," Abbie muttered. "Don't expect me to come to your rescue again."

Abbie sat in the chair outside her trailer and resumed reading the magazine. Sunlight bounced off the pages and caused her to squint even though she was wearing new sunglasses. The last pair had been irreparably damaged when Winston tried them on for size.

Across the courtyard, strains of "Strangers in the Night" wafted over the tops of the trailers. Permanently affixed to the ground, the trailers were laid out in a rectangle and occupied one corner of the five-acre site. In the United States, the research center might have been mistaken for a mobile-home park. A fence defined the perimeter of the compound.

Already the day promised to be a scorcher. The sun hung low in the sky, stoking the chemical merry-go-rounds of plants in the courtyard with an almost artificial brightness. It was not, contrary to what Abbie once had believed, normal weather by Burundian standards. Like most Americans, she had visualized Africa as one big tropical jungle; it had taken considerable readjustment in her thinking to dispel that image.

In actuality, only the area once called the Belgian Congo fit the popular stereotype. Burundi, landlocked between Tanzania and Zaire, consisted mainly of savannah—flat, grassy areas broken up by occasional trees—and green-ribboned rolling hills. Though the country straddled the equator, its high altitude compensated for its location in the Torrid Zone. Temperatures on the Ruizizi Plain, where the capital city of Bujumbura lay, averaged 73°F. It did not normally get this hot—except on anomalies like today.

Today's was a heat that sapped strength and smothered the body in a prickly sweat. It was an African day that pressed every living thing low to the ground.

Except, it seemed, gorillas.

"He's going to do it again," said David, one of Abbie's

students from Brice University, perhaps the one with the most promise in the field. He sat beside her. "Just watch. I'll bet you Joey does it again."

Abbie glanced up from the magazine.

"He gets such delight from it," she said. "That's really perverse, you know? Even for a gorilla. And Fran always falls for it."

"Sort of like Charlie Brown and Lucy," said David. "Each time poor old Charlie Brown thinks Lucy's going to hold the football so he can kick it. And each time she pulls it out from under him."

"You're right. Look. He *is* going to do it. I can tell by the way he's dancing around. Little sadist."

On the far side of the courtyard, Fran and Joey were engaged in a tug-of-war contest. Leaning backward, they pulled on the taut rope. Joey gave an especially hard tug which jerked Fran forward, and, in response, the female gorilla twisted her body to the side and pulled.

At that precise moment Joey released his end of the rope. Fran fell backward, hit the ground, and flipped upside down. The rope cracked past her feet. Joey grunted happily.

Abbie wearily shook her head. It looked as if it was going to be one of those days.

Fran picked herself up off the ground and glared at her playmate. Before Joey had time to retrieve the rope, and possibly entice the female gorilla into another game, Fran scampered to where Abbie sat and plopped down at her mistress's feet. She twined her left hand around Abbie's ankle. Apparently tug-of-war had lost its enchantment for her.

"I wouldn't want to play with him either, Fran." Abbie smoothed the ruffled hair on top of Fran's head. "He cheats."

"Want something to eat, Fran?" David signed to the gorilla.

"Good eat," Fran signed.

"Okay. And how about something to drink?"

The gorilla was momentarily distracted; she swatted a fly from her nose.

"Drink, Fran?" David moved his fist up and down, the thumb extended so that it touched his lip. "Milk?" He made the motion with his right hand of a man milking a cow.

The gorilla yawned, moving her hand in what might have been construed as a gesture of insouciance had it not been for the position of her fingers.

"Beer," she signed.

"Beer?" Abbie sat upright in her chair. "Since when did she start asking for beer? You've been distilling the pombe again, haven't you?"

Pombe, a weak beer made from fermented bananas, was a popular beverage among the students who worked as volunteers at the center. David recently had experimented with brewing it.

"Yeah, but I swear to you, Abbie, this time I got it right. I just dug it up too early last time."

"David, you made the whole camp sick."

"Fran liked it."

"What doesn't Fran like?" Abbie said. "Give her milk."

"All right," David said, leading Fran toward the trailer that served as a kitchen. "Milk, Fran," he signed.

The gorilla stopped and signed, "Beer Dave," and patted the young man's buttocks before resuming her walk. David shook his head and laughed.

"You're such a tart, Fran—"

While the two crossed the courtyard, Joey, who'd been busy sticking his arm in the dirt and licking off the ants that climbed aboard, rolled to his feet in hot pursuit. The ape had an extra sense when it came to the discussion or whereabouts of food.

"Joey," Abbie called to him.

The gorilla swung around to look at her. Abbie made a motion with her hand, universal in its meaning.

"Come here," she signed. "Where do you think you're going?"

"Hungry," he signed, moving a curved hand from his neck to his chest.

"You just ate."

The ape puzzled over her response for a moment.

"Thirsty." He closed his fist and, with index finger extended, touched his throat.

"The faucet's over there"—she pointed—"as you well know."

The ape looked once more in the direction of Fran and David and reluctantly walked to the outdoor spigot. He turned the handle.

In the wild, gorillas are rarely observed drinking water. They rely on dew and on water content in native vegetation. Not so with the three gorillas in Abbie's care. Unlike their counterparts to the north in Rwanda's Virunga range, Winston, Joey, and Fran drank often. And with considerable relish.

Joey bent back his head and a frothy spray poured into his mouth. The water splashed the coarse black fur on his arms and beaded on his flat nose. Underneath the drops, his thick facial skin shone like polished leather. A year younger than Fran, he was, at 155 pounds, heavier than she, and the red cast to his cranial hair made it easy to tell the two apart even at a distance.

After the young gorilla sated his thirst, he twisted the handle to the right, and strolled back toward Abbie. To one unfamiliar with gorillas, his sitting posture might have appeared comical: short legs bent and slightly spread; feet pointed in toward each other, almost as if he were pigeontoed; stomach bulging, practically resting on the ground; long, powerful arms dangling at his sides. He smacked his lips contentedly.

"Ever since that night, we've been together, lovers at first sight—"

From a trailer on the opposite side of the courtyard, the last notes of the Frank Sinatra song rolled out from a cassette. Winston, the big ape, sat against the trailer steps, his feet touching the tape deck. Though barely into his adult years, Winston, at age nine—some three years older than Joey—could not be mistaken for an adolescent. Weighing 325 pounds, he more than equaled the size of Joey and Fran put together, and already had developed, ahead of schedule, the large bony crest on the top of his head that distinguishes an adult male gorilla. His small ears, set back on his head like a human's ears, seemed oddly incongruous.

"—in love forever, it turned out so right, for strangers in the night—"

Larry, a lanky student assigned to Winston, sat next to the tape deck, within reach of a chain that led to Winston's leg. Leg chains were a precaution used when the gorillas were outside.

"—ooh-bi-doo-bi-doo—"

As the Sinatra song played its closing notes, Sal, one of the stray cats in the compound, rolled over in front of Winston. Salvadore was a mystery to the inhabitants of the primate center. By all rights he should have been terrified of the gorillas, but the gray-and-white feline comported himself with nonchalance. Abbie suspected that he was a little addled.

Winston doted on the cat and would carry him about for long periods of time, flopping the animal around in assorted positions. At first, the gorilla's behavior surprised Abbie. Though undeniably fond of her, Winston was not as demonstrative as Joey and Fran. Those two, veritable gluttons for affection, often unnerved the new students with their loving reception. One student compared the enthusiastic reaction his arrival elicited to the sensation a doomed man experiences upon being feted before being led to the electric chair. Winston meted out his affection more scrupulously; cats were high on the list.

Winston picked up Salvadore and, after sniffing the cat, swung him over his head. Sal closed his eyes and drooped unconcernedly around the ape's neck.

"Hey, Abbie," Larry called across the courtyard, "I'm going to take Winston back inside in a bit. He and I are scheduled for the computer this hour, right?"

"Yeah," said Abbie. "You may have to play around with the voice synthesizer, though. It's been on the blink."

"Okay, is there any specific—"

Winston nudged Larry's knee.

"Oh, no, Winston," signed Larry. "Not again."

"Music." Winston ran his right hand along the inside of his left forearm from wrist to elbow and back again.

The cassette deck had clicked off.

"No, I can't stand it. We've heard 'Strangers in the Night' half a dozen times already today. I'm going crazy." Larry turned back to Abbie. "Now, about the computer program you want me to run—"

"Music," repeated the ape.

"*No!* No more Frank Sinatra. Do you understand? Enough of Frank Sinatra!"

"Music now hurry," signed the ape, vigorously shaking both hands next to his head to convey immediacy.

"All right, but a new tape." Larry fished in the pocket of the tape deck and withdrew a cassette. "Bruce Springsteen. Now, that's music."

Winston regarded the cassette with suspicion. Its label was red. The Sinatra labels were white. As Sal the cat stretched and jumped off his back, Winston made a grab for the tape.

"Hold on, now," signed Larry. "You just might like him."

He snapped in the Springsteen cassette and pushed the "play" button. Before the first stanza had played, Winston hit the "stop" button.

"You didn't even give it a chance!" Larry pushed the "play" button.

Winston hit the "stop."

"Come on, Winston. Don't be such a pain in the ass."

Larry depressed the "play." The ape punched no more buttons. When the first song ended, Larry ejected the tape and signed:

"That wasn't too bad, was it?"

Winston reached for the cassette and sniffed it. Gently, he laid it on the ground and squashed it flat with his foot. He returned the mangled tape to Larry.

Larry looked from the ape to the cassette and back again. He snapped in a new cassette. Another Sinatra.

"You bobby-soxers never grow up, do you?" The young

man picked up the tape deck and led the gorilla to the computer trailer.

Abbie, who had witnessed the interaction with wry amusement, rose from her chair and stretched. It was time she got back to work, too. She laid the *Time* magazine next to a book she had started but was having trouble completing: *The Day of the Dolphin* by Robert Merle. It was just too farfetched. Who in his right mind would believe that a couple of porpoises could talk with human beings?

Some people just got carried away.

She had not entered primate research with the intention of becoming a celebrity, although the field certainly had produced its share: Jane Goodall, Robert Yerkes, and now Abbie Guisbourne.

Not long ago, she would have considered coverage in a national magazine a remote possibility at best. Yet as a child, when a teacher asked her what she wanted to be when she grew up, she had replied: "A celebrity." For though she lacked a set ambition at the time, Abbie had not wanted to appear unambitious against the backdrop of classmates who believed Destiny would guide them to Congress or NASA or the Dallas Cowboys.

She needn't have worried. Her senior class president became a used-car dealer. Would-be senators never made it beyond student council. But Fate charted her a more promising course. She eluded the gravitational pull that stultified her peers. In her own single-minded way, Abbie achieved her stated childhood goal—if only by the barest definition—by gracing page fifty-eight of *Time*.

It started at the University of Oklahoma. Interested in the study of language and its antecedents, she quickly became a fixture in the linguistics department. There, she fell in love. Twice.

Her love affair with the one, a graduate student who wore his pants too short, lasted two years.

Her love affair with the other continued throughout her

undergraduate career, and indeed until the end of his life. His name was Arthur. He weighed 184 pounds and had luxuriant red hair.

He was an orangutan.

She worked with Arthur for a year and a half. By the time she started her master's degree, he'd gained a large vocabulary from his computer terminal. Whenever he desired food or drink or even entertainment, he punched the keyboard:

"Please machine gimme water period"

"Please machine make music period"

And on one memorable occasion when Arthur had tired of syntax, he punched, "Dirty machine bad," which, loosely translated, meant "Please machine drop dead period"

But Arthur was another linguist's project; however pleased Abbie was with the orangutan's progress, she had other ideas about how best to communicate with an ape. Channeling all queries and answers through a machine was too impersonal. Abbie wanted to speak to the ape herself.

And that meant sign language.

It was not a revolutionary concept. Ten years had passed since Allen and Beatrice Gardner first taught their chimp, Washoe, to sign. Others followed suit, using gorillas and orangutans, and met with considerable success. Abbie had studied their techniques and was eager to advance beyond their work, not merely concentrating on human communication with the apes, but on communication among the apes themselves.

She ran into problems. Years earlier, Africa had banned exportation of the endangered great apes. The United States, like other countries, was forced to depend on in-house breeding to maintain its populations. The last few years had been unprolific ones ("They just won't fuck," said one exasperated zoo official), making it difficult for Abbie to monopolize one, much less two or three, of a facility's apes.

Primate centers offered no better solution. The few scattered across the country either were involved in their own language projects, such as Yerkes in Atlanta, or were strictly interested in behavioral studies, as was San Diego, and thus unwilling to disrupt the habitat of their animals. In addition, since a recent mauling of a psychology student by an orangutan in Cincinnati, institutions which might have provided Abbie an ape were loath to do so for insurance and security reasons.

The turning point came when a friend, using the hackneyed analogy of Mohammed going to the mountain, suggested she journey to Africa and set up shop in its uncharted hinterland, teeming with primates. The notion had not occurred to Abbie. With buoyed spirits she began the arduous task of obtaining grants. Word of her endeavor spread until it found a sympathetic ear, belonging to the provost of a large and richly endowed private institution, Brice University.

Brice already had established a primate research center in southern Burundi that dealt exclusively with chimpanzees. Little more than a group of tin-roofed huts set in the middle of a government park, it provided spartan living for the anthropologists and students who chronicled the behavior of the local chimps. Seventy miles north of the camp was Burundi's capital, Bujumbura, in which Brice kept a small office overseeing the camp.

It was here, in Bujumbura, that Abbie's project found a home, underwritten by Brice and two geographic foundations. The money was put to immediate use. Aside from the obvious expenditure for the gorillas and trailers, a small sum was spent incorporating the old administrative office.

The first year was hard going. Assailed by constant budget worries, requisition forms, language problems, managerial headaches, and assorted miscellaneous woes—ranging from Fran's arthritis to a drop in the banana market—Abbie was in a perpetual state of exhaustion.

She experienced more than occasional discouragement at the tedious pace at which the gorillas learned. What praise she received from colleagues was all too often attenuated by criticism from others. She became especially sensitive to those who called the gorillas' "speech" a calibrated notch above dog tricks, the result of simple behavior modification. She ranted. And raved.

But it was all worth it. Even five years later.

Her rewards were a sense of fulfillment that had previously eluded her, the admiration of those familiar with her work, and the attention of academic circles. Most telling of all, she felt needed. She'd found a niche that no one else could possibly fill. Yet had she dug deep into her complacency, laid it open under a surgeon's scalpel, she would have discovered that it was not the primate center's dependence on her that was ultimately satisfying. The center relied on her in an emotionless, abstract way, as a cog might appreciate a wheel. Rather, it was the gorillas' need of Abbie that made the unavoidable solitude of her lifestyle bearable. A need based on their unstinting affection for her; their joy in her companionship. That was her satisfaction.

Even so, times were occasionally bleak. She tired of the procession of students coming and then going at year's end. She missed some; couldn't wait for others to leave. Although she'd anticipated the loneliness of working in equatorial Africa, even reconciling herself to a moratorium on relationships with men, she'd never fully adjusted to it. She craved not so much the emotional commitment to one man as merely the simple pleasure of his company.

National recognition was fine, but she was thousands of miles away from the country that now applauded her. She sometimes wondered if the price she was paying was too high.

But those moods always passed. For Abbie Guisbourne, there was no other way to live.

II

With the hand holding the garrote, Bunkeya rubbed his aching lower calf; he'd been standing on the leg too long. The slash wound he'd received on his last mission hadn't yet completely healed. It was of little consolation that the man who'd disfigured his leg was dead. Somehow the knowledge made the wound even more grotesque.

Bunkeya had been with the Front Populaire de Libération, or Popular Liberation Front, for one year. When he'd joined he'd been conspicuous because of an absence of nerves, a veritable automaton. His commitment to fomenting revolution in his home country, Zaire, was both sudden and complete. He'd pursued the goal relentlessly, believing the revolution just months away.

It seemed as if ten years had passed since then. The FPL's attempts to disrupt the Zairian government had proved largely ineffectual. Even Dalam, founder of the guerrilla organization, admitted as much. There had been no concomitant tide of insurgent countrymen. No popular uprising, only counter-attacks. The shape of society stayed the same.

The only changes Bunkeya detected were in himself. At the age of twenty-eight, he felt depleted, broken down. The mental sphincter restricting his emotions had lost its rigidity, and they were leaking out. He supposed his fatigue was an occupational hazard, one made more acute by the influx of younger, more energetic men into the FPL. Like the young man by his side. A boy, really, with a boy's vigor.

"Now, remember," said Bunkeya in a whispered tone, "speed counts here. Speed and silence."

The boy listened with quiet attentiveness to Bunkeya's last-minute instructions. He tapped his foot anxiously and stared at the sentry up the road. Bunkeya recalled the feeling: the terrible anticipation; the rush to re-create the destruction of an enemy which the mind already had imagined, the dangerous simplification of it all.

Well, this boy would learn soon enough. It was time.

Bunkeya tapped the young recruit lightly on the shoulder and motioned him forward. At the same time he handed over the coiled garrote. The boy nearly dropped it, a bad sign. The two moved stealthily down the road until the sentry was within striking distance.

Now, said the pressure of Bunkeya's fingers on the boy's arm. And the boy responded.

It was, as Bunkeya feared, a bungled attempt. The boy telegraphed his intentions to the sentry when, less than five feet behind the man, he took a huge breath of air. The sentry began to turn, and the boy hesitated. He'd forgotten Bunkeya's prime directive to carry out the act in one swift move. Over the head and pull back, twist. Over the head and—

Damn it, the boy was off balance. His legs were in the wrong position; he'd have no leverage now. And look. The sentry had a hand under the wire. The other hand clawed at the boy's cheek, thumb waving ominously like the foreleg of a spider. The boy tugged harder, but the sentry's left hand protected his windpipe. The man kicked backward with one of his legs. His foot barely missed the boy's knee.

Bunkeya swiftly took over. In one quick move he twisted the sentry's hand out from under the wire. With his knee against the small of the man's back, he pulled on the garrote. This time there was no obstacle. The result was instantaneous. The man's arms fell limply to his side, and he crumpled in a heap.

One swift move. Over the head and pull back, twist.

The recruit stood in shamed silence where he'd retreated. He nursed a scratch on his cheek.

"That's how it's done," Bunkeya said calmly. "Not how you were doing it. Remember how I told you to do it all in one motion? That's the key. You paused, and that was your downfall."

"But he turned—"

"Only because he heard you. That'll happen. Did you notice I spread my leg back for balance? That way I protected myself from a kick to my knee or a stomp to my instep. And remember your eyes. They're one of your most vulnerable spots. Guard them, or you'll lose them."

"Yes."

"Now, would you like to try again?"

The boy smiled feebly. "Yes."

"All right." Bunkeya nudged the body on the ground with the tip of his shoe. "Time to get up, Saltwi."

The sentry on the ground stirred and rolled over onto his back.

"Christ," he said, examining an elbow skinned during his fall, "I'm getting too old for this."

The recruit offered the man a hand. Once on his feet, the sentry brushed off his pants.

"Didn't hurt you, did we?" asked Bunkeya.

"Didn't feel a thing here"—the sentry loosened the protective brace around his neck—"but my hand hurts like hell."

"Sorry," said the recruit.

"Don't apologize," said the sentry. "All you need is a little more training. You'll learn."

Would he? wondered Bunkeya as he handed the garrote back to the boy. Given time, perhaps. But time was a scarce commodity these days. The FPL, reeling from losses incurred in the last few months, was churning out new recruits with alarming speed. Alone or in pairs, it didn't matter. Few returned. Too fast; too green.

"All right," said Bunkeya, facing the boy, "this time I want you to—"

From up the hill, a man shouted for Bunkeya. Bunkeya waved an arm in response.

"It seems I'm needed back in camp," he said. "Saltwi, you

take over here. And remember," he admonished the recruit, "nothing is ever totally offensive. Keep your defense in mind."

Bunkeya's calf throbbed slightly as he trudged uphill to the camp. Originally a Belgian mining settlement, the camp, a mile from the village of Iddan, stood in a small clearing amid the high, forested hills of eastern Zaire. The actual mining had taken place a quarter of a mile downhill, its site now marked by scarred land. The mine had been abandoned in the late fifties after its supply of tin and manganese ran out, but the half dozen or so cottages that served as living quarters still remained.

No one in the FPL knew for certain how Dalam had learned of the place. Most Zairian mining took place in the south, in the Shaba province. Bunkeya guessed that Dalam had stumbled across the camp when, like other Katangan rebels who had not fled to Rwanda or Zambia after the disastrous Shaba invasion of 1978, he'd sought refuge in the area around northern Lake Tanganyika.

The day sparkled. Bunkeya stood briefly at the crest of the hill to rest his leg, and savored the panorama. Below in the distance, Lake Tanganyika stretched into the horizon. Although Burundi lay on the other side, some fifteen miles away at this point, Bunkeya liked to think of the view as infinite. The scene did not symbolize home to him—no place did any longer—but at least it evoked a familiarity. It was a place to return to. For that alone Bunkeya treasured it.

The lake was fed by streams from both the Zairian and Burundian sides. One such stream ran alongside the FPL camp, emerging from the surrounding forest for a few hundred feet before disappearing back into its depths. The stream's source was in the mountain range that soared behind the FPL camp, the Mitumbas. As one of many small tributaries feeding into Lake Tanganyika, it was unimportant. As a supply of water for the FPL, it was invaluable. Bunkeya splashed a handful of cold water on his neck.

The cottage to which he was directed, on the extreme left, served as Dalam's office. It took a few seconds for Bunkeya's eyes to adjust to the dark interior and discern the three forms seated around the wooden table. He walked toward them.

Kili, one of Dalam's oldest confidants, sat at the far end of the table. Mpinga sat nearest the door. Bunkeya couldn't recall what first had pitted him against Mpinga, but they were long-standing enemies. Perhaps Mpinga was jealous of Bunkeya's influence with Dalam. Or perhaps it went deeper than that. Bunkeya was a Bakongo; Mpinga, a Balunda. The two Bantu tribes had long been rivals.

Bunkeya crossed over to the far end of the table.

Dalam, seated between Mpinga and Kili, did not stop speaking when Bunkeya entered, but acknowledged the latter's presence with a nod. Bunkeya took a seat.

"—and the other ones are suspect," said Dalam. "But we can deal with those later. We have something more important to discuss." He paused. "Engulu's sentence is to be handed down today."

"Yes," said Kili, shaking his head. "A great loss. It's affected the men. No one expected him to be caught. Not Engulu."

"The sentence will be death," said Dalam matter-of-factly.

"We have always known it would be," said Mpinga. "Engulu knew the risk. You can't kill two Burundian police officers and expect to live."

Dalam's eyes narrowed and locked on Mpinga's. Engulu, like Kili, had been his trusted adviser since the beginning.

"One can expect anything," he said.

In the days before Bunkeya attended these meetings, before he'd grown accustomed to his leader's cryptic ways, Dalam's reply would have bewildered him. No longer. Dalam had a fine appreciation for the dramatic. He understated parts of his speech, emphasized others, and cultivated a theatrical timing to his delivery. What often seemed a vague non sequitur or sudden shift in the conversation was Dalam's way of creating the proper atmosphere in which to unveil his thoughts. One merely had to be patient and wait.

"Lumbawa will be sentenced today as well," continued Dalam. "I anticipate a lighter sentence for him."

"How do you want us to break it to the men?" asked Kili.

Dalam did not answer the question outright. The mood was not quite set.

"We have a total of ten men in Burundi's Rumonge prison at this time," he said. "We've lost three others in our last two missions in Burundi. All on jobs that would have given us no trouble last year. Arsenal pickups and the like. What does that say to you?"

He passed his gaze over each man at the table.

"That we should consider shutting down our operations in Burundi," said Bunkeya, stating a view with which he'd long been associated. It was well known that he believed the FPL had overextended itself, that a radical consolidation of resources was needed. "There could be a leak somewhere. We should reroute our armaments along a different line. We've done it before."

"Anything else?" asked Dalam.

"Yes," said Kili. "Because our experienced men are in jail, we're being forced to use raw recruits. And because of their inexperience, they're being caught. So the number of our men in jail keeps spiraling. We can't seem to break the cycle."

Bunkeya nodded, thinking of the boy with the garrote. The recruit stood a good chance of being caught his first time out. Or worse—killed.

"Exactly," said Dalam. "We can't afford to have all that experience rotting in jail. Especially men like Engulu. I see now it was a mistake to send him to Burundi. Anyone would have done. I shouldn't have risked him. But I did." Dalam leaned across the table. "And now, I want him back."

The bald simplicity of the statement took Dalam's three listeners by surprise. They looked to one another for guidance as to how to respond.

"We all do," said Kili, cautiously. "But it's impossible. We can't break Engulu and the others free from prison. Especially now, when our resources—in terms of both manpower and supplies—are so low. What are you suggesting?"

Only Kili, with his status as Dalam's oldest ally, could afford to speak so openly. Even so, it was clear his question had piqued the FPL leader.

"I'm suggesting nothing," said Dalam. "I'm simply placing the topic in front of you for consideration. I want those men back. It'll take us months, even a year, to recuperate from their loss. We don't have that time. We can't afford another backslide. Everyone here at camp knows that. Everyone knows we came here to regroup and reassess."

Yes, thought Bunkeya, we all know. Perhaps Mpinga best of all. His very presence at the table was a concession by Dalam to appease a faction of men disgruntled with the FPL leader. For the first time Dalam had been handed a challenge from within his ranks. He was treading in shallow water and he knew it.

"To reassess," echoed Kili. "Yes. To figure out where to concentrate now. Not to plan a suicidal prison break-in."

"Bunkeya?" said Dalam.

"I agree with Kili. There's no way to get those men back without destroying ourselves."

Dalam's nostrils flared. "And you, Mpinga? We haven't heard from you yet. What are your thoughts?"

"My thought," said Mpinga, slowly, "is that we can get Engulu and the others back without scaling any prison walls."

Mpinga's comment roused Bunkeya's suspicion. In all likelihood, Mpinga was no more enthusiastic about a rescue scheme than he and Kili, but with the two of them in opposition to Dalam, a perfect opportunity existed for Mpinga to curry favor with the FPL leader.

"We don't need to break in," said Mpinga. "We can secure those men's release through pressure elsewhere. We can use bargaining power."

"And with what do we bargain?" asked Kili.

"With destruction. We switch our next few raids to Burundi. Detonate a few bombs, then demand release of our men in exchange for a truce."

"No," said Bunkeya, almost before the other man finished speaking. "We can't lose sight of our goals. We've got to con-

centrate our efforts in Zaire, not Burundi. This is the nation
we're concerned with. As Kili said, our resources are nearly
depleted. The hotel mission scheduled for Saturday will practically wipe us out as it is." Bunkeya referred to a plan organized weeks earlier. "Maybe later such a scheme will be
feasible. At any rate, we'll have to wait until Goe comes in
with the shipment from—"

"Goe won't be coming in," said Dalam, no trace of emotion
in his voice.

His three lieutenants reacted with stunned silence.

"He was caught early this morning," continued Dalam. "In
Burundi. Soon they'll have as many of us in their jails as we
have here in camp."

Dalam's informational network was legendary. He learned
things hours before anyone else through a grapevine of in-
formants. Early knowledge of events gave him power, and
power gave him an aura of omnipotence. Lately, the correla-
tion had weakened; the news he conveyed was all bad. As
now.

"Goe was scheduled to carry out the hotel mission," said
Bunkeya.

"Yes, I know," said Dalam. "It's yours now."

A chill knifed through Bunkeya. He tried not to let it show.
Mpinga was not as impassive. His reaction to the assignment
instantly etched itself in ugly lines on his face, lines that registered both jealousy and anger. He wanted the mission for
himself.

As Bunkeya watched, the lines on Mpinga's face shifted;
their configuration became more difficult to interpret. Bunkeya
wondered what the man was thinking.

"With Goe gone," said Kili, "retrenchment becomes even
more inevitable. We don't have the capacity to pose the kind
of physical threat to Burundi that Mpinga suggests."

"All right," said Mpinga, "so we can't deal with the Burundians on their ground. We'll bring our dealings with them
here. Work on our own ground."

Dalam's eyes bored into Mpinga's. He was intrigued.

Bunkeya recognized all the familiar signs: the way Dalam sat in the chair, a certain angularity to his posture; the way his hands pressed against each other; the arch of his eyebrows.

"What could we possibly do here in Iddan?" asked Kili.

Mpinga smiled. They had played into his hand.

"We can take hostages," he said, directing his answer not to Kili but to Dalam.

Bunkeya started forward in his chair to object. Never before had they seriously considered a kidnapping. Dalam, encouraged by Kili, favored short missions, ones with as little risk as possible. A kidnapping, by its very nature, implied a protracted length of time.

"A kidnapping would only compound our problems," said Bunkeya. "We can't afford to war with two countries at the same time. Zaire is war enough."

"So you want to forget about our men in prison," said Mpinga. "Is that what you're saying, Bunkeya?"

A malicious grin creased Mpinga's face. He had boxed Bunkeya in a corner. Dalam wanted Engulu's release. Anything Bunkeya said against Mpinga's scheme might be read as opposition to that end. He chose his words carefully.

"Kidnap who?" asked Bunkeya. "If all we wanted was money, we could kidnap any wealthy individual. But to secure the release of our men means dealing directly with the Burundian government, not an individual. And governments don't barter. They can't afford to submit to blackmail. It won't work."

"Something can be worked out," said Mpinga.

"Not with the lack of—"

Dalam waved his hand, peremptorily silencing Bunkeya. "It's worth thinking about. Work on it." He stood, an effective halt to further discussion. The FPL leader was not known for his long attention span.

Mpinga looked relieved that Dalam's intervention had saved his plan from being scuttled by Bunkeya. The latter's astute scrutiny had punctured many ill-conceived plans, all too many of them the scions of Mpinga's imagination.

For his part, Bunkeya's distaste for Mpinga was equaled, measure for measure, by his disappointment in Dalam. The leader's judgment was distorted, a result perhaps of his loyalty to Engulu or of the fatigue that afflicted all of them; the cause was of little concern. What mattered was that it spelled disaster. Bunkeya sensed it as surely as if it had been written on the air itself. And the air today was thin and humid.

As he stood facing the hotel clerk, Bunkeya tugged at the tie around his neck. His shirt collar, damp from the moist air, chafed his skin. He longed to remove the tie, but it was imperative that he look the part of a normal guest. What's more, though he did not let the thought fully mature in his brain, he was not sure he could reknot the tie. Until now, he'd had no reason to learn. Nor had most of those back at the Iddan camp.

He accepted the register and pulled a pen from his pocket. His silver cuff links caught the light from a nearby lamp and gleamed. They had been torn from the sleeves of a colonel in the Zairian army who'd been killed during a skirmish with the FPL and were inscribed with the letter "N." Bunkeya penned the name "Nabwe" and returned the register.

The cuff links were not his permanently, of course, but a loan for the duration of the mission. The FPL owned them, just as it owned the clothes he wore. He would have to be careful with them; they would be needed again.

Such cautious forethought was Bunkeya's trademark. It had been a significant factor in his rapid rise in the FPL hierarchy, as had been his fluency in French, his knowledge of explosives, and his reputation for mental toughness. Though not trained in military tactics or dressed in army khakis, Bunkeya was a consummate strategist, capable of quick, logically formulated decisions. Or so he once had been.

"Avez-vous les autres bagages?" asked the clerk.

"Non, seulement celui-ci."

No, just this one. Bunkeya was amused by the clerk's question, or perhaps the tone, one of barely concealed boredom with the obligatory questions he was required to ask his guests. A single or double room? For how many nights? Do you have any other baggage?

How shocked the clerk would be to discover the contents of Bunkeya's bag, and how unlikely that he would. The man was one of those insipid beings incapable of delving beyond the surface facts. A suitcase held clothes, period. Dull-witted men like him would never understand men like Bunkeya. They did not dream—therefore they would never share Bunkeya's dream of a better society; they had no imagination —therefore they could not imagine a war without uniforms and medals.

Bunkeya contemplated what he could do with other bags like this one: blow the whole fucking city apart, probably. But bags like this were difficult to assemble and their price was high. The latest FPL casualty had been killed while attempting to smuggle one. Luckily, the bag Bunkeya had now was quite enough. This time.

The clerk unhooked a room key from the board behind him and reached for a bell on the counter. Impulsively, Bunkeya grabbed his wrist.

"Don't bother. I can carry my own."

The clerk's eyes widened.

"Monsieur will nevertheless need a porter to show you to your room." A flash of pain passed over the clerk's face. Bunkeya realized that he was unconsciously twisting the man's wrist. He released his hold.

"Of course. I completely forgot. You must forgive me."

Bunkeya's palms were sweating, and the wooden handle of the suitcase slid in his hands. He'd made a stupid mistake. Did the clerk suspect that he'd memorized the layout of the hotel? The man's innocent demeanor did not fool him; he would be closely watched from now on. Suddenly Bunkeya felt the weight of the dead man's clothes on his back as if his body were trying to shed a coil of dried skin. He suppressed the panicked rapidity of his heartbeat; he'd made one mistake, he must not compound it. Breathe, in, out, in. Smile. Release suitcase.

He forced himself to drop the bag. The porter lifted it, unconcerned by the slippery handle. They passed under a crystal chandelier, and Bunkeya concentrated on redirecting his thoughts. He fixed on the flashing sprinkle of color in the multifaceted prisms. It was only the second chandelier Bunkeya had seen in the twenty-eight years of his life. The first was branded into his memory.

It was the day the crowd gathered in the square. The chandelier sparkled through the doorway of the government building as hundreds sought relief for communities devastated, like Bunkeya's, by the year-long drought. The relief never materialized, but something else did. Something horrible. He tried not to think about it.

The porter ushered Bunkeya to an elevator, and they ascended the three floors in silence. The room was down a short hallway. Once inside, Bunkeya bolted the door. He laid the suitcase carefully on the bed, unlocked each of its latches with a different key, and removed the layers of clothing haphazardly, tossing them on the blue carpet. Deftly, he felt for the hidden trigger that released the bottom of the case and depressed it. The false bottom sprang open easily.

The bomb had arrived undamaged. Bunkeya removed the padding and examined the timer and detonator to ensure that their delicate mechanisms were in working order. The briefcase packed among the clothes had weathered the trip in fine condition, too.

A large piece of paper, folded in quarters, fell from the briefcase onto the bed. Bunkeya knew from his instructions what it was and stuffed it into the inner pocket of his jacket.

"Monsieur Nabwe?"

The knock on the door startled him. Bunkeya stood perfectly still, his forehead glistening. He wasn't expecting anyone. Dalam and the others were hundreds of miles away. He rubbed his hand across his face and reproached himself for the slip at the registration desk. The clerk was probably checking up on him. Bunkeya kicked the clothes to the far side of the bed and replaced the false bottom in the suitcase.

"Un instant," he called to the person behind the door.

Rumpling the bed, he placed the suitcase next to the bureau and removed his shoes and jacket.

"Oui?" He opened the door.

"Votre stylo, monsieur," said a bellboy, handing Bunkeya a pen he'd accidentally left at the registration desk.

Stupid. Another stupid mistake. Though the sun was nearly set, Bunkeya sweated anew, a paranoiac luster coating his skin. He reached into his pocket and brought out a crumpled bill.

"Merci, monsieur!" The bellboy's eyes lighted as he curled his fingers around the bill. He was perhaps fifteen.

Had it been another time and situation, Bunkeya might have taken the boy aside and warned him of becoming dependent on another man's money. The boy might not have understood, for he was malnourished and money meant a staving off of hunger. Bunkeya himself had known hunger. He, too, had not understood—until the day his world ripped apart.

The boy departed, and Bunkeya drank from a flask of whiskey that he carried with him, a preface to his two-hour wait. He had not always carried the whiskey—not always relied on its easy sedation. Perhaps it was the unfamiliarity of the hotel or the pile of clothes at his feet, stripped from bodies still warm, that made him seek its solace now. Or perhaps it was simply to deaden the pangs of his disintegration into a man who created enemies from what once had been shadows. He was a stranger, now, to himself.

The resolve he once possessed was gone. With its passing he no longer viewed himself as a revolutionary striving for egalitarianism, but as a mercenary killing because it was a way of life. The transformation sickened him. He could hear the anguished screams that accompanied the blasts in the night in all their tortured, clarion intensity. Once his ears had been deaf to them.

The two hours passed in dull silence. At a quarter to eight, steeped in perspiration, Bunkeya lugged the repacked suitcase and briefcase down a side staircase and into a nearby rest room. He placed the suitcase inside a storage closet next to an old mop and departed with the briefcase.

The restaurant was located just off the lobby. Though many of its diners were guests of the hotel, it catered to the public at large, its main entrance being off one of the hotel's side streets. Bunkeya hoped to see some of the upper echelon of the Zairian army there, but he spotted only one man in uniform. Perhaps Dalam's information was wrong. The restaurant might once have been a favorite spot for the army elite, but apparently no longer.

A waiter appeared at his table. Bunkeya ordered the coq au vin and a half-carafe of red wine, speaking faultless French.

When a party of army officers entered the restaurant, smug with self-aggrandizement, Bunkeya barely could keep himself from detonating his handiwork there and then. He hoped they would sit near his table, very near, and when they did, he noted the general in their midst. Dalam would be pleased. Bunkeya's meal arrived, and he ate it with slow, deliberate bites, giving the military party time to settle in, then he crumpled his napkin on the table.

"Rien de plus, monsieur?"

"Non, merci. Ça suffit. L'addition, s'il vous plaît."

The waiter bumped against the table when he returned with the check, and the briefcase rocked back and forth, teetering on edge for a split second before coming to rest against Bunkeya's foot. Clumsy fool, thought Bunkeya, you could have killed us all. He quickly signed the check and asked directions to the rest room, waiting until the waiter left to bend down, ostensibly to tie his shoe, and press the button on top of the briefcase.

The party of army officers was on its third round of drinks when Bunkeya looked over his shoulder at them for a final time. It was a bittersweet image, for at that very moment a young couple was being seated nearby. As he hurried from the room, his thought of just a moment ago when the waiter bumped the table—*you could have killed us all*—reverberated in his head with new meaning. Bunkeya actually had meant "You could have killed *me*," for it was painfully obvious, as he scanned the faces of those in the restaurant, that the killing of "us" had been his intention from the very start.

In the bathroom, he retrieved his suitcase from the storage closet. He took the folded piece of paper from his jacket and smoothed its creased lines before attaching it to the door of the bathroom. It was addressed to the police and ended with a rough drawing of a crocodile, a symbol known to the various Zairian law enforcement agencies as the signature of the FPL.

To reach the alley and his car, he used a corridor leading to a back door of the hotel. Dalam had instructed him to leave the scene immediately, but Bunkeya did not, choosing instead to circle the hotel until he was directly opposite the restaurant's street entrance. He waited, the car's motor idling.

At that moment, the bellboy who'd delivered Bunkeya's pen appeared on the opposite sidewalk, his arms laden with clothes from the dry cleaners. He was headed for the servant's entrance to the restaurant, which offered a shortcut to the hotel lobby.

Bunkeya did not hesitate. He called to the boy, requesting his help.

"Porteur, j'ai besoin d'assistance."

"Monsieur?"

"Vitement."

The bellboy lumbered across the street, but his face was alive with curiosity. He was ten feet from the car when the explosion ruptured the tranquillity of the block. Bunkeya's eyes closed, but he heard the roar of breaking glass and twisting metal, the sounds of people screaming and moaning as they found their bodies fused to broken concrete, the stench of scorched flesh in their nostrils. And, above the din, he was certain he heard the crying of a young boy.

He opened his eyes and the bellboy stared back at him, still clutching the pile of clothes, his mouth agape. Bunkeya did not wait any longer. He shifted the car into first gear and glided down the street and out of sight. He had stayed for those who cried out. Their suffering would be known to God, for he was their witness; he would carry those screams in his head forever. As he drove, he prayed, at first wordlessly, then out loud. Prayed, did this executioner, that their souls would find a better rest.

III

"Okay, who's got the baseball?" asked Abbie.

"I think Fran took it," said David.

"Fran, have you got the ball?" signed Abbie.

"Come chase hurry," signed the ape.

"Ah, shit," said Abbie. "Fran wants to play hide-and-go-seek. That means she hid the ball again. How many times does this make?"

"That's number four this week," answered David.

"We never should have taught her to play that game. That goes down in the records as our number one mistake: 'Warning to future linguists—Do not teach your gorillas to play hide-and-go-seek. They will turn into kleptomaniacs.' You know, some archeologist will uncover this place in a thousand years and he'll find a graveyard of baseballs. Isn't that right, Fran?"

The gorilla recognized her name and yelled excitedly, a cross between a belch and a grunt.

"Abbie chase," Fran signed.

"First, Fran, please bring back the ball. Winston and I want to play," signed Abbie.

Winston sat unconcernedly on the other side of the court-yard, smelling his foot. He yawned and did a somersault, coating his blue-black fur with dust.

"Chase," Fran signed.

"No, we're not going to play hide-and-go-seek. Now get the ball."

The gorilla didn't move.

"Where is the ball?" Abbie signed.

"Don't know." The ape placed an index finger to her temple and shook her head sideways.

"So you're going to be that way about it, huh? Well, Fran, two can play at that game. David, get us another baseball, will you please?"

Abbie walked over to Winston.

"David will bring us a new ball," she signed. "Fran took the other one."

"Fran bad," Winston signed, passing an open palm in front of his mouth.

"Yes, Fran shouldn't have hidden the ball."

"Rotten bad Fran."

"Yes."

The large ape hooted loudly, reached his arm underneath him, and pulled out a baseball.

"Here ball funny Winston." The gorilla rolled over with delight and brushed two fingers against the side of his nose. "Funny."

"Very amusing," said Abbie. "David, forget the baseball. Winston had it. For once Fran wasn't the culprit. I guess she was trying to get me to play tag, not hide-and-go-seek."

Abbie backed across the courtyard while Winston readied himself. She tossed the ball and he easily snatched it out of the air. He threw it back underhanded.

"Here ball throw," Fran signed, eager to join the game.

"You won't hide it?" signed Abbie.

"No."

"Okay." Abbie tossed the ball lightly. The female gorilla caught it and hightailed it across the courtyard, disappearing behind one of the trailers.

"Damn it, there she goes again. You'd think I'd know better by now. Larry?"—Abbie gestured to another assistant—"Follow her, will you? See where she's stashing the balls."

The young man nodded and ran after the gorilla.

"David," said Abbie, "bring me a football, will you? That's too big for her to hide."

David trudged across the courtyard. "Make sure she doesn't get her hands on this one."

"What's so special about it?"

"It's mine."

"Okay," said Abbie, smiling. "Winston, here comes the ball." She threw a low spiraling pass. The ape caught the ball and threw it awkwardly back to her. "Good throw. Okay, here comes another."

She let loose the football. Winston caught it and hugged it close to his body. The football popped, leaving the confused gorilla with a wad of crumpled leather.

"No, no!" yelled David. "It took me months to get that down here from the States!"

"Ball?" signed Winston, looking for the missing pigskin.

Abbie sighed and eased herself to the ground.

"You know," she said, "playtime is hell."

It was comfortable inside Fran's trailer. Not as cool as Abbie's trailer would be, since the apes were so susceptible to respiratory ailments, but cooler than outside. The intricate ventilation system, designed with humidifiers and refined thermostatic controls, was just one of several precautions Abbie took to ensure the gorillas' health. A standing requirement existed that everyone in the camp undergo tuberculosis tests and chest X rays every six months.

Despite the elaborate safeguards, despite the advantage of operating in the gorillas' native clime, they had still lost Ngagi. Abbie's first ape had died of influenza early into the project. Abbie did not often talk about it. Though the ape was not a human being, nor had anyone at the compound ever treated her as such, Abbie grieved no less for the animal, separated as they were by an intractable evolutionary gulf, than she would have for a friend.

"What took you so long?" asked Abbie when David entered the room with a large box.

"I couldn't find them. Chandra was using the toys with

Joey earlier and didn't put them back." He dumped the box on a nearby table and pried back the top. "Which ones do you want?"

"I'll just pick them as we go along," said Abbie.

The box was filled with stuffed animals. Monkeys. Pigs. Rabbits. Tigers. Many representing animals the gorillas had never seen in real life. Most were rubbed bald, their stitches unraveling, plastic eyes dangling from one thread, mouths stiff with dried glue from prior attempts to repair them. Rather like the refugees found inside Salvation Army receptacles during the Christmas season. Only these toys were brand new.

"Not holding up too well, are they?" Abbie bit off a stray thread from the belly of a frog. "Isn't that right, Fran?"

Fran, sitting in a corner, responded with a belch-grunt.

Abbie sat in front of the gorilla as David pulled a notebook from one of the shelves. The shelves were built high out of the apes' reach, above what the students called "the striking zone."

"David, this is just going to be a drill." Abbie delved into the box and came out with a canary. "Okay, Fran. What is this?" She waved the stuffed animal before the gorilla.

Fran gazed down at her fingers and inspected their fleshy tips. It wasn't a good omen. The three gorillas had short attention spans. If Fran wasn't interested at the outset of a drill, the chances of having a productive session were virtually nil.

"Look here, Fran. Look," Abbie signed, shaking the canary. One of its yellow wings fell off. "Damn!"

The expletive caught Fran's interest and she glanced at the object in Abbie's hand. With a closed fist in front of her mouth, the gorilla extended her index finger and thumb and touched the tips together.

"Bird."

"Good girl," Abbie signed. "Good Fran." She laid the battered bird on the floor and reached into the box for another animal.

"What is this?" she asked.

Fran stared quizzically at the toy, a Scottish terrier. At one time the toy had barked when wound, but its key was no longer intact.

"Bird," the gorilla signed.

"No, no. This is a bird." Abbie picked up the canary. "Bird," she repeated. "Now, what is this?" She held up the dog, carefully, lest it, too, fall apart.

Fran ignored the question.

"This is a dog," signed Abbie. "Dog."

She took Fran's right hand and molded it into the sign for "dog." A technique developed by the Gardners, the couple who initiated the movement to teach sign language to apes, molding entailed shaping the primate's hand into the desired form.

"Dog," Abbie said, pushing Fran's fingers into the proper formation, a curved open hand. She guided the gorilla's hand to her outer thigh.

"Dog," signed Fran of her own volition, touching her thigh.

"Good. Now what is this?" Abbie held up the canary.

"Bird." Fingertips touching.

"Good. And this?"

"Dog." Hand to thigh.

"Good girl. Fran is very good." Abbie threw an arm around the gorilla and hugged her.

"More hug," signed Fran after Abbie released her hold.

"All right, but then back to our lesson. Okay?"

The question was superfluous, but it encouraged Fran to use her vocabulary, currently six hundred words. For everyday use, the gorilla drew from a reserve only half that size.

"Lesson fine," the ape signed.

Abbie gave Fran another squeeze. Contrary to what a layman might expect, the gorilla exerted very little pressure. She let Abbie do the real hugging, an arrangement which suited her mistress fine, since Fran easily could crush a human being's ribs. Possible injury—due to the gorillas' ignorance of their own strength—was a facet of primate research to which Abbie long ago had resigned herself.

"Did we work on colors last week?" Abbie asked David.

"With Fran? Yeah."

"You got the usage rates?"

David flipped through the notebook in which were recorded the most recent of Fran's signs. Hundreds of such notebooks filled the compound's files, along with numerous videotapes that chronicled the progress of all three apes. "Usage rate" was the number of times a gorilla signed a particular word. From this statistic the students gleaned each gorilla's working vocabulary, consisting of those words introduced into the conversation by the ape to a significant percentage. To qualify, the word had to be used spontaneously, not in response to a prompt from the teacher.

"Yeah," said David, finding the figures for the last week, "here they are. Red and black were the only colors that counted."

"Okay. Black it is." Abbie rummaged through the box for an animal that would illustrate the color black.

Hours later, after she'd sorted out the day's jumbled events in a framework of hindsight, Abbie would reason that the sun had made her lethargic. That she was groggy. Why else would she have made the mistake she did?

The mistake was a big one. She chose a black crocodile.

How it got mixed up with the other animals in the box she would never know; it had been relegated years before to one of the back shelves. The pristine condition of the toy should have tipped her off. But it didn't. She had forgotten the special quality to the animal.

Holding the crocodile, Abbie signed, "And what is this, Fran?"

The gorilla screamed.

Often, when a person relates the story of a hunt and describes the capture of the animal, he compares its screams to that of a human, as if this more clearly illustrates the animal's suffering. Even the most skillful raconteurs resort to this imagery in hopes of embellishing their tales with greater pathos. What they do not realize is this: that the most horrifying screams are often not the product of human larynxes. There are others—from the throats of nonhumans who lack our refined vocal cords—that grate nerves so raw that the sound can never be fully purged from the auditory memory.

A gorilla's scream is not human. It slides the range from a high staccato bark to a guttural yell. If a human scream opens a fissure in the mind's cavern, the cry of a gorilla is the implosion of that cavern, compressing whirled, half-formulated thoughts upon one another.

"Shit, Abbie!" shouted David, leaping from his chair. "You've got the croc. Put it down!"

"What?" Abbie scrutinized the stuffed animal in her hand. Her ears rang from Fran's outburst. It took several seconds before she linked cause with effect.

"Damn!" she said. "What in God's name was a crocodile doing with the others?" She dangled the stuffed animal by the end of its tail as though the body, at the very second of her realization, had been coated with a layer of slime.

Abbie jumped off the floor and kicked aside the box of animals in her search for a trash can. Finding none, she tossed the crocodile to David.

"Get rid of it, will you?" Then, directing her efforts to the frightened gorilla, she said, "Come here, Fran. I'm so sorry that scared you. Everything's okay now." She wrapped her arms around the ape.

The crocodile: the dreaded croc, anathema to the three gorillas in the Burundi Primate Research Center. No one in the compound had ever pinpointed the source of their fear—the gorillas had seen a real crocodile only two or three times—but the fear was there, sharp and paralytic. It could be aroused by pictures, or models, or even the simple act of moving one's hands in a clapping motion with the heels of the palms held together, the barest suggestion of a croc's jaws. Occasionally, the gorillas used the motion to threaten one another.

"Abbie's here, Fran. That's my girl. That's my good girl."

The gorilla quieted down.

"Good now? Is Fran okay?"

Fran tightened her hold on Abbie and whimpered.

"Dave?" Abbie said softly, still cradling the ape. "I think we'll dump the rest of the lesson for today. She's had enough. We won't get too far behind if we stop."

As Abbie spoke the last word, "stop," Fran disengaged herself from Abbie's arms and surveyed the room.

"Here"—the ape hesitated before putting the heels of her hands together—"croc?"

"No, all gone," signed Abbie.

Fran heaved a sigh of relief.

"Go outside play," she signed, marching to the door, her fright having miraculously vanished. The rapidity of the gorilla's recovery galvanized Abbie's suspicions.

"You don't suppose this was all an act to get me to postpone the lesson, do you?" Abbie asked David. "I mean, the minute I said 'stop' she seemed to collect herself."

"Outside please," signed Fran.

"I wouldn't put it past her," said David. "But I don't think that was the case this time. She was pretty frightened. Although that last little whimper may have been to make you feel guilty."

"Outside damn me go outside," signed Fran.

"I think she's trying to give you a message," David added.

"All right, Fran. No need to curse. We'll see you later, David."

Once outside, Fran ran a few feet and turned a somersault.

"Personally, Fran, I think you're a fraud. New word for the day," said Abbie.

The ape rolled on her back. "Tickle me," she signed.

"Fran, you got a lot of chutzpah."

"Tickle Fran please."

"All right, ready?"

Abbie dropped to her knees and lunged for the gorilla's torso. Fran squirmed and wriggled and weakly fended off Abbie's hands. Her mouth hung open and she emitted delighted hoots, her gray tongue lolling from one side to the other. Abbie rubbed her hands up and down Fran's body and rolled her back and forth.

"Getting fat, Fran." She tickled the ape under the armpits.

"More more," signed Fran.

"Get up. We're going over there."

"There?"

Sweat dripped down Abbie's back, put there by the minor exertion of tickling the gorilla. They needed someplace cooler.

"In the car," she signed. "We're going for a ride."

"Winston Joey come."

"Winston has his lesson, but Joey can come."

"Good."

Abbie's three gorillas loved to ride in cars, but had been denied the pleasure for nearly a month. Ever since her reprimand from the Bujumbura police, prompted by frightened complaints from local citizens who didn't take kindly to apes on wheels, Abbie had been circumspect about chauffeuring them. The new route she'd plotted led down an old forgotten road. Like most roads in Burundi, save the ones downtown, this one was unpaved; little more, in fact, than a path plowed by the unshod feet of men and animals on their way to Lake Tanganyika.

Normally Abbie tried to limit the outings to either early morning or dusk, times in which the likelihood of being spotted was minimal. It was now nearly midday.

She decided to chance it. The lake promised a propitious change from the dusty compound. There was no danger of the gorillas plunging irretrievably into its depths; they disliked water intensely, even feared it. The aversion was not simply an adjunct to their fear of crocodiles, but an instinct shared by most members of their species.

Best of all, the drive might act as a stimulant to Fran's lagging attention. Precedent showed that a break in the daily routine helped renew the gorillas' interest in conversation. On slow days like today, an unplanned expedition could prove invaluable.

Abbie took Fran's hand and propelled her toward Joey's trailer. Fran waited patiently at the bottom of the steps for Abbie to appear with Joey and Chandra, one of Joey's teachers. When she did, Fran flashed her a sign. Abbie groaned.

"No, Fran, I've told you a thousand times. You can't drive." Abbie strode resolutely to the jeep.

It was one of those days, all right.

Zubi's lunch rattled in his rucksack. He switched the fishing pole from his left hand to his right and quickened his pace. He'd spent the entire Sunday morning completing the last of his lures and was anxious to try them in the lake. They were a source of great pride to him and reflected hours of artful concentration. Thus, he had been particularly angry when, earlier in the week, his younger brother lost most of the lot. For punishment, Zubi banned the boy from today's fishing trip, a decision he was beginning to regret. He missed the companionship.

In the meantime, he had his dog. The animal strayed every so often from his master's heels to investigate a sudden rustle or follow a spreading odor. Yapping and stumbling over feet too large for his body, the dog sprinted awkwardly across the rocky ground. His tongue rolled limply out of his mouth; drops of saliva marked a trail in the dirt.

The rough path the two followed was one Zubi had forged from his house to Lake Tanganyika. It took a little more than a half hour to walk. Zubi knew it would not be long before they approached the dirt road that led to the lakeshore. Past the road was a piece of land that jutted into the lake. Here, Zubi planned to eat lunch, positioned to catch the cool, southeasterly wind.

The dry grass crackled underneath his feet. Small insects, stirred by his footsteps, clung to his clothes. Zubi did not bother brushing them off. Others would replace them, teased by the same magnet that draws all manner of dirt to little boys. He called to the dog, which had stopped to urinate, and adjusted one of the straps on his pack. It was too tight and cut into his shoulder.

As he reached the road, Zubi heard a rumble he recognized as the sputtering of a car's engine. The noise startled him. He'd never encountered anyone on the road before, nor had he spotted evidence, such as an impression in the dirt of a tire's tread, that would have prepared him for today's visitors. He squinted and thought he perceived a car in the distance—a jeep, maybe—jouncing from rut to rut as a ship pitches in a strong gale. There were three, no, four people in the car, but he wasn't able to distinguish their faces. Then the jeep drew nearer and he realized that two of the occupants, though they were jet-black like he, were not human.

Abbie averted her eyes from the road to see why Chandra was laughing. The young black woman, deaf from birth, was seated next to Fran on the backseat. Her lithe fingers moved rapidly, but Fran was not watching them. The gorilla's attention was directed elsewhere, at an object cradled in her hands. Abbie craned her neck, but wasn't able to tell what the object was. It shimmered metallically.

She returned her gaze to the road. Small rocks pelted her arms, sprayed upward by the jeep's spinning wheels. She paid them no notice, concentrating instead on skirting the larger boulders strewn across her path.

The jeep was going no faster than thirty miles per hour, but the cloud of dust it raised, whipped in the air with the ferocity of swarming locusts, made it seem faster. As the car approached the lake, the road narrowed and dipped in the middle. Trees encroached on its rocky shoulders. Abbie eased her foot off the accelerator.

A clinking noise distracted her, and she looked once more over her shoulder. The metallic object that had captivated Fran was a key ring. Its keys hit against one another in rhythm to the swaying of the car. Chandra reached for the ring, but Fran slipped it over her huge gorilla knuckle. As Abbie watched, the ape dangled her hand outside the jeep and admired her new ornament in the sunlight. Suddenly, the keys rattled violently. The car had hit a rut. Abbie, so engrossed with Fran's antics that she hadn't been watching the road, tugged hard on the wheel, and the jeep careened to the right.

Joey, seated beside Abbie on the front seat, was jarred from his seat and hit his head on the roof of the car. He pounded the dashboard.

"Hurt nut nut," he signed, angrily ripping the last of the fringe from the edge of the roof. "Nut nut," "dirty toilet," and "bad bird" were swearwords that the gorillas reserved for the most flagrant outrages. Luckily for Abbie, Joey blamed the uneven ride on the jeep and not on her driving. Fran reacted with the pleasurable grunt that might escape the lips of a roller-coaster enthusiast.

"Pretty finger bracelet," Fran signed, no less enamored of her shiny adornment than a Beverly Hills matron at Van Cleef and Arpels. "Nice pretty."

"Fran," Chandra signed. "Please don't drop my keys. Give me your hand."

The ape brought her arm back inside the car and slid the ring off her finger.

It was not the first time that one of the gorillas had demonstrated an affinity for jewelry. Two years before, Winston had torn a silver necklace from Abbie's neck. The strand was too short to fit around his own burly neck, however, and he lost interest in it, returning it to Abbie with the clasp broken. Although she did not believe that he would make a grab for the necklace again, Abbie had not gone back to wearing it. The scar on the back of her neck was a powerful deterrent.

"Ring, Fran," signed Chandra. "This is a ring."

She pointed to the key ring and repeated the sign for "ring," taking Fran's hand in her own and molding the shape.

"These are rings, too," signed Chandra, removing two silver bands from her fingers.

Fran took the rings and attempted to slide them over her fingers. They stuck on the protuberant tips.

"Ring small bad," the ape signed, cavalierly tossing the two silver bands out the window.

"Fran!"

Abbie stopped the car in response to Chandra's frantic tapping on her shoulder and waited while the young woman walked down the road to retrieve her jewelry.

"There?" asked Joey.

"No, not yet," answered Abbie.

"Now there."

"Joey, we just left a little while ago. Soon. We'll be there soon."

Abbie was beginning to have second thoughts about the trip. There was something to be said for inattentive apes. Chandra stepped back into the jeep and scolded Fran.

"Bad ape," she signed.

"Fran good Fran good good," signed the ape. "Front seat."

"Oh, no," said Abbie. "Fran, I thought we already settled that."

"Front seat front," signed the ape, shaking the seat.

"I think I'm getting a headache," said Abbie.

Normally Fran rode up front with Abbie, but today Joey had been so excited by the prospect of going for a drive that he'd scampered ahead of her. Fran, relegated to the backseat, was noticeably miffed.

"You there," she'd signed to Joey, pointing to the backseat.

Joey had turned his head slowly around and, with an expression reminiscent of Jack Benny, had signed: "Joey here."

"Joey there," Fran had insisted, jumping up and down. But no sooner had she signed the words than a curious transformation occurred. Fran's instincts reasserted themselves. With the suddenness of a computer circuit overriding a previous instruction, she gave way to the male gorilla. Joey, sensing the change in her manner, similarly reverted to the natural hierarchy of their species. He extended his arm. Fran kissed his hand in submission.

Abbie had observed not Fran kissing Joey, but a female gorilla deferring to a male blackback. It was a scene she could have viewed anywhere: in the Kisoro region of western Uganda; near the Rio Muni in Guinea; in the Central Park Zoo in New York City. Such behavior served as a constant reminder

to those at the Burundi Primate Research Center that the apes'
actions should never be ascribed to human motives. Abbie
abhorred those who dressed their primates in baseball caps or
frilly dresses. She did not want to humanize her apes. She
wanted them recognized for what they were: animals. Bright,
sociable, gentle animals. Yet even she occasionally found it
hard not to interpret their actions in "humanese," and had to
remind herself that much of their behavior was the result of
conditioning or mere imitation.

"Chandra," Abbie signed to the young deaf woman, "try to
interest Fran in that key ring again. Maybe she'll forget about
the front seat."

Abbie's right leg and arm were hot from where the sun beat
down on them. The jeep had no side windows, only the front
windshield, and the rushing air tangled her hair. Her sunglasses
slid off the bridge of her nose, and she pushed them back into
place. From a patch of brush ahead a rat scurried across the
road.

"What is that?" Abbie signed to Joey, momentarily taking
her hands from the steering wheel.

The gorilla peered down the road and signed, "Boy."

Christ, thought Abbie to herself, Joey's doing no better with
his vocabulary than Fran.

"No," she signed. "Rat."

"Boy boy," insisted Joey.

"We'll tackle this later," muttered Abbie, swerving to avoid
a hole in the ground.

And then she saw the boy.

He was standing about two feet back from the road, in a
clearing between the trees. Abbie judged the distance between
them to be fifty yards.

She responded to his presence by instantly cutting her
speed. It was an action she would later ponder, for although
the ramifications were unapparent at the time, it would have
startling consequences.

Had Abbie not slowed down, the boy would not have
reached the road at the same time as the jeep, nor would the
gorillas have gotten so excited. But she did slow down, and

before she knew it, the boy was barely ten yards ahead, a stunned look on his face.

Joey and Fran, both sitting on the right-hand side of the jeep, the side near the boy, teetered on their seats and leaned their heads out.

"Catch boy hurry hurry," signed Joey.

The boy started to run down the side of the road, still slightly ahead of the jeep. Abbie was afraid to accelerate lest he dart out in front of her. She finally decided to pass him. The jeep was just about to pull even with the boy when Fran, sitting on her haunches in the backseat, cupped her hands and beat loudly on her chest, emitting a hoot of pure pleasure.

Misconceptions have long surrounded the phenomenon of chest-beating in gorillas. To begin with, the gorilla does not form a fist of his hand but leaves the hand open, the fingers spaced apart and slightly curled. Moreover, the action is not an indication of imminent violence. Dr. Geoffrey H. Bourne, director of the Yerkes Primate Center in Atlanta, Georgia, has this to say:

"At the Yerkes Center the gorillas seem to beat their chests with no particular relationship to anything, and they start it at a very young age. We have seen animals of two years of age beat their chests, and very often the young ones of about four to six, running around in their cage, appear to beat their chests seemingly from exuberance."

He also notes: "A silverback on Mount Mikeno has been seen to beat his chest as he looked at a human, and at that time he was showing neither fright nor aggression."

Just curiosity, it seems.

Zubi could barely believe what he was seeing. The car was bearing down on him. He willed his feet to move, but they were rooted to the spot. The beasts in the car had cast a spell on him. The jeep rumbled loudly, shattering the serenity of the lakeside.

It drew closer, this evil visitation, an image intensified by the dust that trailed the car and filtered the sunlight into haze. The jeep had an eerie, unfocused appearance, like a mirage baked into his skull by the hot sun. He wondered if this was his punishment for treating his brother so unfairly.

"I will let him come fishing with me next time," he confessed frantically to his dog, which barked at the oncoming vehicle. "I promise I will let him come!"

Still the car bore down. Zubi saw two hairy arms reach for him, beckon him, the flicking fingers incomprehensible, and yet, perhaps through a submerged sixth sense nearly lost in the evolution from ape to man, he caught the message, "Catch boy hurry hurry," as clearly as if it had been blared from a loudspeaker.

A face—part human, part beast—leered at him, its darkness a contrast to the whiteness of the woman with the tinted glasses. The beast's eyes were luminous, hypnotic—human. Zubi looked from one face to the other, at the glistening sunglasses, then at the vibrant brown eyes of the demon, and, in the fantastical thinking of a frightened child, concluded that the woman's eyes were lodged in the demon's head. The great beast had stolen her eyes along with her will. Zubi was quite sure that behind those glasses would be nothing more than smooth white skin.

He dropped his pole and forced his legs to move. He did not know where to run. Looking over his shoulder, he saw another creature in back, sitting with a black woman. The four were nearly upon him when the smaller creature hunched forward and let loose a monstrous cry, so loud that it surely must have surged from the depths of hell. Zubi's heart pounded and coursing blood beat a rhythm in his ears. At any second those hairy arms were certain to grab hold and tear him limb from limb.

He screamed and dove headfirst into the side of the road. Brambles ripped his face, knees, and hands. He thudded to a stop against a tree trunk.

And then he ran.

IV

Beans. Beans and leaves.

By his fifth week in Burundi, Evan Olgilvie was so tired of dealing with coffee beans and tea leaves that he questioned the wisdom of his decision to work in Africa. On the one hand, as the sole economic/commercial officer for the United States embassy in Burundi, he'd finally acquired the responsibility he'd coveted. On the other hand, he hadn't anticipated that most of his work would be so inextricably connected with coffee and tea.

Hell, he didn't even particularly like either beverage.

But economy in Burundi was synonymous with the two and fluctuated according to their markets. Virtually every matter that had come under Evan's jurisdiction in the past few weeks concerned their cultivation. The agricultural report on his desk, conducted by a U.S.-sponsored research team, dealt with the viability of turning marshlands in the high valleys into tea farms. Part of the money given Burundi through U.S. Public Law 480 (Food for Peace) was earmarked for farmers whose coffee and tea crops had been destroyed by a freak hailstorm. And one of the bilateral projects proposed by the USAID (U.S. Agency for International Development) focused on improved methods of food storage and marketing, especially with regard to coffee and tea.

The story was the same in the private sector. The only investment American businessmen contemplated in Burundi was the construction of a tea processing plant jointly financed by the World Bank and OPIC, the Overseas Private Investment Corporation. Likewise, the only purchases the U.S. made were of coffee and tea. Lots of each. So much so that the American consumer, unaware that a nation called Burundi even existed, was supplying that very country with a substantial chunk of its national revenue.

Evan found it hard to believe, as he fingered the report on his desk, that he, too, once had been unaware of Burundi's existence. It seemed as though he always had known the hybrid smell of its marketplaces, overripe with the odor of mangoes and dried fish. Always had heard the jangle of copper bracelets and the euphony of Kirundi and French spoken in tandem. Always had seen the bright-colored kangas wrapped around noontime shoppers. It seemed eons ago, not three months, that he had left the embassy in Uruguay.

He wished he had left behind his restlessness as well. Already he felt that familiar disquiet, the desire to do more. He told himself that he was rushing things, that once he was able to tackle the other economic issues at hand, he'd settle down. If only the goddamn coffee lobbyists would leave.

They'd been in town two weeks, armed with fistfuls of diseased beans as well as statistics on the downward swing in coffee quality and yield among Burundi's independent farmers. Their goal was an insecticide refinery that would use pyrethrum, a native crop, to be jointly sponsored by the U.S. and the OCIB (Office des Cultures Industrielles de Burundi).

Evan quashed the urge to tell the lobbyists where they could shove their infested beans; instead he boned up on chemical pesticides.

It was a reaction that fell perfectly in step with the pattern of his life. Doing the Instead. Evan's life, for the most part, had been a series of following through with Plan B when Plan A didn't work; an existence guided by a Fate with a peculiar sense of humor. He always had to settle for second or third choice. The Instead.

He didn't kick the winning field goal at the end of Carthage

High's championship football game. He missed, the team lost, and the scout in the audience left without awarding a state university scholarship. Evan went to college elsewhere.

He didn't score high enough on the LSAT to get into the law school he wanted. He went to work in a bank. His boss, a graduate of Georgetown, liked Evan, and his recommendation paved the road for Evan's admittance to graduate school. But in international relations, not law.

He didn't tell Lila Moretti that he loved her. She married Tony Montgomery.

And then the day arrived that he passed the foreign service exam and was assigned to Uruguay. For a brief, electric time afterward, Evan suspected he finally had broken the pattern. Most first-timers in the State Department landed in places like Surinam or Sri Lanka. Never in countries where they spoke the language or that were of special interest to them. That Evan's first job should find him in a country whose culture he'd studied was unbelievable, truly mind-boggling.

Too good to be true. What had looked like Plan A was really only Plan B wrapped in a poncho.

It dawned on him that he'd been deceived—more by his own expectations than by anything the State Department had told him. As one of several economic officers, he was no more crucial to the operation of diplomacy than a Washington hostess was to the passage of legislation. He quickly found his duties tedious. The heady atmosphere of foreign service which had lured him in the first place turned stale.

He tried to hide his disappointment from friends, filling his letters and telephone calls with noncommittal small talk. The tactic backfired. His silence merely reinforced their image of him as the dashing young diplomat. Glamour, intrigue, exotic women. It was an image mired in their minds with the sticky resiliency of molasses, spooned there by television and flashy novels that equated foreign service with espionage. A hype any publicist could be proud of: a self-perpetuating myth. And about as real as the breakaway props on a movie set.

Evan hated it. All of it. Hated talking with the other bored young Americans, the Monday-morning quarterbacks. So it was with undisguised relish that he regarded his transfer.

"Anywhere will be fine" was what he'd told his colleagues.

His words proved prophetic. Anywhere was what he'd gotten. Upon receiving his assignment, Evan rushed to the atlas to find out where he was going.

Central Africa. A country called Burundi. Four million people. 10,747 square miles. And limitless possibilities for a young economic officer. But that was before he learned about the beans and the leaves. No small wonder his predecessor left him 500 coffee filters in his correspondence files.

Evan pushed aside the filters as he inserted a copy of his latest letter to the coffee moguls. The phone rang.

"Monsieur Olgilvie?" said the operator. "Your call to the States is ready now."

Evan looked at his watch. It was 8:30. Subtract the eleven-hour time difference to California, and presto, it was 9:30 P.M. in San Rafael. A little late, but that couldn't be helped.

"Hello?" answered a voice on the other end. The call was being transmitted through Brussels, and the static was fierce.

"Andrea?" said Evan, loudly. "Hi, it's me. The kid around? Thought I'd wish her a happy birthday."

"Sure. I'll call her to the phone in just a sec. It's so good to hear from you. Guess what? We saw your picture in the paper."

"You're kidding? Where?"

"In the *Chron*. And in *Newsweek*. Same picture. UPI, I guess. You're standing behind the Vice-President. Shana got all excited and cut it out."

"It wasn't really anything. Just a luncheon when he came through on his African tour."

"You look very distinguished."

"What did Mom think of it?"

"She's right here. I'll ask her."

Evan closed the file drawer during the pause.

"She says you look like you've gained weight."

"Just what I wanted to hear."

"Hold on a sec—she also says you look tired."

"Tell her I'm feeling fine. And that I weigh the same as always."

Andrea conveyed the message and laughed.

"She says there's a big difference between kilos and pounds."

"I'm glad she finds it so amusing," said Evan.

"She's only kidding you, Ev. You know that."

"Yeah, yeah."

"So how are things going?"

"Good. The coffee people should be departing soon, the ones I wrote you about. And the other stuff coming in looks real interesting. I tell you, Andrea, this country is fascinating. I still can't really believe I'm here. It's a nice change."

"So you're glad you're there?"

"Who wouldn't be?"

After Andrea hung up the phone—wiping off the sticky chocolate fingerprints that Shana had left—she walked into the living room. Her mother, a woman in her late fifties, was sitting on the patterned divan, reading. As Andrea moved into her line of vision, Mrs. Olgilvie removed her glasses and put her book to one side.

Andrea raised her hands to her chest. Her gestures were small, controlled, and neat. Had her hands been immersed in water, there would have been barely a ripple, so smooth were her movements. But though her sign-language gestures were small, their meaning was expansive. The woman on the divan watched the nimble hands with accustomed concentration, her bluest of eyes peering from beneath translucent lids.

The message: I don't think he's happy.

Evan had only just hung up the phone when Davenport entered his office.

Davenport was in his early forties, and, as Deputy Chief of Mission, was Evan's boss. His face had a weather-beaten, gruff look that matched his personality. He squinted whether in broad daylight or shade.

"Olgilvie, I've got something to take you away from that desk of yours. A little problem for you to straighten out." Davenport ripped a piece of paper from the pad on Evan's desk, scribbled on it, and handed it back. "Here you go."

"What is it?" asked Evan. The paper was covered with curlicues and arrows.

"It's a map. It shows you how to get to the Burundi Primate Research Center. That's where the problem is."

Davenport paused, and Evan felt compelled to comment.

"Primates. You mean like apes?"

"Yes, Olgilvie, that's what primates are," Davenport replied. "The problem is the woman who runs the center, an American by the name of Abbie Guisbourne. She works under the auspices of Brice University—that's back in Connecticut. Anyway, we've received a complaint against her. Seems she was out driving in her car again."

Evan waited attentively for the man to amplify his remarks, but he did not. Davenport's pattern of speech was erratic, and Evan was forever out of sync with it.

"Is she missing a driver's license?" Evan asked.

"No, the apes. The complaint was regarding the apes in the car."

Evan was confused. "Were the apes driving?" he asked.

"No, the apes weren't driving," Davenport said with exasperation. "You don't understand. She's been reprimanded once already by the Bujumburan police for frightening people, but apparently it did no good. She was out early yesterday afternoon with her apes near the lake, and threw a scare into a kid belonging to the deputy foreign minister. Normally, of course, we'd leave something like this to the police, but as a personal favor to the deputy minister, I'm sending you out there."

"And you want me to tell her to quit driving with the apes?" Evan meant it as a statement, but changed his inflection at the last moment.

"Olgilvie, why do you think I just bothered to explain all

of this?" Davenport's question was less a reproach than an expression of bewilderment. "Yes, I want you to tell her to knock it off."

"Right." Evan hastily folded the map and shoved it in his shirt pocket alongside a pack of gum. "I don't mean to be so slow. It's just that as the economic officer I didn't expect to deal with— Never mind, I'll go now."

"Evan"—Davenport softened his tone—"I think we need to have a little talk." His voice was weary, conveying the impression that he'd had this conversation with other Evan Olgilvies, with other young men who had come and gone, whose expectations had been perhaps even higher than Evan's.

"Now, I'm not sure what you were used to in Uruguay," said Davenport. "I dare say it was a whole lot different from here. Some embassies have economics divisions bigger than this entire embassy. But one thing you got to get clear: We aren't like other embassies.

"You and me, see, we make up practically half of this office. So titles don't mean a hell of a lot. Take your title, for instance, Economic/Commercial Officer. That might mean more someplace else, but here, well, we all kind of pitch in together. Right now we have to straighten out Guisbourne and her apes. And you're available. And if we don't send somebody, we're going to have an important Burundian official mad at us. We don't want that."

Evan nodded his head in agreement.

"So you take the embassy car and follow the map and tell Ms. Guisbourne that she either cuts out her joyrides or we'll kick her ass across the border into Tanzania."

"I think I understand," said Evan. He rose quickly, grabbed his coat, and rushed toward the door.

"Olgilvie?"

Evan turned around.

"You forgot something." The keys to the embassy car dangled from Davenport's index finger.

Evan flashed him an embarrassed smile and reached out his hand.

"You're kind of a flake, kid, but I think you'll do all right," said Davenport. "Just remember, the apes will be the hairy ones."

The Burundi Primate Research Center looked remarkably like the temporary classrooms Thurber Elementary, Evan's grammar school, had set up when half the school burned down. The same circle of trailers hooked together. Same jungle-gym equipment in the courtyard. Knee-high water faucets. What was missing were shouts from children at recess. Gone, too, were spitballs and eraser crumblings on the ground.

But this place had something Thurber Elementary had lacked: an ape. Unless his eyes were deceiving him, that was what Evan saw swinging on a rope in the courtyard. Jet-black with a patch of red hair on the top of its head. A gorilla.

Evan parked the embassy car next to the only car in sight, a jeep—the very one, he surmised, in which the infamous rides had occurred—and debated whether to go left or right. A fence with no discernible opening ran the length of the compound. Evan circled to his right and spotted a young black woman near the ape. She didn't hear him when he called to her. He waited a few seconds, hoping she would look his way, then began to climb the fence.

Evan uneasily straddled the wire twists that topped the fence. The ground looked far away. In the process of pulling his right leg over the top, he snagged his pants leg on the wire. The thin material ripped. His toe caught in one of the fence links, and he fell to the soft earth.

Unbelievably, the woman still didn't look his way. She seemed to be playing some sort of finger game with the ape.

"Hello?" he called, dusting off the seat of his pants.

She didn't respond. Evan supposed she didn't realize that he was speaking to her.

"Hello, excuse me, are you Abbie Guisbourne?" he asked, louder.

Her back remained turned to him. Evan walked cautiously

toward her, conscious that he'd caught the eye of the ape. The animal stopped swinging and returned Evan's look with a beady stare.

Evan had never been this close to an ape before. As he drew closer, an old Tarzan movie flashed through his mind. In it, an ape hoisted Johnny Weismuller over his shoulder while the other apes watched. Weismuller, the former Olympian, escaped his simian captors with muscles rippling and loincloth flapping. Evan assessed his pants, ripped at the knee, and his flabby stomach; he and Johnny weren't in the same league. Sucking in his gut, he tried to assume a confident walk, certain that this ape—like other animals—could sense a man's fear.

"Excuse me, but I'm trying—"

A sudden blow to his head sent him sprawling. It packed a considerable wallop and resembled the kind of unintentional hit delivered by a person speaking with gestures to a listener standing too close. Evan hit the ground with great force. Small rocks tore his shirt and gouged his cheek. After Evan regained his breath, his shock gave way to anger and, spitting out the grit lodged between his teeth, he sat up and looked defiantly at his attacker.

Fear set in seconds later when he realized that the black tree trunks in his way were legs. He bent back his head and took in all three hundred plus pounds of the creature looming over him. Its teeth were bared and its forehead contracted spasmodically, moving the crest of fur on top of its head. A toupee endowed with its own will would have seemed no more weird to Evan.

What was perhaps the most frightening feature, however, was the strange coloring of its face: black and red. Red so shiny and bright that it was as if a vein in that huge brow— which, like the chin, receded sharply—had been punctured and had spilled a circle of blood. But the wound was invisible and the blood, defying gravity, did not drip. The creature lunged for him.

Had Evan had his wits about him, he would have known

that the creature was a gorilla with a red circle painted around one eye. He would have known that when the gorilla lunged forward, it was not to attack, but to drop from its bipedal stance, one rarely held longer than a few seconds, to its more familiar posture on all fours.

But Evan's wits were still on the ground. The painted circle, by the time he recognized it as such, evoked images of Indian war paint and intruding wagon trains. He was the intruder now, and the fact that he eventually recognized the creature as a gorilla—the ape's head was now mere inches from Evan's face—did little to assuage his fear.

He screamed. As in a nightmare, no one responded. The woman with the small gorilla continued to smile and move her fingers, oblivious to Evan's predicament. Evan waited for his life to flash before him. Nothing came. He visualized the police telling his family that he'd been eaten. Shades of *Suddenly, Last Summer*. Christ, thought Evan, I'm about to die a gruesome death and all I can think about is a goddamn movie.

The gorilla with the red circle grunted, imposing a small amount of rationality on Evan's disordered mind.

"Somebody do something," he yelled.

The woman in the courtyard finally looked in his direction, but casually, as though she were merely following the stare of the small gorilla on the rope. An expression of disbelief washed across her finely shaped features, and she ran toward Evan.

And past him. Evan sat on the ground, his body shaking, and watched her minister to the red-eyed ape. Something was wrong with this scenario. She was supposed to be aiding *him*.

"Shit, lady, what are you doing? I mean—oh my God— I'm the one who needs the help. Help *me*. That, that ape and the—oh, oh, wow—"

Though he was inarticulate, Evan's mind cleared of Tennessee Williams's movie, and he was able to formulate a plan of action. It consisted of standing up.

"Oh, God, I feel sick. Where's some water?" he asked the woman busily soothing the gorilla.

She didn't answer him. Weaving slightly, Evan bent over and touched his hands to his shins so that blood would flow to his head.

"Look, lady, I'm not hurt. You don't have to worry about being sued. Can you just get me a drink of water?"

She didn't respond. Her face mirrored an inner distress; she wrung her hands.

The gorilla on the rope joined the woman and the red-eyed gorilla. He walked back and forth anxiously. The young black woman patted the ape's head and took his hand in hers. Finally she spoke, her words garbled, an impediment Evan recognized at once.

"I am deaf. Please wait here."

Evan chastised himself for his earlier imprecations against the woman—he, of all people, from his background, to have reacted with such ignorance. He should have suspected her deafness from the beginning. He took a step toward her, but retreated when the red-eyed gorilla made a menacing sound and extended a hairy arm. The woman's finger game with the small ape, in light of what Evan had learned, took on new meaning. It was his way to communicate with her.

"Please," he signed, "don't go. I didn't mean to cause trouble. I'm looking for Abbie Guisbourne."

Evan's fingers moved clumsily, rusty from disuse. The signs did not flow easily, automatically, as they did when he was home. Amesal was so much a part of his private life that Evan felt strangely vulnerable using it under these strained circumstances. He never thought of it as an alternative form of communication. To him, sign language was a symbol of family, of love, and of warmth. That he should be using it here, in such a cold, foreign setting, made the situation even more strange.

The woman seemed surprised and relieved by his command of sign language. She dropped the small ape's hand.

"Who are you?" she signed.

Before Evan was able to respond, a second woman rushed upon the scene. She did not look especially pleased with what she found. A young man trailed after her.

"Just what the hell do you think you're doing to my gorillas?" Abbie demanded of Evan.

Evan was caught off guard by her accusatory tone. Didn't any of these people care that he'd been savagely attacked? He started to answer, but she interrupted him.

"Fold your arms, for God's sake. Can't you see how upset he is?" She pointed at Winston. The red-eyed ape brooded in the background, his lips pursed.

"Fold my—?"

"Your arms, your arms. Cross them."

"I upset him? Lady, he didn't exactly give me a"—Evan decided to take her advice when the great ape bared his teeth once more; he crossed his arms—"warm welcome."

Abbie walked over to the two apes. She gave each one a reassuring squeeze before requesting David and Chandra to return them to their trailers. Winston refused to budge, clearly suspicious of the stranger.

"Winston," she signed, "please go with David. I will come later. The man is good. I am okay with him. Go with David."

Evan focused on the woman's hands. She was forming signs. He didn't quite understand all of them—the Amesal was distorted in some instances—but the impact of what she was doing was undiminished: She was talking to the ape.

And, even more astonishing, the ape seemed to understand.

Winston raised a fist to his mouth and flicked a thumbnail behind his upper teeth. The movement created a clicking sound. "Nut nut," it said to Abbie and the two students. To Evan it said something infinitely more shocking: I *do* understand.

Winston's arms crossed in front of him as he walked away, all 325 pounds of him resting on padded second joints of fingers that were shorter than Evan's. He walked on the outside of his feet, soles turned inward. A large gap separated his prehensile big toes from the rest of his toes. His feet had no balls to them.

The smaller ape, Joey, walked with little hops. Chandra was holding one of his hands.

Abbie's face underwent a transformation from affectionate concern to raging ire, as clearly as if she'd changed Kabuki masks, when she turned her attention back to the stranger in her courtyard.

"So who are you?"

"My name is Evan Olgilvie," said Evan, logily, his mind still grappling with the conversation he'd witnessed between the woman and the gorilla. He had heard of primate language studies, but had never given them much thought. "I'm from the American embassy. I came here to talk to an Abbie Guisbourne."

"Why didn't you come to the office? You frightened the animals to death."

"I couldn't find the office, so I tried asking the woman who just left." Evan found it difficult to talk without gesturing. "Is there any particular reason for me to keep my arms folded?"

"What? Oh, no. He's gone now. That's just a gesture of submission." Abbie resumed her interrogation. "How did you get in here?"

"I, uh, climbed the fence."

"You climbed the fence? That's breaking and entering. Didn't it ever occur to you that the fence might be there for a reason?"

"I'm sorry. I really do apologize for barging in like this. I couldn't find the entrance."

"Sure." She pointed over his shoulder to a padlocked gate with a large sign reading: BURUNDI PRIMATE RESEARCH CENTER, AN EXTENSION OF BRICE UNIVERSITY IN COOPERATION WITH THE BURUNDIAN NATIONAL PARK SERVICES. "Let me see your ID."

"My what?"

"Your identification. If you're from the embassy you'll have a card or something."

Evan fished his card from his wallet.

"All right," said Abbie after examining it, "you pass." She extended her hand. "I'm Abbie Guisbourne. My office is over in that trailer. We can talk there."

She turned her back to him and walked across the court-yard. Evan stared dumbfoundedly after her and then ran to catch up. She made no attempt at conversation, even less of one at cordiality. The trailer's screen door nearly slammed shut on Evan's hand.

"You want something to drink? You look like hell." She ran the two sentences together.

Evan saw a wretched reflection in the mirror over Abbie's sofa: The rip in his pants leg had grown from the knee to the middle of the shin, his hair was mussed, dried blood—drops of which peppered his torn shirt—smeared his left cheek, and he was covered with dirt.

"Yes, please," he answered.

"I've got cold beer."

"That's fine."

She didn't offer him a seat, but he sat on the sofa anyway. On the other side of the coffee table were a couple of chairs. Farther down the wall was a desk with a typewriter. A bed and nightstand flanked the end wall, half hidden behind a bookshelf that jutted out into the middle of the trailer, separating the "bedroom" from the "office." The small refrigerator, which from Evan's vantage point seemed to hold only beer, was to the left of the sofa. Abbie handed Evan a can and sat in one of the chairs, her feet propped on the table.

"So what did I do?" she asked, popping open her can.

No beating around the bush with this woman, thought Evan. Not that he cared. She was no conversationalist; her speech was unembellished and terse. And yet there was some-thing about her directness that intrigued him. Her every word and movement appeared geared toward optimum efficiency and economy.

"It seems that you were driving in your car with the chimps—"

"Gorillas," she corrected.

"Sorry. The gorillas. You recall forcing a boy off the road?"

"I did no such thing!" She banged the beer can on the table.

"That's what the boy claims. His father reported it to one of our officers. The boy says you and the gorillas were driving a jeep near Lake Tanganyika and the apes tried to grab him."

"Oh, shit."

"I take it that means you remember?"

"Yes, but to begin with, we didn't force him off the road. He came out of nowhere and I was as surprised to see him as he was to see us. Fran got all excited and—"

"Fran?"

"One of my gorillas. She got all excited and must have frightened the kid. So he jumped into the bushes. I stopped and went back to check on him, but he had run off."

"The gorillas weren't threatening him?" asked Evan, thinking he sounded like a bad detective parody.

"No, they were still in the car. I went after the kid on foot." She leaned across the table and folded her hands. "Mr. Oliver—"

"Olgilvie."

"Mr. Olgilvie, gorillas are not vicious animals. They're more gentle than human beings, and they would no more dream of attacking a person than . . ." Her voice trailed off as Evan tapped a forefinger next to the dried blood on his face.

"They don't attack, huh?"

"That was the very first time I've ever seen Winston do something like that—and it was completely understandable." She sounded momentarily flustered. "You'd broken into our camp. He's not used to strangers and is very protective of us. Besides, it's a completely natural reaction for the head male gorilla to challenge a trespasser. But it's all a big bluff, a form of intimidation. He wasn't out to hurt you physically."

"A whack on the head? You don't call that physical?"

"I told you it was the first time I'd ever seen him do that!" Her voice was rising to the pitch it had been outside. "He's usually very withdrawn. And in addition he was—" She stopped.

"He was what?"

"Well," she said, reluctantly, "he was sort of doped up."

"Doped up? Did I hear you right? You dope up your gorillas?"

"*No!* Just this once. We had to paint a circle on his face without him realizing it. Look, it's too involved to explain. I didn't ask you to barge in on us, you know. You have no right to be yelling at me."

"I'm not yelling at you," he said, yelling at her. Remembering his position, he lowered his voice; diplomats were supposed to behave with equanimity. "Ms. Guisbourne, let me explain my purpose here. I came—unannounced, I grant you that— to tell you, to ask you, to stop taking your gorillas, gentle animals though they be, on rides in your jeep. A simple request, no?"

"I didn't force that child off the road."

"I'm sure you didn't. However, I understand this isn't the first time this problem has come up. The Bujumburan police warned you once before, I believe?"

"Yes, but I agreed to stick on the outskirts of town and drive either early in the morning or in late day."

"The boy says it happened in midday."

"My watch broke," she said, deadpan.

Evan shook his head slowly from side to side.

"Oh, all right. If it's that big a deal, I won't take them out for any more afternoon rides. Nothing happened to the little boy, did it? I mean he's all right?"

"He's fine."

"You know his name?"

"No."

"Can you get it for me?"

"Sure. Why?"

"I'll write his father a note of apology."

Evan had not expected such a gesture from the woman. He waited for her to say more, but she didn't. One minute reeling off words at a rapid, frenetic pace; the next minute silent. He wasn't able to figure her out.

"That would be nice," he said.

It seemed the appropriate time for Evan to say his good-bye and drive back into town, but he did not want to leave. Not yet. Years with the foreign service had sharpened Evan's ability to appraise people, but few ever had intrigued him as much as this woman. Or were quite so perplexing.

Abbie's obstinacy, her absolute indifference to social amenities, and her self-possession combined to form an unorthodox but compelling personality. She was a person who acted upon things, rather than let them act upon her; a catalyst. The attribute both appealed to Evan and intimidated him, perhaps because he sensed its absence so acutely in his own life, one that flowed with the tide of events.

"You know, I've heard of places like this one that work with primates," said Evan. "What exactly do you do here?"

"We teach the gorillas sign language," said Abbie. "Mainly we're trying to ascertain how advanced their thought processes are. Speech, as we humans know it, is totally out of the question, because—"

"Their vocal cords aren't like ours," Evan signed to her, his fingers regaining their usual dexterity.

"You know Amesal?" she signed back, her face suffused with the unexpected delight of a child who's found a dollar bill on the sidewalk.

"Yes, my mother is deaf."

"Oh," she said, reverting to oral speech. "I'm sorry."

"Don't be. She isn't. So this is a language center?"

"Not really language—that's part of the reason for this study. One of the things we want to find out is whether the gorillas' conversation indicates a capacity for language. We can't claim that yet. All we can say is that they possess a complex communication and thought system all their own. That much we've been able to tap by teaching them Amesal. I guess you'd say that we're hoping to learn if, like us, they've got a specialized framework for language."

As she spoke about the project so essential to her being, Abbie relaxed. Evan watched her with mounting interest. He was less captivated by what she was saying than by what was happening to her. While she talked, another facet of her personality emerged, one of affability.

"So what's the purpose of the red circle you put around the gorilla's eye?" asked Evan.

"Oh, that. We painted that on for an experiment. Since we didn't want him to know it was there, we had to tranquilize him."

"Why shouldn't he know?"

"Well, the experiment deals with self-awareness. We put the gorilla in front of a mirror and— Why don't I just show you? It's kind of difficult to explain. We were just about to conduct the experiment when you dropped in. You got time?"

"Sure. Is this with the big gorilla?"

"Winston," she said.

"With Winston?"

"Yes."

"No, thanks," said Evan. "I think I've seen enough of him for one day."

"Don't worry about it. If he knows you're with me you'll be fine. I'll put you in the back of the room. Come on."

Abbie stood and walked away from him, leaving it up to Evan to follow her. He noted that she walked briskly, with long, purposeful strides, another mark of her economy of movement.

The trailer they entered seemed much larger than the one they'd left, but Evan supposed it was an optical illusion, brought about by the lack of furniture. The makings of a gorilla heaven surrounded him: exercise bars, a metal sloping box, a trapezelike contraption, a couple of tires, rubber balls, brightly colored boxes, and an assortment of blankets.

Evan froze when he caught sight of Winston's hulking form at the far end of the trailer, but, true to Abbie's word, the gorilla made no move for him. The ape's look told another story. Were Evan a magnet for beautiful women, he might have recognized the look from men jealous of his drawing power. But Evan wasn't that kind of man. The biggest response his entrance at a party ever had prompted was ardent praise for his cheese dip.

"Sit there," Abbie insisted, pulling out a chair in the back, but not sitting herself. "David, meet Evan Olgilvie."

David lifted his head to say hello, and resumed tinkering with the videotape camera as Abbie explained the experiment to Evan. She raised her voice to compete with the final stanza of Frank Sinatra's "My Way" issuing from a cassette deck in the corner.

"Remember what I said about painting the circle around Winston's eye without him realizing it? What we're going to record on film is his response once he sees his reflection in a mirror. If he figures out that the circle is on *him*, that'll indicate a high degree of self-awareness, a trait which up until recently was considered exclusive to mankind."

"How will you be able to tell?" asked Evan.

"Just watch."

With David positioned behind the camera, Abbie unveiled a four-foot-tall mirror in the far corner of the trailer. It looked out of place in the room, hardly in the league of the rough-and-tumble items scattered on the floor. Evan envisioned the gorilla slamming a huge fist into the mirror, sending jagged shards across the room. Only later did he learn that it was constructed of hardened plexiglass.

"Winston, come look," Abbie signed to the ape.

The great beast's walk fascinated Evan because it contradicted how he'd imagined gorillas move. Winston walked gracefully, not clumsily, his movements fluid and effortless. This was no lumbering gait, but the perfect coordination of limbs. What made the walk even more mesmerizing was the conjunction of that grace with the inherent strength of the animal. Unlike a lion or tiger, whose massive muscles ripple beneath the surface of their skins, flashing warning signals to their prey like inextinguishable beacons, a gorilla hides his strength beneath coarse fur, unadvertised. He radiates not merely power, but controlled power, as that which belongs to a Michelangelo sculpture.

"Look at the mirror," Abbie signed to Winston. "Good boy. What do you see?"

The ape did not answer. He moved his head from side to side.

"What do you see?" she repeated.

The ape moved closer to the mirror.

"See?" asked Abbie.

And then the gorilla did something which leaped the chasm between man and animal. Staring at his reflection, Winston raised a hand to his face and rubbed the skin around his right eye. The red pigment flaked off onto his fingertips. It was something a human being might do upon finding an unexpected dirt smudge on his face while looking at a mirror. But Winston was no human. As a great ape, he was invading a psychological territory thought to be man's alone: Recognition of Self.

A new understanding of the gorilla flooded Evan. This ape was no brute to be feared, but a sympathetic ally, one with fears and hates and desires, and yes, as now, one who made funny faces in mirrors. Like man, he viewed the world not merely as it felt and looked and smelled, but as it affected him. He assessed every object—each flower he picked, each stone he crossed—not in terms of intrinsic value, but in terms of what it meant to him. That alone mattered. The world was no longer out there, but inside his head, a microcosm of value judgments. It developed as he matured and disintegrated when he died, a world, in a sense, of his own making.

It was immediately clear why Abbie was taking such pains to record the event on film. The ramifications of the ape's deductive reasoning, though immense, were so subtle that they defied translation to paper.

"That's remarkable," said Evan, when Abbie asked him for his reaction. "Can any other animals do that?"

"Only the great apes, and they have to be familiar with the mirror. When they're first exposed to it, they respond to their reflection as though it were a playmate, just as a human infant will do. Gradually they realize that it's themselves. That's what this experiment proves."

"And the other gorilla in the courtyard—he recognizes himself too?"

"Joey? Yeah. So does Fran. In fact, they caught on a lot faster to the mirror than Winston. He still has a few problems."

"What do you mean?"

"Well, there's a danger with any ape that's raised in captivity—even worse with one that's isolated from members of its species—that it'll go through, I guess you'd call it an identity crisis. It gets confused. For example, Washoe—the first great ape to be taught sign language—was a chimp, and the first time she confronted other chimps she called them black bugs, not recognizing them as belonging to her own species."

"So what's Winston's problem? Does he call Fran and Joey black bugs?"

"No, no, that's not his problem. He recognizes them as gorillas, all right. It's just that . . . sometimes he . . . hell, like I said before, I'm not good at explaining things. Let me show you."

Abbie unlocked a cabinet on the far side of the trailer and pulled out a stack of pictures bound with a rubber band. She tossed the packet to Evan. He undid the band and spread the pictures on a nearby table. They were in no particular order. Some obviously were clipped from magazines; others were Polaroid snapshots. Among them Evan saw pictures of gorillas, Abbie, her students, and various celebrities. Although Abbie said nothing as Evan flipped through the selection, he no longer found her silence disconcerting.

"Stay where you are," she cautioned Evan. "He shouldn't get upset if you stay quiet." Abbie patted Winston on the back—the ape was still mugging in front of the mirror—and guided him to the table.

The gorilla paused when he passed Evan and pursed his lips. Perhaps it was a result of watching Winston play with his reflection, but Evan no longer feared the gorilla. Rather, he felt an overwhelming desire to communicate with the splendid animal, even to apologize for his earlier behavior in the courtyard.

"Hello, Winston," he signed, copying the sign Abbie had used for the gorilla's name.

Winston's response was minimal; he unpuckered his lips. Evan counted that a small breakthrough, especially since it coaxed a smile from Abbie.

"Okay, Winston," Abbie signed. "See the pictures?"

"Picture," the gorilla repeated.

"Will you look at them with me?"

"Winston look."

"Some are gorillas. Some are humans. Help me look."

She began sorting through the pictures. Winston cast his eyes in the direction of Evan.

"Winston, will you help me look?"

"Man out." The ape inserted his right hand between the thumb and palm of his left hand, then quickly withdrew it.

"What?"

"Hurry now man out."

"Why?"

"Bad man."

"The man is very sorry he made you mad. Can he stay?"

"No."

"Please, Winston," signed Abbie, "will you help me look at the pictures?"

"Look," relented the gorilla. He hit the underside of his chin with the back of his hand, adding, "Dirty stink man."

Evan found the comment surprising considering it was the ape producing the acrid odor, a smell that Evan would inure himself to about the same time he learned that "dirty" and "stink" were not to be taken literally.

"The man's name is—how does your family sign your name, by the way?" Abbie asked Evan. He showed her, and she molded the name into Winston's hand. The ape practiced the sign and then, looking directly at Evan, signed:

"Dirty stink Evan."

An embarrassed Abbie snatched the animal's hand and redirected his interest to the photos on the table.

"Person," she signed, taking a picture of John Paul II from the group and setting it to her right. The next picture was of Joey.

"Gorilla," Abbie signed, placing the picture to the left.

The third picture was of another gorilla. Abbie placed it on top of Joey's photo. The fourth picture was of Sophia Loren, and this she placed on top of John Paul II. And so on.

"Where does this one go?" she asked Winston, holding a picture of Muhammad Ali.

"That there." Winston pointed to the human pile.

"And this?" A picture of John Kenneth Galbraith. Again, to the human pile.

The next picture was of Winston. The gorilla took the picture between his nimble fingers and, after scrutinizing it, plopped it down on top of John Kenneth Galbraith.

"Winston real gorilla person," signed the ape.

"That," said Abbie, smiling, "is his problem."

"It hurts, Papa, it hurts."

"Shhh. Don't try to talk, little one. I know it hurts."

"Those men, Papa, those bad men. They pushed us."

"Yes."

"I want to go home, Papa." The boy began to cry.

"Soon. I will take you home."

"Where is Salim? I saw him just a bit ago. With you. I saw him just before—"

"Salim is fine." The man smoothed the child's hair back from his forehead.

"Papa?"

"Yes."

"I can see the night."

Bunkeya jolted awake. The little boy's face lingered in his mind like the afterimage of a bright light. He blinked and tried to remember where he was. Sitting up, he looked around the room. And remembered.

He had come in late the night before, proceeding cautiously. One could never be sure how the man on guard would react to a visitor coming in from the dark. Some of Dalam's men were known to be trigger-happy, as often happens with those who feel the weight of a rifle in their hands for the first time. Luckily, the man on duty was an old friend. It was from him that Bunkeya learned about Kili.

"Dead?" Bunkeya had whispered. "But how?"

"No one's sure," answered the guard. "It must have been a heart attack."

Bunkeya reflected on the last time he'd seen Kili. Yes, the man was older than the rest of them, but only in his early forties; he'd been in excellent shape. It did not seem possible that he was gone.

"He didn't cry for help? No one heard him?"

The guard shook his head. "It happened in the middle of the night. We found him the next morning."

"Where is he now?"

"We buried him." The guard pointed over his shoulder. "Couldn't keep him long in this weather. Mpinga said a few words to the men."

I bet he did, thought Bunkeya, but not the words he felt. Nothing could have suited Mpinga better than Kili's early demise. One more obstacle removed in his bid for power. The thought reverberated in Bunkeya's mind.

"How did Dalam take it?" he asked.

"Hard."

As might be expected. Kili's life had been connected with Dalam's since they were boys. Both paralleled the rocky political history of Zaire's last two decades. The two men fought side by side in the early sixties, championing Katangan secession until a United Nations plan, formulated by Secretary General U Thant, reintegrated the Katanga province into Zaire. Their cheers were loud when Moise Tshombe, Governor of Katanga, became Prime Minister in 1964, and their anger explosive a year later when Lieutenant General Mobutu seized control of the government. They fled to the northern shores of Lake Tanganyika, and then to Angola, where they became embroiled in that country's insurrection, but their dreams stayed in Zaire. They returned in 1977, under the leadership of General Mbumba, and held the southern city of Sandoa, eventually losing it to Moroccan-loaned troops in the "Eighty Day War." In 1978 they attacked the mining center of Kolwezi, only to be routed by a battalion of French legionnaires. Soon after, Dalam formed the FPL. Kili came with him.

And now Kili was dead.

The morning sun warmed Bunkeya's back as he walked to Dalam's hut. The FPL leader greeted him with a fierce embrace, but made no comment on Bunkeya's recently completed mission. His grapevine of information already would have informed him of its success. Dalam never discussed matters that were in the past. He was a man solely interested in the future.

Kili, too, was now in the past, but his impact on the future was great. Dalam's grief had reinforced his determination to save the imprisoned Engulu, the last of his old guard.

"The date of Engulu's execution has been set," he told Bunkeya.

"When is it?"

"Too soon," said Dalam, rubbing his temples. "Too soon."

In his cell in Rumonge prison, Engulu had awakened with a sense of dread. The day had arrived. The day his death would be set by the court of appeals in Bujumbura, written in an appointment book as though it were merely a date to have his hair cut or his laundry pressed.

Breakfast remains lay on a tray on his cot. At least they were feeding him well, he thought wryly. Better than anything he ever got with the FPL. He wondered how the others were doing. Lumbawa. And Jumbe. And Kassum. All the friends locked within these walls. He never saw them, not from where he was: death row.

At nine o'clock, they came for him. He joined two other men in the back of a bus for the trip to the courthouse. They did not look at him, but shifted uncomfortably in their seats and stared at the passing streets through barred windows. They must smell my death, thought Engulu. Cowards. Are they afraid they'll catch it like some contagious disease?

It hadn't been his wish to kill the two policemen. Everything had gone wrong on the mission. Everything. The shipment was smaller than expected, and the smugglers escalated their price. False alarms were blown. Engulu checked out the final rendezvous spot, but at the crucial moment the police discovered it.

The two officers died when their car overturned while chasing his. Engulu was charged as if he'd stabbed them on a sidewalk. Not that he wouldn't have if the need had arisen; he'd done it many times before. The irony was to be caught this time.

At least he hadn't divulged anything about the fishing trawler, the FPL's only major asset. Engulu allowed himself a glimmer of pride that he'd kept it secret in the face of the debacle. He assumed the men on board sailed back across Lake Tanganyika to Zaire when he didn't show. He wondered how Dalam took the news of his capture. Perhaps he—

What? What did he expect Dalam to do?

The bus jolted to a stop and Engulu was ushered into a courtroom, the same one in which his appeal had been denied. The judge entered and everyone stood. Engulu remained standing. You're already a dead man, he told himself in an attempt to combat his rising nerves, they can't do anything worse to you. You're already dead.

"Chedial Engulu," said the judge, "this court having found you guilty of two counts of first-degree murder, and having sentenced you to death, it remains only to set a date for the execution of said sentence. Because of the nature of the crime, and the obvious lack of reparation on your part, I see no point in delaying this matter. This court hereby sets July 8 as the date on which you will be taken from Rumonge prison to a designated spot, and there placed before a firing squad. Court dismissed."

July 8. The date burned itself into Engulu's consciousness. Eight days away. Holy Mary, mother of God, eight days. Death was no longer an abstract eventuality, but a hard, cold fact that burrowed into his gut. He crumpled to the table in front of him, hyperventilating.

Holy mother. Eight days.

*   *   *

"July eighth?" said Bunkeya. "It's the third today. Why so soon?"

"His trial was so well publicized—it became a crusade with the government press—that it's whipped the Burundian people into a frenzy," said Dalam. "The judge wanted to expedite matters."

"So he'll be shot to death," said Bunkeya.

"Not if I can help it," said Dalam.

Pictures didn't do Dalam justice. Celluloid simply couldn't capture the real man—the audacious glint in his eyes, the quiet intensity. Dalam did not just sit in a room, he filled it, engulfing those around him in an ideological jet stream.

Bunkeya recalled that Dalam's people, in southern Zaire, when first introduced to the camera, feared it. They believed that taking a photograph of a man robbed him of his soul. Perhaps at one time Dalam believed the myth, and taught himself to transport his "soul"—those elements of ambition and vitality and drive—so that when the shutter clicked, only his physical properties remained to be photographed. An empty hull without spirit.

"What can we do in five days?" asked Bunkeya. "That's so little time."

"We discussed it while you were gone," said Dalam. "I've decided to proceed with the kidnapping."

Bunkeya sat rigid. Mpinga, it seemed, had been hard at work during Bunkeya's absence. With Kili gone, nothing had stood in his way. Dalam, of course, would never admit that his decision was based on anyone's input but his own. Such was his ego that often, after listening to another's suggestion, he became so absorbed in the intricacies of carrying out the plan that he believed it to be his own inspiration. And who among his men would say anything to the contrary?

"I know of your objections, Bunkeya," continued Dalam, "but you must set them aside now. This is our only way. As you yourself said, we have no other resources."

"I still maintain that the Burundian government won't respond to our demands," said Bunkeya. "Not even if we kidnap the President. And it must be a government official, because only the government has the power to release our men from prison."

"It doesn't have to be a public official," said Dalam.

"I don't understand," said Bunkeya. "What good would kidnapping a private citizen do? Our only gain would be money—if there were any wealthy Burundians around, which there aren't. The only wealthy people in Bujumbura are foreigners."

"Precisely," said Dalam. He waited to see if Bunkeya's reasoning would forge ahead without any additional information, a sort of informal challenge.

"You're suggesting we kidnap a wealthy foreigner?"

"As long as he's prominent."

"You've lost me."

"It's not the money we're concerned with here, is it? But pressure. Pressure on the Burundians to release our men. And what better pressure than that—"

"—of another country's government," completed Bunkeya. "You choose a foreigner because that person's government will bring additional pressure to bear on the Burundians to secure his release."

"Yes," said Dalam. "The Burundians could write off their own countryman as a martyr. They can't do that with a foreigner."

"But will they bow to that pressure?" asked Bunkeya, interested despite his misgivings. "Will they be willing to set a potentially destructive precedent for someone who's not even a citizen?"

"It depends on the country of the kidnap victim. If a rift in the relations between that country and Burundi would prove disastrous to Burundi, then yes, I believe they'll bargain."

"So we need to find a country with that amount of leverage."

"Exactly," said Dalam. "Now, the Chinese carry considerable weight. The textile mill they built has contributed greatly to Burundi's manufacturing capacities. Cotton production is up. And the Chinese promise more.

"The most obvious selection is Belgium. It's kept close ties with Burundi ever since Liberation, and continues to dominate imports to the country. The Belgians also contribute sizable aid, have numerous investments in Bujumbura, and were largely responsible for involving the Common Market Development Fund in Burundi's tea production.

"But there's a third country that interests me more," continued Dalam. "It buys more than one-half of Burundi's coffee crop. And since coffee comprises ninety percent of Burundi's exports, an embargo on its purchase would throw Burundi into economic ruin. In addition, this country has endured several foreign kidnappings and long hostage periods over the last few years and is unlikely to take another one sitting down."

Bunkeya interrupted his leader's monologue. There was no longer any question in his mind.

"The United States of America," he said.

"Quite so," said Dalam. A curl formed on his lips.

"Joey's the youngest of the three gorillas. He's six," said Abbie, grabbing hold of the rope dangling from the tree in the courtyard. The sun had dropped in the sky and her shadow ran partway up Evan's leg.

"Swing push more," Joey signed, wrapping his hands around the rope. Abbie pulled him back by the midsection and gave him enough of a push to start him swinging.

"How old are the other two?"

"Winston is nine. He was four when I moved here five years ago. Originally I wanted only young gorillas, because as they get older they don't know their strength and are harder to work with. But now I wouldn't trade him for anything in the world."

"And Fran?"

"She's seven, not yet the adult that Winston is. I'll introduce you to her after her lesson is over."

"Lesson?"

"Yeah. Larry—that's another of my students—is running her through a drill on the computer."

"You've got a computer here? What for?"

"Mainly we use it as a supplement to our regular teaching. Helps us study the gorillas' syntax and stuff like that. Best part about it is that it vocalizes whatever the ape punches in."

"You mean it talks?"

"Yeah, it's got a voice synthesizer. Floored me the first time I heard it. Sounded like the voice of God."

"What's the point of having it speak?"

"For one thing, it reinforces the gorillas' recognition of spoken words."

"They can understand oral speech?"

"Only about fifty words or so. Their names, types of food."

"Planning on teaching them to talk?" Evan asked, jokingly.

"No, it's already been tried."

"You're serious?"

"Yes. A chimp actually spoke three or four words. She was owned by this couple named Hayes and they were able to get her to say 'mama' and a couple other words that I don't remember. But as I mentioned earlier—or you did, rather—the muscles and vocal cords of an ape aren't suited for speech. It's a dead end in terms of study."

Joey jumped off the rope and planted himself at Evan's feet, his arm extended, the palm up as if soliciting money.

"I have the funny feeling that he wants something," said Evan.

"Yes. Your G-U-M," Abbie spelled out.

"My what?"

"In your pocket."

Evan had forgotten the pack of Wrigley's in his shirt pocket.

"Gum," signed the ape, bending two extended fingers from a closed fist into his cheek, and straightening them again.

"That's one of the words he's familiar with, huh?"

"Very familiar. That's why we spell it out when we don't want him to know what we're talking about."

"Is it okay for him to have some?"

"Sure," Abbie said. "As long as you don't mind parting with it."

Evan crouched awkwardly next to the ape, secretly pleased

with himself for having overcome his fear, and reached into his pocket for the gum. His fingers touched the pack and a thought flashed in his mind: Why not take advantage of this opportunity to converse with the ape? Evan let loose his hold on the gum and formulated a number of phrases before settling on "Do you want gum, Joey?" Nice and short, simple. He preferred it to "Here is gum for you, Joey," because, since it was a question, it demanded a response. Evan was about to start signing when the ape waved a hand at him, clearly requesting him to come closer.

Evan hopped a few inches toward the ape. Before he completed his first sign, Joey grabbed for the gum. Startled, Evan jerked his body backward, but the gum, and his shirt pocket, remained in the ape's grasp. For the second time that day, Evan found himself sprawled on the ground with a gorilla leaning over him.

Joey politely handed the pocket back to Evan, drooping it over the supine man's knee, and deftly tore the covering off the pack. With the utmost delicacy, he peeled back the aluminum foil from the first stick and offered it to Evan. When Evan did not reach for it, Joey stuck the stick into his mouth and chewed.

"Good gum like," the ape signed as he walked back to the rope.

A young man dressed in the pseudo-military uniform favored by the young FPL recruits—khaki pants and shirt, a crocodile patch on the left shoulder—entered the room with a stack of papers and then left noiselessly.

Bunkeya studied the pictures in the pile, two culled from newspapers and one from a magazine. The first showed a black man with glasses, dressed in a dark suit. He was seated behind a desk. The second, a white man, heavily tanned, with rolled-up sleeves. The third, a white woman, and next to her, a gorilla.

"All Americans?" asked Bunkeya.

"Yes," said Dalam, retrieving the pictures. "We narrowed the list down to these three, and found out all we could about them. The first is an executive with a large American chemical corporation. The other man's an agriculturalist. The woman's a university linguist."

"How do they stack up against one another?"

"The first keeps regular hours at his job downtown and would be relatively easy to snatch. He also has the advantage of corporate weight behind him. His company has extensive contracts with the U.S. government, and that might be reflected in U.S. pressure on the Burundians. But that's only a guess. In other corporate kidnappings the U.S. government has steadfastly refused to intervene."

"What about the agriculturalist?"

"A government employee, so that's an advantage. Works with another U.S. official. If we took both, so much the better. Problem is he works somewhere in eastern Burundi. His routine is flexible and he keeps no regular schedule. Finding him would take time."

"Engulu's execution is in five days."

"That's the problem. As for the third, she works in a primate center on the outskirts of Bujumbura. She's sponsored by a wealthy American university and operates with a cadre of about a dozen students. If we took some of the students, we'd have the double advantage of pressure from their parents and the university. We're not sure about the security system at her center. It could pose a problem."

"May I read those?" asked Bunkeya, pointing to the papers.

"Certainly."

Bunkeya perused the list carefully. He flipped through the photos slowly, lingering over one particular picture. Finally, he handed the stack of papers back to Dalam.

"There's really only one choice," he said.

"Yes," said Dalam. "I thought you'd see it that way."

"The woman," said Bunkeya, tossing her photo from *Time* on the table. He stumbled over the unfamiliar name: "Abbie Guisbourne."

"Yes. Abbie Guisbourne," Dalam repeated.

* * *

It was embarrassing. First she'd insisted on tickling his ear. Then she'd planted a string of wet, gentle kisses on his face. And now this. Was Evan crazy or was this gorilla making advances?

"She won't let go of my legs," said Evan.

"Fran," signed Abbie. "Come here to me."

The gorilla refused to let go of Evan's legs.

"Oh, my God, what is she doing?" asked Evan.

Fran was rubbing her torso up and down his leg.

"I've never seen her do this before," said Abbie.

"Can you get her to stop it?" Evan's voice was unnaturally shrill. Had he not been so conscious of the heat surging to his own face, he might have noticed the pink in Abbie's cheeks.

"Fran, take my hand. Come here, Fran." Abbie tugged on the ape's hand, but Fran kept a firm grip on Evan's belt. Two of Evan's belt loops broke before the gorilla let go.

"Why did you hold the man?" Abbie signed.

"Beanface nice," the ape signed.

"Beanface?" Abbie signed.

"There man nice."

"What is she saying?" Evan asked. Fran's thumbs, like those of all gorillas, were smaller than a human's and her fingers were less dexterous. Evan was having difficulty understanding some of her signs. Later he would learn that many of them were bastardized versions of the ones he had been taught.

"As I see it," said Abbie, "she's calling you a bean face."

"Is that good or bad?"

"I'm not sure." Abbie signed, "Fran, the man's name is Evan." She molded the correct sign in the ape's palm.

"Beanface," Fran signed.

"Yep, she just christened you Beanface, all right," Abbie said.

"She can call me anything she wants as long as she stays on that side of the room," Evan said, hiking up his pants.

"Let me try to interest her in the computer console one more time. Come on, Fran."

The ape climbed obediently into her seat before the console. Evan crept around to the side and positioned himself at a safe distance to watch. The sudden clack of a motor behind him shattered his already frayed nerves.

"Christ, what now?" he said, spinning around.

"Oh, that. It's a Teletype connected through the computer to Brice's chimpanzee center in southern Burundi. Someone's sending a message."

The machine rapidly spit out letters:

SFX 98

AG

FORGOT TO ADD ONE MORE THING ABOUT MY VISIT WITH RICHE. ARE ALL YOU AMERICANS SO FIXATED BY THE CINEMA? WHILE PRESENTING MY REPORT TO THE ERSTWHILE BRICE BOARD, RICHE KEPT REFERRING TO THE CHIMPANZEES AS CHEETAHS. I COULD NOT UNDER-STAND HOW HE COULD CONFUSE A PRIMATE WITH A FE-LINE (HOWEVER LIMITED HIS MENTAL CAPABILITIES) UNTIL IT OCCURRED TO ME THAT HE WAS THINKING OF THE TARZAN MOVIES.

HE CONTINUED TO CALL THEM CHEETAHS AND I RE-VERTED TO MONOSYLLABIC COMMUNICATION CONSISTING OF "ME MIC. YOU RICHE. ME NEED MORE FUNDS."

IT WORKED SPLENDIDLY. I SUGGEST YOU USE IT NEXT TIME IN THE STATES, LOVE.

—MIC

"Who's he?" asked Evan.

"A very gifted anthropologist, originally from Oxford, studying chimpanzee behavior near Nyanza-Lac. At a place called Muwali."

"A friend of yours?"

"Sort of," she replied, dismissing the subject. "Ready to see the computer at work?" She picked up an orange that Chandra had left from a previous lesson. "Fran, do you want this orange?"

The gorilla depressed a number of buttons, then sat back and watched Evan, her head tilted to one side.

Within seconds, a male voice—unmistakably the product of a machine, jerky and tinny—boomed from the speakers.

"Want Beanface."

An uneasy silence enveloped the room.

"I don't think she meant it like it sounded," Abbie ventured. "See, she hit the 'play' button and she thought it lighted up but it didn't. It should have been 'Want *play* Beanface.' "

"Look how late it is," said Evan. The rumble of the masculine voice seemingly issuing from nowhere, coupled with the lascivious ape, was proving too much for him. "I really want to thank you for the tour. It was most informative."

Evan pulled his keys from his pocket, but accidentally dropped them on the ground. The gorilla dashed over and picked them up.

"Why, thank you . . ." Evan's voice trailed off as the ape ran out the door with the keys in her hand.

"Damn," Abbie said. "How good are you at hide-and-go-seek?"

"Look," said Dalam, pointing to the photograph of Abbie Guisbourne. He put it next to the page in the *Time* magazine from which it had been torn. "Here is a story about Zaire. And here, on the next page, is this American woman. We are as close to the release of our men as our country is to her in this magazine."

Dalam spoke of the conjunction of articles as though it were an omen. This was part of his appeal, too: a strain of mysticism that harked back to the spiritualism of the African shamans. Bunkeya, privy to Dalam's cynical, pragmatic side, knew that the man did not believe the superstition he sometimes preached, that he merely used it as a dramatic tool.

"What do you plan?" Bunkeya asked.

"We take the students and the woman. Hold them as hostages until we get what we want."

"And if not?"

"We kill them."

Dalam was not one to mince words; he meant what he said.

"How is the kidnapping to take place?" asked Bunkeya.

"I'm not sure yet."

"Not sure?" Bunkeya was surprised by the admission. It was so unlike Dalam not to have every last detail of a mission plotted before he presented it.

"I don't know yet how this operation should go. I want you to find that out for me. You have a keen mind for plotting strategy. And a sense for the larger things, as well. A scope."

Another of Dalam's tactics: a fatherly buildup of the other man's sense of self-worth, while covertly directing him toward his own aims. He was very good at it.

"But do we have time?" asked Bunkeya.

"If we move quickly. What I need to know is the layout of the camp. Mainly the security. What guards. The best form of attack and when. Escape routes."

Bunkeya took a mental step back from the conversation and assessed what was happening to him. Dalam's manipulative techniques were sucking him into the mechanics of the kidnapping with the unremitting pull of a vacuum. Bunkeya knew he should fight the pull; his initial opposition to the kidnapping had not waned. More importantly, he had reached a decision in the early hours of the morning. He wanted out of the FPL.

But that decision was counterbalanced by a heavy weight: Dalam himself. With Kili dead, Engulu jailed, and the FPL structure in a state of near collapse, a departure now would be tantamount to betrayal. Bunkeya did not want to stay. The anxiety attacks that had plagued his last missions were steadily increasing. If he tackled a new mission, especially one as strenuous as a kidnapping, it might blow up in his face. But he saw no alternative. He was not a betrayer.

"All right," he said. "How shall I approach it?"

"That's already settled. There's an offshoot to this woman's primate center—a camp studying chimpanzees, farther south. Once a month they send someone up to Bujumbura for supplies. We've learned they have a new man. He was hired in

Bujumbura two weeks ago. His name is Ula. He'll show up at Guisbourne's center this week."

"No one in the center has ever seen him, correct?" said Bunkeya, his mind racing ahead.

"Very astute," said Dalam. "You and I, we think alike."

"How do you want the transfer to occur?"

"On the road from Muwali, the chimpanzee camp. You'll ambush the courier and arrive in his place. No one will be the wiser. Mpinga will be with you. You'll drop him off on the outskirts of Bujumbura. He'll be your contact." Dalam smiled. "I had to give him some part of this. He expected to be doing what you'll be doing, you know."

The prospect of working with Mpinga briefly unsettled Bunkeya. "And what of this Ula?" he asked.

"Eliminate him. And try not to waste a bullet. A man left unconscious in the jungle doesn't survive long. So many hungry animals."

"I understand."

"I'm sure you do."

The jeep bumped along the road, and Evan clung to the handrail attached to the dashboard. He and Abbie had not spoken during the trip. He supposed it was his fault. After the ape ran off with his keys he hadn't felt very talkative. They'd scouted the compound for fifteen minutes in vain. Fran turned up, but no keys. ("Keys gone," the ape signed helpfully.) Abbie volunteered to drive Evan back to the embassy and promised to conduct an all-out search for the missing keys once she returned to the center.

The jeep turned onto Chaussée Prince Louis Rwagasora and pulled to a stop in front of the embassy. Evan stepped down to the sidewalk.

"I'm sorry Fran took your keys," said Abbie. "I'm coming into town around ten-thirty tomorrow, so I'll pick you up, provided I find the keys by then, and you can come back with me to get your car."

"It's not even my car," Evan said.

"Fran didn't mean anything by it. She's just a playful animal."

"Your animals, Ms. Guisbourne, are about as playful as Godzilla. No offense." He stumbled up the stairs to the embassy door.

"Tomorrow then?"

Evan nodded and pushed open the glass door. He caught sight of his reflection as he walked past: his clothes covered with dirt, blood on his cheek and collar, his shirt torn, untucked, and missing a pocket, the pants leg ripped from the knee down, his belt riding above the waistband on one side, the belt loops flapping as he walked. A refugee from a training camp for bouncers.

Davenport took one look at him and said, "Jesus, Olgilvie. What happened to you?"

"Who me?" answered Evan. "Nothing really. I just had my first lesson in primate research."

V

The next morning at exactly ten-thirty Abbie picked up Evan and drove him to the primate center.

"Where did you find them?" asked Evan, as Abbie descended the steps from her trailer.

"Fran stuck them under a blanket," said Abbie. She handed him the keys to the embassy car. They sparkled in the morning sun. "She brought them out when I got back."

"I'm glad they turned up. I would have hated to—"

At that moment Chandra and Fran appeared in the courtyard. The gorilla jumped up and down excitedly. Evan quickly jammed the keys deep into his pants pocket. Fran sat by his feet.

"See?" said Abbie. "She's much better mannered today. Look how happy she is to see you."

Evan looked down at the gorilla's placid face.

"That's happy?" he asked. "How do you tell it from sad?"

"Oh, once you're around them for a while you see all sorts of expressions you didn't see before."

"You know something," said Evan, "I never got one of them to talk back to me yesterday. You mind if I try one more time?"

"Be my guest. You may have noticed that some of our signs depart from standard Amesal. What did you want to say?"

"Might as well start out simple. Is your sign for 'hello' the same one I know?"

"A little different," said Abbie. "Like this." She raised a

flat hand parallel to the side of her face and touched her temple with her index finger before drawing her hand away.

"Hello, Fran," Evan signed, copying the sign.

"Hello Beanface," the ape responded.

Evan was delighted.

"Did you see that? She answered me. How about that? I mean, I know it's nothing to you. You talk to them every day."

"Try something else. You can't lose. You'll never get a more captive audience."

"How are you?" Evan signed, then added out loud, "That was a stupid thing to ask, huh? That's such a human question."

"Not really," said Abbie. "Look."

"Happy," signed Fran, vigorously brushing her hands in flat strokes over her chest.

"Well, look at that!"

"Yes." Abbie petted the ape on the head. "It was nice meeting you, Evan. I'm sorry about the delay with your keys and all. You can assure your superiors that I won't be driving with the apes again in—"

Evan wasn't listening to her. "Let me try one more thing, okay? What's the sign for 'good'? It's slipped my mind."

Before Abbie could respond, Fran shaped her hands into the proper formation.

"My God," said Evan. "She understood me."

Fran belched contentedly.

"She didn't really understand you," said Abbie. "She just recognized the word 'good.' "

"You are good, Fran," signed Evan.

"Tickle me," the ape signed.

"That movement under her arms," Evan said to Abbie, "what does it mean?"

"Tickle. She's asking you to tickle her. She came up with that sign herself."

"You're kidding?" said Evan, ever so lightly scratching the ape.

"No, she'll invent signs for things she doesn't know. Or call it by a sign that's already familiar to her and loosely describes the new object. The first time she saw a cigarette she called it a straw. She'll also string words together to name an object. The first time she saw lipstick she called it face crayon. And just two days ago she called a ring a finger bracelet."

"No wonder I was having difficulty understanding some of her signs."

"That and the fact that the gorilla's lack of manual dexterity causes some problems." She lifted Fran's hand. "See how small her thumb is in proportion to her hand? The size makes it impossible for her to sign things like 'sand' and 'purple,' so we substitute our own signs. Also, we simplify signs. Water, for example, is just the 'W' configuration, then an extended forefinger."

"Clever."

"You watch it for a while and you'll catch on," Abbie said. She signed to Fran, "What time is it? What time?"

"Play." Fran clapped her hands together in front of her body.

"No. Eat." With her thumb and forefinger in an "O" configuration, Abbie touched her fingertips to her lips.

"Eat," repeated Fran.

"Okay, now we go."

"Beanface."

"What?"

"Beanface come."

Abbie smiled at Evan. "She wants you to come to lunch." She signed, "Sorry, Fran. Beanface has to go for a ride."

The gorilla yelled, a clearer protestation than any number of finger formations.

"I think I've got an admirer," said Evan.

"Come Beanface now eat," the gorilla signed, sitting on top of Evan's shoes.

"She's on my feet," said Evan. "What do I do?"

"Come on, Fran. Get off his feet." Abbie tugged on the ape's hand.

"I'd really like to go to lunch, Fran, but—" Evan began, stopping when she interrupted him with a sign. "Why is she rubbing herself like that?"

"Where?" asked Abbie.

"On the shoulder. See? She's got two fingers rubbing her shoulder."

"Oh, Fran!" Abbie said out loud.

"What does it mean?"

"It's the sign for hurt. She's telling us her arthritis has flared up."

"A gorilla with arthritis?"

"Yeah. She's got a real mild case. In the shoulder."

"Shouldn't you do something for it?" Evan asked.

"Ah, she's just faking it. It's a ploy for attention. She doesn't want you to go."

"Are you sure? What if it really hurts?"

"See? She's getting to you already."

"You know"—he glanced at his wristwatch—"I've got forty-five minutes for lunch. I could take it now."

"Sucker."

"How can I turn down an invitation from a female who goes to such lengths?"

Fran belched again.

Abbie smiled. "You'll spoil her."

"I'll have to live with that."

"Okay. The feeding trailer is over here." Abbie led the way. "I sure hope you like bananas . . ."

Fran's appetite, Evan learned, was nothing short of gargantuan. She ate a vast quantity of vegetables, a pint of milk, and a large portion of meat—a foodstuff that wild gorillas never eat. In the jungle, gorillas subsist on bamboo shoots, celery, nettles, bark, thistles, and other vegetable growth. The three in Abbie's care had demonstrated a healthy predilection for cold cuts from the very beginning. Fran was especially partial to bologna. For dessert she had cheese and bananas, and finished by delicately licking her fingers.

"Healthy appetite," said Evan.

"This is nothing," said Abbie. "Out in the wild they eat anywhere from twenty to forty pounds of fruits and vegetables."

"Per day?"

"Yeah."

"So will this meal hold her for the rest of today?"

"Are you kidding?" Abbie laughed. "This is already the third time she's eaten. And she'll eat again in another couple of hours."

"That's unreal. What's her favorite food?"

"She likes peanut butter a lot. Loves beer, but I don't let her have it."

"Beer?" Evan wiped a smear of mayonnaise from the corner of his mouth.

"Yeah. It's less that I'm protecting her from the evils of alcohol than it'd cost me a mint to keep her supplied."

"Banana," signed Fran, rubbing one index finger on top of the other. Abbie handed her one.

Evan gulped down the last of his milk. "So you've been here five years?"

"Sure have."

"You plan on being here for much longer? Five years must seem like a long time."

"Well," said Abbie, popping a last shred of sandwich into her mouth, "it's taken me till now to get my Ph.D. That's what brought me here in the first place. I can't think of anything that would give me as much satisfaction as this. You know, five years for someone in primate research really isn't that long. Dian Fossey spent thirteen years studying the mountain gorillas in Rwanda."

She washed down the sandwich with a glass of orange juice. It did not surprise Evan that she finished eating before him. Here, too, she wasted no time.

"It's hard to explain to an outsider," she continued. "I guess it boils down to belief in my work. Sort of like one of those intangible beliefs in a deity. If you believe, you don't need explanations. If you don't believe, there's no explanation that will ever suit you."

"Have you been back to the States at all?"

"Sure. I go back to make my token reports to Brice. Hand in

papers. I try not to be gone too long, because the gorillas go into a blue funk and won't eat."

"You don't miss life back there?"

"Some of it. But this is home now."

The door to the trailer flew open.

"Excuse me," signed Chandra. "I didn't realize you had company."

"That's all right," signed Abbie. "What is it?"

"Larry is ready for the experiment with Winston."

"Good, thank you. Can you take over Fran?"

"Of course."

"Well, Evan," said Abbie, "would you care to finish your lunch with a visit to Winston?"

"What kind of mood has he been in lately?" asked Evan.

"Fine. Only broke two necks yesterday."

Evan smiled, relieved that she possessed some sense of humor where the gorillas were concerned.

"In that case," he said, "lead on."

The trailer they entered was the same one in which Evan had watched Winston the day before. The single change: a bunch of bananas suspended from the ceiling. A young man stood next to the sitting gorilla.

"Larry?" said Abbie. "This is Evan Olgilvie, the man from the State Department who stopped by yesterday. Larry Caruthers."

"Nice to meet you," Larry said. "Abbie, I've got the camera set up even though I wasn't sure you wanted it. You want this on tape?"

"Yeah, although I'm not counting on much."

"What's going to happen?" asked Evan.

"We're trying to test Winston's ability to use tools. What we do is place food where he can't reach it, either up in the air or behind something. Then we lay a stick on the floor and see if he'll use it to get the food. So far we've had no luck. Unlike chimps, gorillas just aren't tool users."

Larry positioned the gorilla under the bananas and, stepping over the baseball bat left on the floor, took his place behind the camera.

"That's your idea of a stick?" asked Evan.

"Well, we had a branch the first time but Winston started to eat it, so this time we got something a little more solid."

"And you want him to hit the fruit down with that bat?"

"Right. We haven't given him any instructions or anything. It's just up to him."

"Fine. I think I'll just stand back a bit."

Winston anxiously circled below the fruit. He tentatively stood on his feet, then dropped to the floor and paced. Evan recognized the gorilla's agitation from their encounter the day before. Suddenly Winston jumped, his long arm extended in the air, and tried to grab the lowest banana. He missed and thudded back to the floor.

Vibrations from Winston's landing rattled the trailer windows. The gorilla could not have more dramatically illustrated the enormous span of those strong arms had he tried. Evan imagined the destruction the ape could wreak with a baseball bat in his hands. He stepped back a few more feet.

"Just want to give him some breathing room," he mumbled.

Winston resumed pacing the floor. He pirouetted at the far wall and abruptly stopped. Something caught his eye. Evan followed the ape's line of vision and reasoned that the object of interest was a stack of tires in the corner. Winston proved him correct by pulling the tires into the center of the trailer, directly under the bananas.

The gorilla stepped on the first tire but was short of the lowest banana. He picked up a second tire, threw it on top of the first, and clambered aboard. The top tire teetered unsteadily. With a yell that could have set off a cavalry charge, Winston pushed himself off the stacked tires—which immediately became unstacked—and grabbed the bunch of bananas.

"Well done," said Evan. Abbie and Larry wore glum expressions. "Not well done?"

"Next time we run this I'll have to make sure there's nothing for him to climb on," said Abbie.

"But didn't he successfully complete the task?"

"Yes, but he didn't use a tool. Those tires don't constitute a tool. The stick does. Hell, I guess the idea's just never going to occur to him. Thanks a lot, Larry. You can give him the rest of his lunch now."

Winston happily peeled a second banana. Abbie walked outside, and Evan followed her.

"Where's the third one?" he asked.

"Joey? In his trailer. He hasn't been very energetic today. I've got to check and see how he's doing."

"I won't take up any more of your time then," said Evan.

"I'll walk you to your car."

At the gate, Evan reached into his pocket and produced the car keys.

"Thanks for lunch. Tell Fran I appreciated it."

"I will."

Evan opened the car door, but instead of entering, he leaned against the frame.

"I don't suppose you'd be able to get a babysitter for them tonight."

"For who?"

"The gorillas. I thought maybe you and I could have dinner. Believe it or not, I've yet to see the Bujumburan night life."

"I appreciate the offer, but I don't think—"

"Look, I'll be honest with you. I don't know how you've managed to survive this place for five years, but I can tell you that I'm pretty tired of eating dinner by myself." He laughed. "God, that's a switch. In Uruguay I complained all the time because I always had to go out for dinner. At any rate, I could do with a little companionship. What do you say? Look on it as your good deed for the day."

"All right," she said, smiling. "When shall I expect you? Or would you prefer I meet you somewhere?"

"No, I'll come here. How about seven?"

"That's fine. See you then."

During the drive back into town Evan tried to figure out what made Abbie Guisbourne tick. She seemed perfectly normal on the outside, but she had to be a little crazy to devote all her time to three gorillas. How could someone so apparently rational let herself become so emotionally attached to a bunch of animals?

Before entering the office, Evan stopped to buy a wicker-work doll from a street vendor. For Fran, the little girl of a friend of his, he told the vendor.

The old man winked.

"The timetable has been moved up," said Dalam. "Ula, the delivery boy, leaves tomorrow for Bujumbura. You and Mpinga must leave today in order to intercept him."

Bunkeya did not question how Dalam got this information, nor why the man who relayed it did not simply substitute himself for Ula. Bunkeya already knew the answer: He was the best at such things. The damnable best.

"All right. How will we know him?"

"He'll probably be the only one traveling the road. Look for a Land Rover. It'll have a sticker from Brice, Abbie Guisbourne's university, on the windshield. He'll approach the primate center around noon."

"And Mpinga?"

"He'll separate from you once you've disposed of the courier, and check back with you tomorrow night. You'll arrange the details with him. If you've had time to scout the compound, give him your suggestions then, and he'll report back to us. Depending on what you say, it'll go off the next day or the day after. Here are your papers for the border check. Mpinga has the rest of your gear."

"Fine."

"We'll see you in a few days."

"Yes."

Dalam left the room without saying "good luck." There was no such thing as luck in the FPL. Bunkeya's luck was in his mind and in his hands and in his nerve.

Abbie's hands were covered with markings from a green Kadopen. She took a twelve-by-twelve-inch sheet of white construction paper from the pile and lazily drew a couple of intersecting lines on it. Her thoughts were elsewhere, on the young embassy official who didn't treat her as though she were an oddity. She sensed in him the potential to understand why she did what she did, why it was important. Few people ever did, not even her own family, and she was tired of being labeled an eccentric.

Abbie held her drawing to the light and added two more lines.

"Okay, what does this look like to you?"

David and Chandra, busily scribbling their own drawings, looked in her direction. The two students capped their Kadopens.

"Frankly," said David, "it looks identical to the bird you drew."

"Does it? I don't want these drawings too complete, you know. The whole point is to test how well Joey can recognize everyday objects from sketches made out of a few lines. To see how advanced his sense of abstraction is."

"Well," said David, "if he's going to make any sense out of that thing he better have the abstract appreciation of a Picasso."

"Be fair. Doesn't this look like an airplane to you? See the wings and the tail? Hell, we've got enough of these anyway. I'll go get Joey."

The trailer next door reeked of peanut butter and jelly sandwiches, a smell not unknown to the camp since Joey, like Fran, doted on the sandwiches, eating one at every 2 P.M. feeding. Abbie entered just as the ape consumed a last bite. Larry was at the counter cutting vegetables. Abbie stood quietly in the doorway and watched the two. Joey, signing the word "quiet," much as a human being might speak to himself, sneaked up on Larry and lightly bit the student on the hip.

"Damn it, Joey, knock it off."

Abbie laughed and stepped into the room. "What does he want you to do?"

"He wants some more C-A-N-D-Y. I told him I wasn't going to give him any more, but he hasn't given up." Larry rubbed his hip. "Who taught him to get attention that way, anyway? My ass is covered with bruises."

"No one taught him. He thought it up all by his little self, didn't you, Joey?" Abbie bent down to the gorilla and signed, "Are you being bad to Larry?"

"Good happy."

"What did you eat?"

"Candy." He brushed his lower lips with two fingers.

"Joey, you're signing the wrong thing. You ate a sandwich. Sandwich," she repeated.

"Sandwich," signed the ape. He extended his right arm and thrust his curved hand upward. "Up me hurry."

"Where?"

"He wants you to lift him to the cabinet," said Larry.

"Key." Joey bent two fingers at the knuckle and rotated them clockwise on the palm of the opposite hand. "Open please gimme key."

"Why?" asked Abbie.

"Bottle there candy."

"This gorilla has a one-track mind," said Larry.

"Open key hurry."

"No more candy." Abbie shook her head and maneuvered Joey toward the door. "We're going to have to hide that bottle of M&Ms, Larry. We'll be in number three."

David and Chandra had winnowed the sheets of paper down to about a dozen when Abbie and Joey entered. The plan was for Abbie to lay the papers face down in her lap, then hold them up one at a time and ask Joey what he saw. At no time would Abbie know what picture she held, so she could not inadvertently transmit information about the picture to the ape. This method of experimentation, in which the experimentor is "blind" to a certain part of the procedure, was used to legitimize test results. The exercise began.

"Look, Joey." Abbie held up the first drawing, a picture of a sketchily delineated boat, a triangle on top of a half-circle, no more. "What is this?"

"Paper." The gorilla hit the heels of his hands together.

"Way to go, Joey," David said, his laughter carrying across the trailer. "How's that make you feel, Abbie? Outsmarted by one of your own gorillas."

"This is a boat," Abbie explained to the ape after she'd turned over the drawing. "See the boat? I'll draw it." She traced a finger over the geometric figures. "Make boat. See the picture?"

"Boat," signed Joey.

"Yes, that's right." She moved on to the next picture, a flower. "What is this?"

"Flower." He touched his nose with a curved hand.

Chandra unobtrusively recorded his response in a ledger balanced across her knees.

"Okay," Abbie continued, "and what is this?"

The ape scrutinized a picture of a hat.

"Don't know," he signed.

"Think."

"Brush." With spread fingers, he rubbed the back of his forearm.

"What is this?" Abbie held up a picture of a telephone.

"Paper bad nut nut!"

"What?"

"Damn no want."

"Joey—"

"Bored Joey gimme paper."

"I don't think he's too wild about this test," said David.

"Ah, I think he's pissed because he didn't get more candy with lunch," said Abbie. "What do you want to do, Joey?"

"Pen please draw."

"You want to draw a picture?"

"Pen."

"Okay." Abbie reached behind her and pulled a pad of construction paper and a Kadopen from the table. She uncapped the pen.

Joey took the pen and smelled it. He clumsily drew a few lines on the paper and, when satisfied with his drawing, presented it to the three human beings in the room.

"Damn!" said Abbie. "He wants us to guess what it is!"

"What picture?" asked Joey.

"All right. I'm game," said David. "A bird?"

"No." The ape shook his head.

"A clown?" asked Abbie.

"No."

"We don't know, Joey. What is it?" signed Abbie.

The gorilla added a few more lines.

"He's out to make us look dumb," said David. "He'll keep adding lines until he's filled in the whole picture."

"A cat?" signed Chandra.

"What is it, Joey?" asked Abbie.

"More think," signed the ape.

"He's not going to tell us," said David. "Little stinker wants us to sit here until we figure it out."

"Please, Joey," signed Abbie. "We don't know. What is it?"

The gorilla turned the drawing toward himself. For a moment Abbie thought he was going to add more lines. Instead, he motioned them to come closer and, when assured of an attentive audience, signed:

"That nothing." He tossed the paper on the floor.

"Smart-ass," said Abbie.

Joey beat his chest.

From his seat on the bus, Bunkeya viewed the glistening waters of Lake Tanganyika. In a short while they would reach the Burundian border. Bunkeya's second thoughts about the kidnapping no longer mattered; he could not pull out now.

He stretched his leg, and the large scab on his lower calf pulled uncomfortably. The wound was finally healing. Four rows ahead, next to a woman whose hair was wrapped in a blue kerchief, sat Mpinga. Bunkeya's worries about the viability of his and Mpinga's partnership had not lessened. He recalled the conversation that took place early that morning, and how it started: with the rifle.

"Your satchel's in the corner," Mpinga had said, packing his backpack in silence. Bunkeya did likewise. A series of familiar snaps and clinks disturbed the quiet, and Bunkeya glanced up at his companion. Mpinga had snapped shut the folding stock of his rifle, a near copy of the American infantry's M16, and was sliding it into the bottom of his rucksack.

"What's that for?" asked Bunkeya. "You won't be needing it. Not yet."

"Don't try to tell me what to pack or not to pack, Bunkeya. I've done fine without you."

"It'll only cause us problems if it's detected."

Mpinga secured the flap of the rucksack.

"I said leave it." Bunkeya grabbed the man's arm.

Mpinga twisted out of Bunkeya's grip. "You handle your part of this mission and I'll handle mine."

"There are no neatly defined parts here," said Bunkeya. "Whatever you do affects me."

"You may be in charge of this mission, Bunkeya, but you're not in charge of me."

"Believe me, it wasn't my idea to head this kidnapping. But that's how Dalam saw it, so you and I are going to have to try to get along. You listen to me, and I'll listen to you."

"Listen to you? Whose idea do you think this mission was? Mine. I've worked every detail out. If anyone should do the listening here, it's you."

"You can forget that idea," said Bunkeya. "We're on the same side, remember?"

"For today," said Mpinga, throwing his rucksack over his shoulder, "but you never can be sure about tomorrow."

The sharp reduction of the bus's speed brought Bunkeya's thoughts back to the present; they'd reached the border. The passengers began to file out the doors. Bunkeya lifted his backpack and joined the queue. Ever since Burundi and Zaire had aligned themselves with Rwanda in the CEPGL, La Communauté Economique des Pays des Grands Lacs, passage between the two nations had become a perfunctory affair. Only rarely did a guard search a traveler's possessions.

Mpinga was four places ahead of Bunkeya. The line moved quickly. When Mpinga's turn came to have his visa stamped, he slung his backpack off his shoulder and to the ground. It hit an iron leg of the table and pinged, the noise made when one metal connects with another. The sound aroused the curiosity of the border guard stamping Mpinga's visa. He stooped to the ground. Mpinga stood woodenly next to the table as the guard opened his satchel.

Bunkeya rapidly assessed the situation and saw only one possible solution. He stepped out of line and rushed forward, dragging his right leg behind.

"Please," he shouted. "I have to get through. I can't stand much longer. My leg." He limped his way to the guard investigating Mpinga's pack. "I've hurt myself."

Bunkeya lifted his pants leg and ripped his fingernail along the length of his scab. The wound bled anew. He let the leg collapse underneath him.

"Help me. I can't walk."

The guard quickly closed Mpinga's satchel and helped Bunkeya to his feet. Bunkeya leaned on the man and hobbled to a nearby bench. From the corner of his eye, he was able to watch Mpinga retrieve his backpack and ascend the stairs to the bus.

Blood trickled into Bunkeya's shoe while he waited for the guard to return with his stamped papers. His calf ached. Sunlight beat down on him, and flies alighted on his face and neck. Finally, the guard brought his papers and assisted him onto the bus.

Mpinga's face showed neither gratitude nor apology when Bunkeya passed by his seat; rather, his eyes flickered with resentment. Bunkeya was not surprised. The man had been shamed. He would not easily forget it. The episode pushed their uneasy partnership onto even more precarious ground.

As the bus lurched forward, it occurred to Bunkeya that one of them would probably destroy the other before the mission was completed. The disturbing part was that he was not certain who the corpse would be. He reached inside his satchel for the flask buried there, and by the time the bus pulled into the Bujumbura station, he no longer cared about corpses or hidden rifles or curious border guards. He was beyond caring.

*   *   *

Evan felt like an oversized teenager when he asked Davenport to lend him the keys to the embassy car. He half expected the deputy chief to demand that he be home by ten, and was boyishly pleased when Davenport grumbled his assent.

The day had passed slowly. More precisely, Evan had caused the day to pass slowly, glancing at the clock at neat intervals of forty minutes. He was either more bored by the inflation report he had to read or more intrigued by Abbie Guisbourne than he thought. Apathy or anticipation. He supposed it was a combination of both that had set him to watching the minute hand.

Six-thirty eventually rolled around, and Evan drove to the outskirts of Bujumbura. He parked outside the primate center, and Abbie appeared in the courtyard, the setting sun highlighting her hair. She wore a blue cotton dress.

"We can't go," she said, flinging open the gate.

These were not the words Evan expected from this vision of loveliness.

"Joey's sick," she said. "Damn, I should have kept a closer watch on him this afternoon."

"What's wrong with him?"

"I'm not sure. He threw up all his food. Could be a virus or something."

"Did you get anyone over here to check it out?"

"Of course I did," she said irritably. "A zoologist I know. He thinks Joey ate something that disagreed with him."

Why is it these things always happen to me? wondered Evan. A beautiful sunset, a lovely woman, an exotic country. A sick gorilla.

After following Abbie to the sickroom of the ailing ape—who looked to Evan the picture of a healthy ape, but what the hell did he know?—Evan noticed a slight improvement in her spirits. Chandra and David managed to convince her that Joey was improving and promised to watch him carefully. Abbie agreed to take a break from tending him, but adamantly refused to leave the camp.

"I'm sorry I ruined your plans, Evan," she said.

"It's perfectly okay," he said, thinking to himself: Next time I'll stand you up for a vomiting gorilla and see how you like it.

"I could use a drink. Want one?"

"Sure."

They walked silently to her trailer. For the first time, Abbie waited so that Evan was able to walk beside her. The trailer was dark—the sun had set while they were visiting Joey—but Abbie switched on only the lamp on her desk.

"Hope you like Scotch. We're sort of limited here."

"Fine." He sat down on the sofa.

She carried the bottle to the table and poured two drinks.

"I didn't mean to be so snappy before. Sorry." Abbie curled up in the chair opposite Evan and took a healthy swig from her glass.

"That's all right. I understand." He didn't.

"It's just that ever since Ngagi died, whenever one of the gorillas gets so much as a stuffy nose, I tend to fly off the handle. You happened to walk in on one of those occasions."

"Ngagi?"

"Yeah." She downed the drink. "When I started this place we had four gorillas. Ngagi was the oldest female, a little younger than Winston. The sweetest disposition you could imagine. And God, what a memory she had. She was quick, too. Anyway"—Abbie leaned forward—"you want another drink?"

"No, thanks. I'm still working on this one."

"Anyway"—Abbie poured herself another Scotch—"she got pneumonia. It happened so fast. I'm still not sure how. She was gone before we knew it."

"I'm sorry."

"You must think I'm crazy still mourning an ape. But you know, they have such a way of getting to you. It's like they remind you of everything good that's possible in man because they're so warm and gentle. And when you see something like that die—I don't care if it's a human being or an animal—it takes a long time to forget.

"I always worried about what effect her death had on the

three remaining gorillas. Fran spent a lot of time with Ngagi in her trailer, but we wouldn't let her in when Ngagi got sick. Right after Ngagi died, Fran somehow got back in the trailer when no one was there. I'm not sure whether she tried to wake up Ngagi or what, but when I walked in—"

Abbie put down her glass and rested her chin on top of her folded hands.

"When I walked in, Fran was covering Ngagi with straw. We'd had a bunch of it around for a test we were doing, and Fran found it. She didn't stop when I came in the room, just kept at it, scooping up handfuls and laying them over Ngagi. I closed the door and watched her. I knew I shouldn't let her be so close to Ngagi and yet I couldn't seem to do anything else. I guess I stood there for maybe ten minutes, not moving. Not saying a word. Fran covered Ngagi until all that was visible was her face, and then—I remember it so clearly— Fran reached out her hand and touched Ngagi's face and gently covered it, too. Then she retreated to the corner."

Abbie drained the last dollop of Scotch.

"Throughout the next few weeks, Joey and Winston would ask for Ngagi. Ask where she was, where we had taken her. Joey even thought he might have done something to make her go. But Fran never asked. She never signed Ngagi's name again. Winston and Joey stopped asking soon after that. I know they hadn't forgotten her. They just stopped asking . . ."

As if struck by a Joycean epiphany, Evan no longer found Abbie's attachment to the gorillas strange or extraordinary. Through the telling of her story, Abbie had provided him with the glimmerings of an understanding. She was not so much the pragmatist he thought, but an idealist, a woman whose work was tied into a dream she had conjured years ago. All that dedication, that relentless perseverance, was a magical step leading to the realization of that dream.

"The name Ngagi . . ." he said. "It has a beautiful sound. What does it mean?"

"Well, it's never been accurately translated. It's a Pygmy term for 'gorilla.' I guess loosely defined it means 'night chaser.' "

"What does that refer to?"

"The Pygmies believe it's the gorilla's yell in the morning that invokes the sun to rise, thus putting an end to night. So gorillas are 'the ones who end or chase the night.' Without them, the world would be plunged into eternal blackness. Eternal evil. They're the ones who bring light and warmth and joy to the earth."

"It's a nice concept," said Evan. "Makes you wonder how it got started."

"Oh, there's a bunch of stories like that," said Abbie, lazily enunciating her words as the Scotch took hold. "The Wabembe tribe near Fizi, Zaire, calls the gorilla 'kinguti.' The story behind the name is that a long time ago, a group of lazy men retreated into the forest and never came out again. They're believed to be the ancestors of the gorillas. And you know something?" she added, laughing. "Damned if I don't believe it myself sometimes. Those apes can be incredibly lazy."

A knock sounded on the door.

"Abbie? You in there?" asked a voice.

"Yeah, come in."

It was David, a big grin plastered on his face. "Come with me," he said. "I've got something to show you."

The three made their way across the courtyard to Joey's trailer. Inside, Larry, Chandra, and two other students were crowded around the gorilla. Evan stood on tiptoe to see over them; Abbie pushed her way through to the ape's side.

Joey was sitting up, eating, and reveling in the attention. He blinked at his admirers.

"I think whatever it was that he had has passed," said David, triumphantly, as the ape washed down another glass of milk.

"He's got his appetite back," said Abbie, excitedly. "How is Joey?" she signed to the gorilla.

"Gimme gumdrop hurry," signed the ape, eliciting a whoop from the crowd.

"I'd say he's recovered, all right," said Abbie, her left arm squeezing the ape. "Okay, everyone. I don't want him too excited. I'll put him to bed."

The students filed out of the trailer, leaving Abbie and Evan. The two sat quietly while Abbie stroked the gorilla's fur. Evan felt a bit like an intruder. Joey yawned and clutched a blanket to his body.

"God, I feel so relieved," said Abbie.

The Teletype machine behind Abbie clattered. Joey stirred slightly in her arms.

"Another message from your friend?" asked Evan.

"Yeah," said Abbie absentmindedly, her attention on the ape.

Evan, for lack of knowing what else to do, stood and read the message:

SFX 083

AG

    NEW MAN ULA COMING DOWN TOMORROW NOON. NORMAL REQUISITION AND MAIL POUCH. (PLUS A QUART OF SCOTCH FOR ME, THAT'S MY LOVE.)

    CHIMPS SEND THEIR REGARDS.

                        —MIC

"Says something about a man coming down tomorrow," said Evan.

Abbie gently laid the sleeping gorilla on his side and joined Evan behind the Teletype.

"Yes," she said, reading. "I figured they were getting low on supplies." She tore the message off the machine. "Come on. Joey's asleep. We can leave now."

Outside, there was a light breeze. A few leaves had fallen on the embassy car.

"You never got any dinner," said Abbie. "Can I offer you something from the kitchen?"

"Don't bother," said Evan, consulting his watch. "I've got to be going. Early day tomorrow."

"Sorry about this evening."

"Forget it."

"No, I don't want to forget it," said Abbie, almost stridently.

"You know, there's a lot of people who can't understand why these gorillas mean what they do to us, or why we put in all the time we do here. And the reason they don't understand is that they've never had the opportunity to work on something that really mattered to them. On something important.

"But I do have that opportunity," she said. "I may be a workaholic. I may have sacrificed too much. But working here is like walking a tightrope. Every day brings the fear that the gorillas will stop learning, or retrogress. Any little thing can throw them off. So I keep at it. Especially now, with all these books out disclaiming this type of study, and project funds being cut off. That only makes what we do here more important."

Important. That was the key, thought Evan. What Abbie said about those other people applied to him as well. He had never worked on something he considered truly important, something worth the sacrifice, the dedication. Something that was not just a job, but a dream. He envied her the sense of commitment he had never known.

"God, I'm sorry," Abbie said, suddenly. "I don't know what came over me, lecturing you like that." She paused, fumbling for the right words. "Shouldn't have drunk so much, I guess. Good night."

She turned and left Evan alone in the courtyard. Evan slid into the car seat and turned on the ignition. The evening had been a confusing one, but he was too tired to dwell upon it. He would think about it in the morning. Depressing the clutch, he sped off into the cool Bujumburan night.

VI

He had been sitting by the side of the road for over an hour, his heels sunk in the soft earth to keep him from slipping down the incline. The terrain was a marked contrast to the heavy woods around Iddan. Burundi: "Country of a thousand and one hills." Bunkeya recalled the phrase from a sign he had seen near the border.

He contemplated joining Mpinga, sitting downhill under the shade of a tree, but Bunkeya was afraid that the minute he left the road, Ula's car would come into view. He stayed where he was.

Rushing water echoed softly in the background. Bunkeya had picked a spot not too far from the primate center, near a bridge that ran over a small stream. It was a section of the road that ran straight for nearly a quarter of a mile, probably the longest such stretch in the entire road, one infamous for its endless curves. The site gave Bunkeya a good view of oncoming traffic, of which, true to Dalam's words, there had been precious little.

As he wiped the sweat from his brow, Bunkeya thought about other waits and other killings. A sentry killed with a garrote. A businessman shot in his car. He tried to remember why each had been targeted for assassination. The reasons had seemed so terribly obvious at the time. Why should they escape his memory now? In his mind he envisioned a long white wall, and in front of it, lined up like targets of a firing squad, the men who had died. They did not blink. Their dead eyes bored into him. Bunkeya wished he had closed their eyes when he'd had the chance.

He heard a soft drone. The jeep appeared on the road. Bunkeya rose and started walking toward the primate center, his back to the approaching car. He looked over his shoulder. Good. Only the one man at the wheel. Bunkeya had had his share of surprises on missions: extraneous people in the way, premature detonations, the wrong men stepping out of buildings. He didn't much care for surprises.

When he judged that the car was fifty yards away, Bunkeya turned and waved at the driver, and stepped into the middle of the road.

The driver applied his brakes and leaned out the window.

"Can I help you?" he asked.

Bunkeya smiled broadly and jogged around to the driver's side.

"Hi," he said. "You must be Ula. Abbie's been waiting for you."

"I got started late," the man said, anxiously. "I hope I haven't messed up anyone's schedule."

"Relax." Bunkeya leaned against the car door. "Abbie knows you're new. She won't care. Just tell her a tree fell on the road and you had to move it."

"Yeah, okay. Thanks." The driver smiled.

"Don't mention it."

"Who are you?"

"I'm Nabwe," said Bunkeya. "I run the chores for the center. My car broke down about a kilometer back. You probably passed it, as a matter of fact."

"Didn't see it, but I'd be happy to give you a lift. Hop in."

"Great. Say, I unloaded the car—I was carrying a bunch of expensive tools which I didn't want to leave out in the open. I tried bringing them with me, but they got too heavy so I dumped them under a tree. Right over there, down that hill. You mind helping me with them?"

"Not at all."

The two men walked along the road.

"You work for Abbie—I mean, Mlle. Guisbourne—long?" asked Ula.

"No, not long."

"You got a job like mine, sounds like. Picking up supplies and stuff. I've got the requisition lists Professor Fielding gave me in the glove compartment," Ula said. "This is my first trip."

"You'll get used to driving this road in no time at all. Pretty soon it'll be a snap."

"Yeah. I suppose so."

"The tools are just down here," said Bunkeya, stepping off the road.

Pebbles unearthed by their footsteps rolled down the steep hill. They neared the edge of a cluster of trees.

"Say, why were you out this way?" asked Ula. "Bujumbura's in the opposite direction. What did you need out here?"

Bunkeya didn't answer.

"So where are the tools? Did you have them in a pack?" Ula scanned the ground. "Which tree are they under?"

"Right there, I believe," said Bunkeya, pointing to a musanga tree.

The courier bent down.

"Well, I sure don't see them—"

Bunkeya's hand shook as he reached for the knife inside his clothes.

"You don't suppose somebody—" Ula faced Bunkeya. "What's that you've got there?"

Bunkeya accidentally dropped the knife to the ground.

"Wait a minute. What's this— Oh, God!" Ula stumbled backward. He started running up the hill.

Mpinga's shadow wavered on the ground, and Ula fell. It was over in seconds.

"Hey, Abbie?" David stood in the trailer doorway. "The new courier from Muwali just showed up. Ula. You want me to bring him over?"

"Never mind. I'll come out. Tell him I'll be there right away."

"Okay."

Abbie finished scribbling a few last lines in her notebook and set it back on the shelf. She rubbed her eyes before going outside. David had opened the gate and the Muwali Land Rover was sitting in the courtyard. A tall, lean man was standing next to the jeep, talking with Larry.

"Ula?" Abbie extended her hand. "Abbie Guisbourne."

"Nice to meet you, mademoiselle," said Bunkeya.

"Abbie, please. I trust you had a pleasant trip."

"Yes. A few things slowed me down. I'm sorry if I'm late."

"Don't worry about it. You look hot. Why don't we hold off on the supply forms until after you've had something to drink."

"Thank you. I'd like that."

"I wouldn't mind something cool myself. You've met Larry?"

"Yes. We introduced ourselves."

The three walked to the kitchen trailer. Abbie sat Bunkeya at one of the outside tables while she and Larry fetched the iced tea. When she placed a glass before him she was struck by the contrast between this man and the boy who had been the previous Muwali courier. The new courier was much older. He exhibited a maturity and confidence unknown by the other. They spoke in French; his command of the language equaled her own. Abbie found it puzzling that this man, who seemed suited for any number of jobs, had taken the position as a supply runner.

He drank and asked a few polite questions about the work the linguists did and the operation of the center. When Abbie asked him about his home life, he changed the subject. Rather, he maneuvered the conversation so adroitly that Abbie almost did not detect the evasion.

Her curiosity mounted. What was someone this skilled in manipulating conversation doing in the forests of southern Burundi?

"So," she said, when he'd finished his drink. "You've got the requisition forms from Professor Fielding?"

"Yes. They're in the glove compartment."

"We might as well get the ball rolling."

"Okay. I'll get them."

Bunkeya swung his legs over the bench and rose from the table. He had walked only a few paces when Winston and David emerged from the nearest trailer. Abbie stood to deflect a panicked response—the reaction Winston often elicited from a visitor—but quickly realized that her intervention this time was unnecessary. The courier was totally in control. With one glance he sized up both the chain around the gorilla's leg and the unconcerned expression on David's face. He did not miss a step. Abbie was flabbergasted. If fear registered somewhere in the man's dark eyes, she did not see it. She vowed to monitor the courier closely.

"I'm sorry. I hope Winston didn't startle you," said David, rotely. He, too, sensed the man's exceptional calm. He dropped Winston's chain so that the ape could get a drink of water.

"You let them go loose like that?" asked Bunkeya.

"During the day, yes. I don't believe we've met. I'm David. I take it you're Ula."

"Yes. Pleased to meet you." Bunkeya shook David's hand. "Excuse me for just a minute, will you? I was just about to get something from the car."

Bunkeya popped open the glove compartment and pulled out the papers that Ula had mentioned. Mpinga's muddy footprints were clearly visible on the passenger side of the jeep. Bunkeya leaned down and rubbed the caked impressions into a fine layer of dirt. He riffled quickly through the papers before handing them to Abbie; she scanned them with cursory interest.

"Okay. There's nothing major here," she said. "We should have you on your way in no time."

"About how long is 'no time'?"

"I wouldn't think you'd have to stay here much more than a couple of days."

"Say Friday then?"

"Yes, I suppose so." Abbie was bewildered by his concern over the date. "I don't know if Professor Fielding told you, but we'll be putting you up and feeding you. You won't have to worry about anything."

"That's fine. You mind if I look around in the meantime?"

"No, not at all. If you have any questions, feel free to ask."

"I will," Bunkeya answered.

"Fran? Fran?" Abbie signed. She was having difficulty keeping the gorilla's attention. "Please look here. It's time for your lesson."

"No."

"Fran, please help Abbie count. How many balls are on the table?" Abbie set out three small red balls, the kind used for jacks.

The ape did not respond.

"How many?"

Fran picked up one of the balls and threw it off the table.

"Bad, Fran. This isn't playtime," Abbie signed, though she did not think the ape had thrown the ball in play. She retrieved the ball and placed it back on the table. "How many?"

The ape swept an arm across the table and the balls flew against the trailer wall.

"Nothing," she signed.

On another occasion, Abbie might have thought Fran's action clever. But the gorilla did not knock the balls off with any intention of being clever or funny. She'd been cantankerous for hours. Abbie let the balls lie where they landed.

"Are you going to pick them up?"

The gorilla ignored her.

Annoyed, Abbie scooped the balls off the floor and dumped them in a container. She had been working hard at trying to teach Fran the concept of numbers for weeks, and was disappointed that the gorilla was not cooperating.

Her mood changed, however, as her thoughts turned to Joey and his stomachache. Maybe Fran was suffering from the same malady. Or her arthritis might be flaring up. That would explain her crankiness.

"How are you, Fran?" Abbie signed.

"Finish." The ape's hands, palms up, rotated inward until her palms faced the ground.

Abbie wasn't sure whether Fran was asking that today's lesson be concluded or merely was signing incorrectly.

"How are you?" Abbie repeated.

"Different."

What the hell kind of answer was that? It made no sense.

"Fran," Abbie signed, "you are signing wrong things."

"Dirty Abbie."

"Fran, why are you mad?"

"Belly hurt."

That clinched it. Abbie was certain that Fran had eaten the same thing that had upset Joey's stomach.

"Come, we'll get you some medicine." As Abbie stood, she mentally reviewed all that the gorilla had eaten that day and compared it to what Joey had eaten yesterday. Fran continued to sit.

"Don't you want your belly to feel better?" asked Abbie.

"Belly fine."

Abbie was confused. Was the gorilla lying about her stomach? Fran had displayed none of Joey's nausea or lack of appetite. In fact, she'd just finished another hefty meal. Her only symptom was irritability. Perhaps she was jealous of all the attention paid Joey by the students earlier in the morning.

"All right then, we'll continue our lesson."

"Have Beanface in," Fran signed.

So that was it: a lovesick gorilla.

"Beanface isn't here," Abbie signed.

"Nut nut," signed Fran.

"So how big will he get?" Bunkeya asked.

"Oh, God," answered Larry, eager to share his expertise, "Winston could get anywhere in the four-hundred-to-five-hundred-pound range. That's like two hundred kilos. He's a big gorilla."

"And the others?"

"Fran will be smaller than the two males, but female

gorillas can get huge, too. Both males and females tend to get especially large when they're in captivity and sedentary. In the wild they usually don't weigh as much."

"That size must mean a lot of power. Have you ever gotten hurt by one of them?"

"Me? No. You know, they're really very gentle. The worst thing that's happened here is one guy got his arm broken."

"What happened?"

"Well, the guy was a real asshole. He deserved it. Seems he dangled some food or something in front of Winston—sort of teasing him, the jerk—and Winston got understandably irritated and grabbed the guy's arm. But you're not going to have to worry about anything like that, if that's what's prompted this question. The gorillas are perfectly safe. You'll be fine."

"Just curious, actually," said Bunkeya. "So if the gorillas are irritated or excited, they can get violent?"

"Well—"

"I realize that they rarely do, but it could happen, right?"

"In the case I just mentioned it wasn't violence that broke the guy's arm. It was a case of Winston not knowing his own strength."

"What about fear? Are they afraid of anything?"

"Yeah. Crocodiles scare them. So do strange noises. Same sort of stuff that scares people. Like even though they don't know what guns are, they'll pick up on the aggression in a person holding a gun. They sense things."

"I would think they'd get violent if they were frightened."

"They don't often get frightened," said Larry. "Luckily."

"Can they fear for others as well as for themselves?"

"Sure. About the only times you see a gorilla charging someone is when he's protecting another gorilla."

"So they're loyal?"

"Yes."

"To humans as well?"

"Definitely. Those animals arc devoted to Abbie. They make the best watchdogs in the world."

Enter the first hitch to a smooth mission, thought Bunkeya.

"So if anyone were to threaten Abbie, the gorillas would come to her aid?" he asked.

"Not just her aid. They'd tear the fellow to pieces."

"They've got the strength?"

"Sure do. They can crush you if they want."

"The smaller ones, too?"

"Don't let their size fool you. They've got many times the strength of a human."

"I wouldn't want to meet up with one of them on a dark night," said Bunkeya.

"Okay, hoist away."

Abbie let go of the bunch of bananas, and Chandra pulled on the rope.

"Keep going." Abbie watched the bananas rise higher in the air. "That's it, keep going. Okay. Stop! Secure it right there."

The young deaf woman did not hear Abbie's words, but read Abbie's many gestures perfectly. She knotted the rope. The bananas twirled slowly in the sunlight, a piñata separated from its Cinco de Mayo celebration.

"Winston, come over here," Abbie signed to the ape sitting across the courtyard.

The big gorilla left Joey's side and planted himself directly under the dangling fruit. He arched his neck.

"Look, Winston," signed Abbie. "Bananas there. See the banana?"

It had been Abbie's idea to move the tool experiment outside. She'd planned to suspend the fruit from a tree until Chandra pointed out the flaw in that idea: Winston would simply climb the tree to get at the bananas. Though not particularly fond of tree climbing, a reluctance usually shared by all but the young of his species, Winston was quite capable of scaling trees that might discourage a human being. With this in mind, the two women rigged a rope over the trailer.

There were no footholds in the sheer trailer wall. Nothing for Winston to grab or stand on. It seemed, thought Abbie, that they'd finally established a control situation, one in which all the variables were eliminated.

"Come on, Winston. You can get those bananas. Come on, big guy."

As Abbie anticipated, Winston tried jumping for a while. When that didn't work, he ran his hand along the trailer wall, feeling for protrusions by which to pull himself up. After that, too, proved unsuccessful, he sat back on his haunches and looked imploringly at Abbie. Guilt assailed her conscience. Her only consolation was that Pavlov must have felt the same way making his dog salivate every time a bell rang.

Joey adopted a posture similar to Winston's, hunkering on the ground, hands loosely draped over his knees. Abbie had not planned for the smaller ape to take part in the experiment —she wanted to test him independently at a later date—but let him stay when it became obvious that he was intrigued.

"You can do it, Winston," signed Chandra. "Get those bananas."

Abbie checked her watch. Five minutes had passed. The baseball bat, coated with a fine layer of dust from Winston's aerobatic flurries, lay untouched where she had placed it.

"Look," signed Chandra to Abbie.

Joey had joined Winston and was sniffing the baseball bat.

"He's going to pick it up," signed Chandra.

The two women watched anxiously as Joey lifted the bat and turned it over in his hand. He signed something to Winston.

"I didn't see what he signed. Did you get it?" signed Abbie.

"No," signed Chandra. "But I bet it had to do with the bat."

Wrong. What the gorilla actually had signed was "Joey ride," a request that he be allowed to climb on Winston's back. This became quickly apparent to the two women when Joey laid down the bat—like Winston, he had failed to grasp its significance—and clambered onto Winston's back. Reaching up, the smaller gorilla grabbed the fruit, slid off the big gorilla's back, and landed on the ground with the prize clutched in his arms. Winston broke off and peeled the first banana. With half of it sticking out of his mouth, he invited Joey to chew on the end, a symbol of trust in the gorilla kingdom.

Also a symbol of some crafty teamwork, thought Abbie, reproaching herself for not having foreseen this outcome and prevented it. She picked up the baseball bat and retired it to the recreation box in one of the trailers.

Another joyless day in Mudville.

"I realize the gorillas are fine watchdogs," said Bunkeya, "but surely you've got other security measures here?"

"Of course," said Larry. "We've got locks on all the doors and an electric fence that we turn on at night."

"No guards?"

"We've got one man, Juste, who keeps a watch over the camp. He also doubles as our maintenance man. Professor Fielding must have mentioned him."

"Yes, I just forgot."

"You probably do the same sort of stuff in Muwali, huh?"

"Yes. But we're isolated there, you know. No one really comes by much. We've got rifles in case a lion or some other animal invades camp."

"I remember Abbie telling us about Professor Fielding's marksmanship. Is he really that good?"

"I don't know," said Bunkeya. "I've never seen him shoot."

"That's right, how could you? You're new. Well, I don't think we have any rifles around here. But Juste's got a gun. He pulled it out the time the poachers showed up."

Bunkeya made a mental note about the gun and asked: "Poachers? When was this?"

"Oh, years ago. I wasn't here. They usually operate near the Virunga range. Dian Fossey has been fighting them for years. Pretty much singlehandedly they've reduced the world population of mountain gorillas to virtual extinction. They cut off the gorillas' hands and heads and sell them for souvenirs. Or else they sell them to the Kwa. You familiar with them?"

"Yes," answered Bunkeya. "But why would the Kwa want the parts of a gorilla?"

"Witchcraft, that's why. They consider those parts of a gorilla to be powerful witchcraft weapons against an enemy. Dr. Groom of Cambridge University once found a silverback whose ears, tongue, genitals, and even the terminal phalanx of each little finger were cut off. It's a grisly business. Apparently the poachers who set the traps outside the compound here didn't realize that we don't let the gorillas run around unsupervised. Luckily, nothing happened and they left. Juste got real conscientious for the next couple of weeks and carried his gun around."

"Fascinating," said Bunkeya.

Mpinga wandered desultorily around the marketplace, hardly glancing at the batiks and wood carvings and terracotta pots artistically arranged in the merchants' stalls. Shoppers bustled around him. A man wrangled with a vendor over the cost of a wicker basket, ultimately convincing the craftsman to drop thirty francs off the price. A woman examined a thin copper bracelet. All around, currency and goods changed hands.

To Mpinga, the vibrant outdoor market was nothing more than a convenient place in which to wait. As such, it was a poor choice. The noise and jostling crowd intensified his restlessness. He resented having to kill the hours, aimlessly drifting through the streets of Bujumbura, while less than five miles away Bunkeya laid the underpinnings of the kidnapping. Twelve empty hours stretched before him, more than half a day. Twelve hours of boredom until he was scheduled to meet with Bunkeya and carry the man's report back to Dalam. A delivery boy. That was all he was, a glorified delivery boy.

It was all Bunkeya's fault. Without him this would have been Mpinga's mission from start to finish, his chance to show the men in Iddan that he could lead them as well as Dalam. Better, in fact. But Bunkeya had spoiled that opportunity; just as Kili had nearly spoiled it. Mpinga did not intend to let Bunkeya thwart his plans any more than Kili. Somehow he had to regain the upper hand.

As the bright equatorial sun signaled high noon, Mpinga sought shade under a palmyra tree and contemplated his next move.

"You know about the boat patrol, don't you?" asked Larry.

"I know that each side keeps watch for smugglers, yes," said Bunkeya.

"Then you know that Burundi and Zaire share Lake Tanganyika, as do Tanzania and Zambia. Oh, there's a line of demarcation out in the middle of it, some border line, but I don't think much attention is paid to it."

The information about the Burundian patrols was not news to Bunkeya. He already was aware of their existence. When planning Engulu's entry into Zaire from Burundi, Bunkeya had rejected sending him on land, and had instead planned a route across the lake in a fishing boat, to avoid suspicion. But Engulu had not needed the boat. He never made it to the lake.

As with the other items unearthed by Larry's conversation, Bunkeya mentally filed the fishing boat away for future reference. His brain operated with the precision of a miniature computer, sorting and reviewing material, latching on to what first appeared to be random bits of information, only to gradually, slowly, have them fall into place. A plan was forming, all right, growing around a single purpose as surely as a crystal develops out of itself in a fine, mathematical pattern. It was only a matter of time.

The lunch served on death row is the same lunch served to the other prisoners in Rumonge prison. A lukewarm stew. Bread. Carrot mixture. The clothes those particular inmates wear is the same as is worn elsewhere in the complex. The cot, the same. Often the crimes are the same, for even the most impartial judgments are subject to man's fallibility.

But the mental set of those men is not the same. The men on the row carry a special burden. Each reacts differently to the terrible knowledge that death waits around the corner. Some find God. Some lose their grip on reality. And others, in a last-ditch effort, try to cheat the system.

The man in cell #23442 was one of those. Engulu's death was three days away. As he lay back on his cot and digested his meal, he no longer rejected the idea of his death, or found it unfathomable. With each passing second, its very inevitability struck him like a hot spark from a blazing fire. His disbelief gradually gave way to insurmountable anger.

Anger that he, one of the FPL's most active members, should leave this world on such a passive note. Engulu didn't want to be remembered by the men in Iddan as a martyr who died bound and blindfolded, but one who, even in the end, played a part in the sequence of events.

Thus, the death had to be by his own hand.

He recalled his conversation with a man who had delivered the FPL a shipment of Armalite rifles, and how the man had spoken glowingly of a colleague in the Japanese Red Brigade. The terrorist had killed himself rather than be caught. He had taken charge of his life. This was what Engulu wanted. To be in charge.

He reached under his blanket and fingered the fibrous sheets. He was not yet ready.

Evan's excuse for driving to the primate center during lunch was to see how Joey was faring. In actuality, he was unable to fight the strange lure the center had for him. Perhaps it was the sense of purpose that abounded there, one which Evan, floundering in what he perceived as a vague, bureaucratic mire, found reassuring. Perhaps it was the woman herself, Abbie Guisbourne.

Now that he was before her, on the opposite side of the picnic table, he found she was still very much of an enigma. Last night had revealed part of her complexity, but not all of it. She was speaking to him, but he was not listening. He concentrated instead on her gestures, hoping to detect a subtlety of her character, contained in the toss of her head or the roll of her eyes, that would lead him to a complete understanding of her, and of why her life was a source of envy to him.

"What's wrong?" asked Abbie. "You seem to be thinking about something else. Am I that boring?"

"Sorry. I was just thinking about Joey. I'm glad he's better."

"Wish I could say the same about Fran. She's been in a rotten mood. I think you're the cause."

"How so?" Evan cracked a walnut and dug the meat from its shell.

"She's lovesick."

"Oh, really?" Evan cracked another shell. It wasn't until he popped the nut into his mouth that he considered what Abbie had said. He nearly choked. "You don't mean over me?"

A strange scenario played in his mind: Boy meets Girl. Boy and Girl become Friends. Boy gets Gorilla.

"Who else?" asked Abbie.

"Doesn't she know that I'm a man and she's a gorilla?"

"It's not really that big a deal, Evan," said Abbie. "I only told you because I think it would boost Fran's spirits if you'd stop by later."

"You need to ship in some more little boy gorillas," grumbled Evan.

"I'll keep that suggestion in mind," said Abbie. The slight smile on her face disappeared as she looked up from the table. She pointed across the courtyard. "Have you met Ula yet?"

"Who?" Evan shielded his eyes and studied the man walking with Larry. "No, but I saw him when I drove in. Who is he?"

"He's the courier from our chimpanzee camp down south. The one Mic Fielding sent up for supplies."

"This the first time you've met him?"

"Yes. I'm not sure what to think of him."

"How so?"

"I mean I can't figure out why he took this job. The couriers have always been young men before. Boys wanting to see what exists outside their villages. He doesn't fit that type."

"Maybe he just needed the money and this was the only job available."

"I suppose. But he gives an air of, I don't know, maturity. It's hard to believe this was the only job he could find."

"Ask him."

"I tried. Sort of."

"What does that mean?"

"He's coming over here. Do you know French?"

"Yes."

"Okay, you talk to him, see what I mean." As Larry and Bunkeya neared, Abbie said, "Hi. You two had lunch?"

"Yeah," said Larry. "We just finished."

"Ula," said Abbie, "I'd like you to meet a friend of mine, Evan Olgilvie."

The two men shook hands.

"So nice to meet you, Monsieur Olgilvie. Do you work here too?"

"No. I'm with the American embassy."

Evan thought he detected a slight change in the man's expression. It passed quickly, the split-second speed of a subliminal ad flashing "Drink Coca-Cola" on a movie screen.

"I understand you arrived this morning?" asked Evan, hoping to hear in the man's voice a hesitancy, a strained modulation, that would confirm what Evan thought he'd seen in the courier's face.

The voice that responded was firm. "Yes. Larry's been walking me around the compound. Quite a fascinating place."

"You've met the gorillas?"

"One of them. He appeared rather suddenly in the court-yard."

"Let me guess: Winston, right?"

Bunkeya looked to Larry for confirmation. "Yes, I believe that was the one."

"He looks meaner than he is," said Evan.

"He didn't look particularly mean," said Bunkeya, evenly.

Evan recalled his own encounter with Winston in the court-yard and tried to imagine the courier in the same situation. Abbie was right. The African exuded a surety about himself. Evan doubted that this man would have panicked.

"What brings you to the primate center, Monsieur Olgilvie?" asked Bunkeya, sitting opposite Evan. "Nothing wrong, I hope?"

"No, I mean, yes—originally I came here because Abbie had taken the gorillas out on a drive, and had scared some of the people around here, and"—why did he feel compelled to explain all this?—"anyway, I'm just here for lunch. A social visit."

"I see. Have you been here long? In Burundi, I mean."

"No," said Evan, trying to slow his rapid-fire answers. When ill at ease, as he was sitting before this man, Evan accelerated his speech. "Just a few weeks actually."

The man was pumping him for information, decided Evan. Having dealt with his share of smooth operators, Evan recognized the telltale signs, however well couched in polite conversation. What disturbed him was not the man's technique, but why he was employing it. What did he hope to learn?

"And what do you think of Africa?" asked Bunkeya.

"I like it fine," said Evan. "Takes some getting used to for a foreigner, but every new country does. I'm happy to be here. Are you a native of Burundi?"

Evan asked the question merely to put the man on the receiving end for a while. He was surprised when the courier's eyes narrowed and the scowl that had flashed just seconds ago returned. This time Evan recognized it for what it was: suspicion.

"Yes, I am," replied Bunkeya.

"What did you do before getting the job with Professor Fielding?"

"Different things. Here and there."

"Do you have a family?"

"No." Bunkeya's eyes broke contact with Evan's for a fraction of a second.

Evan decided not to push the limits of his minor interrogatory skills; the man was not about to reveal any more than he wanted to. Even so, Evan garnered some satisfaction from the conversation. The courier's voice was steady, but his face was not able to conceal an inner turmoil. And Evan detected it.

"You'll have to forgive me," said Bunkeya. "I'm afraid the drive up here is starting to catch up with me. I'm rather tired. I hope you won't mind if I excuse myself."

"Not at all," said Evan.

"Larry, show Ula to his quarters, will you, please?" asked Abbie. When the two men were out of earshot, she asked, "So what do you think?"

"You're right," said Evan. "I certainly never would have matched him with the job of a courier. I don't think he'll stay with it very long. He gives the appearance of running from something. Maybe the law. You want me to check up on him?"

"No," said Abbie. "It's not that important. He'll only be here a few days. I'll talk to Mic about him later."

"Okay, whatever you say." Evan took another walnut from the bowl and cracked it. He flipped the shell in his hand. "Hey, I just got an idea how to cheer up that lovesick gorilla of yours."

"How?"

"By playing a little game with her. Let's go."

Walnut/Jellybean Test—Trial #1

Evan sat opposite Fran, his elbows on the table. The gorilla was overjoyed to see him, and sat in mute rapture as he scooped out the walnuts and arranged three shell halves in a row on the table. A sack of jellybeans lay next to Evan's foot.

"Okay, Fran," he signed, as Abbie drew up a chair for herself. "You want to play a game?"

"Happy play," signed the gorilla.

"Here are three nutshells." Evan pointed to each one. "Here is a bean." He took a jellybean from the paper bag and held it before Fran.

"Bean," she repeated.

"Good. I put the bean under the shell. Look."

He lifted the walnut shell on his right and slid the bean under it.

"Now, where is the bean?" he asked.

Fran pointed to the correct walnut shell.

"Yes." He lifted the shell and gave the bean to Fran. "There it is. And you get to eat it. Good Fran. Now look. I am going to get another jellybean"—he reached underneath the table and pulled out a large orange bean—"and, oh, it's a big one. I'm going to put the bean under the shell. Now look. I am going to move the shells."

He slowly switched the position of the shells.

"Now, Fran, where is the big bean?"

Fran studied the shells, then Evan. Leaning across the table, she raised her hand and pointed.

"There big bean," she signed.

She was pointing at Evan's face.

Bunkeya did not know what to make of the man from the American embassy. Could Dalam's plan have been leaked? It seemed unlikely. And yet what was the embassy officer doing in the compound? Bunkeya did not like the questions the man asked him. Nor was he pleased to learn that the man had been in Burundi only a short time. Perhaps the Americans had caught wind of the plan some time ago. Who knew to whom Mpinga had told his grand scheme before presenting it to Dalam? This Evan Olgilvie hardly looked the part of a special agent sent down to Africa to avert a kidnapping, but appearances could be deceptive. If such was the case then Bunkeya's time was wasted.

And a life wasted. Only now did Bunkeya let his thoughts turn to Ula. He and Mpinga had hidden the man's body beneath brush off the side of the road. Mpinga had not commented on the strange paralysis that had afflicted Bunkeya. Perhaps he assumed it was clumsiness. Bunkeya knew better. For the first time, the very first, he'd been unable to surmount his emotions while on a mission. They had finally bested him. He would always remember the numb, unresponsive feeling in his arms, just as from now on he would count the days until it struck again.

All this ran through his mind as he walked beside Larry. Unwittingly, Bunkeya had selected the most garrulous person in the compound with whom to converse. Coaxing information from the young man about the operation of the primate center was effortless, just a handful of questions interspersed in the right places. Bunkeya wanted to know more about the diplomat in the courtyard, but did not press the student. He waited as Larry related a story about his first session with the gorillas.

"That's truly fascinating," said Bunkeya, after Larry finished talking. "They behave a lot like humans."

"Yeah, in some ways."

"Tell me, what was this incident about the gorillas scaring people that Monsieur Olgilvie mentioned?"

"Oh, every once in a while Abbie takes the gorillas out for a drive. Last time she did the embassy got a complaint and Evan was sent out here."

"I see. So he's not here because of anything serious?"

"Nah."

"Do you know where he was before he came to Burundi?"

"Uruguay. I was there once, you know. Guess it was back in 1977—"

As Larry talked about his South American tour, Bunkeya returned to his analysis of Evan Olgilvie. Perhaps the man was simply what he appeared to be. It could be a coincidence, his being here at this time. Still, better to take no chances. Bunkeya decided to start laying the foundations for Dalam's plan this afternoon, without waiting to discuss them with Mpinga. And that meant driving into Bujumbura today.

For even as Bunkeya conversed with Larry, his mind was

calculating the best way to execute the kidnapping. He'd nearly completed the plan, working out its kinks as smoothly as a rope maker might restore pliability to an old rope through the generous use of emollients.

"Larry, I'm going to have to go into town soon," said Bunkeya. "What's the best route in?"

"You just follow the road until it jogs to the left and then go straight. That'll take you to the heart of town. It's too bad you didn't speak up earlier. Juste just left. He could have picked up whatever you needed."

"That's all right. These are just personal things."

"You sure you don't want to rest first? I know you're tired."

"No, thank you. I seem to have gotten a second wind from somewhere."

Bunkeya pulled the Land Rover out of the gate, and the key chain hanging from the car's ignition hit against his leg. He examined the trinket on the end of the chain, a medallion of sorts, on the back of which an inscription read simply, "Du K.M." So, it had begun. Already Bunkeya had affected someone he'd never seen. K.M., the man or woman who had given Ula the key chain, would grieve in a few days' time. The dominoes had started to fall. By the time of the actual kidnapping, now just an embryo in Bunkeya's brain, their clatter would be deafening, touching people around the globe.

Bunkeya gunned the accelerator and sped down the road leading to downtown Bujumbura, the city where Engulu was being held. He had not thought of the city in those terms before, but now he wondered if the trooper who had taken Engulu's possessions had felt the same inescapable roll of events press down on him. Bunkeya stared at the Burundian people as he passed, but was unable to hate them for decreeing Engulu's death. They were like him—pawns. To hate them would mean unleashing the self-hate that brimmed below his surface. Bunkeya saved his hate for others.

He asked a woman on a corner where the library was, and found it without difficulty, checking twice to make sure he was parked legally. Bunkeya knew that trifling errors often ruined the best-laid plans. Libraries were almost non-existent in Burundi, as they were in Zaire, but Bunkeya had had greater exposure to them than most of his countrymen. From a nation with a 20 percent literacy rate, Bunkeya had emerged an educated man, largely for the convenience of the Belgian colonist who taught him. Most Zairians could not recognize their own names.

Bunkeya wandered around the building until he entered a room on African heritage. When he saw the walls covered with tribal art, he knew he would find what he needed.

Walnut/Jellybean Test—Trial #2

Having decided it was pointless to continue the walnut-shell test with Fran, Evan asked Abbie if they could try the game with Joey.

"But Joey isn't the one who needs cheering up," she said.

"I know, but now it's gotten to be a challenge to teach one of them the game."

"Look, I've spent five years trying to teach them games a lot simpler than this one. You can't do it over a lunch break. They won't catch on."

"Just bring in Joey."

"All right." She smiled. "But don't take it personally if he doesn't cooperate."

When she returned, and Joey seated himself on the opposite side of the table, Evan commenced with his instructions.

"Okay, Joey," signed Evan. "Here are three nutshells. They are empty." He picked up each of the shells.

Joey scratched his head phlegmatically. His left arm drooped across his stomach.

"Here is a bean." Evan held up a red jellybean.

The change in the gorilla was instantaneous.

"Gimme bean Joey eat," he signed, the left arm, lifeless just seconds ago, now outstretched across the table.

"No, I'll give you a bean later. Right now we play a game.

I put the bean under one of the shells." He placed the jellybean under the walnut shell on his right. "Where bean?"

"That there," pointed the gorilla.

"Good. Now—"

"Gimme bean damn now."

"First play. Then bean. Okay. Now watch. I move shells, then you tell me where the bean is. Look."

Evan rotated the shells, but as he was doing so, he accidentally tipped over the sack of jellybeans at his feet. He bent down and quickly scooped them up.

"Okay, now where is the bean?" he asked the gorilla.

Joey scrutinized the shells and pointed to the middle one. Evan lifted the shell and turned it on its side.

"No, not there."

The gorilla pointed to the shell on the left.

"No, not there either."

Joey pointed to the shell on the right.

"Yes, here is—" Evan stopped abruptly. There was no jellybean under the shell. "What the hell happened to the bean? Where did it go?"

The gorilla pointed to his mouth.

"Bean here," he signed, swallowing.

The bag on the seat jostled as Bunkeya drove the Land Rover back to the compound. He had bought the contents at different spots, moving at an almost leisurely pace as he selected the right paint and beads, the right type of stone. Bunkeya had a keen eye and a good memory, and he wanted to duplicate the picture in the library book as well as he could. He did not worry that its authenticity would be quickly disproved; by that time he would be long gone. The plan, still crystallizing within him, was almost complete.

He paused as he rounded a bend in the road and caught sight of Lake Tanganyika beyond the trees. It was a spectacular view. Once, in Zaire, Bunkeya had thought that the lake stretched into infinity. Now, on its opposite shore, he knew for certain, as his intellect had always known—refuted only by the mystical in everyone—that the lake had a perimeter. As did life itself.

He pressed down on the accelerator.

Walnut/Jellybean Test—Trial #3

"Winston. Here. Look here, Winston," signed Evan.

The big ape eyed Evan suspiciously.

"Sit here, Winston, please."

The ape didn't move.

"Evan will not hurt Winston," Abbie signed. "I'll be right here with you."

Winston snorted and sat opposite Evan.

"Okay, let me try explaining this again. Winston, here are the shells," signed Evan. "I put a bean under the shells. Then I move the shells. You tell me where the bean is. Okay?"

"Good now," the gorilla signed.

"Here we go." Evan slid the shells around on the table. "Now, where is the bean?"

The gorilla studied the three shells on the table and then, forming his right hand into a fist, rapidly pounded each one. They shattered into fragments. He sifted through the rubble with his fingertips until a blue jellybean could be seen.

"Bean there," the ape signed.

Evan tossed the shells into the wastebasket.

Bunkeya stored his purchases under his cot and exited from the trailer just as Evan drove out of the camp. Bunkeya's instincts, which he trusted as he did no man, told him that he had nothing to fear from the embassy officer. The man was harmless. His instincts also told him that if trouble were to develop from any quarter, it would be from Abbie Guisbourne, now closing the gate after Evan, whose cool intelligence Bunkeya had readily perceived. He was certain that she had relayed her misgivings about him to the embassy officer. Evan, in turn, had revealed those misgivings to Bunkeya through the tone of his conversation. They were all chasing each other's suspicions.

He headed for the kitchen, passing Abbie as she sat at a picnic table next to her trailer. She smiled at him. A stack of blue notebooks lay before her.

"Larry said you'd gone into town," said Abbie. "Get everything you want?"

"Yes, thank you."

"You didn't get lost going in?"

"No," said Bunkeya. "Larry gave me directions. Besides," he added, recalling that Ula had been hired in Bujumbura, "I know this area. Professor Fielding hired me here."

"That's right," said Abbie. "I'd forgotten."

Bunkeya doubted her sudden forgetfulness. She was trying to pry information from him; he saw no reason not to do the same with her. If this mission was to proceed without a hitch, he would have to be able to anticipate her moves. That meant becoming acquainted with her mode of thought and, as a corollary, her potential as an adversary.

"Good thing you do know the area," continued Abbie. "Larry's directions have been known to land people right in the middle of Lake Tanganyika."

"I can see how. It's certainly close enough."

"The lake? Yes. I like being near it. When I'm sick of this place, I go there to relax. Lately I've taken to painting it, but I'm afraid I'm not very good."

"You couldn't ask for a better subject. I've seen some magnificent sunrises over that lake in my day."

"Yes," said Abbie, a slight frown to her brow. "The colors are beautiful." She shifted her position in the chair. "You speak French beautifully. Where did you learn it?"

"As a boy I worked for a Belgian farmer." True enough, but in Zaire, not Burundi.

"I see. Wewe wasema Kiswahili?"

"Yes, I speak Swahili as well," said Bunkeya.

"Sisemi vizuri sana."

"On the contrary, you speak it quite well."

"Natondi yo."

"You're welcome—"

Seconds after the words escaped his lips, Bunkeya realized his error. Abbie had led him into a trap. She'd said the words "Thank you" not in Swahili, but in Lingala, the lingua franca of Zaire. He had replied to words of which, as a native Burundian, he should have been ignorant.

"So," Abbie said, looking at him curiously, "you know Lingala as well."

"As you do, I see," said Bunkeya, stalling for time to think. How had she known to toss the language at him like that?

"I'm afraid those are the only two words I know in that language—a pity when you think that Zaire is only just across the lake. How did you happen to learn?"

Unexpectedly, Bunkeya found himself playing the role of the pursued in this game of cat and mouse. He racked his brain for an answer, one that would not fuel further questions.

"I lived in Zaire for many years. You see, I am a Hutu. For many years I was a refugee in Zaire."

For one familiar with Burundian politics, as was Abbie Guisbourne, Bunkeya's explanation was a brilliant display of resourcefulness. The Hutu and the Tutsi, Burundi's two main ethnic groups, had been at odds for centuries. In 1965 and 1969 two violent clashes had taken place, harbingers of a bloody massacre in 1972 in which a hundred thousand Hutus were killed. An equal number fled the country.

"I'm sorry," said Abbie. "It must have been hard."

"It was," Bunkeya replied. "I'm curious. How did you know that I would understand Lingala?"

'You mentioned the sunrises over Lake Tanganyika. Here in Burundi, we see only sunsets. That meant you were watching from the other side of the lake. In Zaire."

"I see."

Their conversation ended shortly, and Bunkeya returned

to his trailer. It was all too clear what kind of adversary Abbie Guisbourne would be: a formidable one. He would have to watch his step around her until the actual kidnapping.

And, he suspected, even after that.

"I can see the night, Papa. Is it that late?"

"Yes, little one. It grows late." Bunkeya passed a hand over the boy's sun-drenched face.

"I tried to hold on to Mother's hand. I did. I held her hand very tight. But then the people and the noise and the hurt, and everyone pushed and I tried to hold on, but her hand pulled from mine."

"I know you did, Gise. You are a good boy."

"Is Mama all right? And Salim?"

"They're fine." Bunkeya clenched his eyes shut and then opened them. He tried not to look at the covered bundle across the yard, next to the other soiled bundles that had once been children.

"I was so scared, Papa. So scared. I'm not now. Now that you're here. But I was then. Why did they do that?"

"I don't know. I don't know. They are—" Bunkeya choked on the words.

"You aren't afraid of them, Papa?"

"No, baby, I'm not afraid of them."

"It's wrong what they did. They shouldn't hurt people." The little boy was crying. Bunkeya cradled the child in his arms, afraid to hug him too tightly. The fragile little body could not withstand much more pressure. "It hurts, Papa. When will it go away?"

"Soon, Gise, very soon."

"I don't ever want to come back here."

"You won't. I won't let them come near you, either."

"I'm so sleepy." The boy's eyes fluttered ominously. "I— I . . . wish . . ."

"What do you wish, Gise?"

But the boy's eyes had closed. He didn't hear his father.

Bunkeya removed his hand from where it supported his son's head. It came away red.

In the twilight of one of Abbie Guisbourne's trailers, where he had retreated to take a nap in anticipation of his meeting with Mpinga, Bunkeya clutched the pillow before him and screamed, just once, into it.

VII

Bunkeya ushered in the night with a sigh of relief. This was much more his element. Dark hollows that offered sanctuary. Star-lighted paths. While others feared the dark for what lurked around the corner, Bunkeya welcomed it for the cloak it provided him as he waited on that same corner. Night's cool breath filled him with a sense of inexhaustible strength. While the sun was berthed halfway round the world, he could not be defeated.

That was how it once seemed. Here, in this camp, the night was indistinguishable from the day in terms of how he felt about himself. Never before had his presence been known to so many while he was on a mission, and though disguised in a false identity, he was robbed of much freedom of movement. He was especially cautious when, after the lights had gone out in the compound, he stole outside the fence to meet Mpinga.

As he neared a cluster of trees, he shone his flashlight in an arc, twice, and stopped for a reply. A flicker of light greeted him, three flashes, and Bunkeya walked forward, flashlight held straight ahead. From behind a scarred tree, a figure emerged.

Larry wasn't able to fall asleep, so he warmed a pan of milk on the stove. He'd never tried this remedy before and had little faith in it, but what the hell, it beat counting sheep. The trailer he shared with two other students was set back from the courtyard, and when he walked to it carrying the glass of warm milk from the kitchen trailer, he saw a light reflect off the bushes. He figured it was his imagination, or the hazy half-dreams of an insomniac, and ascended the stairs to his trailer. Seconds later, the light flashed again. This time he knew it was real. Damn it all, just when he was starting to feel drowsy. He walked over to investigate.

"You haven't been waiting too long, I hope," said Bunkeya.

"No, not too long," said Mpinga. "It took me a while to walk here."

The two men spoke in hushed tones. Mpinga smelled a trace of gin on Bunkeya's breath. "What have you come up with?" he asked.

"Coming into camp and kidnapping the woman and her students will be no problem," said Bunkeya. "The security is lax except for one man who has a gun. As far as I could find out, he's really more of a maintenance man than a guard. He doesn't patrol. I'll take care of him beforehand."

"How many people in the compound altogether?"

"Fifteen. That's counting three students per gorilla, a cook, an administrative assistant, the guard, and a couple of part-time employees. Then there's Abbie Guisbourne, of course. Some of the people leave at the end of day. Like the cook."

"And how many of us will be required?" asked Mpinga.

"An equal number. Enough to man a fishing trawler. Tell Dalam that I recommend transporting the hostages to Iddan across Lake Tanganyika on the boat that was readied for Engulu's mission. You'll have a bit of a walk on this side of the lake, but it'll be worth it. It's too risky to attempt conveying them across the border on land. The boat can carry them without suspicion."

"All right. What about the Burundian patrol?"

"They're mainly concentrated at night. So you'll go in the day."

"Isn't that risky?"

"On the contrary, it reduces your danger. Burundi and Zaire share the lake waters for commercial enterprises like fishing. It won't seem strange for a Zairian-registered boat to be in Burundian waters, especially since the trawler has all the proper papers and equipment on board. Of course, you'll have to keep normal fishing hours. The kidnapping will have to be carried out in early morning. If you're stopped for any reason by the patrol, it will be on your way over, and everything will be in order. You'll be anglers, nothing more."

Mpinga nodded for him to go on.

"There's a spot just south of here that will do well for a rendezvous. I'll show it to you. An uphill walk. Our people will come into camp, take the woman and her students, and the rest will fall into place."

"It sounds too simple."

"There're only a few minor complications. The American woman has a friend in the U.S. embassy. He was here earlier today. I don't think he suspects anything, but his very presence bothers me. He may not be as innocent as he looks."

"What do you plan to do about him?" asked Mpinga.

"Nothing for now. But if he gets in the way . . ." Bunkeya did not complete the sentence. "As for the other complication: The gorillas are let outside in the day. Often in the early morning when they're restless. They're very protective of Mlle. Guisbourne and her students, one of whom assured me that if any of the humans in the camp were threatened, the gorillas would rise to their defense. And they're nothing to be taken lightly. They can't be around when we strike."

"How exactly do you plan on getting rid of them?" asked Mpinga, a note of derision in his voice.

"I've already given that my attention. It won't be as difficult as it seems, although it may make the camp a little more security-conscious. We'll get to that later. In the meantime, the men in the cottage closest to the river will have to move. We can put the hostages in there. Since it was originally the miners' storage room, it has a lock. We'll move the—"

The tall grass behind Bunkeya rustled. Mpinga ducked, and

Bunkeya circled around to intercept the eavesdropper. When he recognized the intruder as Larry, Bunkeya relaxed. He stepped on a twig which snapped loudly. Larry dropped the glass he was carrying.

"Ula? Is that you?" asked the student, straining to see the figure poorly defined by the pallid moonlight.

Bunkeya hesitated, then stepped forward.

"Yes. Larry? Was that you out here with the light?"

"No. I saw the same thing. I think there are some men up ahead talking."

"Have you heard what they've been saying?"

"Not much," Larry whispered, "just something about a mining cottage by a river. About moving men out of it. I wasn't close enough to hear them before."

"Well, I don't hear anything now. Whoever they were, we've probably scared them off."

"Maybe we should—"

Larry never completed his sentence. A rock crashed down on his head. Mpinga raised another one over the crumpled form.

"No," said Bunkeya, grabbing the man's arm. "He's just one of the students. There's no need to dispose of him. He heard nothing."

"What do you plan to do with him then?" asked Mpinga, nudging Larry's inert body with his foot. "How do you explain what happened when the others ask you?"

"The same way I eliminate the presence of the gorillas from the courtyard. I hadn't thought it would take place this soon, but everything is ready. You stay here. We've got some work to do. And afterward," Bunkeya said, almost as an afterthought, "you're going to have to beat me up."

"With pleasure," Mpinga replied.

Abbie burrowed her head in the pillow and curled herself into a tight ball. It was a futile attempt. The scratching noise that had woken her passed through the goose down and settled in her eardrums with the harshness of fingernails dragged down a chalkboard. Her resolve snapped like a thread of spun sugar.

Once, in a former apartment, a wind-driven branch beating against a windowpane had made that sound. Reluctantly, she turned on the light by her bed. The glare hurt her eyes. The clock on the nightstand read two o'clock.

Abbie groaned and threw on a thin bathrobe. The scratching stopped. She sat on the bed and listened. The noise came again from outside her door.

Abbie stomped to the end of the trailer. Probably Sal trying to get in after an evening's crawl with the other tomcats, she decided. With the loving annoyance pet owners reserve for their pets, Abbie unlocked the door.

"All right, you little bastard—"

Larry lay collapsed on the steps. He raised his blood-caked face to her. The hand that had been scratching the door fell limply next to Abbie's foot.

"Oh, my God," she gasped, locking her arms under his and dragging him into the trailer. "Larry, what happened? Who did this?"

Abbie yelled to the trailers across the way, calling the names of her students until lights flicked on in the windows. Her voice reverberated in the courtyard as if amplified by an unseen microphone. One of the students rushed out his door and nearly tripped down the steps, his bare feet skidding over small pebbles.

"Get the car, Alex," Abbie called. "Bring it in front of my trailer and then come get me."

The student jackknifed in midstride and ran in the opposite direction.

Others began pouring out of doorways, an assembly line activated by Abbie's shout. David reached the trailer first and charged up the stairs. Abbie was on the floor, wiping Larry's face with a washcloth. The wound in the back of Larry's head was obscured by sticky, blood-matted hair. Lights from the arriving jeep streamed through the doorway.

"All right," Abbie said to David. "Help me carry him to the car." Though Abbie hated to move the young man, especially since he might have a concussion, she saw no way to avoid it. She sat in the backseat and, using the sweater she'd brought as a cushion, laid Larry's head in her lap. Alex sat in the driver's seat.

"Get us to the hospital as fast as you can without running us off the road," she said. To David, she added, "Wake up Juste. I want a check on everyone else to make sure they're okay. And get the police."

The car roared off, its taillights fading in the distance like dying flares. David called the police, then joined the circle of frightened young people outside. A roused Juste prowled the grounds with his gun drawn.

"Is everyone here?" asked David.

"What happened?" asked one of the students.

"Larry's hurt. Abbie's taking him to the hospital. She didn't explain what happened. I don't think she knows."

No one spoke for a few seconds. The picture the group formed was an eerie one, adumbrated by light streaming from the open trailer doors. Shadows played upon the students' faces, distorting an eye here or a nose there and investing the gathering with a ghoulish air, one more suited to a cabal of witches than a handful of bewildered students. The one flashlight in the group, held by a student who'd just joined the circle, pointed straight up to the sky. Its dim beam was visible for only a few feet, as though blocked by an impenetrable dome that had descended supernaturally over the group. David broke the spell conjured by the night air.

"So is everyone else okay? We all here?"

The students actively engaged in counting one another, their lips moving silently, relieved to be occupying their minds with even this most mundane task—anything to keep their imaginations from running rampant.

"All here," said a young woman named Sara. "Wait a second. What about the courier from Muwali? Where is he?"

A murmur of concern arose from the group, gradually giving way to xenophobic fear as the same thought crowded each student's mind. Yes, the outsider, where was he?

"Let's go check him out," said the young man with the flashlight. "He's in number four. Larry set up a cot for him."

The mention of their injured colleague's name sent an angry ripple through the students. They moved en masse to the trailer, no less frenzied than the torch-bearing townspeople on their way to destroy Frankenstein's monster.

With a politeness incongruous to the group sentiment, David knocked on the trailer door. When no one answered, he knocked again, harder. He tried the doorknob.

"It's open," he said to the people behind him.

The cot was empty.

"I don't see him—" David's declaration was interrupted by a shout from the student with the flashlight, who, unable to crowd inside the trailer, was lazily aiming the beam along the fence.

"Look!" he said. "Over here. Come quick."

The students flooded back outside. David pushed his way to the front, where the flashlight bearer stood.

"Right there," said the young man. "Under that tree."

"What, that lump?" asked David.

And then the lump moved.

When Abbie returned to the compound, she noticed a slight lightening of the sky. Not quite dawn breaking, but a decreasing pitch to the blackness that had enveloped the hospital. The adrenaline she'd been running on for the last hour had left her; she was fatigued and her reflexes were slower than normal. When she stopped the car to unlatch the gate, it took her a few seconds to understand why another car was in the courtyard. The police, of course. She was surprised they were still around. Some of the students ran outside when they heard the rumble of the jeep.

"How's Larry?" asked David. "Is he going to be okay?"

"He'll be fine," Abbie replied. "He's got a concussion. I left

Alex at the hospital with him. One of us will have to drive there in a while and switch places with him."

"Mademoiselle Guisbourne?" said a man standing to one side of the students.

"Yes?" answered Abbie. She turned off the engine.

The man walked into the beam from the car headlights. The gold braid on his cap and shoulders shone. He seemed phantasmic to Abbie, as water shimmers with unreality to a person helming a lifeboat hour after hour.

"Captain Karuhije, Mademoiselle Guisbourne. Bujumbura Police Force," the man said, doffing his cap.

"Nice to meet you, Captain," Abbie said, jumping down from the jeep. "David, have you checked the gorillas? With all this ruckus they may need calming down. The last thing I need right now is an agitated gorilla."

"Um, no. They haven't made any noise, and we've been sort of busy ever since the police arrived," said David, guiltily. "God, Abbie, I'm sorry. We just sort of forgot about them."

"It's all right. Take Chandra with you. Start with Winston." Abbie turned her attention back to the policeman. "Sorry, Captain. Just had to get that out of the way. Have you found anything?"

"Not really. Just the eyewitness report from your courier."

"Juste?"

"No, Ula. The other man who got hurt."

"Oh, my God, I left before I heard about him. Is he all right?"

"Yes. Pretty beat up, but he strikes me as the kind of man who didn't leave the opposition looking very pretty either."

"He fought someone?"

"Yes, the two men who were prowling around your compound. The ones who knocked out your student."

"What were they doing here?"

"We don't know yet. It's kind of hard to see what's been disturbed. So far your students haven't found anything missing. If burglary was the intruders' motive, they didn't do too well."

"What were Larry and Ula doing outside?"

"Seems they each saw a light shining outside the fence. Went out to investigate and joined forces. Larry got hit first, and then Ula tussled with the two men."

"Is Ula still in the compound? I should go see him."

"Some of the students have been with him. I think he's trying to rest now. As for—"

"Hey, Captain," shouted a young officer. "Captain, over here."

Abbie and Captain Karuhije rushed to where the policeman was standing. He pointed to an area just outside the fence.

"That's where Ula says he lost consciousness. And a few feet away, this." The policeman directed his flashlight at a clump of bushes.

There, illuminated, was a tree, part of which had been painted red, and propped against it, two spears with feathers. On the ground, a pattern of beads and feathers and stones was arranged.

"I know that sign," said the captain, snapping his fingers. "That's the tribal insignia of the Kwa. And the Kwa—"

"—kill gorillas," said Abbie, numbly. She broke into a run to the gorilla trailers, passing Chandra and David as they left Fran's trailer. "Have you checked on Joey yet?" she yelled.

"No, we just finished with Winston and Fran," said David, who, seeing the wild expression on Abbie's face, began to run, too.

Pictures of mutilated gorillas flashed before Abbie as if in a slide show. Great gaping mouth with bloody tongue stump. Slashed neck. Fingers cut off: one, two, three, four, five. Like the child's game gone berserk. This little piggy went to market. Slice. This little piggy stayed home. Slice.

Abbie's heart pumped faster. She had seen a blackback killed by the Kwa near the Virunga range in 1979. She knew what to expect. Bloody holes on the side of the head where the ears had been, white cartilage poking through. Teeth pulled. Wet, red mass between the legs. And always, fingers gone. One, two, three, four, five.

Hot air seared Abbie's lungs. With the police officers trailing after them, Abbie and David threw open Joey's door. Abbie held her breath. One, two, three—

Joey was asleep in the middle of the room. All in one piece.

"God, he can sleep through anything," said Abbie, scooping the ape into her arms.

Joey yawned when the light was turned on. He seemed confused by the attention, greeting his visitors with:

"Party time."

"No, Joey," signed Abbie, ruffling his fur. "It's not party time. How are you?"

"Happy good good."

Abbie smiled at Captain Karuhije. "He says he's feeling fine."

"Right," said the policeman. "Whatever you say."

"Fran and Winston?" Abbie signed to Chandra, who'd just joined them.

"Just fine," signed the student, slightly out of breath. "Fran was real grumpy at being woken up."

"What a relief. Oh, I'm sorry"—Abbie addressed the befuddled policemen—"have you met my assistants? Chandra and David?"

The two policemen nodded.

"And this is Joey."

The young officer, who'd kept his distance from the ape, felt the need to respond.

"He has nice . . . fur."

"These are policemen, Joey," signed Abbie, molding the sign into the gorilla's hand. "Policemen."

"Policemen," Joey signed back.

"Good. Now I'm going to hand you over to Chandra while I talk with these men."

Abbie and the policemen left the trailer. Outside, the first rays of morning sun were hitting the compound. They accentuated the lines of sleep deprivation that creased Abbie's face.

"Something like this happened to you once before, I believe," said Captain Karuhije.

"Yes, how did you know?"

"One of your students told me. Can you recall what happened that time?"

"There's not much to recall. No one was hurt then. Some poachers came down here and set up a couple of traps outside the compound."

"Were any of the gorillas harmed? I understand—you'll forgive me if I appear indelicate—that the Kwa butcher gorillas."

"The gorillas were fine."

"And those men never came back?"

"No. Not until now."

"If these are the same men," said the captain. "We'll do all we can to try to find them. In the meantime, as a safety precaution, keep all your doors and gates locked at night, if you don't do so already. I'd especially keep close watch over the gorillas. We don't know whether those men were aiming to come in and were scared off by Ula and your student, but I'd be careful for the next few days. Keep your gorillas inside."

"I couldn't agree more," said a man's voice.

Abbie and the captain turned to see who had spoken. Bunkeya emerged from his trailer.

"Ula. Should you be up?" asked Abbie. "Are you well enough to be walking about?"

"I'm fine, thank you." Bunkeya sported a makeshift bandage over his right cheek. "I agree with the captain. Those men probably won't come back, but I assure you"—he touched his cheek—"they're dangerous. It isn't worth endangering either ourselves or the animals."

"Yes, Mademoiselle Guisbourne," continued Captain Karuhije, "try to keep a low profile for a while."

"My gorillas aren't going to like being cooped up all day long," said Abbie.

"Better restless than harmed."

"True."

"Good, we'll be leaving now. You give us a call if anything else turns up."

"Will you be seeing Larry?"

"Yes, after he's better," said Captain Karuhije. "Thank you for your help. We'll be in touch."

The policemen left. Abbie ran her fingers wearily through her hair.

"Night, Ula," she said, though it was clearly morning. "I'm going to get some shut-eye. I'm glad you weren't hurt too badly. Tell the others I'll be up in a couple of hours."

"How's Larry?" asked Bunkeya, walking alongside her.

"He'll be fine."

"Was he conscious?"

"Yeah, but not very lucid."

"What did he say?"

"He mentioned your name a couple of times and mumbled something. I expect he was trying to tell us that you'd been hurt, too. See you in a while."

"Right."

Abbie climbed the steps leading to her trailer and vanished inside, leaving Bunkeya to greet the day. The African paid little attention to the magnificent sunrise, his eyes riveted instead on Chandra and Sara, who were dismantling the Kwa display of feather and stone. Gingerly, he touched the bandaged welt under his right eye. Perhaps he should have let Mpinga have his way with Larry. By saving the student's life, Bunkeya might very well have endangered his own. The young man might suspect his complicity. Bunkeya grimaced. His nerves were returning. And with them, the mistakes.

"Bad banana," Fran signed, throwing a banana across the room.

"Bad, Fran," signed Abbie, still groggy from her nap. "This is lunch. Now is the time to eat."

"Later."

Fran was in a cranky mood. Chandra, whom Abbie had relieved, attributed it to lack of sleep. The disruption in the night had undoubtedly disturbed the apes.

Well, my darling, thought Abbie, I'm not feeling too keen myself. She patted the gorilla on the shoulder.

"What's wrong, Fran?"

"Nothing."

Abbie suspected that the root of this tantrum lay deeper than lack of sleep. At any moment she expected to see the sign for "Beanface."

"How about an oil bath? You skin looks dry."

To keep the gorillas' skin supple, Abbie periodically slathered the three apes with baby oil. It was no easy task. Joey invariably tried to drink the bottle.

"Go away," signed the ape.

This was not the first time Abbie had been told to get lost by one of the gorillas. Nevertheless, the rejection wounded her.

"Abbie wants to stay."

"Go." Fran moved to a corner.

"All right. I have better things to do than watch you pout." Abbie made sure there was fresh water and food in the room, and left. Chandra might be right. Maybe all the gorilla needed was a nap.

Fran waited until the door closed and, with her body braced against the wall, curled her fingers again and again into the same sign: Hurt.

A few miles down the road from the primate center, in that area beyond the reaches of modernization where the land reverted to rolling, wooded hills, a pack of hyenas were trampling the brush. Their gait was distinctive: The limbs on one side of the body moved together, then the limbs on the other side, shoulders higher than hindquarters. There were perhaps sixteen in the pack, their noses broad and snubbed, their jaws empowered with an awesome skull-crushing capability.

Carnivores, unmistakably. As such, it was with a rush of excitement that the pack discovered a man's corpse shoved under the shrubbery. And the jaws went to work.

Had it not been for the sudden appearance of a car on the road above, which frightened the pack, nothing would have remained of the dead body. As it was, those pieces that did remain were horribly mangled.

Farther down the road, say, eighty miles, where the rolling hills gave way to dense tropical growth, a bronzed Englishman dabbed his brow with a crisp handkerchief. It was mid-afternoon. His knees were tired from crouching and he was hungry, so he left the hiding spot from which he'd watched a confrontation between two chimpanzee groups, and cleaned a place to sit. He opened his knapsack and removed a small checkered cloth, which he laid on the ground. On top of the cloth he spread a number of insulated containers that held his lunch. He'd been told that the anthropologist who preceded him in Muwali had subsisted largely on canned tuna. He shuddered at the thought.

A red-tailed monkey swooped by, chattering at the top of its lungs. The noise lost itself in the surrounding jungle. The Englishman took his knife and spread a dollop of caviar on a Fortnum and Mason water biscuit. He washed this down with a sip of Pouilly-Montrachet, '61. It had been a good year. A nice bouquet.

The man's name was Mic Fielding.

"Cheers." Evan raised his glass to face level. The wine it held was considerably more modest than the wine Mic Fielding had drunk just hours before in southern Burundi.

Abbie's elbows were on the restaurant table and her chin was propped in both cupped hands. The remote gaze of her eyes suggested a multitude of concerns brewing within her. She sat upright when Evan made his toast, but did not reach for her glass.

"It was a mistake coming here," she said, bluntly. "I shouldn't have left the primate center."

"Abbie, the whole point of going out for dinner was to give you a break."

"I know, but—"

"Look, the police found nothing. You've got Juste and the students taking shifts in the courtyard. Relax. The gorillas are in no danger. They're safely locked in."

"But they don't understand why they're being kept inside. It really bothered them today. Especially Winston."

"Abbie," said Evan, "it's all going to work out. We came here for you to be able to unwind. That was a bad scare you had this morning. You have a right to be uptight. But the doctor says Larry's going to be fine. And Ula is just a little beat-up, that's all."

"Yeah. Ula." She played with a piece of bread on her butter plate.

"What? I say something wrong?"

"No, just that I can't quite make heads or tails of him. You know, he lived in Zaire."

"So?"

"Nothing really. He was just real secretive about it. I practically had to pull it out of him."

"It's no crime for a person to want to keep his private life to himself." Evan unfolded his napkin. "You aren't thinking he was involved in the attack this morning, are you?"

"Oh, no. Nothing like that. Maybe I'm making too big a deal out of it. Lack of sleep does that to me. Getting shocked out of bed in the middle of the night doesn't exactly do wonders for you."

"And that's why we're here," said Evan, raising his glass once more, "to try and salvage part of the day. The evening, at least."

"You're right. I've got to wind down a little."

She smiled and raised her glass. Before Evan could clink the rims together, she stopped smiling and lowered her hand.

"It's just that when something happens that could affect the gorillas I get all weird. Actually, I don't even think the gorillas were in danger this time. I'm not sure it was really poachers."

"What do you mean?" asked Evan.

"I think the scare this morning could have been a scam organized by the local residents who aren't so hot on our being here."

"That's a pretty drastic move, Abbie. What makes you suspect them?"

"I guess maybe the way things were arranged this time. Last time we had poachers, they just left the traps, no neat little sign attractively displayed by a tree. And it was a freak thing. We hadn't been at the center that long and the poachers didn't know the gorillas were kept inside a compound. But now we've been here for years. People know about our operation."

"Whoever left that display is long gone. No harm was done. Try to stop thinking about it."

"There was harm done. You're wrong there. This whole episode has set the gorillas back. They're sensitive animals; they know when something's gone wrong, and it affects them. Boy, will I be happy when I don't have to clean up so much."

"Clean?"

"Yeah, Fran's reaction to being locked up all day was to throw stuff around her room. And on top of that she went to the bathroom right in the middle of her trailer."

"Maybe she couldn't hold it in."

"Fat chance. When we first toilet-trained the three of them —how did we happen to get on this topic over dinner?— anyway, when they were first taught, it was Fran who needed the additional instruction. Not to use the setup inside, mind you. But to learn that it was permissible to go outside as well. See, whenever she felt the urge, she'd run like hell from wherever she was, in the yard or whatnot, and go rattle the door to her trailer. Funniest goddamn sight you ever saw. The little moron. It was such a revelation when she discovered that the great outdoors was one big dumping ground. Such a happy, relieved look on her face."

Evan laughed along with Abbie, but their laughter was not enough to lift the shadow of the day's events. He realized that Abbie felt as trapped in the restaurant as did the gorillas behind their locked doors.

"Let's go," said Evan, crumpling his napkin on the table and standing.

"What are you doing? We haven't eaten yet."

"I know, but I got this sudden craving for a peanut butter and jelly sandwich, and I know this little place that makes the best around."

"Does it happen to have live entertainment?" asked Abbie, smiling.

"As a matter of fact, it does. Of course, you have to like animal acts."

"Sounds good," said Abbie, rising. "And thanks."

The fingers clenched rapidly now, spasmodically, signing over and over again, hurt hurt hurt HURT . . .

Evan's rumbling stomach split the quiet of the moonlight-splashed courtyard. For the second night running, his dinner date with Abbie Guisbourne had not included dinner.

"Joey all right?" he asked Abbie as she emerged from the gorilla's trailer.

"Yeah, he's fine," said Abbie, smoothing a lock of hair from her face. "I appreciate your coming back with me."

"My pleasure."

"You want to see Winston with me?" she asked.

"You go ahead. I think Winston and I are still on a plateau of mutual distrust. I'll wait out here."

Evan shoved his hands into his pockets and whistled. On the steps of a nearby trailer, David sat writing a letter, awaiting his turn as watchman for the center. Evan stopped whistling and listened to the night sounds.

"He's fine," said Abbie, stepping from the trailer. "What's wrong? You just jumped a foot."

"Nothing," said Evan, taking a deep breath. "Just wasn't expecting you to jump out like that."

"Jump out? Evan, I was just walking down the stairs—"

"Now to Fran, right?" said Evan, catching Abbie's arm and smiling—a transparent attempt to change the subject.

"Yes. This time you better come in with me. I wouldn't want the night crawlers to get you."

"So I'm a coward. I'll live longer that way."

"You know," Abbie said, steering a course across the courtyard, "you're not the only one who finds it spooky here. This center has a strange feeling for me now. I'm not sure I can explain it. It's as if your house was burglarized. One moment, it's so secure to you. Seconds later, it's so terribly vulnerable. I mean, on top of worrying about Larry and the gorillas, I'm angry because my private space has been invaded. I don't feel comfortable here, like there's something wrong. Everything looks the same but I know that it's not."

"That feeling will fade," said Evan. "With time."

"I guess so. Anyway, two down and one to go," she said, as they approached Fran's trailer. "Be prepared to get smothered with attention."

Abbie fumbled with her keys at the door. She slid the right key into the lock, turned the knob, and reached her hand inside the trailer to turn on the light.

The light snapped on. And it reflected red.

Blood. Blood splattered everywhere. On the floor, collecting in small puddles. Along the baseboard, smeared. On the lower walls, dripping.

Abbie recoiled at the sight. Her face blanched. Evan pushed her aside. He was not prepared for what he saw. Patches of blood trailed to the back wall as though someone had taken a paintbrush and slapped a red streak across the floor. He hoped it was some kind of sick joke, that it really was paint. Then he saw the bloody imprint of a hand on the wall.

Evan fought the impulse to be sick, and picked his way through the spread of crimson. Some of the blood spattered his left shoe and he very nearly panicked, smitten by an irrational fear that the blood would spread up his leg if he didn't immediately wipe it off. He blocked the gruesome image from his mind and kept moving. His heart strained wildly against his breast.

The playthings in the room were upended. Brightly colored boxes obstructed Evan's path, and he moved them cautiously, afraid of what he might find behind them.

He found more of the same. More blood, as if the dam

holding it in the body's reservoir had burst. Evan never dreamed that a living thing held this much blood.

And then a groan. It came from the corner. Evan breathed heavily through his mouth. An awful thought struck him: Perhaps there was more than one victim behind the last group of boxes.

Sweat ran under Evan's collar. He cursed himself for making Abbie leave the compound. Though he'd heard the Kwa described as mutilators, the heinousness of the term had not sunk in. Now, faced with this grisly field of red, he understood what to die of mutilation meant.

Drops of sweat filled his eyes, and he blinked rapidly to dispel them. Why was he moving so slowly? The far wall seemed to be curving toward him, distorted, as though seen through a fish-eye lens. He was no longer able to hear Abbie's gasps, only his own tortured breathing.

He took another step and skirted a box to his left. The groan came again. Evan stopped dead in his tracks. A foot stretched out from behind a stack of tires: a gorilla's foot, the hair wet with blood. Evan's lips were dry and his tongue was raspy, a sheet of sandpaper against the roof of his mouth. Summoning all of his strength, he took one last step and peered around the tires.

Fran looked up at him, feebly. By her side was a newborn gorilla.

Pig—as Fran named the new gorilla, presumably because the infant's protruding nasal region reminded her of a pig's snout—weighed four pounds at birth and was perfectly developed. Her hair, a medium brown, was sparsely distributed over her body except for a jet-black tuft on her head that looked as though it had been slicked down for a documentary on the fifties. Her face was pink and wizened; her eyes were closed. Evan remarked that her ears seemed much too big for her head and her limbs too thin and spidery, but he was assured that this was normal.

"I should have considered the possibility of her being pregnant," muttered Abbie. She had recovered quickly from the shock of entering the blood-spattered room, and was drinking a cup of coffee in the kitchen. Chandra had been posted outside Fran's door. "What with her being so irritable and excitable and the stomachache. God, I'm so stupid. I thought she was jealous because of the attention you were paying me and not her. See? That's what happens when you try to impose too many human standards on apes. You screw up. I was trying to assign her human attributes instead of concentrating on her own primate characteristics."

"Don't be so harsh on yourself," said Evan. "Pig's fine. Nature took its course. Although"—Evan leaned back in his chair—"it does sort of escape me how you could have missed that Fran was pregnant."

"It happens all the time!" Abbie grew defensive. "Believe it or not, it's extremely difficult to detect a pregnancy. Hell, it's hard enough just figuring out what sex a gorilla is. You should try it sometime."

"No, thanks."

"Do you know that this same thing happened in the New York Central Park Zoo—and mind you, they have all those hot-shot veterinarians and zoo people there. Their female gorilla, Lulu, gave birth, and no one had suspected that she was pregnant. I think that was in 1972. They named the baby Pattycake. Gorillas have such big abdomens to begin with, who can tell if they get a little bigger?"

"I wasn't criticizing you," said Evan. "Just curious."

"Then there's Dian Fossey's 1978 study which recorded that only two of the nine cases of pregnancy in her gorillas had been suspected."

"I believe you, okay?" Evan said. "Are the births always quite that . . . messy?"

"No. According to all that I've read, the majority of the blood is deposited within one nest. Looking back across the trailer, it seems like Fran made a series of nests. I don't know why. Maybe because she never had an older female gorilla around to emulate. Usually a large amount of blood like that and a series of nests means a nonviable birth."

"But Pig is quite viable," said Evan.

"Yes, luckily."

"This may be tacky to ask," said Evan, "but who's the father?"

"Winston. Joey's only now beginning to mature sexually. It's a little early for Fran, too. I really hadn't thought she'd be able to conceive yet."

"You hadn't taught her about the birds and bees yet, is that it?"

"No," said Abbie, seriously.

"I was joking."

"I'm not."

"You mean you honestly would have taught her? How does one go about instructing a gorilla in sex education?"

"Oh, there are films," said Abbie in an offhand manner.

"Come on, you're pulling my leg. I don't believe it."

"I'm telling you the truth. When zoos and primate research centers discovered how difficult it was to breed gorillas in captivity—the low sperm count and all—they started making films of gorillas fornicating. In case they didn't quite know what went where."

"Gorillas are dumber than I thought."

"Think about it," said Abbie. "If you'd been brought up in captivity—the only male of your species, never having seen another human being—and there was this woman in the corner, you think you'd know what to do?"

"Damn right I would," answered Evan. "Ingenuity's always been one of my strong points." He shook his head. "Gorilla porno films. What will they think of next."

"They're not porno films. They're only about thirty seconds long."

"That's all? Poor Fran. What do they call these movies? I remember we had one in junior high school that was about venereal disease and was called something like *A Quarter Million Teenagers*. Only every year they had to revise the title. *Half a Million Teenagers. A Million.* I don't think the titlers were very farsighted."

"I believe in some circles they're called *Monkey See, Monkey Do*," she said, dryly, a remark that sent Evan into a paroxysm of laughter. After he recovered he said:

"You should be real proud that you have two astute gorillas who figured out where everything went all by themselves."

"Such virtuosity I could have done without. I think I've had my share of surprises for this week."

"Admit it. You're excited about Pig."

"Yeah, I am. The only problem is that Fran isn't turning out to be the best mother."

"What do you mean? It's only been a couple of hours."

"That's exactly what I'm talking about. She should have formed an attachment to the baby by now. Instead she's refusing to hold Pig. And every time Pig crawls into her arms Fran refuses to help the baby find her breast."

"Why?"

"It's another problem with gorillas in captivity. They reject their offspring sometimes."

"How do you go about counteracting that?"

"Well, like the sex films you were laughing about, there are films for female gorillas which show other female gorillas fondling and nursing their babies. Unfortunately, we don't happen to have any lying around."

"You're about as farsighted as the namers of my junior high school film."

"Yes, but I've got a backup plan."

"What's that?"

"You'll see."

Mpinga laboriously reported Bunkeya's findings to Dalam. He showed the FPL leader the maps of the primate center and of the nearby coastline. He meticulously outlined the schedule of attack. No fact was too small for him to report. He wanted Dalam assured of his objectivity. Only then could he mention the role he planned for himself.

"—and Bunkeya is certain that this so-called Kwa scare

that you two devise ¹ will not unduly alter the primate center's security precautions?" asked Dalam.

"No. A few vagrant poachers aren't enough to really concern the police. Any additional security measures will be carried out by the center's inhabitants. Nothing we can't handle."

The FPL leader seemed satisfied with Mpinga's itemization of the plan. He clasped his dark hands on the table.

"Yes, it will work," he said, after a short pause, "but time is short. We must start moving."

"Yes," said Mpinga. His mouth grew suddenly dry as he mentally composed his next sentence. He hated to admit it, but Dalam still held a mysterious sway over him. "I'll need time to instruct the men before I lead them across Lake Tanganyika."

"You plan to lead them?" Dalam arched one eyebrow.

"Yes, of course," said Mpinga. "Bunkeya and I agreed it would be best. I'm already familiar with the rendezvous point and the layout of the camp. The terrain. Anyone else leading the assault would only have to defer to my judgment in the end."

Mpinga had picked his words carefully. Their impact was not lost on Dalam. Were the FPL leader to assume command of the expedition, as he had planned, his position of authority would be undermined by Mpinga. Better not to go at all.

"I see," said Dalam. "Well, I'm sure Bunkeya knows what he's doing." He rose from his chair. "Let's inform the men."

Mpinga practically leaped from his seat. He did not care that Dalam probably suspected his duplicity. Only one thing mattered: He'd regained the upper hand.

"I feel like a complete ass," said Evan.

"You're doing just fine," said Abbie. "Just keep at it. Fran ignored all the rest of us, but since you're so special to her she seems to be paying attention to you."

Evan and Fran sat opposite each other. In the gorilla's lap

was the wrinkled little Pig. Evan held a stuffed gorilla toy used for the vocabulary drills. He wasn't wearing a shirt.

"Okay, now hold it up to your chest."

"Jesus, Abbie. Do I have to do this?"

"You're our last shot. Otherwise we'll have to take away the baby and feed her ourselves. So please, grit your teeth and do it for Pig."

"Shit. Okay, Pig, for you." Evan cradled the stuffed animal in his arms, an unnaturally tight grin on his face. He positioned the head of the toy over his right breast.

"Make sure Fran can see what you're doing," said Abbie. "Angle yourself a little more toward her. That's good. Now move the gorilla around a little more."

"Do you mind?" said Evan. "I don't need any backseat advice. I'm going to nurse this gorilla the way I goddamn feel."

"See, Fran?" Abbie signed to the gorilla. "Beanface hugs baby. You hug your Pig-baby too. Please, Fran."

Slowly, tentatively, the gorilla mimicked Evan's pose and brought the newborn gorilla to her chest.

"Now if we're lucky the baby will do the rest," murmured Abbie.

Sure enough, Pig began searching around on Fran's chest—straying once to the region of the armpit, to Fran's obvious annoyance—but finally she located her mother's teat and began suckling.

"She did it," said Abbie.

"Thank God," Evan said, lowering the stuffed animal.

"Don't you dare! You keep that toy up to your chest until Pig's finished. I don't want Fran letting go until the baby's had her fill."

"I hope word of this doesn't leak out to the Bujumburan community," said Evan. "I don't think a diplomat who breast-feeds stuffed animals has much credibility."

Abbie paid him no attention.

"There, I think she's done. Yeah. You can put down the stuffed animal now."

"Swell."

"You did fine work, Evan. Better than any film could have."

"Thanks. I'll have to write it down on my résumé some-day." Evan walked to where his shirt was draped.

"Wait a sec," said Abbie. "I think Fran wants you."

"What is it, Fran?" signed Evan.

"Beanface come."

"What, Fran?" Evan drew closer.

The gorilla cuddled her infant, stroking Pig's head, then pointed at Evan.

"Beanface daddy," she signed.

"Oh, God . . ."

VIII

The sun streamed through the window of Abbie's trailer and fell in a line across her pillow, gilding her hair. She did not want to get up yet. It had been a long night.

The breast-feeding gimmick had worked far more successfully than she'd imagined. She recalled a similar attempt at the Columbus zoo in which a woman breast-fed her baby outside the gorilla enclosure. That demonstration failed, largely because the male gorilla, Oscar, fascinated by this facet of the human female anatomy, hogged the window and wouldn't let Toni and Joansie, the two female gorillas, watch. Abbie had foreseen as dismal a result for their experiment—until she thought of using Evan.

He certainly was an interesting combination, this Evan Olgilvie. He had a wonderful gentleness and sensitivity matched by a keen intelligence that sometimes got misplaced in the shuffle. And there was strength there as well. He was not a man, she sensed, who would accept a defeat easily. He might not win, but he'd do his damndest to rebound for the next time.

Abbie yawned lazily. Joey and Winston would be awake by now and restless, she reckoned. She didn't look forward to keeping them locked inside again, especially since the clatter in the night had alerted them that something out of the ordinary had occurred. Something called Pig.

Only now was Abbie able to contemplate Pig's arrival with any objectivity. Until this moment all her energies had been concentrated on coping with the unexpectedness of the birth. She'd forgotten what a delight it had been raising Winston, Fran, and Joey, how every one of the first signs they'd learned had been a momentous occasion. Pig would be even more of a challenge, opening avenues of study in maternal behavior and the relay of language.

But Pig. What sort of name was that? No one was sure whether Fran truly intended naming the newborn gorilla "Pig" or simply was making an observation. Nonetheless, Pig was what she'd been called, and Pig was what she would remain.

Abbie harbored no doubts, however, as to the nature of another of Fran's signs. Chandra admitted that she'd demonstrated "daddy" to Fran while Abbie and Evan were in the kitchen, but in reference to Winston. It was only happenstance that the gorilla practiced the sign on Evan, not yet comprehending its meaning.

Happenstance or not, Evan's enamoration of Pig clearly bordered on that conferred by fatherhood. Abbie had had to drag him away from the infant. It seemed Pig had gained an "Uncle Evan." And Abbie had lost sleep, again.

She was about to remedy that situation. Turning over on her stomach, Abbie yawned once more, and drifted back to sleep.

The cot already was made, corners folded neatly in and under, blanket smooth and taut. Nothing remained to show that Bunkeya had stayed in the trailer. He had taken it all with him.

The trailer next door was a startling contrast: clothes strewn around the room, a few empty beer cans tossed indiscriminately into paper bags. Juste was sleeping peacefully, a blanket rumpled about him, his legs dangling off the bed. He snored. It was the deep sleep of a man who had tied on one too many with his newfound friend, the courier, Ula.

The room was disorderly, but to Juste there was method in

the disorderliness. As he had explained to his new crony, he knew where everything lay in the room: how many layers of soiled socks had to be lifted to reach his keys; how far to reach under the bed for his shoes; which drawer held his gun and which held the ammunition.

When he woke, it was unlikely he would think to look for his gun. Both it and the ammunition were missing, but Juste would find this out too late.

Bunkeya stood at the edge of the lake and scanned the horizon. A small gust shook the limbs of the trees around him. It had not taken as long to walk from the compound to the shore as he had thought, and he was early. He swung the pack off his shoulders, untied it, and pulled a square mirror from its inner pocket. Then he resumed his vigil.

Although it was still early morning, Bunkeya knew that the boat would have been out on the water for some time, fishing. He caught a glimpse of something in the distance and squinted. Still too far off to tell. He waited, the breeze tugging at his pants leg. The approaching object took on the characteristics of a ship, as a flower unfurls its petals in time-lapse photography.

Bunkeya tilted the mirror so that sunlight bounced off it. Primitive, this signaling device, but effective. He waited for the return signal, barely managing to step out of sight when a Burundian patrol boat hove into view.

"That's it. Over there."

Mpinga followed the outstretched arm of one of his men and leaned against the rail. A brilliant light flashed in the distance.

"Can we stop fishing now?" asked the man.

"Not yet," answered Mpinga. "I want to make sure. Besides, we'll need a full day's catch in case anyone decides to check our haul. As it is, we'll be far below the norm."

"Damn," said the man to another. "I hate doing this." He scooped up a handful of bait and threw it into a bucket. A few of the small fish fell to the deck, where they slid under his shoe. He walked unconcernedly over them, scraping his shoe on the side of the boat as he adjusted a rope.

"Company," said Mpinga quietly, pointing to the Burundian patrol boat. He spat on the deck.

A dozen heads turned west, in the direction of the oncoming boat. A dozen sighs sounded, minutes later, when it passed by without stopping.

So far, so good.

Bunkeya had picked a spot on the shore not too far from the primate center—a small natural harbor. The fishing trawler remained stationary in the choppy water as the Burundian boat moved out of sight. Before long, a small boat put out from the trawler. This was the part of the plan that Bunkeya dreaded. He disliked operating within a group. One could never be sure of the soundness of another man's judgment or the celerity of his reflexes. Particularly when, as on this windy morning, the men he saw before him were all strongly aligned with Mpinga, and two or three were still boys.

"And Dalam?" asked Bunkeya when the men from the boat assembled in front of him.

"Back in Iddan," replied Mpinga. "He decided I should handle this part."

Bunkeya made no comment. It was hardly the time for cross-examinations. He briefed the group and organized them into two squads, one headed by himself, one by Mpinga. They trooped silently up the incline which led to the back of the primate center. The soft breeze that had acted as a tranquilizer on Bunkeya's taut nerves was cut off by a grove of trees. And as the lake vanished from view, so did all hope of turning back.

*   *   *

Abbie and Chandra were crossing from the kitchen to Joey's trailer when they spotted a man off in the distance, traversing the five-acre site.

"Is that Juste?" asked Abbie, using her hand as a visor.

"He's up early," signed Chandra.

"Yes," answered Abbie. "Wonder where he's been?"

The two women took a few more steps, their conversation returning to talk of the gorillas, but stopped when from the third trailer down, one housing the students, a figure dressed in green khaki emerged. The man roughly pushed one of the students through the doorway.

"What the hell do you—" Abbie stopped short when she saw the rifle clutched in the man's hands.

Frantically, she pivoted toward Juste, but he was not where she expected. The man entering the camp was another green-clad figure. He, too, carried a rifle.

Another trailer door swung open. Another man emerged, this time empty-handed. A third man. And a fourth. They were swarming through the camp, spilling out of the brush as though called forth by an invisible piper. One of the invaders approached her.

"Come with us, Mademoiselle Guisbourne. I'd prefer it if you didn't put up a fight. It'll prove useless."

"Go where? Just what exactly do you think you're doing? This is private property."

"We can use force."

"I don't understand what's going on here. I demand an explanation."

"There's nothing to understand. You're being kidnapped."

"What? That's ludicrous."

The compound was filled with activity now. Damn it, where was Juste? Why hadn't he alerted them? Scuffles broke out around her. Past Chandra's terrified face Abbie saw a man in green prod Juste with the end of his rifle. Juste's head was bloody and his hands were bound in back of him. Abbie's thoughts darted swiftly to the six or seven people still eating breakfast in the kitchen.

"You can't be serious," she said, loudly. "You won't get anything for us. We're American citizens."

A scream pierced the air, and out of a trailer a man dragged Sara, Abbie's administrative aide. The young woman thrashed in her captor's arms.

This can't be happening, thought Abbie.

Disbelief. Fear instills a number of reactions, many of them organic in nature. Rapid pulse. Tense muscles. Butterflies in the stomach. Dryness of the throat or mouth.

Other reactions are mental. An inability to concentrate. Confusion. And often a sense of unreality, that this couldn't be happening: disbelief.

After World War II, a survey was taken on the symptoms of fear reported by fliers in combat missions. Seventy percent of the 1,985 flying officers and 2,519 enlisted fliers who participated in the study reported experiencing disbelief at the sights and sounds around them. In psychological jargon, a surfeit of external stimuli overloaded their normal processing abilities. In layman's terms they felt like characters in a book watching imagined atrocities.

Of course, that was war.

"Mademoiselle Guisbourne," said the terrorist, "I won't ask you again. Please come with me."

Abbie felt light-headed and disoriented, as though standing on a cliff between absolute panic and total detachment, waiting for a stiff wind to blow her one way or the other. She forced herself to concentrate on the man before her.

"Our government won't barter for our release," she said, struggling to retain her composure. "Surely you know that. You can't go anywhere with us. The police are probably on their way right now."

Abbie's voice failed to carry the conviction of her words. It cracked in mid-sentence. As she spoke, two of the interlopers entered the kitchen but exited empty-handed. The students in that trailer had fled into the brush after the first signs of commotion. This knowledge gave Abbie a modicum of support. With her returning lucidity came the realization that these men, whom she'd first taken for Kwa poachers, were like no tribesmen she had ever seen. Their mien was paramilitary.

"I don't know who you are, but—"

The next thing Abbie knew, a rifle was shoved in her back and she was jabbed forward. Tears smarted her eyes. It was insane. Who in their right minds would want to kidnap them? What could these men possibly hope to achieve? The questions jumbled kaleidoscopically in her head.

Like cattle, she and the other captives were prodded to the end of the courtyard. A young man with bad teeth began to bind their hands while his companions scurried in and out of trailers. They darted across the courtyard with the mechanized rapidity of targets in a shooting gallery. Only six of us caught, Abbie counted. Thank God. Only six.

"Don't bother with those trailers," a voice snapped. "Mpinga should have told you that those contain the gorillas."

Abbie did not recognize the voice at first. The curt tone threw her off. His manner always had been so controlled when he talked to her. Unnaturally so. And then it clicked. She whirled around.

The strange courier from Muwali faced her.

"Ula," she said under her breath, the name suddenly odious.

He returned her look with the stoicism she expected and resumed giving orders.

The shock of the revelation helped check Abbie's rampaging emotions. Her thoughts channeled in a single direction: They were being kidnapped; in a few hours their disappearance would be investigated. Somehow, if she could manage it, she had to leave their trackers a clue.

And then she saw Joey.

The gorilla was watching the embroilment in the courtyard through the window of his trailer. His teeth were bared and the top of his head contracted with anger.

The activity in the compound was still frenetic. The invaders' search became much less methodical. They went through the trailers for anything they could carry. Food. Blankets. A disagreement broke out between two men near Abbie's trailer. Others joined in. So, thought Abbie, there was disunity among these men, whoever they were. Now was her chance.

Taking advantage of the kidnappers' disorder, Abbie inched toward Joey's trailer. With as little movement as possible, she began signing to him. She did not have much time. The boy with the bad teeth had finished binding all but one of the students. She would be next.

The young gorilla did not follow the movement of her hands. Patiently, Abbie signed the name "Ula" to him, spelling it out over and over again: U-L-A. She followed it with "Tell Evan," but had little hope the message would be delivered. Since none of the gorillas was familiar with the manual alphabet—it was too complex for them to handle—the finger letters were gibberish to Joey. It was unlikely the ape would be able to remember the signs, much less form them with his fingers. The letters required a greater degree of dexterity than any gorilla possessed, Joey in particular. Years earlier he had ripped tendons in his right hand, which hindered some of his signs. But it was Abbie's only chance.

"Joey, look here. Joey, tell Evan 'Ula.' Ula. U-L-A."

She saw no need to add that they were being kidnapped: that much would be apparent soon enough. Moreover, she had no idea where they were being taken or by what group. The only clue she could leave was the name of the man who had arranged the kidnapping.

Abbie asked Joey to repeat the signs, but he was so agitated that he did not respond. She was jerked away before she was able to see him tentatively repeat the formations.

The rope that was used to bind Abbie's hands cut into her wrists. She winced as it was knotted. To her right, Sara cried softly. Fortunately, except for the gash on Juste's head, the others appeared unharmed. Alex attempted to whisper something to Abbie, but got out only a few words before a rifle butt rammed into his stomach. He doubled over on the ground.

Across the courtyard, a trailer rocked on its foundation.

David remained crouched behind the cabinet in Fran's trailer. He had taken refuge there when the men invaded the camp, partly to escape detection should one of the invaders glance inside, and partly to shield himself from Fran's outburst. The gorilla had responded to the attack on the camp with an angry display of pent-up energy. She slammed against the walls, and tossed blankets and boxes and tires around the room in a rage. She set the trapeze swinging violently, an action that fascinated the newborn Pig, who sat undisturbed on a rug in the corner. As Abbie was led away, Fran barked loudly, a sharp, piercing sound that startled the marauders outside.

One of Mpinga's men, lagging behind to complete the sweep of the compound, walked over to the trailer to see what had produced the noise. At the same time, Fran perched herself on a stack of tires and looked out the window.

To David's surprise, the ape recoiled and barked again, this time in fright.

The man with the crocodile emblem on his shoulder passed by.

"Hello, this is Evan Olgilvie. Can I help you?"

"Evan, it's David McCreary." The young man's voice broke unexpectedly. "We got trouble."

"What's wrong?"

"I'm down at the police station. There was an attack on the compound. They took Abbie and some of the others."

"What? Who took them? The Kwa?"

"We don't know. A gang of men. I hid in Fran's trailer. A bunch of others were in the kitchen and were able to run into the brush. They heard a couple of the men talking about a boat. Sounded as if they were going to take Abbie and the others across Lake Tanganyika."

"Good God. Was anyone hurt?"

"Not among us. I'm not sure about the ones who got taken."

"When did this happen?"

"Early this morning. We were afraid to return to the center for the car, so we walked into town."

"How many were taken in all?"

"Seven. Abbie, Juste, Chandra, Sara, Tyler, and Alex. And the courier from Muwali, Ula. At least we think those are the ones who were taken, since they're missing."

"And the gorillas?"

"Untouched."

"Okay, how long are you going to be at the police station?"

"We're going back to the center with the police now. It'd help if someone could come down. The police were about to notify the embassy anyway."

"All right. I'll meet you there."

Evan replaced the phone receiver in its cradle. Here it was, what he'd been waiting for, a break from the tedium of agricultural surveys and industrial reports. A sudden end to the lethargy that surrounded his work. A plummet into the world of high stakes and diplomatic furor.

But he'd never gambled on this being the form it would take. Evan Olgilvie desperately wanted his old world back.

Engulu's hands shook. How many times had he tied the knot? Ten? Twelve? It just wasn't right. One more try and he was satisfied. He let the rope, made of strips of twisted sheets tied together, fall free from where it was secured to the ceiling. It swung back and forth, its shadow bisecting the far wall. The slight motion brought a tightness to Engulu's chest. He took a large breath.

Stupid of them to build the cells with so many places from which to hang a rope. Engulu had picked a section of pipe over the sink. It was fastened to the ceiling with bolted clamps and had a one-inch gap. Just enough to permit the passage of a rope. He tugged on the rope until he was convinced it would hold his weight. He didn't want anything to go wrong. Get it over and done with as quick as possible; no lingering. That was all that mattered to him. A clean exit. That was the way to die.

Sounds produced by exercising men came in through his window. The day's first recreation shift was in the courtyard. Engulu was sorry that he couldn't be outside just now. Death inside these dank charcoal walls was not how he wanted it, but he was content to pick the time and means of his death, if not the place.

The rope stopped swinging. The time was now. With extraordinary calm, Engulu stepped on the edge of the rickety cot, which he'd shoved against the wall. The bed nearly tipped over. Engulu shifted his weight and the metal legs settled back on the floor. He listened to the creaks outside in the passageway. No guards, just the groans of old wood.

The absurdity of the situation made him laugh. All his life he'd worried that men like the prison guards would kill him someday. Now he was worried that they'd try to prevent his death. It truly was a world without meaning.

His laughter subsided and he took the roughly fashioned noose in hand. He rubbed the coiled sheet between his fingers, and briefly contemplated the irony that the last object he would touch would be the instrument of his death. He placed the noose over his head and tightened it around his neck. The rope lodged against his Adam's apple and he instinctively gagged. He loosened the knot. It would be tight soon enough.

He thought of his family and his life in Dilolo, a town in southern Zaire. This was the image he had decided to carry with him. Not the image of this wretched cell and its dusty corners, but one of a better time. He recalled the circular thatched hut he'd lived in and the cows he'd tended and the women he'd known. And he remembered the tribal dances. Dances that shaped his consciousness as no outsider could understand. Stylized movements that formed a link to a second world, a world of spirit. The familiar beat sounded in Engulu's ears. His muscles tensed. The steps began. Whirling, clapping in a dialogue between just him and the drummer. Faster, faster. Long skirt flapping, feathered headdress molting, sweat coating the body.

Engulu began to sway. The drummer came down again and again on the tanned surface, the cadence only for him. The cell was gone. The drummer's beat reverberated around him. Faster. Jump high, spears thrusting to one side. Quick, furious, ritualized steps. Crouch low, jump high.

Engulu's calf muscles tensed, ready for the push. His feet moved. The syncopated throbbing intensified. Flying colored beads blurred his vision. Legs kick, dive low. Jump high. Jump—

"Engulu."

The voice came from another plane of existence. Somewhere Engulu was not. The weaving, pulsing dance continued.

"Engulu, are you there?"

The urgent voice pierced through the diaphanous world of Engulu's making. Slowly, his mind registered the question. His body was warm. The noose around his neck was cool with sopped-up moisture.

"Engulu?"

Again the voice. It was coming from below his window. Should he reply? It could be his last contact with the human race. Engulu stood at a threshold. The dance was still going on. He could remain in its ranks until it ended, or break away. He did not think he would be able to find his place again if he left. The voice, hoarse and insistent, tugged at him.

"What?" he finally answered, the word exploding from his mouth like a trapped air bubble.

"Have you heard?"

All Engulu heard was the sound of receding drums. The dancers were leaving.

"Heard what?"

"There's been a kidnapping. Dalam has taken a group of Americans. Do you realize what that means, Engulu? They'll bargain for you. You're going to get out of here."

The drummers were gone. There was only the voice.

"Do you hear me, Engulu?"

"Yes, I hear you."

The conversation ended with the sharp command of a guard in the courtyard. Engulu listened as soft footsteps on the loose red earth retreated. He slipped the noose over his head. His legs trembled as he stepped to the floor, and he collapsed.

The dance had drained him.

The police swarmed across the grounds of the primate research center with the assiduity of a colony of ants moving a piece of bread in a transparent mail-order farm. Occasional rumbles sounded from the gorillas' trailers. Upset and restless and hungry, the three apes battered the trailers like punching bags.

So far the police had come up with nothing. No apparent motive. No leads of any kind except for the sketchy descriptions of the green-clad men by the remaining students. The Kwa incident of the other night was tossed about, but was dismissed as not bearing on the case. Poachers were after gorillas, after all, not people. The police officers sedulously reconstructed the sequence of events. Their hypothesis: A ransom note would be forthcoming.

Not exactly the brilliant deduction Evan hoped to hear. Nor would the news buoy Davenport's spirits. Had the Deputy Chief of Mission not been busy contacting the ambassador, the State Department, Brice University, and the CIA, he would have journeyed to the primate center himself. As it was, he was forced to let Evan stand in his place. Reluctantly. He'd told Evan to call him the minute anything developed. Nothing had.

Evan stood to one side as the police scooped samples of blood from the ground and placed them in plastic bags, to be typed back at the station. He hoped that Abbie hadn't resisted the invaders, that she'd gone peaceably with them. In short, that the blood wasn't hers.

"Yes, I agree," Police Captain Karuhije was saying as Evan

drew near, "even though we notified the patrols on Lake Tanganyika to board any suspicious vessels, I don't think they'll turn up anything. It took a while for the students who escaped to get to us. The kidnappers have probably reached their destination by now."

"What about air patrols, sir?" asked a policeman.

"They've been alerted as well. So far, they've sighted nothing. It looks as though the kidnappers are calling the shots from here on out. We'll just have to be patient until we get a message from them."

"That's all?" asked Evan, incredulously.

"Yes, Monsieur Olgilvie. There's not much else we can do. It's highly likely that the kidnappers were headed for Zaire. We have no authority there. Beyond informing the Zairians and checking on the activities of a few groups here, we're pretty much at a stalemate. It's international now. These men were professionals. They didn't leave much for us to go on."

"But the Kwa angle—"

"We have men checking on that. It may lead somewhere. Or it may not. Believe me, I don't like waiting any more than you do. Neither do my men. But unless you can produce a more informative witness, Monsieur Olgilvie, that's where it stands."

A more informative witness. Where the hell was he supposed to find one?

"Now, Fran," Evan said, prying the gorilla's powerful arms from his legs.

"She's pretty upset," said David.

"I can see that," said Evan.

"Beanface Beanface," Fran signed, releasing one arm from Evan's legs.

"Joey and Winston are upset, too," said David. "Especially Winston. I don't think it'd be a good idea to go into his trailer just now, in case you were thinking about it."

"I really can't say I was," grunted Evan, pulling Fran's hand from his pants leg.

"We're just sort of leaving him alone until he calms down. Laura has been signing to him through the window, to reassure him, but he's still upset. He refuses to sign back."

"It's no wonder," said Evan. "Hearing all that noise and screaming outside. You say Fran was watching out the window?"

"Yeah."

"How is Fran?" Evan signed to the gorilla.

"Bad," signed the ape.

"Did you see the men?"

"Nut nut!" She reburied herself in Evan's legs.

"Fran," Evan signed, "did you see the bad men?"

She whimpered.

"No one can hurt you now, Fran."

"Man animal hurt."

"What hurt? Is Abbie hurt?"

"Abbie go."

"Did you see the men?"

"Nut nut dirty toilet."

"Damn," Evan said, patting the ape. "I can't understand a thing she's signing."

"Well, she had a big shock," said David. "Whatever she saw outside the window really scared her, because she screamed and wouldn't go to it again."

"You didn't see what she saw?"

"No. I was hiding behind the cabinet."

"Okay, one more time." Evan took the ape by the hand. "Fran, who is hurt?"

"Man animal hurt."

"Hurt how, Fran?" signed Evan.

The gorilla hesitated and then, whimpering as before, moved her hands in a clapping motion, the heels together.

"Crocodile?" said David and Evan together.

"What crocodile?" signed Evan.

"Man animal crocodile." Fran gave a frightened bark.

"She must have been real frightened to compare this experience to a crocodile," said David.

"Are you sure that's what she's saying?" asked Evan.

"What do you mean?"

"She's just making a comparison?"

"Yeah, what else could it be? There aren't any crocodiles this far from water."

"I guess. I always thought it was a lot more clear-cut talking to apes with sign language."

"Nope. A lot of it's open to interpretation. Often the gorillas sign nonsense. Some of their conversations never do make sense. You've just been lucky to see some that do."

"Yeah. I guess so. Is she going to be okay?" Evan asked.

"I hope so," said David. "A trauma like this is always difficult to handle with the apes—even worse when you're as understaffed as we are now. To tell you the truth, if Abbie doesn't come back soon it could cause permanent damage to this study. I'm sure it's already set us back months."

He walked Evan to the door.

"But the really bad thing is not what's happening to the study but to the gorillas themselves. Emotionally, I mean. They don't understand what's happened. And there's no way I can communicate the concept of a kidnapping to them. I just don't know what to do."

"I'm sure you're doing everything you can, David. Abbie knows that. If I can help you in any way, you know I'd be more than happy to assist you."

"Thanks, I appreciate it."

Neither of them mentioned what would happen if Abbie Guisbourne never came back.

Captain Karuhije adjusted the sunglasses on the bridge of his nose and cleared his throat.

"Well, Monsieur Olgilvie," he said, "I suppose you'll be reporting all of this back to your embassy."

"Yes, I will."

"I noticed you called some of the students by name. Do you have some other connection here?"

"Connection? No, not really. That is, I was here a few times this week on official business. I didn't know anybody here before that."

"I see."

How can you, thought Evan, when even I don't understand my connection here. Last week, he had not known of Abbie Guisbourne's existence; now he felt a strange obligation to help find her. If she were not found, all her work, all that dedication, might go down the drain. Evan did not think he could bear to watch the gorillas' deterioration. There was nothing crueler than taking a living being from its original state to a seemingly more advantaged one only to return it from whence it came.

"How are the animals doing, by the way?" asked Captain Karuhije.

"They're in a pretty shaky state. This hasn't been the greatest week for them, what with Joey getting sick, and Pig being born, and Fran afraid of the crocodile—"

"The what?" asked the policeman.

"The crocodile. She's deathly afraid of them. She thinks she saw one today."

"The gorilla? How do you know this?"

"I know sign language. She told me."

"So what exactly did she 'say' about this crocodile?"

"Nothing much. Something about a man or animal wanting to hurt her, I think. It wasn't very clear."

"Can you remember exactly?"

"Why do you want to know? Is it important?"

"It may be. There's a terrorist organization in Zaire called the Front Populaire de Libération which uses a crocodile for its symbol. This kidnapping isn't their usual type of operation, but you never know about some of these groups."

"Let's go find out," said Evan.

"How? Go talk to the gorilla?"

"Sure. You said you wanted a reliable witness. We may just have found you one."

*   *   *

Fran behaved admirably, considering Evan was asking her to relive the ordeal again in front of a stranger. But now that Evan had a focus to his questions, her answers made a lot more sense. It turned out she had indeed seen a crocodile: the facsimile of one on a man's shirt sleeve.

Evan translated the ape's answers on a sheet of paper for Captain Karuhije. The captain handed the transcript to a young officer.

"Captain, how do you want me to list it in my report?" the officer asked.

"What?"

"To whom should I attribute it?"

The captain removed his cap and smoothed back his hair.

"Hell, list it as Mlle. Fran Gorilla."

"Mlle. Gorilla?"

"You heard right. Only I don't want a word of this leaking to the rest of the men. Or the press. Tell them we're operating on the assumption that this was perpetrated by a Zairian organization, the origins of which we are not at liberty to disclose."

"Who shall I say tipped us, sir?"

"A reliable eyewitness."

"Yes, sir." The young officer departed.

"This is a hell of a way to run a police investigation," muttered the captain.

The crossing in the fishing boat was not too rough. Luckily, it was the dry season in this part of Central Africa. In the rainy season, monstrous thunderstorms developed over the lake and raised hellish swells of water. Still, the reek of fish permeating the hold engendered a general seasickness among the hostages.

They were a miserable-looking lot. Abbie's hair was half in and half out of her ponytail. Juste's wound had bled considerably, as facial lacerations are apt to do, but it appeared superficial. Chandra was in fairly good spirits, although she had squirmed throughout the voyage, trying to find a comfortable position; it was difficult with her hands bound behind her back. Sara, Tyler, and Alex were faring as well as could be expected. Sara's face was blotched, and Alex complained of nausea and chewed his lip nervously. Tyler was silent.

The man in the corner keeping watch over them appeared unaffected by the roll and stench of the ship. A rifle lay across his knees. He was the only kidnapper the hostages had seen since boarding the ship, but Abbie did not attempt to talk to him. She'd ceased trying to understand why they were being taken, where to, and by whom. The questions merely taxed what little reason she had left. All she hoped for now was to arrive at their destination safely.

This they did, after being blindfolded and transferred to a jeep, in which they rode for miles over unpaved roads, jostling against one another. Once they were in camp, their blindfolds were removed, and they were bunked in a dark hut near a stream. A sentry was posted outside. The door, containing the room's only window, a barred one, was locked after them. In a short while, it was opened by a man who asked Abbie to accompany him.

"What for?" she asked.

"To see Dalam."

"Who's that?"

"You'll find out."

"I don't want to leave my students," Abbie said.

"They'll be fine," said the man. "We wouldn't have brought them all this way to harm them now."

The man's logic was irrefutable. As Abbie and he crossed to another cottage, she got her first clear view of the camp, and, concomitantly, an appreciation of its isolation. Nothing but forested hills. She thought she saw the sparkle of Lake Tanganyika over the scruffy grass that led downhill to the edge of camp. A kingfisher sailed over her into a msulula tree, landing in thick foliage bowed with red and orange fruits.

The cottage they entered was spartanly furnished and splashed in oddly cast shadows and light. The result was almost Kafkaesque. Abbie sat in one of three wooden chairs across from Dalam. Bunkeya stood behind the FPL leader.

"Ah, Mademoiselle Guisbourne," said Dalam. "How nice to see you. I trust your trip here was not too uncomfortable?"

Abbie said nothing. She looked with hatred at Bunkeya.

"I hope you're not going to be like this for your entire stay here." Dalam paused and smiled. "Now I'm sure you've quite a few questions you'd like answered. Let me see if I can help. You're a hostage of the Front Populaire de Libération, Mademoiselle Guisbourne. I suspect you haven't heard of us. Oh, forgive me, would you care for something to drink?"

Abbie shook her head.

"Very well." He smiled again, a grin as eerie in this setting as that of the Cheshire cat. "My country—this country around you, Zaire—it means everything to me. Everything. Only right now it is sick. And we—we're trying to make it well again. But the only way we know how to do that is with war."

"I don't understand what this has to do with us," said Abbie. "You know my country won't pay for our release."

"How nice to hear your voice. It quite matches your face," said Dalam. "And yes, your State Department is rather firm on the matter of ransoms. But it's not your State Department we're concerned with. Rather, Burundi's."

"I don't understand."

"You see, we merely want a trade of sorts. You for our men in Burundian prisons. Your country may not pay for you, but"—Dalam pulled the *Time* clipping from his pocket—"a certain university would hate to see you harmed. And there are your students' parents as well, of course. They'll pressure the university; the university will pressure the U.S. government; the U.S. government will pressure the Burundians; and before you know it, you'll be free and my men will be back."

"Why are you telling me this?"

"So that you'll understand that we're not animals, Mademoiselle Guisbourne. We're traders. We'll try to make you and your group as comfortable as possible. Tell your students that. If you cooperate with us, you'll find that things will go quite smoothly. All right?" He gestured with his right hand. "Take her back to the others, Bunkeya."

Bunkeya. So that was the man's name. Abbie took an instant dislike to the sound of it. She rose and followed him out of the room.

"You were never hired by Professor Fielding, were you?" she asked as they trudged across the hill.

"No," he answered, taking long, powerful strides.

"Is the real Ula alive?"

"No."

To her surprise, Bunkeya guessed her next question and answered it.

"No, I wasn't the one who did it."

Bunkeya, for his part, was not sure why he volunteered the information. Abbie Guisbourne unnerved him. If only she would break down and cry or scream. But she remained in control. With every second, in fact, she gained strength. Perhaps his discomfort stemmed from the fact that she reminded him too much of himself, as he used to be. And perhaps this explained why he felt compelled to clear himself of Ula's murder, the question he had seen in her eyes.

"Why so many of us?" asked Abbie, stopping on the incline. "Why couldn't you just have taken me?"

He did not answer immediately, but Abbie was certain, unless her previous instincts about the man were wrong, that he would.

"You can figure that one out for yourself. There's more pressure with numbers."

"Five is as good as six. Can't you release one of them?"

"It's not up to me. Dalam decides."

"The man in the room?" she asked.

"Yes."

"Listen, there's one of my students—you must have noticed him—a young man named Alex. He's terrified. Give him a statement explaining your reasons and he'll go and tell the authorities what your grievances are."

Yes, mused Bunkeya, this woman was very much like him

in some ways. Already she was trying to run the kidnapping from the inside.

"They can't just be wrapped up in a pretty package. It'll all come out with the ransom note."

"Dalam said you were at war."

Bunkeya stopped before the storage cottage and nodded to the guard, who unlocked the door.

"We are at war, Mademoiselle Guisbourne," he replied before leaving. "But Dalam and I, our wars aren't the same. Tell the others you'll be fed in an hour."

"Speak up, Olgilvie, I can't hear you. All these damn reporters in the hallway," said Davenport, pressing the receiver to his ear.

"I don't have anything else to report, I said," shouted Evan.

"All right, then. I'll see you back here."

"Yes, later. I've got a few more things to do here."

"What things?" asked Davenport, but he didn't follow up the question. Evan heard him talking to someone on his end. "Yes? Oh. Okay. Evan?" Back to full force. "I've got to hang up. You get back here when you can. It's a madhouse."

Evan hung up the phone and sat back miserably in Abbie's chair. He had reported his few findings to Davenport, and the deputy chief had responded by telling him that he, Davenport, would be handling everything to do with the kidnapping from now on, with help from State Department and intelligence personnel being flown in to Bujumbura. Evan would return to his regular duties and pick up the slack.

As Evan digested this disheartening piece of information, David came into the trailer with news from the Teletype machine. Brice University had decided to send a proxy to Bujumbura to represent its interests. Its choice? The elusive professor of anthropology, Mic Fielding.

Bunkeya stayed with the hostages while they ate lunch, but he did not eat with them. Abbie had told the others about her meeting with Dalam, and they were calmer. At least now their enemy was known, their fear localized. Abbie moved her plate closer to Bunkeya, and spoke in a low voice, out of the others' hearing. She did not want to disturb their fragile adjustment to the surroundings with her questions. For the first time since they'd arrived, the students were chatting among themselves.

"How long before the authorities are contacted and know that we're safe?" she asked Bunkeya. She disliked having to deal with the man, but it seemed he was to be their liaison, and she had questions that needed answering.

"I don't know," he answered.

"Will we be allowed to send any messages outside?"

"That depends."

"On what?"

"On how long you're here."

Abbie took a bite of ugali, porridge made from ground cassava root and dried dagaa, a fish caught in Lake Tanganyika. In the same monotone as she'd asked the other questions—for she sensed that this was a man who respected control, perhaps above all else—she asked:

"Will we be killed if your demands aren't met?"

"I don't know," said the African, his gaze unwavering.

Abbie sensed the man was telling the truth. He was no more interested in dodging the issue than she. Knowing that, she altered the tack of her conversation.

"You're an intelligent man," she said. "Surely your reason tells you that this course is a destructive one."

Abbie thought she saw Bunkeya smile.

"Reason," he said, "is just a tool to figure out how to satisfy our emotions. I find it odd that people always split the two, saying one is ruled by the head or by the heart. The two are intertwined. The more logical a man, the more he satisfies his emotions."

"And what emotion are you satisfying?" Abbie asked. "What war are you fighting?"

"We've talked enough. I'll look in on you later."

* * *

"Come on, Joey. Be good. It's lesson time," said David

Evan sat on a stool eating an orange while David cajoled the gorilla into depressing the lighted lexigrams on the computer console. With the primate center so shorthanded, Evan had volunteered his lunch hour doing odd chores. Not exactly the work Davenport might have stiffed him with, but at this moment Evan didn't really give a damn about the deputy chief or his coffee reports. Put a layer of mulch over them and maybe they'd write themselves by fall.

David and Joey had been at the keyboard for over half an hour, and so far the gorilla had pressed only one button: "sad." A gross understatement, thought Evan. Had the voice synthesizer contained a dial for emotional intonation, he would have set it at "lugubrious."

"Damn!" In frustration, David slapped his hands on his thighs. Like the other students, David had refused the government's offer to fly home, electing to stay with the gorillas in hopes of instilling a semblance of routine back into their lives.

"I just don't know what else to do," he said. "I've tried to bribe him with food all morning. He won't touch any of it. Can you believe that? Joey not wanting a piece of candy? He just sits and stares. I can barely get him to sign anything."

"Is this how he always reacts when Abbie's gone?" asked Evan. "What about her trips to the States for reports and fund raising?"

"On those occasions he and Fran and Winston are told for a long time in advance that she'll be gone. Besides, it's not just Abbie he's missing. I'm sure he's wondering where Chandra and the others are. Especially after the screaming in the courtyard."

The young man held up an old tennis shoe.

"Joey," he signed, "tell the machine what this is."

The gorilla made no move toward the console. David reached over the ape and pressed a series of buttons.

"This is a shoe," the machine intoned. The sentence, composed of colored lexigrams, flashed simultaneously on the projection screen.

"And this, Joey, what is this?" David asked. "Tell the machine."

Joey ignored the banana in David's hand.

"Ah, hell. I'm going to see if anyone's returned from town with the licorice I ordered. I've never once seen him turn that down. Be right back."

Evan nodded and offered Joey a section of orange. The gorilla showed no interest in the fruit. He pulled on his lower lip and stuck a finger in his ear. Finally, he punched a string of buttons on the console. There was a delay of a few seconds before the message reached Evan's ears.

"Joey good come back Abbie."

Come back, Abbie. So that was it. The gorilla had decided that it was his fault that Abbie had left. He was offering a pact: He would be good from now on if she would return. Evan recalled that he had reasoned in much the same way as a child. Now all he had to do was convince a 150-pound gorilla that he was being too hard on himself.

"I'm so sleepy." The boy's eyes fluttered dangerously. "I—I wish . . ."

"What do you wish, Gise?"

"I wish you would kill them all."

His son had never said that. And yet Bunkeya had lived out the last year as if that had been his dying child's request, the unholiest of tenets. For wasn't that what he'd meant when he'd told Abbie that his war differed from Dalam's? Bunkeya had fought in many battles, but never in the name of Zairian revolution. His war was one of vengeance only. As a vehicle for revenge, the FPL had served him well. But had it served the best interests of Zaire?

Thoughts dormant for over a year spilled into his deliberation. He did not think he would be able to complete this mission. His commitment was gone, his self-worth negated, his sanity slipping. The inner mechanism that had governed his psyche for twelve months was quickly eroding.

It was a battle fatigue unlike any with which he was acquainted, and it thundered down on him like a steadily growing
avalanche. A fatigue produced not by Dalam's missions, but
by a skirmish within himself, between his actions of the last
year and his previous life. And now this conflict was breaking
through to the surface, as water, accumulated drop by drop,
eventually tears the finest parchment. He could no longer
engage in his war, the one of vengeance.

His son was wishing for something different now.

Winston had been fed a sedative with his food and was
noticeably calmer. He no longer violently banged or threw
boxes against his trailer walls. Even so, Evan decided to wait
a while longer before visiting. His first encounter with the big
ape, from which he still sported a lump on the back of his
head, had proved that sedatives did not totally control the
gorilla's actions. He stayed instead with the saturnine Joey,
who was still refusing to cooperate with David.

"Evan," said David. "I think he wants you."

"What?"

"Joey keeps signing your name."

"No, he's not," said Evan. "He's not even looking at me.
Just playing around with his fingers."

"No, you're wrong. Look closely. See? There's the sign for
Evan. And that looks like—" David stopped speaking as he
crouched next to the gorilla.

"What's he signing?" asked Evan.

" 'Tell Evan'—that's what he's signing: 'Tell Evan.' "

"Tell Evan what?" asked Evan. He, too, knelt by Joey. "Tell
Evan what, Joey?"

"Tell Evan," the gorilla signed tentatively, forming his
fingers into a series of awkward configurations. First, a hand
with the four fingers stretched out parallel to one another, the
thumb clenched to the palm; second, a hand with just the index
finger and thumb extended, as if parodying a gun; lastly, a fist,
the thumb overlapping the curled index finger.

"I can't believe it," said David, dazed. "Those are letters. He's signing the manual alphabet."

"I didn't know you'd taught it to the gorillas," said Evan.

"That's just the point. We haven't."

"Where did he learn it then?"

"I don't know. This is the first time I've ever seen one of the gorillas sign a letter."

"Abbie," Evan said, excitedly, "it must be a message from Abbie."

"Look," said David, "there he goes again. 'B,' isn't it? And —'L.' Is that an 'L'?"

"Yeah, I think so. You're the expert here at reading his signs. B . . . L . . . A. That third sign is an 'A.' What's this fourth sign?"

"He's just repeating 'Tell Evan,' " said David. "So we've got a 'B,' an 'L,' and an 'A.' What does it mean?"

"I don't know. It doesn't say anything. B-L-A. But it must mean something."

"Hell, Evan. We don't even know if this *is* a message from Abbie. I don't know where Joey picked this stuff up. Could be he's just playing around and by coincidence is signing letters."

"That's too big a coincidence. He must have the order confused." Evan combined the letters out loud. "How about B-A-L? Bal. Ball? Maybe Joey didn't realize she was repeating the extra 'L.' Does 'ball' mean anything to you?"

"No," said David.

"You sure?"

"Yeah, I'm sure."

"Okay, let's see . . . A-L-B. Alb. No, damn it, that's nothing. L-A-B. Lab? Could that be it? Is there some laboratory around here? A chemist? Does Abbie know someone in science?"

"No, not that I know of—"

"Well, think about it!"

"I am," said David, angrily. "Look, Evan, if you want to act like Sherlock Holmes, fine. But don't get on my case about it. I'm worried about Abbie and the others as much as you are. Probably more. You haven't worked with them day in and day out for a year like I have. You've only known Abbie a few days. So don't try to order me around."

"I'm sorry," said Evan. "You're right, David. I guess I'm reacting to the fact that I feel so powerless to help them."

"We all feel that way," said David.

"I know, it's just that you'd think someone in the State Department would be able to . . ." He didn't bother explaining. Earlier, he had told David of his conversation with Davenport. "So do you think Joey has a message for us or not?"

"Who knows? Could be, but it's pretty discombobulated. We can't even be sure he's getting the letters right. Or whether these are just three of maybe seven or eight Abbie signed to him."

"Yeah." Evan bent over and petted the gorilla's head. "Guess we're never going to know what's locked up there. You be good now, Joey. David, I'm going to take off."

"Hey, Evan?" said David, contritely, trying to make up for losing his temper. "You know, Larry is fully conscious now, but he's going to have to stay in the hospital for a while. I know he'd appreciate it if you could help him get something off to his parents so they don't worry. Maybe through the State Department."

Evan saw through the young man's ploy to restore his sense of usefulness. He smiled.

"Yeah, maybe I can. I'll stop by on my way back."

Evan softly closed the trailer door. All the while the young gorilla in the corner signed to himself: B-L-A, B-L-A, B-L-A, B-L-A . . .

Dalam folded his hands and sat forward in the wooden chair, Mpinga to his left and Bunkeya to his right.

"Now, our first demand is the prison exchange. Then the money," said Dalam. "Are we in agreement? Five million American dollars?"

"Yes," said Mpinga.

"Had we not gotten hold of the woman, Abbie Guisbourne, our bargaining power would have been greatly diminished," said Dalam. "Sounds like a marketplace, doesn't it? And that's where we have the advantage over our American friends. We know how to barter. They don't."

"We tried to get the ones who fled into the brush, but it was impossible," said Mpinga.

"Do not construe my statements as criticisms, Mpinga. When I want to criticize you, I'll let you know," said Dalam, coolly. "These six hostages suit us very well. The important thing is to have the American woman. Without her, we'd have nothing. She is the cornerstone of this whole scheme."

"We'll also have to supply the names of our men in Burundi whom we want released," said Bunkeya, steering the conversation back to the matter at hand. "That is our first priority."

"Yes," said Dalam, "that and the demand for arms and ammunition. I think that will be sufficient."

"When will we send this to the Burundian government?" asked Mpinga.

"As soon as possible. Only I think as an extra inducement we should include a nice picture of our hostages. It will give the American papers something to run next to their stories and increase pressure from the States. Yes, I think that will have an impact on the emotional Americans."

"May I suggest one more addition?" Bunkeya asked.

"Certainly."

"Have a courier deliver the photo and our demands."

"A courier?" asked Mpinga.

"Yes, one of the hostages," said Bunkeya.

"What?" asked Mpinga. "Let one of them go?"

"The boy, I believe he is called Alex," said Bunkeya, directing his comments to Dalam, "let him deliver the message. It will be a sign of our goodwill. That we intend no harm to the Americans. All we want is a simple business transaction."

"Yes, the Americans are businessmen. They will understand that."

"But there's no need to let one of them go," said Mpinga.

"I rather like the idea," said Dalam. "Very dramatic. Very convincing. Why this particular boy? Why not one of the others?"

"He's a very nervous type," said Bunkeya. "It'll be better for us if he's gone. Otherwise he might spread a panic."

"Fine. He'll be the one to go then. We'll start drawing up our demands. Yes, a goodwill gesture." Dalam's eyes glistened. "I do hope the authorities respond to it. It'll seem a pity to have to dispose of the others if they don't. Oh, well . . ."

"Anything else you want me to tell them?" asked Evan.

"No, that'll do it," said Larry, smoothing the sheet on his hospital bed. "Just want to make sure they don't panic. My mom, she's a rock. But my dad will have them both on the first plane over here."

"Don't worry." Evan stood up to leave. "I'll get this message to them."

"Evan? Before you go, could you tell me about the kidnapping? No one around here will tell me anything. Guess they don't think I'm strong enough to handle it yet."

"There's really not much to tell beyond what you already know. Seven of them were taken captive by a Zairian terrorist organization, and it's believed they crossed Lake Tanganyika into Zaire. That's about it."

"There's been no ransom demand?"

"Not yet."

"What about that guy who got clobbered when I did? Ula. Was he taken too?"

"Seems so."

"God, talk about bad luck. Guess I won't get my answer."

"What answer?"

"Nothing really," said Larry. "Just something I remember from the night the poachers came. I'm not sure if I made it up or if it really happened. I wanted to verify it with Ula."

"What was it?"

"Nothing important. Forget I brought it up. It seems sort of stupid to worry about catching a couple of small-time poachers when Abbie and the others are being held hostage."

"I'm sure the police would still be appreciative. What was it?"

"Just something I thought I heard one of the poachers say. Something to do with moving men out of a house by a river."

"That's it? That's all you remember?"

"Yeah. One more thing. He mentioned mining, I think. Then he stopped talking and I ran into Ula coming around the other side. Next thing I knew, I was hit over the head."

"Did you tell anyone else about this?" asked Evan.

"No, like I said, I just remembered. Not exactly the most incriminating piece of evidence, is it?"

"It might be. You never know. I'll report it to Captain Karuhije for you. You get some rest now."

"Okay. Thanks for stopping by, Evan."

"Sure."

As Evan walked out of the hospital, he reviewed what Larry had said. It left him inexplicably uneasy, akin to not remembering which of two jigsaw puzzles was missing the final piece. A link seemed to be missing from Larry's story as well, but Evan blocked it from his mind. The kidnapping was, as Larry said, far more important.

Mpinga sat at one of the outdoor tables and whittled a piece of wood. His cuts were ragged. Gouges, really. Large chunks flew in the air as he chopped with his knife.

He raged inside. At the meeting he'd been treated by Dalam and Bunkeya as though he were nothing but a schoolboy. His inclusion in the FPL's so-called executive council was a sham. He was being shunted to one side; humiliated.

Mpinga rued the day he suggested the kidnapping. At the time he thought it would put him in Dalam's good graces, but things had not gone that way. The irony was that he didn't even care about the men in Rumonge prison. They were all loyal to Dalam. Excessively loyal. As far as Mpinga was concerned, they could go to hell. The entire mission could, for that matter.

His whittling became more controlled. He handled the knife with greater care, less slashing. His pace slowed, and he applied even pressure to each cut. The chunks became shavings.

An idea slowly presented itself. He had created the mission. Could he not as easily destroy it? Since Dalam had taken credit for the kidnapping, it would be seen as another failure for the FPL leader in the men's eyes. A failure Dalam couldn't afford if he intended to retain the reins of leadership.

But how to do it? Mpinga pondered the question. What had Dalam said? "Abbie Guisbourne is the cornerstone. Without her we have nothing."

The solution was that simple. Abbie Guisbourne would have to exit the scene. Mpinga's hands crafted the stick of wood into a tapered form. His knife was patient now.

Better yet, he could kill two birds with one stone. Bunkeya could be brought down as well. And what better way to get rid of the man than at Dalam's order. The reason?

Because it would appear that Bunkeya had killed Abbie Guisbourne.

Mpinga was well pleased with himself. In his exuberance, he made a false cut with the knife and the piece of wood split in half. He tossed the two halves on the ground. Only after he'd left did a sudden gust of wind blow the parts together.

"And do you know the irony of this?" asked Mic Fielding, brushing a tsetse fly out of the Land Rover. "One of the reasons I jumped at the chance a year ago to study in Muwali was that I wouldn't have to cope with administrative crap. Abbie Guisbourne would be handling all of that. And now, what happens? Someone kidnaps Abbie and I'm told to act as the official representative of Brice University and negotiate for her release. What bloody luck."

"Do they know who's taken them yet?" asked the driver.

"What? Oh, no. The computer gave just a few scant details. Seems they were snatched early in the morning. Six of the Bujumburan staff. And Ula. Poor boy. He's worked less than three weeks for us and he gets involved in this."

"Well, if we meet any of the kidnappers along the way, we'll be prepared." The driver patted the rifle he always carried with him.

"I doubt we'll run into them. Apparently they escaped by boat."

"Will the university pay?" asked the driver.

"I can't really say. Probably not. Can't start a precedent. They might create some sort of fund—paid by private individuals, like the parents of the students—in which they'd have a hefty investment. We'll have to wait and see what the terrorists demand."

"They may have to be paid some other way," said the driver, patting the rifle a second time.

The gesture did not go unnoticed by Fielding.

"Perhaps," he said, dabbing at his brow with a handkerchief.

It was a splendid day, or rather morning, for though they'd been on the road nearly four hours, it was not yet noon. It took time to wind through the dense tropical growth around Muwali and to traverse the rolling hills. Having traveled the road from Muwali to Bujumbura umpteen times, Fielding knew that presently they would pass into the flatter lands paralleling Lake Tanganyika. He sighed and replaced the handkerchief in his breast pocket. The drive was not an unpleasant one, and under normal circumstances Fielding would have reveled in the passing scenery, which, no matter how often he saw it, escaped the monotony of other landscapes. But the circumstances now were not normal, and aesthetic contemplation seemed somehow improper. And Fielding was, if nothing else, proper.

The car swerved around a familiar curve and gathered speed as it rattled down an incline and onto a straight section of road that stretched for half a kilometer. On Fielding's side of the car, the earth receded sharply, sloping at a forty-five-degree angle down to a gully below. Trees and brush obscured the dry riverbed from view.

A small blue monkey in one of the trees bordering the gully swung with lightning speed to its outermost branches. Silently, Fielding compared the movements of the monkey with those of the chimpanzees he studied. Fascinated by the supple gracefulness of the primate, he did not return his gaze to the road for some time. When he did, he was startled by the sudden proximity of an ugly object stretched across it. From the size he guessed it was a mongoose. Or perhaps, though the thought repulsed him, one of the very monkeys that so enchanted him. Fielding supposed it had been struck dead by a car.

The Land Rover drew closer to the object on the road. Around its perimeter was a pool of blood laden with red-brown lumps dried by the sun. Though Fielding was not the squeamish sort, the gore turned his stomach. He reevaluated the cause of death. Something had literally ripped it open. Fielding could only guess which scavenger lurking beyond the brush deserved credit for the kill. A hyena, maybe, though why it had abandoned its victim in such a desultory manner was a puzzle. A red smear leading up the hill and onto the road indicated that the dead thing had been dragged.

Fielding averted his eyes. No use staring at it any longer; nothing could be done. Yet when the driver skirted the corpse, swerving to the left-hand side of the road, Fielding looked again.

And then his calm veneer exploded.

"Jesus Christ! Stop the car! Stop the bloody car!"

"What is it?" asked the driver.

"Just reverse. Stop when I tell you."

The driver shrugged and, thrusting the car into reverse, steered backward until Fielding told him to halt. Fielding jumped from the jeep and backtracked to the object in the road. He stared with disbelief. What he suspected he'd seen from the car was no illusion but grim reality:

A human arm. Where the elbow had been now was a ragged, pulpy stump. Two of the fingers were missing, and the once jet-black skin was covered with a layer of dirt and caked blood. Flies and maggots crawled across the flesh and burrowed into pockets of muscle, exposing tendons and ligaments to the harsh sunlight.

Mic Fielding, normally unsqueamish Mic Fielding, hugged his stomach and barely reached the side of the road before he threw up. His choice of location was unfortunate.

When he opened his eyes he saw that his vomit was spattering the severed head of the courier, Ula—spilling from his own mouth into the gaping, mutilated orifice of the boy.

Fielding screamed, but bile blocked the sound. The scream ricocheted inside him with a ringing madness. He scrambled to the jeep, horrified. For an instant, the boy's dismembered head seemed to float in front of him. It stared from its one good eye, the other lost in the bloody gorge that had been the right side of a face, now a bowl of desiccated bone and baked flesh.

Lunging for the safety of the jeep, Fielding screamed again. And this time it could be heard. Quite clearly.

The madness took longer to push out.

IX

When David's call came through that afternoon, Evan was slumped over his desk reading a coffee report.

"Evan?" The young man's voice shook. "I've got some bad news."

The phone froze in Evan's hand.

"What?" he asked.

"They've found one of the hostages. Dead."

"Who?"

"Ula, the courier from Muwali."

Evan let loose an audible sigh and passed a sweaty hand across his forehead.

"Where did they find him?"

"A few miles from the center, on the road that leads up from Muwali. Professor Fielding spotted him on his way here. He's pretty shook up. They haven't determined the time of death. It seems—" The young man's voice faltered.

"What, David?"

"It seems some wild animals got to him. He was pretty well mangled, but enough remained to identify him."

The phone slipped a fraction of an inch in Evan's hand. He regretted that he'd been so wary of Ula, the strange courier. All that reserved intensity, that brooding silence, the mystery of the man, gone. The brutality of his end, the absolute savageness of it, was in some ways harder to accept than the extinguishment of the life itself. Evan hoped that the man was long dead, and not in the throes of dying, when he was ripped apart by the jungle scavengers.

"Evan, are you there?"

David's quavering voice returned Evan from the imagined scene of Ula's death to the nine-by-fifteen dimensions of the embassy office. The floor beneath his feet was slick. The chair was hard and solid.

"Any signs of the others?" Evan asked.

"No. Just Ula."

"Why did they kill him? The cops got any clues?"

"Not really," said David. "He might not have been co-operating with the kidnappers. Or else he was sacrificed as a message to us that they mean business. To set the tone for when we receive the ransom note. Since he wasn't American, they may have figured that he was expendable."

"Christ. I wish they'd hurry up and deliver that note."

Though he did not voice his concern to David, Evan was bewildered by the body's discovery south of the primate center, when the terrorists, if they had taken the hostages across Lake Tanganyika as believed, had proceeded due west. Were the kidnappers deliberately trying to confuse the authorities? Perhaps he and Captain Karuhije had placed too much importance on Fran's sighting of the crocodile. The kidnapping might very well turn out to have no connection with the Zairian-based FPL.

The Front Populaire de Libération. It was an organization whose extent, intent, and makeup were largely the product of hearsay. Despite Davenport's repeated instructions that he not involve himself in the case, Evan had secretly read the scant embassy file on the terrorists after he returned to the office. The file raised more questions than it answered. One thing was instantly clear: Kidnapping was not the group's forte. Murder was. If Ula was indeed the FPL's latest victim, then time was of the essence in negotiating for Abbie and the students' release. This was not a gang of men with whom to trifle.

"Okay, David," Evan said into the mouthpiece, "thanks for calling me. I'll relay the information to Davenport in case he hasn't heard. He's been meeting all morning long with Burundian officials."

"One more thing, Evan. Professor Fielding's on his way to

meet with you people. He should be showing up at the embassy any time now."

"All right. We'll expect him. How are the gorillas doing?"

"Not great. A little less agitated, I think, but they still aren't communicating much. I think we'll let them out later. It can't hurt."

"Joey sign anything more?"

"No."

"Okay. I'll try to come out later if I can to help out," Evan said. "If you want me to, that is."

"Sure. We can use the help," said David. "See you later."

"Yeah. Bye."

The phone conversation left Evan restless and unable to concentrate on his work. Discordant images crowded his mind, of Abbie, of the gorillas, of Ula's mutilated corpse, and lastly, of Professor Mic Fielding. Evan tried to envision what the man would look like: Oxonian, equestrian and champion sharp-shooter, a Leo with egotism rising. Therefore, tall, rather lean, a toothy smile.

His image was not far from the mark, Evan realized as the Englishman stood before him. Fielding was four or five years Evan's senior, a man grown craggy from exposure to the elements. A deep tan concealed the telltale ruddy complexion peculiar to the British. He was the archetype of the dashing English hero, straight out of the epics about the French Foreign Legion. Even his moles looked distinguished, like the penciled affectations of a pompadoured retainer in Louis XVI's court. And that voice. Sonorous and decidedly upper-class, it flowed from a mouth accustomed to Bloody Marys, nicely chilled, served on steamy Riviera beaches. Confidence radiated from his pores.

Evan was quite sure he was going to dislike the man.

"Mic Fielding," the professor stated, offering his hand. He had a firm grip. "David told me I'd meet you here."

"Won't you take a seat," said Evan. "I wish we could be meeting under more pleasant circumstances."

"So do I." Fielding sat down, crossing his legs. "Well then, my information is that I'm to meet with your man Davenport."

"Right," said Evan. "He's just down the hall. His secretary's gone to tell him you're here. I understand you've been in contact with Brice?"

"Yes," said Fielding. "They're in a bit of a panic up there, as you might imagine."

"Any special instructions to you?"

"No, not really. We're all rather new at this."

"I was wondering if you could tell—"

Evan was interrupted by Davenport's arrival. The Englishman rose from his chair.

"Thank you for occupying the professor until I could break free, Olgilvie," said the deputy chief.

Evan recognized the note of dismissal in Davenport's voice. He threaded his way to the door with as much nonchalance as he could muster.

"You're going?" asked Fielding. "I rather assumed from what David had told me that you'd be working with us." The next sentence Fielding directed to Davenport. "Inasmuch as Mr. Olgilvie is so well acquainted with the primate center and its personnel, and fully briefed on the kidnapping—as well as having dealt with the police—I think it would be helpful if he could stay. Of course, I realize there are other urgent embassy matters to attend to—"

"Yes, certainly," said Davenport, on the defensive. "I don't know what I was thinking. Pull up a chair, Olgilvie."

No doubt about it. Evan was certain he could grow to dislike Fielding if he put his mind to it. Nothing rankled as much as falling in debt to a total stranger. With a few words from that perfectly shaped mouth, Fielding had achieved what no amount of grumbling from Evan had: He was now part of the team.

"Now," said Fielding, authoritatively, lacking only the Charatan pipe that would have set off his tailored jungle clothes, "I realize that I'll be meeting soon with the Burundian officials, but before I do, perhaps you could clue me in as to where they stand."

"Of course," said Davenport. "Well, I spent most of the morning with Juki Kombi and Cwandu Sando, heads of the intelligence community here. The Burundians are being very cooperative and diligent. They've sent out helicopters and have had men scouting the area, questioning anyone who might have seen the kidnappers, checking the brush, that sort of thing. By the way, I was sorry to hear about your man, Ula. A shock for us all."

"Yes," said Fielding, his face somber. "It is."

"In addition," continued Davenport, "the police have been charting all movements of known antigovernment groups in the area. Including those of the FPL."

"The Front Populaire de Libération," said Evan, expanding the abbreviation less for Fielding's sake than to legitimize his own presence in the room.

"Yes," said Fielding. "Dalam's group."

Evan refrained from further comment. He reminded himself of a grade-conscious classmate at Georgetown who, faced with a desire to make herself known to a professor but not possessed of a particularly inquisitive mind, interrupted a lecture on the Scottish Home Rule Movement to ask if the crop in the background of the slide was wheat or barley.

"And the results of the investigation so far?" asked Fielding.

"Nothing concrete yet. The police found an eyewitness—a woman, I believe—who confirms that the kidnapping is the work of the FPL. She's asked to remain anonymous. Scared, naturally."

Naturally, mused Evan. A gorilla's only human, after all.

"And you, Mr. Davenport, have been in consultation with your government, I take it?" asked Fielding.

"Yes. Representatives from our State Department and CIA will be arriving shortly from Washington."

"What about the Zairian authorities? You've been in communication with them?"

"Of course," said Davenport. "Our embassy in Kinshasa is working hand in hand with us here. Preparations are now being made for a joint meeting of American, Burundian, and Zairian authorities. You'll be included as Brice's representative."

"Excellent."

"Perhaps you'd care now to enlighten us about your communications with Brice?"

"They've been quite limited. The university anticipates a lengthy confrontation with these terrorists once they make themselves known. Rather like the Stanford case in 1975. I'm afraid Brice finds itself in the same sticky position that each of the governments involved does. We can't afford to start a precedent by submitting to blackmail. Brice is awash with students from affluent backgrounds. It would be disastrous for us if we paid ransom for these five. Before we knew it, we could have a whole slew of abductions."

"But the Caslin College case—" said Evan, referring to a well-publicized kidnapping of two Massachusetts college seniors.

"Yes, those students were ransomed, but Caslin didn't pay out of its own pocket. That money was paid through a private fund established by individuals. Such a network could be set up at Brice if the monies involved aren't too excessive."

"I understand your position," said Davenport. "Unfortunately, all any of us can do right now is speculate and plot possible responses. We're operating in the dark until that ransom note comes." Davenport tugged at his shirt sleeve and checked his watch. "I'm afraid I have to leave. I'm supposed to be meeting with Ambassador Stevens right now. Nice to meet you, Professor Fielding. Olgilvie here can answer any of your other questions. We'll be in touch."

Outside in the hallway, after Davenport had taken his leave, Fielding asked Evan:

"Do you happen to know who the eyewitness is?"

"One of the gorillas," Evan answered.

"One of Abbie's? Good God. Which one?"

"Fran, the female."

"Fran? I should have known. You know, she once had an enormous crush on me."

"She did?"

"Yes. I know it sounds crazy." Fielding chuckled. "Animal magnetism, I suppose."

Evan walked along in bruised silence. Although Abbie had warned him not to humanize the gorillas' behavior, Evan had believed that Fran considered him special. Her apparent indiscrimination wounded him more than he would admit, a dejection which suggested a deception by Aphrodite herself, not the flirtations of an unscrupulous ape.

"—and I thought it was really quite cute," said Fielding. "I remember— Hey, what's wrong? Don't tell me she's infatuated with you now? Didn't mean to disenchant you."

"Nah." Evan shrugged, silently cursing Fran for not having had the fortitude to resist Fielding's charms. "Hell, she's just an ape."

"You know, personally, as much as I admire Abbie's dedication, I think those apes of hers are just parroting human action. Mind you, it's always valuable to study any primate behavior, but I think the focus of her study is all wrong. Herbert Terrace and his chimp Nim pretty much proved that, now didn't they? Apes just aren't capable of the intricacies of language."

"But they can communicate," said Evan, rising to the absent woman's defense.

"Sure, but why waste—I mean, spend her life on that? In Muwali we study primates as they should be studied, in a natural environment. But Abbie's stubborn."

"She happens to think her work's vital."

"Of course it's her decision what she does. Is there something personal in your defense of her?"

"What do you mean?"

"You know her well?"

"Only a few days. Why?"

"Just thought I heard a little something more in your protestation."

Evan pondered Fielding's remark as they headed outside. Had his morose reaction to Fran's attachment to Fielding been a sublimation of other emotions?

"Yes, a remarkable woman," said Fielding, picking an invisible piece of lint from his shirt. "Great legs."

* * *

Bunkeya primed the camera so that it was ready to shoot. He and Mpinga had argued all morning about how the picture should be taken, against what background, what arrangement of the hostages. Bunkeya tolerated the man's grumblings for what they were: projections of his anger that Alex was being released, that his feelings on the subject had been ignored.

"What if he describes to the Burundian authorities where we are?" Mpinga had asked earlier.

"He doesn't know where we are," replied Bunkeya.

"But he can tell them we took them across the lake."

"The authorities will know that by now. Some of the students scampered into the brush, remember? We didn't get them all. They saw us leaving."

"We would have gotten them if I had been in charge," mumbled Mpinga. "The boy knows that we're uphill from the shoreline."

"This lake is hundreds of kilometers long," said Bunkeya. "We kept the hostages out on the water so long that they have no idea how far down the shore they are."

"You've anticipated everything, haven't you?" When Bunkeya did not answer, Mpinga said, "Retreating again behind that impenetrable exterior?"

"I might talk if the company were more appealing."

"To you, no company is appealing. God knows what Dalam sees in you."

"That's it, Mpinga, isn't it? That's what really bothers you —that Dalam relies more on me than on you."

"And why shouldn't it?" said Mpinga. "I've sweated and struggled with this group. I was here at its formation. Here when half of our men were slaughtered in one assault. I've gone forward with it, and I've backslid with it. And you come along and think you can take over."

"Take over? It's you who wants control, Mpinga. That's why you're here. Don't attribute it to me. When Dalam ignores you, it's like a red-hot spike driven into your gut."

"At least I joined for a reason. A commitment you never had. You've just hidden yourself in our ranks. You don't belong with us, Bunkeya. You've driven yourself into a corner with your silences. The men don't know you. Only Dalam supports you, and if he goes—"

Bunkeya's ears pricked up at the sound of treason. Mpinga cut short his tirade.

"You should quit, Bunkeya. Quit while you can. Before—" He lowered his voice as another man entered the room. "Before your life is on the line."

He left the room.

"What have you done with him?" demanded Abbie. "Where have you taken Alex?"

"He's with Dalam," said Bunkeya, standing in the hostages' cottage.

"What does he want with Alex? Alex can't tell him anything. He's just a frightened young man. He knows nothing."

"Dalam isn't trying to get information from the boy."

"Then what?"

"He wants a message delivered. The boy will be a courier."

"What does that mean?" asked Abbie. "He'll be a courier like Ula was and pay for it with his life?"

"No, he'll deliver the message alive. It was your suggestion, after all."

"My suggestion?" Abbie's brow furrowed. "You mean you're sending him with the ransom note?"

"Yes."

"Is this another of Dalam's ways to make us feel comfortable?"

"No," said Bunkeya. "It's mine. And it's not meant to make anyone comfortable. It's meant to keep someone alive."

Bunkeya stood flush in the doorway, Abbie to one side of the door frame. A guard was stationed just outside. It was his voice greeting Mpinga that made Bunkeya turn.

"All right, we're ready now," said Mpinga, joining Bunkeya and the guard. He did not see Abbie around the corner. "The boy understands and is over there"—Mpinga pointed—"with an escort. He'll be blindfolded and sent on his way as soon as we get the picture done. One of our guards just spotted a group of fishermen heading down the road from Iddan, but they won't present any problem—"

Mpinga saw the flicker of an arm behind the door frame. He reached inside and yanked Abbie forward.

"So. An eavesdropper," said Mpinga. "Why didn't you tell me she was right there?"

"You didn't ask," said Bunkeya.

"Does she understand Swahili?" asked Mpinga.

"Yes," said Abbie, pulling her arm from his grasp. "She does."

And then the man did something neither Abbie nor Bunkeya expected. He smiled. An ugly smile.

"Doesn't really matter, does it?" he said, walking away, suddenly unperturbed that the camp's location was no longer a secret, that Abbie had overheard him mention Iddan.

"Can you tell the others we're going to move them up to a different cottage?" said Bunkeya. He, too, appeared unconcerned by what had transpired. "We'll be taking a picture of you to send with the boy. I'll be back to get you in five minutes." He turned his back to her.

"Wait, I—" Abbie intended to thank him for releasing Alex, but when he faced her again, her gratitude faded. This was the man who had arranged their abduction; she could never forgive him for that. "I want to know what the ransom is."

"Five million of your dollars. Exchange of prisoners and guns. Anything else?"

"No."

"Five minutes then."

Bunkeya motioned to the guard and the door swung shut. The metallic click of the lock sealed not just the room, thought Abbie, but their fates. The hostages—at least she— now knew where they were, near Iddan. Such knowledge was dangerous. Especially with dissension in the camp. The animosity between Bunkeya and Mpinga was not difficult to detect. Abbie hoped that the hostages would not be used as pawns between them. Of the two, she preferred Bunkeya. He was a known commodity. He would listen to reason. And his treatment of Alex meant that she had touched something human in him.

But the other man had the crazed mien of a fanatic. "Doesn't really matter, does it?" he'd said. What was that supposed to mean? The fear Abbie had suppressed since their arrival surged anew as she reflected on his veiled threat. She had to use this new information about Iddan before he used it against her. But how?

First, however, she must tell the four people at the back of the cottage to prepare themselves for the picture. Out of sheer force of habit, she began speaking to them in a combination of speech and sign language.

"Okay, everyone, we're going to have to move—"

She held her hands to her face, and slowly moved them back and forth, forming different signs.

"Abbie, what is it?" asked Sara.

At that moment, the guard unlocked the door.

"Oh, nothing," said Abbie, deliberately loud. She turned her back to the doorway and continued speaking. "We're just going to have our picture taken."

But to the people in the room reading her hands, she was saying something entirely different.

While Bunkeya opened a window, Mpinga tied the hands of the five hostages in front of them, commenting that he did not want any trouble from them. Bunkeya thought the action unnecessary, but made no issue of it. The arrangement probably suited Dalam's fancy. There was something inherently dramatic about having the hostages bound.

Bunkeya fiddled with the camera; his nerves were on edge. He'd been wrong to agree to carry out this one last mission for Dalam. Had it been like previous operations, he might have been able to pull it off. But a kidnapping entailed the holding of hostages, and that meant time to get to know one's captives.

The five people seated before him had names and voices and faces. In short, identities.

Bunkeya had heard stories about kidnappers who became emotionally attached to their hostages. Such intimacy had not developed here, but respect had. Bunkeya admired Abbie Guisbourne's strength and courage, her tenacity. Mpinga's earlier comment, and its insinuation that she would not survive, needled Bunkeya. He did not think he could stand by and let the hostages be killed. They would be six too many among the dead faces against the white wall in his mind, staring forever at him.

Mpinga was nearly finished tying the hostages' hands. Bunkeya walked up and down the row of wooden chairs on which Abbie and her students sat, a poster of a black crocodile looming above them. Their faces were blank. Too blank. What were they hiding?

Mpinga tied a last knot and signaled to Bunkeya that he was finished.

"All right, everyone," said Bunkeya, holding the Polaroid camera at eye level. Such cameras were favorite bribes from foreign visitors to Zairian customs officers. "I'm about to take the picture. Don't move."

No sooner had the words left his lips than Bunkeya realized how totally unnecessary his request was. The five hostages had kept rigid the entire time he'd held the camera, almost as though they were posing. There was a unity among the five, the camaraderie of desperate people. They were pulling together, closing ranks in tight-knit bond for an aim that Bunkeya had not yet deciphered. He studied them as the flashbulb popped.

"Okay, we'll wait for that one," said Mpinga. He pulled out the picture, which reeked of chemicals, and placed it on the table.

"One more," said Bunkeya.

"But this one will be fine, I'm sure," said Mpinga. "Just wait for it to develop."

"One more, just to be on the safe side. We may need another picture of them later. And this time with them standing up." Bunkeya walked to where Abbie sat and assisted her in rising from her chair. The others rose hesitantly. "Now, group together so we can see you." Bunkeya arranged two of the hostages in front, and three in back, staggered so that all five faces showed.

"A little closer," he said, keeping his eyes trained on Abbie's face.

"They're too far," said Mpinga, exasperated by Bunkeya's manuevering. "You won't get their bodies in."

"Don't worry. It'll be a head shot. Right above the shoulders. That way the American papers will have a clear picture of their faces."

A current of anxiety crossed the hostages' faces. They turned toward Abbie in unison. She did not acknowledge their looks, but continued to stare straight ahead, suppressing whatever discomfiture she felt. Her eyes, however, betrayed her. Bunkeya knew he had struck a nerve.

"Now," he said, softly, "don't try to move and ruin the shot. We'll just have to take it again." He released the shutter and a flash of light bounced off the worried faces. "Fine. You can sit if you like while we see how this one turns out."

Before them, a miracle of modern technology. As Mpinga and Bunkeya watched, the two pictures developed, and mere specters of human beings gradually incorporated into bodies. With the snapshots side by side, Bunkeya assessed the hostages' poses. And then he knew. Knew the reason behind their solidarity. It was there, captured by the silver halides of the film, so blatant and yet so remarkably subtle. A dialectical triumph.

"I prefer the long shot of them," said Mpinga.

"Yes," said Bunkeya, locking his eyes on Abbie. The woman did not move a muscle. He had not judged her qualities incorrectly. She was a laudable opponent, but even the best opponents needed hope. "The long shot is better. Send that one."

He did not expect to see relief register in her face, but once again her eyes betrayed her.

*   *   *

Evan hadn't seen Winston since the walnut/jellybean test. The ape's actions were still erratic, so Evan stayed on the far side of the courtyard. The big gorilla was lolling in the sun under the watchful eyes of the students. Fran and Pig sat next to him.

"Fine animals, aren't they?" said Mic Fielding as he joined Evan.

"What did you say?" asked Evan.

"Great specimens of healthy primates."

"Is that how you view the chimps you study? As specimens?"

"Of course not. I'm not that clinical. But don't be put off by my objectivity, Evan. Abbie and I are scientists of a sort. These animals aren't pets, although I think Abbie sometimes forgets that."

"She doesn't forget," said Evan.

"Perhaps. At any rate, as behavioral researchers we're trained to be objective. I'd nullify my study were I to get emotionally involved with the goings-on of the chimpanzees. It's torture to watch an infant chimp be killed by another of its kind. To watch as the skull is cracked open and the brain scooped out like some ambrosial delicacy. But it happens. And I'm there to witness that, and report it, and see if it sheds any light on what we know about animal and human behavior. I wouldn't be able to do that if I let my emotions get in the way."

"Only proves I could never be an animal behaviorist," said Evan.

"No," Fielding said, dryly, perusing Evan. "I don't think you could."

At that moment Fran caught sight of the two men and barked. Pig, out in the big outdoors for the first time, sat contentedly on her mother's lap.

"Why, it's Fran, isn't it?" asked Fielding. "Is that her baby with her?"

"Yes. She's called Pig."

"How marvelous. The makings of an ideal study."

"Yeah." Evan visualized Fielding following Fran through the course of a day, waiting expectantly for her to dash out Pig's brains.

"Fran," signed Fielding. "Hello, Fran."

The ape ignored the Englishman. She wrapped a sinewy arm around Evan's leg.

"See the man?" Evan signed.

Fran peered up into Evan's face. Adoringly, so he thought.

"That's Mic," he signed. "Do you remember him?"

The gorilla scratched her nose. "No."

"Sure she does," Fielding said, squatting next to her. "Fran, remember Mic?" he signed.

Fran chewed on Evan's pants. "Tickle Beanface."

"In a minute, Fran," signed Evan.

"She must have forgotten me," said Fielding.

"Seems that way," Evan said.

"Well, uh—" It was the first time Evan had seen Fielding at a loss for words. "Come to think of it, I was taking Abbie's word for it that the ape had a crush on me. I really only saw her once or twice." He changed the subject abruptly. "Got to get back into town now. Need a ride?"

"No," said Evan. "Thanks all the same." He basked in vindication as Fielding throttled out of the compound.

"I see you're getting along with the indomitable Professor Fielding," said David, emerging from a doorway.

"He's not quite as indomitable as he likes to appear. Where's Joey?"

"Getting dried off. He left the faucet running. Again. Second time he's done that since Abbie was taken. I'm not sure if he's absentminded or just pissed off."

"I'd say the latter."

"Probably. I sure wish these three would stop blaming Abbie's disappearance on me. I'm tired of cleaning up after them."

"Winston acts like he's doing better," said Evan as the big ape yawned.

"I think it's helped him a lot to get outside."

"Think it's safe for me to pay my respects?"

"Yeah. He's pretty calm."

Evan cautiously approached the big ape. Winston was rolling over on the ground.

"Hello, Winston," signed Evan. "How are you?"

"Sit." Winston tapped the back of two fingers from his right hand against the flat palm of his left hand.

Evan debated whether the gorilla had signed incorrectly or really had meant for him to sit. He played it safe and joined Winston on the ground.

"How are you?" Evan repeated.

"Blue man bad," signed Winston, pounding one fist on top of the other.

Blue man? The ape repeated the sign for "blue." Evan suspected Winston was referring to Fielding's blue shirt.

"Why?" he signed.

"Dirty stink," signed the ape.

"I don't like him much either," signed Evan.

He was certain that a flicker of understanding appeared in those gorilla eyes. Winston responded, "Good," and hesitantly added the unfamiliar configuration "Evan."

"Good Evan." It was the first time the large ape had used Evan's name spontaneously. The ice between them was finally thawing. Ironically, Mic Fielding's arrival had worked its first rapprochement, not between terrorist and public authority, but between man and ape.

The gorilla rolled away from Evan and drummed his fingers on the back of his chin. The action produced a teeth-rattling sound. He picked a white flower from a weed, and plopped next to where Pig was sprawled across her mother's leg. Winston tickled the little ape under the chin with the flower. Pig gurgled.

Serenity, for a moment, in the gorilla household. But not for long. Joey arrived in the courtyard, and shook the last drops of water from his coat while standing only a few feet from Winston. The large ape responded with a loud cough,

which the younger gorilla rightly interpreted as a reprimand.
The confrontation was blessedly brief. Strangely, it reassured
Evan that the gorillas were coping in their mistress's absence.
Winston seemed to be taking command of the situation,
assuming the natural responsibilities of the eldest. It would
take years before streaks of silver-gray sprouted on his
back, distinguishing him as a member of the exclusive order
of silverbacks, but already he was demonstrating their
sapience.

David threw Joey a ball, which the red-topped gorilla
ignored. It rolled past Winston and under one of the trailers,
where, despite the big ape's efforts to dislodge it, it remained.
Paying no heed to the various branches and sticks that would
have extended the reach of his arm, Winston kicked the trailer
in frustration.

So much for sapience.

Dalam studied the ransom note for a last time. He reread
its demands, block-printed on the thin piece of paper, and sat
back in his chair, dissatisfied. The note read like a shopping
list. It lacked the single element so fundamental to Dalam's
campaign: a dramatic flair. With pen in hand, he tried to
remedy the matter.

He composed a short diatribe against the government of
Mobutu Sese Seko and added it to the note. When calling for
Engulu's release, he praised his imprisoned colleague for his
revolutionary zeal. Lastly, he changed the section that stipu-
lated how the Burundian government was to respond to their
demands. Rather than have the FPL monitor all broadcasts
from the official government radio station, the group would
tune in only twice a day, at nine in the morning and three in
the afternoon.

The alterations helped, but still, the note lacked urgency.
It stated that failure to comply with the conditions would
endanger the hostages' lives, but the threat was unspecific.
There were no time limits.

And so, without the knowledge of his men, Dalam added

a new condition to the note. Satisfied at last, he folded the paper and sealed it in an envelope, and with it, the fates of several dozen people.

The warden at Rumonge prison had a problem. July 8 was the start of his vacation, and months ago he had promised a trip to his family. His wife and children had never been outside the city limits; their excitement, like his, was great. It would be the first vacation he'd earned since being appointed warden, and he had already purchased the proper tickets and made the necessary reservations.

July 8 was also the scheduled date of execution for Rumonge's most notorious prisoner, the police-killer and terrorist Chedial Engulu. The warden had not expected the court to recommend immediate execution, but it had. Now, as he sat in the chair he'd filled for only one year, he mulled over his predicament.

He could not be absent from the execution; the government and its media tools would crucify him. But he could not start changing the dates of his vacation, either; everything would be booked up. There seemed to be only one solution.

Move up the date of the execution to the seventh. After all, the public was clamoring for the man's death. An overzealous warden would be more readily excused than a negligent one. He would find some reason—a mix-up with the firing squad, a shortage of cells. Something. The court of appeals judge would approve the change; he was an old friend.

With considerable relief, the warden signed the new order and went back to reading his travel folders.

Abbie played with the food on her plate, stirring it in swirling patterns while she contemplated the latest turn of events. She knew that Bunkeya had caught on to their trick, and yet, after putting them through the torture of the second picture, he had selected the first.

Was he taunting her? Had he sent the second picture instead? But why the act? She was baffled and desperately wanted to talk to him.

The others had carefully avoided the subject of the two photos after they returned to the cottage. They quietly ate their meal. Like Abbie, they, too, were baffled, but they did not panic. She had, indeed, chosen her students well. Little had she known when she'd read those innumerable résumés, boasting a thousand different accomplishments, that the traits she'd sought in her research assistants were the very ones now helping them through this ordeal: patience, optimism, stamina, hope, courage, integrity. Above all, an overriding belief that setbacks are never permanent. The young people before her filled her with pride.

A jangling at the door sent a shock wave through her system. She nervously shoved her plate aside. Bunkeya appeared in the doorway.

"Is everything all right?" he asked.

"Yes, everything is fine."

"You're not eating? Is there something wrong with the food?"

"No, it's okay. I guess I'm just a little claustrophobic. Is there any chance I could go outside for some air?"

Without even stopping to think about it—as if he had expected her request—Bunkeya stepped to one side of the doorway. Abbie walked across the threshold and breathed deeply. The guard near the door reached for her but returned to his post when he saw Bunkeya follow. Bunkeya nodded, and the guard closed the door.

The sun was nearly set, and a light breeze trickled in from the north. Abbie stretched her legs. To her surprise, they were genuinely cramped. She kneaded the stiffness in her calves and walked to where the stream rushed downhill. She followed it for a little way until she had a view of the lake. Bunkeya did not attempt to restrain her. When she sat, he remained standing.

In the twilight, the fishermen from Iddan were readying their canoes for the evening's expedition. Night was the time to catch dagaa, the sardine-sized fish used in preparing ugali. With kerosene pressure lamps attached to the bows of their crafts, the fishermen pushed off from shore, their nets at their feet.

It was a spectacular sight, both beautiful and eerie. The pinpricks of light reflected softly in the water. All along the coast, similar platoons of men were on the lake, their lamps like torches held by nymphs heralding the arrival of Neptune. And to welcome the god, a chorus of sound. A group of fishermen had spotted a large shoal, and began singing and stamping their feet and banging their paddles against their boats. The cadence carried to where Abbie sat, then diminished in volume so that it became just another murmur of the surrounding wood.

"It's lovely here," said Abbie. "Hardly the type of place I would have expected to find the FPL."

"Anyone can appreciate beauty, Mademoiselle Guisbourne."

"Not anyone. I don't think the man who helped you take the photo of us today can see beauty." There, she'd broached the subject of the photo. The African did not seem to notice. Or chose to ignore it.

"Mpinga? That's true. Beauty is not practical; it has no function. Thus, it is of no value to him."

Abbie did not dare question the African outright about his behavior at the photo session. She tried a circuitous route.

"Did Alex get off all right with the picture and ransom?"

"Yes. He'll be in the authorities' hands by early tomorrow morning."

"I'm glad Dalam let him go," said Abbie, as close to an expression of gratitude as she was able to get. "Alex doesn't have a strong constitution. He was starting to break."

"Even those with the strongest constitutions break, mademoiselle."

Bunkeya's comment caught Abbie by surprise. "Of course, under harsh circumstances," she said, talking off the top of her head. "It's just harder to imagine some people breaking than others. Say, like you."

"That's because you don't know me. You don't know Africa." His gaze was granite-hard.

"I'm sorry," said Abbie, sensing she had touched a hidden core of the African. "I didn't mean to imply that you were inhuman."

"Yes, you did. Don't apologize." Bunkeya shifted his gaze to the lake. "I had a family, once. It was a year ago. We lived in a place called Kitwach. Farmers mostly. Some livestock."

The muscles in the side of his neck tensed, veins protruding like sinewy ropes.

"So, one day the dry season came. And it didn't go away. Our rivers dried up, and so did our crops. Our livelihood. One of my brothers, he said, 'We'll go and talk to the provincial government and they'll help us.' So we went to a huge square outside the government building. Others were there, too, milling about. From all over. All with the same idea. And we waited.

"The square became more congested as people poured in from far-off villages. We were all standing, an ocean of people, more than I'd ever seen in my life. An old man in front of me, he fell over, twice. They had to carry him away.

"I could see the lights in the building's great hallway. Big crystal ones. And people were jammed inside, stepping on one another. Then they closed the doors. People yelled at the guards. A man shouted but he was struck down.

"My son . . ." Bunkeya paused for a moment. "My son, Salim, was hungry. We left the others and tried to make our way to the side of the square. People started pushing us. Shoving. They were trying to get to the doors. I held my son by the hand, but we couldn't break free from the crowd.

"The crowd grew stronger, and pressed us against one another. And then the rumor started. I heard people yelling: 'Get to the doors. They're handing out food there. Get to the doors.' I began to lose my balance. A panic set in. The crowd absorbed my efforts to break out, and redoubled them against me. I pulled my son closer to my side and we were sucked back into the middle of the square. It was like a whirlpool.

Sometimes it would be calm and then, in the next moment,
it would surge forward, with tremendous force: taking your
feet off the ground, shoving elbows into bellies, knees into
groins. People screamed. Some fell to the ground. My son and
I, we were forced farther into the center of the mass, whipped
there. He couldn't breathe. I lifted him above my head and
told him to wrap his arms around my neck.

"He was there a long time, as wave after wave sent us
scrambling. I wouldn't put him down. But then a quiet period
came. I didn't hear the screaming. I thought it might be over.
I was fooled and put him down. The next thing I knew, he
was ripped from my hand. I tried to fight against the wave of
people. I remember scratching and hitting those around me,
trying to pry people's legs apart with my own. Finally, I dove
down under them. It was a nightmare of tangled limbs. I
couldn't get up again. My chest ached. The pressure pushed
me forward, forcing me down. I struggled but I was losing.

"And then the wave changed, slowly, to the other side. I
felt something under my knees. It was a body. The leg was bent
and twisted under the torso. An arm flung across the chest.
A young woman. I didn't bother trying to help her up. Instead,
I used her as a base to get my footing back.

"Seconds later, I found my son. Someone had used him."

Hot tears blurred Abbie's vision. She did not brush them
away.

"I held him aloft. I suppose I knew he was dead even then.
He was so limp, so lifeless. But I wouldn't let myself believe
it. I held him up until the blood drained down from my arms
and I thought I would scream in sheer pain. We were there
forever.

"Then, finally, it began to break up. I was propelled to one
of the fringes of the huge square. It took me hours to find my
family. My other son, Gise, was still alive. He talked to me.
Such a good boy. He was worried about his mother and
brother. And then he, too, died.

"Sixty people died that day. Forty were children. The rest
old people. Suffocated to death, most of them. There were

assorted ones who were trampled or maimed, but most died because they couldn't breathe. More than a million square kilometers in this country and my sons died because there wasn't space enough to breathe. All because a corrupt provincial official who'd siphoned off the relief money wouldn't open his doors.

"My wife—well, you asked what it is that breaks a person. I was broken, too. Oh, I didn't know it at the time, but my actions weren't those of a sane man. I found that I was suffocating—as surely as my sons—only slower. I tried to do something about it. But I took the panicked way, clawing and scratching at all the other innocent people around me.

"And now, there's a calm moment and I can breathe and think once more. Only I'm afraid of being fooled again." Bunkeya looked at Abbie for the first time since he'd begun his story. "I don't expect you to understand. I don't really myself."

A silence ensued and then, in a thick voice that sounded strange to her, Abbie asked:

"When did you say Alex would reach the authorities?"

"Sometime in the early morning."

Abbie nodded and wrapped her arms around her upper torso.

"I'd better go back. The others will wonder what happened to me."

The stars lighted their way as they trudged up the hill. They walked without speaking to each other. Abbie Guisbourne had no more questions to ask.

Before settling the apes in for the night, David put Pig in a makeshift diaper. He was tired of cleaning up after her and, for the first time, truly appreciated the accomplishment Abbie had wrought in toilet-training the three other gorillas. He left Pig and Fran in Evan's care as he made his final rounds.

Evan had arrived for dinner and agreed to stay afterward to help David. One of the storage cabinets in the trailer was open, and he moved to close it. The shelves were filled with taped cartridges. Evan cocked his head sideways to read the labels on the end: "Fran, A 22, Chandra, Abstract"; Winston, F 7, Larry, Picture Rep"; "Joey, M 11, Vince, Intro." On a whim, he chose the last tape and carried it to the videotape machine.

The first few minutes weren't of Joey, but of Fran, a much younger Fran. The tape had been recorded years before—an obvious inference, but one Evan was proud of making. A week ago he wouldn't have been able to tell one gorilla from another, much less recognize a particular gorilla in a film taken of her at an earlier time.

Fran, however, was not the object of his attention. Abbie was. It was she who was signing to Fran. Impulsively, Evan leaned over and adjusted the videotape machine so that it showed the tape in slow motion. The reduced speed infused Abbie with a fuzzy unreality, much like Evan's recollections of her. Their time together had passed so quickly that it seemed dreamlike. Separated from her for nearly as long as he'd known her, Evan found it easy, with each passing frame, to think he had imagined her.

It wasn't as if they had been especially close. He barely knew the woman. But that was, as Hamlet said, the rub. He would never know if the flimsy beginnings of their friendship could have been built into something more solid. It was this that nagged at him. He did not know her well enough to say that life wouldn't be the same without her, only enough to wonder what would have happened if they'd been given a chance. That was the mark she had made on his life.

The television screen flickered and abruptly the image changed from Fran and Abbie, to Joey and a young man whom Evan did not recognize. Perhaps the mysterious "Vince" of the label. His speculation was confirmed when Abbie came into the picture:

"Okay, Vince," she said. "First we've got to come up with a sign for your name."

Joey could be seen chomping a piece of licorice in the background. His black figure blended with the shadows.

"We can't just spell it out?" asked the young man.

"No," answered Abbie. "Takes too much time. Besides, the gorillas don't know the manual alphabet. That's beyond their understanding."

"What's the sign for your name?"

"It's the letter 'A' "—Abbie formed her right hand into a fist—"placed next to the ear. We usually try to do a variation on the first letter of the name."

"Okay," said Vince. "How about the letter 'V' touching the right eyebrow?" Vince had extraordinarily lush eyebrows.

"All right, let's give it a try."

Abbie crouched next to Joey.

"Joey," she signed. "This is Vince. His name is 'Vince.' "

"Hello, Joey," signed Vince.

"Vince," repeated Abbie, reaching for Joey's hands. She molded the sign for "V," the index and middle fingers spread straight out like a victory sign, the other fingers and thumb curled in toward the palm. Then she touched his eyebrow with it.

"Vince," she signed once more, waiting for the ape to repeat it.

Joey modified the sign. He touched his eyebrow with all four fingers stretched out, parallel to one another.

"That's what I suspected," said Abbie.

"What?" asked Vince.

"I wanted you to see this for yourself. See how he won't keep his two little fingers down? They keep popping up. That's because the 'V' letter, like the 'U' letter, which is practically identical, pulls these ligaments here." She pointed to the back of her hand. "A gorilla's hand is normally dexterous enough to hold that position, but Joey accidentally ripped those ligaments. He doesn't like to hold those fingers down. So if we can avoid creating new signs with that formation, we do."

"So what are we going to use for my name?"

"See the sign he's forming now? It's the letter 'B' touching the eyebrow. Since that's easier for him to sign, we might as well use it. All right?"

"Sure. After all, 'B' and 'V' are pronounced the same in Spanish. I'll just call him José instead of Joey," joked Vince.

Evan stopped the tape. He rewound it.

"—That's because the 'V' letter, like the 'U' letter, which is practically identical—"

He ran it forward.

"—After all, 'B' and 'V' are pronounced the same in Spanish—"

Evan turned the machine off.

Told to form the letter "V," Joey formed the letter "B." If told to form the letter "U"—identical to the sign for "V" except that the index and middle fingers were parallel and not spread—would he not then also sign "B"?

B-L-A. Joey's cryptic message to Evan: "Tell Evan, B-L-A." B-L-A. Could it not have originally been U-L-A?

Ula, the courier from Muwali.

"Tell Evan, Ula." That is what Abbie had signed to Joey immediately before she was dragged off by the kidnappers. Somehow Ula had played a part in the kidnapping. But what? Evan's thoughts swiftly returned to the present.

Ula was dead. Whatever information he might have had to offer was forever sealed.

Or was it?

"I'm sorry to make you go to all this trouble, Sergeant, but it's rather urgent that I look through the files tonight."

Evan peered over the counter as the policeman rifled through a stack of manila folders.

"That's quite all right, Monsieur Olgilvie. Always happy to assist the American embassy. Let's see. Here it is." The officer pulled out a folder and dumped it upside down on the desk. "Watch, ring, wallet. Just what exactly are you looking for?"

"I'm not sure. I guess we'll start with the wallet."

"Not much there. A little money. Driver's license. Pictures of friends or relatives."

"Turn that around toward me, will you please?"

"Sure." The officer handed the open wallet to Evan. "Just a plain ordinary driver's license. Name. Address. Picture."

Just a card with a picture.

But not, as it happened, a picture of the man Evan knew as Ula. A man who, if Evan guessed correctly, was now in possession of the six hostages from the Burundi Primate Research Center. A member of the FPL. And dangerously alive.

Mpinga saw the tears glistening on Abbie's face as she and Bunkeya walked back to the cottage. More importantly, so did the guard on duty, a young man of an impressionable nature. Those tears suggested a plan to Mpinga.

He did not know what had caused her to cry. Probably just exhaustion. But the story he concocted, one that would soon spread throughout camp, had a clear explanation: Bunkeya had forced himself on the woman, threatening to kill her if she did not let him have his way, and she had submitted.

Such a story would make the sudden death of Abbie Guisbourne less of a shock. With the hostages' testimony that Bunkeya had removed her from the cottage in the dark of the night, Dalam would arrive at the only logical conclusion: Bunkeya had wanted his way again, only this time the woman had put up a fight.

And so she had died.

Rather a perfect scheme, thought Mpinga.

Abbie returned to the cottage hungry and cold and confused. She knew the others were concerned by her frazzled appearance, yet she sloughed off their questions. Bunkeya's story haunted her. She could not shake the image of his sons crushed between a hammer and anvil made of human bodies. She only half listened to the conversation taking place on the other side of the room.

"—but so what?" Tyler was saying. "Even if they do get the picture, nothing will happen."

"The police will figure it out, Tyler," said Sara. "We've just got to wait for it to pay off."

"How can it? They still won't know how to find us."

"Tyler," said Juste, "you just calm down. There's nothing we can do except sit tight."

"Yes," signed Chandra. "It's not easy for any of us."

"You're crazy," said Tyler, jumping to his feet. "All of you. You're just going to sit here and do nothing. Well, not me."

"Tyler, sit down," signed Chandra.

"Come on, Tyler," said Sara. "We can't do anything. You're just making matters worse."

"What do you mean we can't do anything? We can try to escape. Have you forgotten that?"

"Be realistic, will you?" said Sara. "We don't know where we are, and there's a bunch of armed terrorists outside. We don't stand a chance."

"One person could do it," countered the young man. "One person alone has the best chance. You distract them and I'll go for help. That's a jungle out there. Even they couldn't find me."

"You'd get lost," said Juste.

"No, I'd follow the river. It leads straight to the lake. Just follow it down—"

"No, Tyler," said a new voice. "And that's final."

All four hostages looked to Abbie Guisbourne. She had not stirred from her position in the corner of the cottage. Her knees were drawn up to her chest.

"No, Tyler," she repeated. "There'll be no escape attempts as long as I'm in charge."

"Abbie, we're not in an academic environment any longer. You're not my teacher here. I can do—"

"I said no!" She shouted the words across the room. "Do you have some stupid romantic notion of making a hero of yourself? We're not playing a game here. Stop being so naive."

The young man had never seen Abbie so angry. He sat back on the ground, but as an act of temporary conciliation only, not capitulation, a distinction the others would not detect until it was too late.

* * *

Mpinga timed it so that he entered the food line just behind the young man assigned the night guard. They joked about the monotony of the dinners, and walked to a table together. The guard was flattered by Mpinga's attention and, emboldened by his sudden rapport with the older man, slipped into the idle palaver of intimates.

"Anyway," said the guard, "I don't feel like standing watch tonight. Those people sure as hell aren't going anywhere. They don't even need a guard."

"I agree," said Mpinga with false empathy. "I'd tell you to skip it, but you never know when Dalam might come along. Or Bunkeya."

"Yeah, Bunkeya came by earlier," said the young man. "To talk with the American woman."

Mpinga smirked.

"What's wrong?" asked the recruit.

"Just your use of the word 'talk,'" Mpinga said, nonchalantly.

"I don't understand."

"Surely you know?" Mpinga lowered his voice and tossed out the first strands of his spider's web. "I mean, you've been guarding them all this time."

"So?" said the young man, confused.

"I understand this last time she was pretty upset," Mpinga continued. "Came in crying, didn't she?"

"Yes," said the guard, remembering, "she was crying."

"Well?" said Mpinga.

"Well what?"

"You are young, aren't you, my boy?" said Mpinga, clapping the recruit on the shoulder. "It seems Mlle. Guisbourne was less than enthusiastic about yielding to Bunkeya's, as you put it, 'talk.'"

"Yielding?" The guard's eyes widened. "Oh."

"Exactly. It appears even Bunkeya has desires. Only no woman in her right mind will come near him. So he has to take. Ask anyone here. They'll know what went on down that hill." Mpinga shoved the guard a glass of beer, certain the

young man would question no one, since it would suggest
naiveté on his part. "Here, drink up. I tell you what: I'll take
over your shift tonight."

"No, I couldn't let you."

"Nonsense. It isn't fair the way Dalam has only you younger
men standing watch. We should all have to take our turn. Just
don't tell anyone or else we'll both catch hell. What do you
say?"

"I am pretty beat. All right. Thanks. I'll remember this."

"I've no doubt you will," said Mpinga.

Tyler rolled over from his left side to his back, and flung
his right arm under his head. The grass mat left a crisscross
impression on his face like a tic-tac-toe game. He stared at
the ceiling of the cottage and listened to the rhythmic breathing
of the others. It was dark and it was quiet and his stomach
was full. He'd eaten the portions of food left by Abbie and
the others on their plates. Let them waste away if they wanted.
He needed his strength.

The FPL had made one mistake already. It had never frisked
the hostages, an understandable oversight. The students hardly
looked the type to conceal dangerous weapons. Tyler himself
had forgotten all about his pocketknife until a few hours ago,
when he'd automatically reached for it to snip off a hangnail.
He always carried the pocketknife with him. It was a Swiss
Army make, complete with tweezers, scissors, toothpick, can
and bottle openers, and a screwdriver.

And two very sharp, very sturdy knives. He'd used them
to slice hunks of bread and chop kindling and clean fish. His
plan for them now was quite different. He eased the longer
of the two from the red body and quietly snapped it into place.
The blade was cold to the touch. He ran the edge along the
back of his hand, and then closed the knife and repocketed it.

Morning would arrive soon enough.

* * *

Mpinga stamped his feet on the red earth as he watched the last of the FPL men turn in for the night. He'd let the young guard stand the first part of the watch so that no one would know Mpinga had relieved him. The young man had been effusive in his thanks, never once suspecting the older man's ulterior motive. He would not know about the deception until later, when, in a panic over leaving his post, he would be willing to say anything to protect himself. Even that Bunkeya had asked him to open the door to the hostages' cottage.

Mpinga waited another hour. The night was moonless. Even so, he pulled his cap low over his face before inserting the key into the door lock.

Tyler heard the slide of the bolt as it receded into the metal lock. To his ears, the sound signaled the arrival of morning as shrilly as a rooster's crow. The sun would not rise for several hours, but he did not take the time to contemplate the disparity. Shinning across the floor to the door, he stood, then flattened himself against the wall, pocketknife in hand.

The snap was quite audible this time.

Mpinga twisted the key one revolution and pushed the heavy wood door ajar.

"Mademoiselle Guisbourne?" he said, standing back from the door and exposing as little of himself to the hostages as possible. His voice was pitched high in imitation of the young guard. "Bunkeya needs to—"

He heard the click first. The gleam of the knife in his flashlight beam followed a split second later. Then the beam caught Tyler's startled face, which reflected an inchoate realization that the young sentry he'd planned on overpowering had metamorphosed into a man of consequence.

Mpinga's decision to stand back from the door proved propitious. The knife missed its mark and passed harmlessly through his shirt. The African's next move was the result of long years of guerrilla warfare, an environment in which enemies were not neutralized until they stopped breathing.

He did not reach for the hand that had wielded the errant blade, but jumped to one side and unsheathed the knife he'd brought to use on the Guisbourne woman, the knife stolen from Bunkeya's satchel. He plunged it forward, and a scream ruptured the quiet of the cottage. A body slumped next to his feet.

The hostages jolted awake in various stages of commotion. Mpinga shone his flashlight on the ground. Tyler lay gasping on his side, hands clutching his abdomen. A red bubble burst at the side of his mouth.

The young man's pocketknife was clearly visible in the shaft of light. It was opened to the screwdriver.

X

Before departing from the police station, Evan left a message for Captain Karuhije to telephone him as soon as possible. Too excited to sleep, he called Mic Fielding and asked him to describe Ula, the man hired as the Muwali courier. Fielding's description contrasted sharply with Evan's recollection of the man who had driven into the primate center. More convinced than ever that there had been two "Ulas," Evan briefly outlined his hypothesis to Fielding.

One: The FPL had somehow learned that Fielding had hired a new courier and that the new man was scheduled to make his first trip to the Burundi Primate Research Center.

Two: The real Ula had been ambushed on the road up from Muwali and replaced by the false Ula, a member of the FPL. The body had been dumped at the side of the road. This explained the discrepancy between the location of the body and the western route taken by the terrorists after the kidnapping.

Three: The Kwa scare had been a ruse perpetrated by the false Ula and his contact when they were discovered by Larry.

Four: The hostages were being held somewhere across the lake in Zaire. Before being hit over the head, Larry had overheard a comment about moving men from a cottage by a river. Obviously, the men in question were FPL members forced to make room for the hostages.

As Evan enumerated his points a peculiar exhilaration stole over him, its genesis both the respect in Fielding's voice as he complimented Evan on his perspicacity and Evan's own astonishment at having exhibited such deductive prowess.

But after Evan hung up the phone, whiling away the night hours while those less clever than he slept, his marvelous deduction lost its marvel. What had he really uncovered? Simply that Ula, the false one, was one of the kidnappers, and that the hostages were being held in a mining cottage by a river in Zaire, a country the size of the United States west of the Mississippi, with literally thousands of rivers and mines. It didn't exactly narrow things down.

He regretted telling the police sergeant that his message for Captain Karuhije was urgent. He considered calling and downgrading its importance, but it was too late. The phone rang.

"Monsieur Olgilvie?" The captain's clipped voice bounced off Evan's eardrum. "How did you know about it before the rest of us?"

"What?"

"Your urgent message. The one you left with the sergeant. How did you find out so early about it?"

"You know, too?"

"Would we be talking like this if I didn't know? So how did you find out?"

"One of the gorillas, Joey—"

"Not those apes again. How did he know?"

"Abbie apparently flashed the name to him before she was dragged off."

"Whose name? Alex's?"

"No," said Evan, confused. Their conversation reminded him of an Abbott and Costello routine. "Ula's."

"What are you talking about?"

"I'm talking about the man who posed as Ula, the courier from Muwali." Evan wondered if the conversation would make more sense were it not six o'clock in the morning. "He was part of the kidnapping. That's the message. The Ula who's in your morgue isn't the same one who arrived in Abbie's camp. The dead one is the real courier."

"Good God," said the captain. "I thought your message was

about Alex Golding, one of the kidnapped students. He showed up at the primate center about five minutes ago as a messenger from the FPL. He's got the ransom note with him."

"I hadn't heard a word about it," said Evan. "Where is he now?"

"On his way here."

"Did he tell you anything about the others?"

"He just barely arrived. But he's got a picture of the others. That gorilla was right about the crocodile she saw. There's apparently a poster of one in the picture. The FPL never was one for subtlety. Now this story about Ula, you want to run it by me again?"

"I think it'd be better to explain it in person," Evan said.

"Okay, but hold off for a while. We'll need an hour or so to talk to the kid."

"Fine. See you soon."

Abbie winced as the first light of dawn streamed through the barred window. Her eyes were raw, the lids puffy and red. She had not slept a wink since being shocked awake. Nor, she knew, had any of the others.

Tyler was dead, she was certain of it. He was still breathing when the FPL carried him out of the cottage, but his skin was white and moist, and he made odd gurgling noises. The blood pumped out of him like oil from an uncapped gusher. Abbie's gaze lingered for just an instant on the dark red stain on the floor. She and the others had bunched in the corner, as far away from the stain as possible.

Tears smarted her irritated eyes. That stupid, stupid boy. If he'd listened to her, he'd still be alive. She clenched her fists. The worst of her fears had been realized.

And they'd only just completed their first twenty-four hours in the hands of the terrorists. She shook in dread of what the next twenty-four would bring.

* * *

Mpinga had not slept either. He'd passed the time examining the story he'd told Dalam, probing it for weak spots: The young guard became sick while on duty and Mpinga replaced him; he opened the door to the hostages' cottage after hearing a strange noise from inside, and, without provocation, Tyler attacked him. Not the most airtight story, but its simplicity lent it a certain cogency. Dalam seemed to accept the explanation.

Mpinga had heaved a sigh of relief, as had the young sentry, when the FPL leader returned to his cottage. The sentry had stuck to the story line Mpinga fed him, but his manner, as he'd stonily faced the older man before retiring, was sullen and resentful. Mpinga did not care. The important thing was that the young man would not talk. All that remained was to replace Bunkeya's knife before it was discovered missing.

And to devise a new plan, of course.

Alex Golding sat at one end of a small table, his face wan, blue eyes rimmed in dark shadows. His hands cradled a cup of coffee, but he did not drink from it. He used it as a pacifier for his trembling hands while he talked to the two policemen seated next to him.

Evan was ushered into an adjoining room, through whose doorway he caught sight of the pallid youth. He immediately was greeted by Fielding. The Englishman was seated on a folding chair by a side wall.

"Hello, Evan. Welcome to the dawn brigade," Fielding said cheerily, exuding charm even at this disgustingly early hour. He'd been equally chipper the night before when Evan telephoned. "Have a seat."

"What are you doing here?" asked Evan.

"It was my trailer that Alex burst in upon."

"I didn't realize he'd been returned directly to the primate center."

"He was returned to the shoreline, actually. He walked into camp."

"Where's the captain?" asked Evan.

"The captain is right here," said a voice behind Evan. "Nice of you to come, Monsieur Olgilvie, though I guess we didn't really need you. Monsieur Fielding here straightened me out on the Ula switch, and how the gorilla told you about it."

"Just wanted to save time, old chap," said Fielding.

"How considerate," said Evan with the kindred appreciation of an overweight man whose friends have eaten the last of his favorite cake to save him the calories.

"But since you drove all the way here," said the captain, "let me tell you what we've learned. The hostages are fine. They're being held, as we suspected, by the FPL on the other side of Lake Tanganyika in Zaire. Mode of transport was a fishing boat, but since they were out on the water for such a long period of time, and blindfolded, Alex can't really give us a good estimate of how far down the coast the FPL camp is. All he said is that it's in a forest up a group of hills, on the rift escarpment. A little cluster of cottages on a carved plateau of sorts."

"A mining camp," said Evan.

"Could be," said Captain Karuhije, nodding his head thoughtfully.

"That isn't a guess," said Evan. "I thought Fielding told you?"

"Told me what?"

"About the conversation Larry heard before getting clobbered by the fake Ula. One of the speakers mentioned a mining camp."

"You didn't say that over the phone," said Fielding, defensively.

"You sure about this?" Captain Karuhije asked Evan.

"Positive."

"This may give us our first break in pinpointing the FPL camp," said the policeman, excitedly. "I'll have to get a man over to the hospital to talk to that student."

"What about the ransom?" asked Evan, anxious to know the whole story before the captain rushed off.

"Steep. The note mentions five million American dollars,

release of ten political prisoners, assorted specifications for arms."

"Where's the note right now?" asked Evan. "I'd like to see it."

"So would I. I only barely saw it before Intelligence took it for analysis. You can see the picture of the hostages, though. I'll get it for you." He returned with the Polaroid photograph. "Nothing much here that helps. At least we see that they're alive and healthy."

Evan held the photo by the edges, as one would handle a phonograph record. He had never been presented with evidence from an official investigation before, and having it in his possession made him nervous. The glossy surface shimmered in the light. He tilted the picture to get a sharper image.

The captain was right. Nothing special about the picture. The five hostages were seated under a huge FPL sign across the top of which slithered a black crocodile, its mouth open. It looked as if the animal were about to bite off the hostages' heads. Evan stared at Abbie's face, comforted by the fact that though she was tense, she showed no signs of physical abuse. He prepared to hand back the picture when an oddity caught his eye.

"Their hands are tied," he said.

"Yes," said Captain Karuhije. "But only for the picture. Alex told us that when they were locked up they weren't bound."

The policeman reached for the photograph, but Evan tightened his hold on it. Something about the picture wouldn't release him. He concentrated on it, searching out the most minute detail. He looked at the crocodile. He stared at the bound wrists. A nascent idea found its way into the eddies of his thoughts.

The hands. The hostages' hands. That was what made the photo odd. Each left hand was perfectly straight. Each right hand was curved, shaped. Molded. Though the placement of fingers differed with each right hand, the staging was undeniably deliberate. They were signing, sending a message.

Each right hand was a letter of the alphabet. As Evan looked from hand to hand, he read the message out loud:

"I-D-D-A-N. It says 'Iddan.' "

"What does?" asked the captain.

"Their hands. Look at their hands," Evan said with increased conviction. "They're spelling out a name."

"Where? I don't see it."

"They're using American Sign Language. See how Abbie has her little finger raised? That's an 'I.' And the others follow. Those two are 'D's. See the raised index fingers? And then an 'A,' and an 'N.' Iddan."

"That sly Abbie." Fielding clapped Evan on the shoulder. "We shouldn't have underestimated her."

I never have, Evan almost said.

"Pretty clever, all right," said Captain Karuhije, momentarily distracted by a note an aide handed him.

"But what the hell does 'Iddan' mean?" asked Evan.

"I don't know," answered the captain, "but we'll find out even if it means pulling in all my men to do so. This may be the factor that'll break open this case, provided—"

"Provided what?" asked Evan.

"Provided the hostages are still alive when we get to them."

"What do you mean? Look at the picture. They're fine."

"For now. There's a complication," said the policeman, waving the note handed him. "Apparently, the ransom has a series of deadlines we must meet. Every day at three o'clock we've got to announce compliance with a different demand over national radio. One of them involves an FPL member sitting on death row in Rumonge prison. His name's Engulu, and his execution is set for three this afternoon. If that execution takes place, the FPL vows to carry out a similar execution with a hostage. Just as they'll do if their other demands aren't met, until they've killed them all, one by one."

One by one. Evan hoped that Abbie Guisbourne didn't top the list.

*   *   *

The scream came from down the hill. Sara's scream. Abbie jumped to her feet and grabbed the bars over the small window in the door. She wasn't able to see anything. Suddenly, the bars were ripped from her hands and the door swung open. Sara ran inside, her blond hair straggly, tears tracking her mottled cheeks.

"What happened?" asked Abbie, enfolding the frightened young woman in her arms.

"They lied to us about the ransom," Sara said between sobs. "One of the guards told me I'd better enjoy the afternoon because it might be my last one. I asked him what he meant, but he just smiled. The other man, the one outside this hut, said that there was an ultimatum attached to the ransom. Unless the authorities in Burundi halt an execution scheduled for today, the FPL will start killing us. One of us will be murdered. Like Tyler. And that awful man—"

The young woman gasped for air.

"—he said that it was going to be me first."

"He was just being sadistic, Sara. Don't pay any attention to what he said. We wouldn't be of any use to them dead, now would we?"

"But Tyler—"

"Tyler was a mistake. Try to calm down, now. Chandra, take care of Sara for a moment, will you?"

Abbie wished she could believe her own assurances. After last night's ordeal, and Bunkeya's subsequent confirmation earlier in the morning that Tyler was dead, anything was possible. Perhaps Dalam had been fooled by Mpinga's story, but she had not. The man had entered their cottage last night with the intent to murder. There had been no suspicious noise, just as there had been no sick guard; they were part of a hastily concocted excuse. Mpinga had entered the cottage to kill her, of this Abbie was sure. Tyler simply chose the wrong time to try to escape.

Abbie rattled the doorknob. "I want to see Bunkeya," she said to the guard on the other side of the door.

"He'll be by later," said the man, turning away.

"I don't think you understand," said Abbie, coldly. "Monsieur Dalam told us that we would be kept comfortable. I don't think he'd like to find out that you disobeyed his orders."

Abbie paced the floor while the guard delivered her message. It was more fury than fright that consumed her. One of her group had been inanely slain. A bitter rage exploded in her. Bunkeya's arrival provided her a vent.

"One of my students says there's some sort of deadline with the ransom," she said to the African. "Why didn't you tell me about it? Was this your idea of being merciful?"

"I didn't know anything about it until just a few moments ago," Bunkeya answered. "It was something Dalam added without consulting anyone. He parceled out the demands. One has to be met within every twenty-four-hour period or he kills one of you."

"What is this execution Sara mentioned?"

"One of our men in Rumonge prison is on death row for killing two policemen. He's to go before the firing squad today. The ransom note demands his reprieve."

"But that doesn't give the authorities enough time."

"When the note was written, the execution wasn't to take place until tomorrow. For some reason it was moved up one day. We just learned about the change."

"Then Dalam can't possibly adhere to his threat against our lives," said Abbie.

"I wouldn't count on that."

"Well, what would you count on?" she said, angrily. "You expect me to return to those three people in there and tell them we're going to pick straws? God, to think I actually believed that you were truly sorry about Tyler's death. You're no better than the rest of them. A human life is nothing to you. That boy had every right to live. Every right—" She turned away in disgust, and nodded at the guard to unlock the door.

"I'll speak to Dalam," said Bunkeya to Abbie's back as the guard twisted the key. "I'll see if something can be worked out."

Abbie said nothing. Without turning around, she stepped

into the cottage. In the dark gloom, she was barely able to discern the three figures in the corner. The whites of their eyes, disappearing with every blink, were a strange contrast to the darkness. Disembodied and red-lined, they epitomized what the hostages' second day of captivity was developing into: a deathwatch.

Evan plugged a finger over his left ear. He pressed the telephone receiver close to his right, and asked Fielding and Captain Karuhije to lower their voices. Davenport sounded a thousand miles away.

"Can you repeat that?" asked Evan.

"Yes," said Davenport. "Ambassador Stevens has already talked to the Minister of Justice, I said. The minister agrees that Dalam must not have known about the change in the execution date. He doesn't know if the FPL is serious about the hostage threat, but has someone in his department working on a reprieve for the terrorist in Rumonge."

"How long will it take?" asked Evan.

"It may be a while. Since the man was convicted not only of murder, but of political crimes against the state, the reprieve has to come from the Supreme Court."

"So why the delay?"

"The Supreme Court isn't based in Bujumbura, Olgilvie, remember? It's in Gitega."

"Damn," said Evan. Gitega, the ancient seat of the Bami, traditional rulers of the Tutsi, was a city of several thousand people, sixty miles southeast of Bujumbura.

"And what makes matters worse," said Davenport, "the court's in recess. No one's exactly sure where the justices are."

"That's just great." Evan twisted his watchband nervously. It was 8:22. In less than seven hours a man Evan had never met was scheduled to go before a firing squad. Though the man was a stranger, his life—rather, the continuation of it— was of paramount importance to Evan. Not for the first time since he arrived in Burundi, Evan cursed the miserable communication and transportation lines outside downtown Bujumbura.

"Is Fielding still there?" asked Davenport. "Let me talk to him, will you?"

Evan called Fielding to the phone. The Englishman made a series of affirmative sounds into the receiver before hanging up.

"What was that all about?" asked Evan.

"I'm needed at a meeting Ambassador Stevens has arranged with some of the Burundian ministers. The Zairian ambassador will be there as well, and the—"

"We've got it," interrupted a young policeman, running into the room. "We know what Iddan is." He eagerly placed a scrap of paper down on a side table and Captain Karuhije, Fielding, and Evan gathered around him. "It's a fishing village on the Zairian side of Lake Tanganyika. About a hundred fifty, maybe a hundred sixty kilometers from the lake's northern end, southeast of the town of Fizi."

"Any mines there?" asked the captain.

"We don't know yet. A lot of mining establishments were set up in the vicinity of Fizi. We've got men checking it out."

"Good work," said Captain Karuhije.

"Thank you, sir," said the policeman, beaming. He retreated to a back room.

"What do you do now with this information?" asked Evan.

"Nothing," said the captain.

"What do you mean?"

"We lose control of it from here on out. This information goes on to a higher level, to the men M. Fielding will be meeting with. It's up to them whether to act on it or not."

"Which reminds me," said Fielding, consulting his watch, "I'd better get going. See you later, Evan. Captain."

Fielding passed a police lieutenant on his way out the door. The officer handed Captain Karuhije a folder.

"Captain, there's been a murder downtown. You want Ndabeme on it?"

"I'll be right there." The captain shook Evan's hand. "Sorry to rush, Monsieur Olgilvie. Thanks again for making the trip down here."

The room that had been bustling with activity just seconds before was suddenly empty. Evan picked up the scrap of paper with the crudely drawn map of Iddan on it, and tucked it into his pocket. He knew he was expected back at the embassy, but on his way out of the police station, he set himself a different route, to the court where the FPL ball had been tossed: the Burundian Ministry of Justice.

The clock outside the cell read 11:15. The grapevine was wrong. Or it had been unprepared, as Engulu had been, for the one-day advancement of his execution. He shouldn't have let his hopes be raised. He should have taken his life while he'd had the chance. Now it was too late. His bed was stripped clean.

Engulu buttoned his blue work shirt, and noticed that one of the buttons was hanging by a thread. He was about to bring it to the guard's attention, but stopped himself. What did it really matter? He'd be dead before the button fell off. He tucked the shirt under his waistband.

Engulu didn't know what had gone wrong. He knew for a fact that a stay of execution was one of Dalam's ransom conditions. Earlier that morning he had overheard talk that he was to be removed from death row, but hours had passed since then and he'd heard nothing more.

Taken off death row. Engulu smiled bitterly. Taken off, yes, but in a pine box.

Lunch brought no encouraging words. The turnkey placed a tray on Engulu's cot and lingered at the door.

"Special lunch, you know. Potatoes. Corn. Beef. The works." The guard lowered his voice. "You want anything else, Engulu? Cigarettes, maybe? A beer? I can get you a beer."

"No," said Engulu, dully. "This is fine."

"Okay," said the guard, sticking his hands awkwardly into his pockets. "I'll get the tray later."

At first Engulu ignored the food, but a tantalizing odor filled the cell. He picked up the tray and laid it across his knees, where it tilted to one side. The juices from the meat slid to one end of the plate, and collected in a red-brown pool.

Engulu placed the tray back on the cot. He wasn't very hungry.

Seconds after he learned that Supreme Court Justice Jamal had been contacted in Gitega, Evan hurried to the office of John Moyo, assistant minister of justice. More than two and a half hours had passed since Evan arrived at the ministry. Each minute of waiting had been like another granule of salt rubbed in an open sore.

The assistant minister looked shrunken behind his large desk. He massaged the bridge of his nose where his small glasses pinched, and motioned Evan to a chair.

"Yes," he said as Evan sat, "the justice agreed that the hostages' lives depend on a stay of execution. He was most emphatic."

Thank God, thought Evan.

"But he won't grant it," said the assistant minister.

"Why not?" asked Evan, anger coloring his cheeks. "We're not asking for a pardon. Just a reprieve. Why can't he do that?"

"Because," said Moyo, "to do so would compromise the court. Justice Jamal says that the Burundian judicial system must be an apolitical entity. If this Engulu is reprieved—while others sentenced for the same crime are not—then justice is a travesty geared toward political ends."

"Bullshit," muttered Evan under his breath. A nice story, this talk of an untarnished court, but he didn't buy it. Not in a country where the court system, in the last decade, had turned a blind eye to heinous political manipulations. The worst: a gross indifference to prosecuting the murderers of over 100,000 Hutu tribesmen executed in the genocidal campaign waged by government forces in 1972 and 1973. Evan suspected the justice didn't want the responsibility of granting a reprieve with such grave political repercussions without prior government approval.

"Does he know that his decision could have serious consequences on the relationship between your country and the United States?" said Evan.

"Undoubtedly," replied the assistant minister, giving the impression that he, too, suspected the justice of less moral concerns. "But there is another way. The court can't grant the stay of execution without violating its integrity, so we have to go to a political figure who can. Someone who can override the sentence without damaging the judicial system's or his own reputation."

"Who can do that?" asked Evan.

"There's only one man," said the assistant minister. "The President."

What time was it? Engulu lacked the courage to look outside his cell. His fingernails were bitten to the quick. He hadn't done that since he was a child. Nervous habits shed long ago were returning to him in droves. He tapped his foot against the side of the cot.

The guard had removed the tray of food more than half an hour ago. He'd shaken his head when he saw the untouched meal, and once again had asked Engulu if there was anything he wanted.

Twelve-thirty, maybe. One? It didn't really matter. What good was an extra fifteen minutes to him now?

He hadn't even killed the fucking policemen. They'd killed themselves. Engulu reviewed his long career with the FPL. They'd all killed themselves, all the people he'd seen die. If they hadn't taken the stances they had, or represented the values they had, they'd still be alive. They had chosen death. It wasn't Engulu's fault. They'd been on the wrong side; he'd been on the right side.

And yet, sides didn't matter in the end. They all went young

sometimes, the right and the wrong. All the prisoners in Rumonge knew it. An old Tutsi proverb served as their motto:
Uwakiz'ubusore aba agize Imana. Give thanks to God if you live long enough to grow old.
From Chedial Engulu, no thanks would be forthcoming.

"Have you ever been in a helicopter before?" shouted the assistant minister over the roar of the whirling blades.
"No," said Evan. Nor did he ever want to again. His stomach lurched as the helicopter flew over the frothy waters of Lake Tanganyika. Somewhere on the lake the President and his family were enjoying a second day of respite from the exigencies of politics. That vacation was about to end.
The helicopter pilot tapped the assistant minister on the back. The presidential yacht lay stationary in the water below, small waves lapping at its clean white sides. The Burundian flag was barely visible. As the helicopter tilted forward, Evan once again felt queasy. The source this time was not airsickness, but the realization that everything depended on what the man on that toylike boat decided, and whether his decision came in time.
It was 2:37. Twenty-three minutes left.

Bunkeya had kept his promise. He had spoken to Dalam on the hostages' behalf, and now the FPL leader wanted to talk to Abbie in person. As soon as she saw Dalam's face, Abbie knew that Bunkeya's words had achieved nothing. The FPL leader was immovable. Too tired to kowtow before him any longer, Abbie put the question to him bluntly.
"Do you plan on carrying out your threat?"
"I hope it doesn't come to that," he said, almost apologetically.
"That isn't an answer."
"Perhaps I have a better one. Do you know why the crocodile is the FPL's symbol, mademoiselle? Because it's

native to Zaire. It will always be here, part of the land, indestructible. And yet the crocodile has an unusual relationship with a small bird that eats the parasites living off it. Often, the bird settles near the crocodile's jaws. Occasionally the crocodile bites down and the bird is killed. The crocodile did not want to kill the bird—you see, the bird was doing him a service—but nevertheless, the bird is killed."

Dalam folded his hands on the table. He had long, delicate fingers, perfect for a piano keyboard.

"Is that an answer?" he asked, and then he smiled.

A big crocodile grin.

Engulu paced the perimeter of his cell. Until now he never imagined he would be sorry to leave its cramped austerity. Any minute, that's what the turnkey had told him. Any minute now.

Engulu had turned down everything they'd offered him in the way of comfort. What a barbaric custom, to comfort those about to die. They should kill him quickly and get it done with. That was how Engulu always had handled his missions, with speed. He was never cruel. But this way, drawing out the actual execution into a ritual of religious consultation and will revisions, this was cruel. They threw a man's impending death in his face and called it solace.

So he waited alone and in sepulchral silence, willing himself to maintain his dignity. It was his last self-challenge. He'd surmounted all the obstacles life had strewn in his path, and now wished to die as he had lived, his honor intact.

The guard appeared at the cell door. With him were three prison officials. "It's time," he said.

There was no dramatic half-mile walk down a patchily lighted corridor. The men accompanied Engulu to an area outside the prison where the rifle shots would not be heard by the inmates. A crowd of people had gathered, and they gawked unashamedly at Engulu. To one side six men of indeterminate age stood together in the perfect harmony of

minds committed to a single goal, his execution. Engulu had
been told that men rallied to volunteer for the squad; only the
lucky few were chosen. These six.

As they led him to one end of the yard, Engulu wondered
which of the six had the gun with the blanks. One nonlethal
rifle to appease all six consciences. It seemed an unnecessary
precaution. These men, so eager to draw blood, would probably all claim the killing shot.

Two stakes stood upright in the yard, and Engulu was
strapped to one of them. The other was not to be used today.
Its past employment was verified by a series of nicks and
stains running along the wood grain. Despite his best efforts,
Engulu was unable to control the frantic beating of his heart.
The last thing he saw before a hood covered his head was one
of the riflemen jogging in place.

Engulu had not expected the hood. The air inside became
warm and stuffy. The loose-weave material let in a diffused
light, and he imagined himself standing on the edge of a great
hole. He began to panic. He hadn't wanted this. He was
supposed to die in the sunlight. The great hole loomed. Any
minute now, and the shove would come, and would it hurt,
please, don't let it hurt, and he would fall, and any minute
now—

The President's message was relayed to the firing squad
before the men had even hoisted their arms, but by that time,
Engulu had fainted. The great hole—that vast, unknown void
—had engulfed the African in its dark underworld.

Three o'clock arrived and the radio sputtered. Word filtered
down to the men in the Iddan camp. Bunkeya walked to the
hostages' cottage and said just two words through the window:
"He's alive."

XI

Voix de la Révolution, the official government radio station of Burundi, carried the news at precisely 3:02 P.M. The announcement was of particular interest to the inhabitants of a downtown Bujumbura conference room. No ordinary room, this, but one in the bowels of the state bureaucracy, a cavern of antiseptic whiteness and chrome, now filled with American, Zairian, and Burundian officials. Ambassador Leslie Stevens had been there most of the day, as could be deduced from the pile of cigarette butts in the ashtray nearest him. The others in the American delegation, including Davenport, Fielding, and embassy officials from Zaire and Kenya, as well as two intelligence operatives from elsewhere in Central Africa, were equally frazzled.

The Burundians were huddled on the far side of the rectangular table and included the ministers or assistant ministers of Defense, Information, and Foreign Affairs, the director of the PJP (Police Judiciare des Parquets), the presidential chargé d'affaires, and the army chiefs of staff.

Zaire's delegation, smaller in size than the American or Burundian contingency, was headed by the Zairian ambassador to Burundi, J. Babia, a man with both questionable ambassadorial credentials and badly fitting dentures.

Evan sat behind the participants, still unsettled by the afternoon's events, especially the harried flight to Rumonge prison. He listened quietly as the representatives conferred. Opinions were stated, then qualified. Tempers flared and rhetoric

bounced, reverberating with eloquent double-talk. It seemed
to Evan that the diplomats were caught in a vortex, reasoning
with the specious circularity of an injured shark trying to feed
on itself.

"And so," Ambassador Stevens said, as Evan's foot fell
asleep, "I recommend that we follow the FPL's demands in-
sofar as to prepare a radio broadcast for tomorrow—which
they will monitor—and at such time broach the subject of
negotiation, explaining that we need time to arrange a transfer of prisoners and money. With their man Engulu saved
from the firing squad, they should be agreeable. Surely they
can't object."

"They can and will," said a man at the far end of the table,
standing. "You don't know the FPL."

"Monsieur—?"

"Colonel Ubalijoro," said the man, head of the Division
d'Armes Spéciales (DAS) of the Burundian army. He was not
tall, but his exquisite posture gave him the illusion of height.
His orotund voice projected to the corners of the room. "You
go in and get your hostages now, or there won't be any hostages to get later."

The officials in the room stirred uneasily, talking among
themselves.

"Colonel," said Ambassador Stevens, "it's our responsibility
here to pursue all peaceable means available to us."

"The FPL isn't likely to respond to peaceable overtures,
Ambassador. I know. I've dealt with them before."

"Not in a kidnapping," the ambassador retorted. "You
can't predict how flexible their conditions and deadlines will
be."

"Who expected the terrorists in Iran's British embassy in
April of 1980 to abide by the deadline they'd set?" countered
Ubalijoro. "No one. That is, until the first body was tossed out.
I'm not suggesting you abandon your attempts at negotiation,
just so long as you have a backup plan."

"And that plan would entail military intervention?" said
Ambassador Stevens. "No, Colonel, I think we should limit

our discussion for right now to less drastic means. I'm sure the Zairian armed forces—certainly my country's Defense Department—will solicit your expertise concerning the FPL if it is required."

"But prudence dictates that this assemblage consider other—"

"Of course, Colonel. I'm not advocating narrow-mindedness. I just don't want to splinter the discussion right now. We'll get to everything in due time. Now, I know that I, for one, could use a small break. Let things cool down. How does everyone else feel? Ten minutes?"

The assembled officials murmured approvingly, eager to dispel the tension gripping the room. All but Colonel Ubalijoro. The ambassador's curt dismissal had rubbed him the wrong way. He was noticeably piqued as he strode from the room. Evan assumed the colonel's reaction was the product of a wounded ego, or, less likely, of a genuine belief that negotiation would doom the hostages.

Either way, thought Evan, a man well worth watching.

"Come on, Evan," said Fielding, smoking a cigarette as he sat on a low white concrete wall outside the building. He flicked the ashes on top of a water sprinkler. "Don't get so wrought up. They're doing their best to figure a way to get the hostages out safely."

"It's just not moving fast enough," said Evan.

"I'm sure the FPL will respond to Ambassador Stevens's negotiation idea. They don't want to get backed into a corner any more than we do. They'll stall."

"What if they don't?"

"They will," said Fielding.

"You never met the fake Ula, Mic. He radiated determination."

"There aren't a whole lot of alternatives."

"Shit." Evan paced the small courtyard. "It's a mess in that room. Three governments, three times as much talk, three

times as much delay. Disorganization, disagreement on what
to do; disagreement on what *not* to do."

Fielding rolled the cigarette between his fingers. He was
weary of the young economic officer's complaints—as though
the burden of freeing the hostages fell on Evan's shoulders
alone. He replied in a cross tone:

"That room is positively crammed with experts on anti-
terrorism. They'll figure something out."

"But no one's listening to the experts," said Evan. "Look at
that Ubalijoro fellow. The minute he tried to talk, no one
would listen."

"That's because he's your typical military hawk. Thinks
bombs provide the solution to any problem."

"How do you know that? Do you know anything about
him?"

"No, but I don't have to. It's written all over him."

"Well, I'd like to know more about him."

"Why?" asked Fielding.

"Just curious."

"I'd forget about the colonel if I were you, Evan." Fielding
dropped the cigarette butt to the ground and stubbed it out
under his shoe. "Our ten minutes are up. Time to go back
in."

Evan followed the Englishman through the oversized doors
to the conference room. He looked to where Ubalijoro had
been sitting with the Burundian delegation.

The seat was empty.

During his years of captivity in a North Vietnamese POW
camp, a young G.I. kept his sanity by building a house in his
head. An entire house, step by step. He started by mentally
drawing the lines of the blueprint, complete with electrical
wiring and gas and water pipes. Then came the actual construction: digging the foundation, mixing the concrete, saw-
ing the wood, pounding each and every nail into each and
every board. Step by step. Cutting the glass for the windows.

Shingling the roof. Each step performed at the pace it would have taken had he used his muscles and not just his mind.

At the end of his incarceration, the house was completed. The POWs were sent home. The soldier was sane.

But no one ever convinced him that the house he built didn't exist. For that man, the structure was as real as Monticello or Windsor Castle. It existed, all right, but as a piece of real estate accessible only by a convoluted path of neurons and nerve synapses, on the steep precipice of his imagination.

Abbie Guisbourne remembered the story of the soldier, and like him, she tried to divert her thoughts from her grim surroundings. She outlined an itinerary for the four gorillas, and wrote a report, complete with punctuation, informing Brice University of Pig's birth and her concomitant plans.

Unfortunately, her choice of "work" was not as providential as that of the soldier. His house was a detachment from anxiety; her gorillas were an addendum to it. They would be missing her sorely. In the primate center of her conjuration, Abbie signed to Winston, Fran and Joey, but they did not answer.

"Stop it, Joey," signed David, tugging on the leash connected to the ape's foot.

Joey had defecated in the yard and was flinging handfuls of excrement against the trailer walls.

"Goddamn it, Joey. Knock it off."

David was at his wits' end. Joey had been difficult all day, his behavior fluctuating from one extreme to the other; he'd signed only a few words. David had tried everything to entice the gorilla into conversation, but nothing worked. Joey's malaise was insidious. Both its cause and cure resided more than 100 miles to the east, in the person of a young American woman.

Unfortunately, for the ape and the man, a panacea as elusive as Jason's Golden Fleece. And not an Argonaut in sight.

"What the hell do you suppose they're up to?" asked Evan, folding his arms on the shiny surface of the conference table.

"Damned if I know," said Fielding. "Whatever it is, they're taking their jolly time about it."

Five of the seats in the Burundian delegation were still empty. Nearly half an hour had elapsed since the other committee members regrouped.

"Look," said Fielding, "I think that's them coming now."

The oversized doors to the conference room swung open, and the missing representatives entered in single file. As they took their places, the Burundian Minister of Defense spoke.

"Gentlemen, I apologize for the delay, but my colleagues and I were engaged in speculations that I think will interest you. Like you, Ambassador Stevens"—the minister nodded in the direction of the American contingent—"the Burundian military has no desire to escalate this situation with the FPL into an armed confrontation. But it's our feeling, and an adamant one, that we should be prepared for such an eventuality."

So, thought Evan, he had not misjudged Colonel Ubalijoro. The man had spent the last half hour developing a united front.

"What we propose is this," continued the defense minister. "A small squadron from our Division d'Armes Spéciales will be sent into Zaire to scout out the position of the terrorists, without—and I repeat—without making contact. This will be no armed raid. We simply want to gather information on the location and strength of the FPL should the occasion arrive that aggressive action is called for. The expedition would be for exploratory purposes only."

The defense minister paused to give the officials around the table time to absorb his proposal.

"Isn't that risky?" asked Ambassador Stevens.

"There is a small element of risk, yes."

"How can you be sure you won't blunder upon them? You could place the hostages in even greater danger."

"We have their camp pinpointed. According to Police Captain Karuhije's information, the FPL site is an old mining camp located above Iddan, a village near the shore of Lake Tanganyika. We know from the returned hostage that they're situated in the hills, near a stream. It is our belief that it is here."

The minister drew a circle on a large map standing at one end of the table.

"From an old Belgian mining map, we know that there's an abandoned mine there. It produced tin, I believe. The FPL must have discovered it and appropriated it for their own. Its layout matches the returned student's description."

"When would you plan on launching this surveillance?" asked Ambassador Stevens.

"As soon as possible. Tomorrow."

The ambassador's face went slack.

"We need to know as much as we can about the FPL's situation," said the minister, "so that if Dalam refuses to negotiate when the next twenty-four-hour period expires, we'll have accurate information."

"This seems too hasty," said Ambassador Stevens. "We need more time to consider all possible difficulties that could arise from such an expedition."

"The DAS squad is perfectly capable of dealing with any unexpected problems. They're experts in guerrilla warfare. To prevent detection, as few as possible will go. Colonel Ubalijoro here will lead them."

Immediately the room flooded with whispered exchanges as the delegates discussed the desirability of the expedition and of Ubalijoro's designation as leader.

"Christ," said Fielding to Evan, "that's the guy who's all ready to go into the camp and blast the FPL out."

Ubalijoro sat calmly with his arms folded. Evan marveled at his restraint. As if in response to Fielding's comment, the defense minister added:

5 *Jamey Cohen*

"Of course, the entire operation will be under the control of our generals. Colonel Ubalijoro will be under their orders."

"I'm afraid," said Ambassador Stevens, "that in the end this discussion is a premature one. After all, the final say belongs to the Zairians, since the camp is located within their borders. Anything else constitutes invasion."

From his seat at the far end of the table, Colonel Ubalijoro broke his self-imposed silence. Once again, his voice filled the corners of the room:

"We have no wish to usurp Zaire's rightful jurisdiction over this matter, or pose a threat to her sovereignty. And that is why we have secured her permission first."

Ambassador Stevens turned to the Zairian ambassador. "Is this true?"

"I have just finished speaking with President Mobutu," said Ambassador Babia, rising. "Under the circumstances, with the difficulty involved in deploying our forces to that section of the country, he has accepted Burundi's gracious offer. But he stresses that the expedition be exploratory in nature. If an assault of any kind is required later, it will be undertaken by Zairian forces alone."

His words echoed hollowly in the conference room.

The truth was the Forces Armées Zairoises (FAZ) rarely handled anything alone. Western military experts used words like "incompetent" and "impotent" when describing the FAZ. Their nations continually sent trainers and equipment to Kinshasa. And troops. Lots of them. More often than it liked to admit, the Zairian army was bailed out of a sticky situation by a foreign battalion.

The most glaring example occurred in March of 1977, when 1,500 Moroccan troops were needed to repel invading Katangan insurgents. President Mobutu called it a "moral defeat" for his men, and blamed bad strategical leadership; experts blamed the corruption riddling the Zairian ranks. Because of embezzlement by high-level government and military officials, soldiers were infrequently, if ever, paid.

Embarrassed by his country's poor showing, Mobutu re-
vamped the armed forces. He purged "disloyal" elements; de-
ployed soldiers throughout the country rather than solely in
Kinshasa; merged his military and presidential staffs into one
unit; and assigned the Kamanyola division, reputed to be the
army's top-notch outfit, to the Shaba province on a permanent
basis.

It didn't help. The second Shaba invasion, in May of 1978,
generated another disastrous performance by the FAZ, suggesting that Mobutu's changes were more deleterious than
helpful. His purges, which produced no discernible reduction
in corruption, cut army strength by 25 percent. Worse, a foiled
plot against Mobutu led to the arrest of over 250 military
officers in early 1978, thus further reducing manpower. Some
officers were dismissed, some imprisoned, some executed.
Many were of field-grade quality, trained in Belgian, French,
British, and American military academies. Their departure
crippled the FAZ both professionally and morally.

As a result, the FAZ was largely ineffective against this
second wave of insurgency. A combined force of 700 French
Foreign Legionnaires and 600 Belgian paratroopers was required to dispel the invaders. Other countries helped: Egypt
and the United States lent air support, which included eighteen
C-141 jet transports; several African nations, among them
Gabon, Togo, Senegal, and Morocco, formed a security force
to patrol the volatile area. A tenuous peace returned.

Government sources high in the Kinshasa bureaucracy said
that Mobutu could not afford to suffer this kind of humiliation
again. When a small skirmish broke out on the Angolan
border in early 1981, huge numbers of troops were mobilized.
They were still there. Thus, it came as no surprise that Ambassador Babia accepted Burundi's offer to probe the FPL
camp. Zaire had no men to spare, and what information the
Burundians divined could prove crucial to the success of any
Zairian-launched rescue attempt. Nor was it surprising that
Mobutu was stern in his warning that Burundi not change the
exploratory nature of its mission. Unpublicized help was one
thing; a military attack within Zaire's borders by a foreign

country was an altogether different thing. The face of an
entire government was at stake.

"Well, I sure hope he knows what the hell he's doing," said
Evan after the meeting had ended. "If the FPL catches sight
of Ubalijoro's men, it'll be bad for Abbie. I wish they'd decided to go all the way in, or stay the hell out. Not this half-
assed approach."

"I thought you'd be pleased by the development," said
Fielding.

"You heard anything more about this Ubalijoro?" asked
Evan.

"Only what a few of the others were saying. He's shrewd.
Clever. Very ambitious, always looking out for the gold star.
He's bucking for brigadier general. That's why there was so
much dissension when the defense minister said that Ubalijoro
would be leading the squad. His reputation precedes him. He
takes risks. They've always paid off, so far." Fielding removed
a pair of sunglasses from his shirt pocket. "I'm going past the
embassy. Need a lift?"

"No, thanks," said Evan. "I'm going to stick around for a
while. I'll get a ride back with Davenport."

"Suit yourself."

Evan sat down on the concrete wall enclosing the patio and
waited. But not for Davenport.

Colonel Ubalijoro emerged from the building nearly ten
minutes later. He was alone, exactly what Evan had hoped.

"Colonel Ubalijoro?" said Evan, walking up to the Burundian. "Could I speak with you?"

Ubalijoro did not break stride. "I'm afraid I've got an awful
lot to do, Monsieur . . . ?"

"Olgilvie. Evan Olgilvie. I'm with the American embassy."

"If you want more assurances for your government that
my team won't—"

"That's not what I want to talk to you about. I'm not here representing my country."

"What's on your mind?"

"Could we sit down?"

"No, I'm afraid not. I'm in a hurry."

Evan chose his next words carefully. "I've been thinking of a way to turn your exploratory expedition into a rescue operation."

Ubalijoro stopped walking. "I'm sure you're aware of the impossibility—"

"I'm aware of a way of getting around that impossibility," said Evan, determinedly. "A way where none of the blame falls on you, and all of the credit."

"Is this some sort of trick?" said Ubalijoro, growing angry.

"Not in the least. You're the only man who can carry out my plan."

"And what might that plan be?"

"You're interested then?" asked Evan.

"It never hurts to listen," said Ubalijoro, "if you're quick about it."

"Well, as I see it," said Evan, "there are two obstacles in the way of your rescuing the hostages. One is that as a Burundian military officer you can't attack the FPL without violating Zairian territory and creating a diplomatic furor. Two, you can't go against the orders of your commanding officers."

"Those are the problems. So?"

"There's a simple way to get around them."

"Like what?"

For the first time since instigating the conversation, Evan felt a nervous twinge. He was dealing with a man he didn't know, whose ruthless cunning was well attested. The proposal he was about to present was, to put it mildly, outlandish. Regardless of the outcome of the scheme, he'd be fired by the embassy. And to cap it all off, he wasn't even sure he could ensure Abbie Guisbourne's freedom. But he'd gone this far.

"Well," he said, swallowing his trepidation, "it involves adding a few extra personnel to your squad . . ."

It was her last chance. Abbie had no choice but to approach Bunkeya. Not if she wanted to live. She waited until they were alone on the hill, and then it all came pouring out.

"—no one will know it was you who did it. Look, I don't know why I think I can trust you, but I do. I don't think you want Dalam to go ahead with his plans any more than I do."

"Even if I wanted to get you out of here," said Bunkeya, "you'd be caught. Or you'd get lost in the forest."

"Then if you can't release us, go to the police yourself. Or leave an anonymous tip. I'm going to be straight with you. I know you realized that we sent a message in that photo, but still, you let it go through to the authorities. Since you don't read sign language, I'll tell you what it said: Iddan. We spelled out the name of this place—"

"You shouldn't be telling me this."

"—so the police would know where we are. Only I don't think they're going to get to us in time. We need your help."

From behind a nearby tree, Mpinga listened intently to the ensuing conversation. His first inclination was to inform Dalam of Bunkeya's duplicity and of the imminence of a rescue attempt, but it was quickly overridden by a second, more consuming thought of self-interest. Why tell Dalam? There might be a way he, Mpinga, could use what he had overheard to his own advantage. He listened for a few more minutes, then crept quietly back to his cottage.

"The entire idea is insane," said Fielding. He accidentally knocked over his iced tea and it spilled on the ground outside Abbie's trailer. "Crazy. Have you lost your mind, Evan?"

"I'm not asking you to go along with it, Mic. Either of you." Evan glanced at David. "I just want you to listen to him. Think about it as an exercise in logic, as Ubalijoro does. Like solving a puzzle."

"A puzzle? You have lost your mind."

"You say this colonel came up with the idea?" asked David.

"Yes," lied Evan. The plan sounded more credible coming from the Burundian's mouth. "He thinks it'll work. There's only the smallest kind of risk when the hostages are led out."

"There's no such thing as a tiny risk in my book," said Fielding.

"Where's all that blue blood of yours, Mic?"

"Still in my veins, thank you. And that's just where I want to keep it."

"For God's sake, I'm not asking you to commit yourselves. Just meet with the man. For right now, treat it as a game. Something to figure out all the angles of."

"Evan, there are so many things that could go wrong," said David. "How do you know you can trust Ubalijoro? Are his superiors aware of the plan?"

"You mean the generals?" asked Evan. "No, they aren't. But it's a good plan, believe me. It'll work."

"Yeah, that's what they said about the Charge of the Light Brigade," muttered Fielding.

"Please, just meet with Ubalijoro and his men tonight. You'll get the whole plan then. Every detail. And if you don't like it, we won't go."

David and Fielding exchanged skeptical shrugs.

"All right, Evan," said Fielding, finally. "We'll go to your meeting. But I'm not promising anything."

"That's all I ask," said Evan.

Bunkeya sat cross-legged on the same spot where he'd stood the night before with Abbie Guisbourne. Antennaed insects crawled across his bare legs, and red sod, fine and powderlike, clung to his skin. Water in the nearby stream rushed easily over a fallen branch stuck between both banks. Bunkeya dislodged the branch and the current swept it downstream. It drifted out of sight.

Bunkeya pondered the journey the branch might take: winding east through overgrown forest, tumbling into Lake Tan-

ganyika, then abruptly changing direction as it entered a
westward system of tributaries leading to the Zaire River; and
from there, after a long voyage through rapids and falls, tor-
tuous bends, and unnavigable stretches, to its ultimate destination, the fathomless depths of the Atlantic Ocean.

A journey of unpredictable twists and turns—one that
spoke to Bunkeya not only of a changing river, but of a changing man.

He sat by the stream a while longer.

"Calm down," said Fielding. "Have another drink." He
lifted the open Scotch bottle and poured a shot into David's
glass.

David balanced the drink precariously on the arm of his
chair as Fielding returned the bottle to a spot between them
on the ground. Their shadows, cast across the primate center
courtyard by the late afternoon sun, resembled the elongated
figures of an El Greco.

"I can't help it," said David. "The idea of meeting with
Ubalijoro makes me nervous. You can imagine what I'll be
like if we really go through with this plan." He absentmindedly
scratched Joey's head. The gorilla sat on the dirt to the left
of David's chair.

"Look," said Fielding. "I'm not too wild about any of this
either. But Evan's right, there isn't any harm in meeting with
them."

"That sounds like you want to go along with the plan," said
David with alarm.

"Want? Yes. I'd do almost anything to get Abbie and those
students out of there. But wanting and doing are two very
separate things. I don't plan on participating in some ridicu-
lous adventure unless there's a very high chance of getting out
in one piece."

As the two men talked, Joey picked up the bottle of
Scotch and smelled it. He swished the alcohol around, and
some of it spilled onto his fingertips. The ape smelled his

fingers and licked them. Then, raising the full bottle to his lips, he chugged its contents, part of which splashed down his throat.

"I never was much of a gambler," said David. "Too much of a coward."

"You probably never thought the risk was worth the possible gain, that's all," said Fielding.

Joey rocked softly against David's chair. Neither man noticed him. He was signing to himself.

"Whereas Abbie and Chandra and the others are worth the gain," said David. "Is that what you're trying to tell me?"

"I'm not trying to steer you one way or the other. Good Lord, I haven't even made up my own mind yet. And I don't intend to—not until I've got a better understanding of this expedition than I do now. The worst mistake you'll ever make, David, is if you feel compelled to participate through guilt."

Joey, meanwhile, was swaying to unheard music. He rolled tipsily over on the ground.

"He's in a good mood," said Fielding, nodding toward the gorilla.

"It's about time. He's been in bad spirits all day long. I kept him out here hoping he'd perk up."

Fielding reached into his breast pocket and withdrew a box of cigarettes and matches. The action caught Joey's interest; he rolled over to the Englishman and unsteadily pulled himself up by the chair arm.

"This is the friendliest he's ever been to me," said Fielding, sticking a cigarette in his mouth. He struck a match.

Joey blew out the flame.

"What the devil—?" sputtered Fielding.

The gorilla hooted happily.

"Hasn't he ever seen a match before?" asked Fielding.

"Sure, lots of times," said David.

Fielding struck another match. Joey blew it out, too.

"Hey. Stop that."

Joey shook Fielding's chair. A second later the gorilla grabbed hold of one of Fielding's shoelaces and tugged.

"Goddamn it," cursed the Englishman.

As Fielding bent down to retie the lace, Joey snatched the matches from the chair and ran across the courtyard.

"Joey, give Mic back his matches," signed David.

The ape danced around the courtyard and waved the pack.

"Joey," signed David, "please."

"The hell with cordiality," grumbled Fielding. "Come here, ape."

Fielding took hold of the pack, but Joey held firm. The Englishman leaned closer to the gorilla and sniffed.

"Why," he said, "this ape is soused."

"He's what?" asked David.

"Drunk. Look at the bottle." Fielding pointed to the nearly empty Scotch bottle, which had rolled beneath David's chair.

"Holy shit," said David.

Joey wrenched the matches from Fielding's hand, and grabbed the rope swing suspended from the courtyard tree. He twirled from it with one arm outstretched. When Fielding approached, the gorilla let go of the matches and the pack sailed over Fielding's head. Joey made great loops in the air, still holding on with only one arm. With his free hand, he signed.

"What's that he's saying?" asked Fielding, dodging the flying ape.

"It looks like—"

"Airplane airplane," signed Joey, spinning on the rope.

"—airplane?" said David, uncertain he'd read the sign correctly.

"Good God," said Fielding, "the animal is deranged."

"No, no, gorillas are very imaginative," said David. "There's one in California named Koko who's even engaged in make-believe tea parties."

"How quaint," said Fielding, ducking as Joey completed another circle.

"Evan's due here at any minute," said David, beginning to panic. "We can't go off leaving Joey loose like this. You go to the meeting. I'll get him down."

"Nonsense. We can both go. I'm not going to let an inebriated ape change our plans. All we have to do is position ourselves so that one of us can grab him. You go over there."

"Airplane," signed Joey, taking a swipe at Fielding's ear.

David made a few halfhearted lunges for the swinging ape. "This isn't working," he said.

"I can see that," said Fielding. His face was filling with color. "Have you got anything better to suggest?"

David shrugged. "Maybe if you pretended you were an airport . . ."

Ubalijoro leaned back in his chair and studied the three non-Africans: a student, an economic officer, and a Briton with a penchant for questioning his every statement. Not the makings for a raid on Entebbe, certainly. And yet they were a deceptive lot. Who'd have credited the American economist with the imagination and daring to concoct a rescue scheme? Or the surprising courage to want to carry it out? If the other two possessed comparable hidden traits, the operation just might work.

"And if we don't agree to go?" asked Fielding, for what seemed to Ubalijoro the hundredth time.

"Then the mission reverts to an exploratory expedition," sighed the colonel, wishing he knew what magic words might convince Fielding, but at the same time appreciative of the Englishman's caution—a perfect counterweight to Evan's reckless determination. "You stay here. And we all take our chances that the FPL is bluffing about their twenty-four-hour ultimatums."

Fielding nodded. He sensed Ubalijoro's growing impatience with him, but ignored it, refusing to pass judgment on the plan until he was assured the Burundian was not holding back anything.

As Fielding understood it, the plan was this: The civilians—Fielding, David, and Evan—would follow the Division d'Armes Spéciales squad out of Bujumbura and over the border into Zaire, maintaining a safe distance to prevent any later speculation by authorities about a link between the two groups. Simple enough. Slightly modified travel documents would get them that far.

On a road cutting across eastern Zaire which originated in Bukavu, the two groups would rendezvous at a point below Fizi nearly parallel to the fishing village of Iddan. From there, each group would set off on foot toward the abandoned mining camp, the civilians approaching from the north, the DAS team from the east. Once the latter reached the FPL camp, a plan of attack would be devised. It would be relayed by radio to the civilians, who, now led by Ubalijoro, would position themselves within the forest cover, hidden, but close enough to receive the DAS signal.

Now the tricky part: The camp would be stormed and the hostages released. If all went successfully, retreat would take place along the old road leading out of the mining camp, assuming it was still passable. This would be faster than retracing the path made through the surrounding tropical growth. As the civilians escorted the hostages out, the DAS team would protect the rear.

"Why not use the mining road to enter the camp in the first place?" asked Fielding.

"The FPL probably uses it," said Ubalijoro. "We'd run the risk of encountering the terrorists before we even reached the camp. Our element of surprise would disappear if we were spotted by sentries posted on the road."

As he listened to the African, Fielding removed a handkerchief from his breast pocket and mopped his brow. A waft of Scotch tingled his nostrils. He recalled, with dismay, that he'd used the cloth to wipe Joey's booze-laden saliva from his arm after the scuffle to return the gorilla to his trailer. Fielding stuffed the crumpled handkerchief back in his pocket.

"Why do the civilians, as you call us, even have to enter the camp?" asked Fielding. "Couldn't we wait by the side of the main road?"

"For one thing," said Ubalijoro, "it'll be helpful to have

you near when we're rescuing the hostages. They'll recognize you and that will ensure their instant cooperation. But more importantly, the minute you set foot back in Burundi with the hostages, you're going to be besieged with questions from reporters. You'll have to have seen the camp to answer those; we won't have the opportunity to brief you on the way back.

"What's more, and this is important, the hostages must be under the impression that the story you tell the reporters is the true one—that it was all your idea to rescue Mlle. Guisbourne and her students, and that the DAS stepped in only to keep you from getting slaughtered. That is the story this operation hinges on. The hostages must believe it, otherwise, with the stress they've been under, they may inadvertently reveal the truth under questioning.

"And lastly," added Ubalijoro, "there is the matter of the distraction."

"What distraction?" asked Fielding.

"A distraction?" echoed David.

"Yes, I discussed this with M. Olgilvie earlier. I suppose he forgot to mention it to you," said Ubalijoro, fully aware that Evan scrupulously had avoided telling Fielding and David, just as he knew the American had lied to them about who had originated the rescue scheme.

"Let me refer you to the map we've developed from the released student's information." Ubalijoro indicated a sheet of paper on the table. "From what he told the police, our best chance of taking the camp comes if my men stream down the hillside behind it, emerging at a point just next to the access road. However, when my men move down that hill to attack, they'll encounter a blind spot, right about here"— Ubalijoro stabbed an area on the map with a pencil—"where they won't be able to monitor the movements of the terrorist camp."

"That's all right," said Fielding. "We civilians can relay any changes to the DAS team over the radio."

"No. For you civilians to see the movements of the FPL you might have to leave the cover of the forest. I don't want that.

Instead we need a distraction here"—he pointed to a spot in front of the camp, on the Lake Tanganyika side—"in this cleared area leading downhill to the old mine. A distraction that'll focus the terrorists' attention away from the camp and allow my men to move quickly through the blind spot."

"What has this distraction got to do with us?" asked Fielding. "Why don't you just set off a bomb down there?"

"You forget, Monsieur Fielding, that the DAS team is on this expedition ostensibly for surveillance purposes. It wouldn't be carrying bombs."

"Throw a grenade then."

"It would require a man with a throwing arm better than mine to make sure it landed where we wanted it. Besides, I don't want a violent distraction. The last thing we need is to have the FPL all jumping for their weapons. We need something nonviolent and prolonged, something that will hold their interest long enough for the DAS team to reach camp."

"Like what?"

"I'm surprised it hasn't occurred to you. M. Olgilvie suggested it the minute I told him of our problem."

"I would have told you earlier," said Evan, sheepishly, "but I thought that if you knew about it beforehand, you wouldn't have agreed to tonight's meeting."

"Knew about what?" asked Fielding.

"What's the distraction?" asked David.

"The gorillas," said Evan.

The two men turned pale.

"This must be a joke," said Fielding.

"I must admit," said Ubalijoro, "that I reacted in much the same manner when M. Olgilvie broached the subject to me, but I've had considerable time to think it over. The more I mull it over, the more feasible it becomes. And that's the main reason why you civilians must go down to the camp—to direct the gorillas."

"Feasible," said Fielding. "You call that feasible?"

"But how would we explain to the newspapers why we brought the gorillas along?" asked David. "That'll prove to them that there was collusion between us."

"No," said Ubalijoro. "You'll explain that you brought them for the same reason—as a distraction. You'll say that you knew three men couldn't possibly hope to get into a terrorist camp and free five hostages without some sort of diversion."

"In addition," said Evan, "we can tell the papers that we brought the gorillas along for their strength and frightening presence."

"Oh, Lord," said Fielding.

"You know as well as I do, Mic, that a lot of people think of gorillas as violent. Having them along will make up for the fact that there are just three of us in the eyes of the newspaper readers. And, after the raid, all the attention will be paid to us and the apes—the unbelievability of it—thus taking the limelight away from our connection with Ubalijoro's men."

"This is the stupidest idea I've ever heard," said Fielding. "Even the American public isn't that gullible."

"They'll believe it because the facts will back it up," said Ubalijoro. "The gorillas will actually be there at the camp, a perfect nonviolent, prolonged distraction. While the FPL watches them, my men move from above."

"But the gorillas are afraid of crocodiles," said David. "What if one of the terrorists is wearing the FPL emblem? Or what if one of them gets scared and tries to shoot the gorillas? Abbie will never forgive us if something happens to them."

"The distraction will take place in seconds. My men will be there before anything like that can happen. Also, you forget that the FPL is accustomed to living in a forest. Animals are curious bypassers to them. They know the true nature of the gorilla. As for the gorillas, they'll never get close enough to the FPL to see the crocodile emblems.

"So what will it be, gentlemen: In or out?"

The decision was reached some two hours later. Project Ngagi, as Evan code-named the rescue operation, was most decidedly on.

*   *   *

On the way back to the Burundi Primate Research Center, where Evan was to spend the night with David and Fielding so they could be ready for tomorrow's early start, the three men quarreled as nervous exhaustion took hold of them.

"I don't want to talk about it anymore," said Evan. "If you're going to think that I got you committed to this thing without your consent, well, that's just your problem."

"You knew the minute we agreed to go to the meeting that there was no way to back out," said Fielding. "And really, the gall of keeping the idea about the gorillas from us."

"Will you two stop arguing," said David. "I'm sick of it."

"What do you know?" said Fielding, "he can talk. I had my doubts about that during the meeting."

"What was I supposed to say?" said David. "If you thought it was all such a bad idea, why did you agree?"

"I got tired of being the lone holdout—"

"Christ," said Evan, "I need a drink. I can hardly wait to get to Abbie's Scotch."

Silence encased the car as David and Fielding arrived at the same thought. David cracked his knuckles.

"About that Scotch, Evan . . ."

XII

Evan glanced in the rearview mirror as he slowed for a chicken that was crossing the road in front of the jeep.

"What's he eating?" he asked.

"What did you say?" Fielding leaned over the front seat.

"Joey. What's that he's chewing?"

"How should I know?"

"Well, check, will you?"

"Stick my hands in that gorilla's mouth? Forget it."

An exasperated Evan pulled the jeep over to the side of the road. Fran, who was next to him on the front seat, grunted as Evan got out of the car and walked around to the passenger side. The apes were in markedly improved spirits since being informed that they were going to "see Abbie and bring her home."

"Okay, Joey," Evan signed to the gorilla in the backseat. "What's in your mouth?"

The gorilla extracted what appeared to be a strip of seat upholstery.

"Bad rotten," signed the ape, tossing away the fabric.

"Whatever it was," said Fielding, sitting to Joey's left, "he didn't much care for the taste."

"I suppose that we should be happy that he's got his appetite back," said Evan, returning to the driver's seat. While he pried Fran's hands from the steering wheel ("Drive drive Fran drive," signed the gorilla), the jeep David was driving pulled up behind them.

"Anything wrong?" asked David.

"No," yelled Evan over the rattle of the two engines. "Joey just had something in his mouth. How's Winston doing?"

As if on cue, the big gorilla began to climb out of the second jeep. David coaxed the animal back onto the seat.

"He's fine. Shouldn't we get rolling again?" asked David. "We don't want to get too far behind Ubalijoro and the DAS men."

"Relax, David. We don't want to get too close to them either. You doing okay?"

"Fine, just fine." The young man gripped the wheel tightly.

"Okay. We'll be at the border soon."

Evan shifted the car into first and steered back on to the road. David followed.

"If he was any finer," said Fielding, "that steering column would break off in his hands."

"He'll be all right," said Evan. "He's just nervous and scared." He shifted into second, adding, "Like us."

The car picked up speed as it followed the road leading out of Bujumbura. Dawn had barely broken, and the waters of Lake Tanganyika glistened in the early-morning sunshine. Cooking fires crackled beside a few of the conical huts they passed, the smoke curling in the soft breeze. The tranquility was broken by a sudden outburst from the backseat.

"Stop that!" Fielding repeated.

"What?" asked Evan. "I'm not doing anything."

"Not you," said Fielding *"Him."*

With the gleeful exuberance of an autograph hound badgering his favorite movie star, Joey had entrenched himself on Fielding's side of the car and was cuddled up against the Englishman. The expression on Fielding's face as he tried to fend off the ape was one of aristocratic indignation.

"Back," he said. "Back!"

"Tickle play," signed Joey, leaning against Fielding's arm.

"Let go of my hand, Joey, or I will be forced to resort to violent means."

Fielding extracted his hand, but Joey retained possession of his wristwatch. Fielding snatched it back.

"All right," he said, "that does it. I'm moving up front. Stop the car."

Evan pulled the jeep to the side of the road once more.

"You," Fielding said to Fran, "in the back."

Fran blinked her eyes.

"Fran," signed Evan. "Please get in the backseat."

The gorilla scrambled to the vacated spot.

"Why is she along anyway?" grumbled Fielding once the car was moving again. "Who's taking care of Hog?"

"That's Pig."

"Whatever."

"One of the students," said Evan. "I had to let Fran come. She saw us taking Winston and Joey and got terribly upset. Especially when Joey signed Abbie's name to her."

"But who's feeding the infant? I'm surprised she would abandon it like that."

"She's not abandoning Pig. It's unusual for a mother gorilla to leave her baby, yes, but most mother gorillas don't know sign language. I told her Pig would be taken care of. There are such things as baby bottles, you know."

"It's downright unnatural. We'd never dream of interfering like that with our chimps in Muwali."

"Oh, God, Mic, don't start on about those chimps of yours again."

Fielding started to balk, but held his tongue. Like Evan, he recognized their bickering for what it was: an outpouring of nervous energy. Neither had ever engaged in an expedition with so much at stake, or with so little knowledge of what awaited them. He nudged a box on the jeep's floor with his foot.

"What's this?" he asked.

"Ammunition."

"Oh," said Fielding, removing his foot from the box. "You ever shoot?"

"No," said Evan. "I understand you do."

"Only clay pigeons. On the family estate in Devon, you know. Never anything living. I abhor hunters. After all— *Will you stop that!*"

Joey had stuck a finger in Fielding's ear.

"Calm down, Mic. We're approaching the border. And you in back"—Evan signed to the rambunctious apes—"stop it."

The border gates were only fifty yards off.

"Tickle tickle," signed Joey, waving a hand perilously close to Fielding's ear.

"If I ever do break my pledge against hunting," muttered Fielding, "I want you to know, ape, you'll be the first to go."

"Shhh." Evan stopped the car, and a Burundian guard did a double-take at the sight of the gorillas. "Sit down," Evan signed to Joey.

The gorilla sat on the seat, but every once in a while he reached out a hairy arm and poked Fran.

"Hello," said Evan, with false congeniality. "My name is Evan Olgilvie. I work with the American embassy in Bujumbura. We're coming inside your country with orders to deliver these animals to the university at Kinsangani."

The guard warily eyed the gorillas, and then studied Evan's diplomatic pass and the papers Ubalijoro had provided.

"You can see we're on a most extraordinary assignment. We can't afford to be held up. These animals are quite ill."

Joey punched Fran in the stomach and she yelled and climbed on top of him, giving him a mock bite on the shoulder.

"Clearly the behavior of sick, sick animals," said Evan. "Now, this man beside me is Dr. Mic Fielding, head veterinarian for the renowned London Zoo, and that man in the car behind us is an American zoologist. I have all the visas here. This is most urgent business. I'd appreciate it if you could pass us through quickly."

"Yes, monsieur," said the guard. "Those gorillas don't look well at all. You know, I've never seen apes transported like this before. They must really trust you, Doctor."

"Dr. Fielding?" Evan jabbed Fielding with his elbow. "Dr. Fielding, the guard is talking to you."

"Yes," said Fielding. "We have a most unusual relationship."

"Have a safe journey."

"We will. Thank you," said Evan, depressing the accelerator. Joey waved at the guard as the jeeps rumbled by.

*   *   *

The road deteriorated as it turned south. As in Burundi, few roads in Zaire were asphalt. Of the more than 85,000 miles of roadway, most were dirt-paved; some were surfaced in gravel. Despite foreign assistance in developing the Zairian Office des Routes, the roads were poorly maintained. In the rainy season, many became impassable, miring man and beast alike in knee-high sludge.

As the two jeeps skirted the village of Uvira on the northern top of Lake Tanganyika, its passengers received disbelieving stares from the few passersby, mainly Bantu-speaking Furiiru carrying baskets of vegetables on their heads or leading an occasional cow. The gorillas, less active now, gazed appreciatively at the passing scenery.

Gradually, the number of thatched huts declined and the woodland grew more dense. The road, which had hugged the shore of the lake, began to twist and turn, no longer following the natural curve of the shoreline. Once in a while, a pocket of habitation could be seen through the forest, marked by an acre or two of shrubby land cleared by natives.

But where man was not, the forest thrived. It was an alien, overgrown splendor that swiftly engulfed the two jeeps. After several hours of travel, the road veered west, past the town of Fizi, and into the formidable hills of eastern Zaire. Evan noticed a whirr in the jeep's engine as it bore the strain of the ascent, as well as a change in the surrounding greenery. The vegetation was more lush, the air more moist. They were climbing the rift escarpment.

The Great Rift Valley is a geological depression of approximately thirty miles in width which stretches from Ethiopia to Mozambique. It marks the eastern boundary of Zaire, and encompasses Lakes Mobutu Sese Seko, Kivu, and Tanganyika. On either side of the valley rises the rift escarpment, which in Zaire melds with the Mitumba mountain range to form the Eastern Highlands region. It is the most rugged section of the country, extending from Lake Idi Amin to the southern end of the Shaba province, with widths ranging from 50 to 350 miles.

Vegetation in the area is perhaps the most diversified in all of Zaire, changing with the elevation, from lowland savannahs and woodlands, to dark evergreen riverine forests and swamps, to extensive gallery and montane forests. Because of the region's proximity to the valley's chain of lakes, parts are often covered with misty clouds, a result of moist air blown in off the lake waters.

It is a work of nature at her finest. And for the hunter and hunted alike, it can be a welcome ally or a treacherous foe.

By the time the two jeeps rendezvoused with the DAS, Evan and the others found themselves deep in a strange, flamboyant world of tropical flora. They had little time for adjustment. Ubalijoro's scouts had sighted the old mining road a short distance away. Since the mine had been abandoned years earlier, the forest should have reclaimed the road. But it was clear. This fact, along with the mine's location directly above Iddan, led Ubalijoro to believe that they'd found the FPL camp.

A chill went down Evan's spine. From the corner of his eye, he saw David swallow nervously. Even the gorillas reacted with appropriate stillness. The forest's beauty suddenly turned malevolent.

The DAS men camouflaged the jeeps as Ubalijoro explained that they were at an elevation of more than 1,400 meters, a height that defied categorization as either hill or mountain. Far below lay Lake Tanganyika and the tiny village of Iddan. If the old Belgian map was accurate, the mine was a little less than one mile due east. Evan hoped the estimate was correct because, as David previously had warned, gorillas rarely travel more than one or two miles in a day. The mile that loomed ahead, from the appearance of the surrounding environs, would not be an easy one.

"Well," said Fielding, "at least it's downhill."

"Yes," said Ubalijoro, handing Fielding a rifle. "We'll be sneaking down behind them."

"I'm glad they didn't decide to settle in the mountains," said Evan, pointing behind him, to the west.

"It's from those mountains that the lake gets its water. With any luck, we'll come across the river that the boy in the hospital mentioned and be able to follow it down. Ready?"

"I think so," said Fielding. He patted the rifle. "Is this really necessary?"

"I thought you knew how to handle a gun."

"Yes, I do, but—"

"Then it's necessary."

With Ubalijoro and one of his lieutenants joining its ranks, the civilian group began trudging through the heavy undergrowth, gradually losing sight of the DAS team, which veered off at an angle to approach the camp from the east. Short, knobby trees interrupted the brush, as did tall trees with clusters of shiny leaves. The latter were musangas. Known for their phenomenal growth rate, they reached heights of over forty feet within five years, but died by the age of twenty. Somehow they managed to exist in the impenetrable undergrowth.

"There?" signed Joey.

"No, we're not there yet," signed Evan, disturbed that the gorilla was impatient already. He handed Joey a piece of gum.

The going got steadily slower. Evan had expected that the gorillas would impede their progress, but the opposite proved true. The apes carved an easy path through the luxuriant forest, unfazed by the thickets that clawed Evan's torso and legs. He cursed the musanga trees that he'd admired just minutes ago. Only as a forest ages, its branches spreading to form a canopy, does vegetation on the forest floor die from lack of sunlight. Because of the short life span of the musangas, no canopy formed over this section of the escarpment. Sunrays streamed in, and the undergrowth spread unchecked, a rampant mass nourished by the fertile earth.

Ubalijoro kept them on course by consulting his compass.

After about ten minutes that seemed hours to Evan, they encountered a wall of interlacing lianas and thorny branches,
a lattice of vegetation.

"It's pliable," said Fielding, pushing against the tangled
vines.

"Yes," said Ubalijoro. "We should be able to get through
it. It won't be easy though."

"But how thick is it?" asked David.

"Only one way to find out," said Evan. "Climb a tree."

He chose one of the knobby trees with branches low enough
to the ground to let him get his footing. About twenty feet in
the air, he crouched in the crook of a branch and surveyed
the scene.

"It's not that bad," he called to the men below. "The undergrowth thins out into a sort of valley."

"All right," said Ubalijoro. "We'll try it. Come down."

"Okay, just a second." Evan squinted in the sunlight. Beyond the valley he saw the edge of a forest vastly different
from the one in which they were traveling. Its trees rose high
in the air, dwarfing the one holding Evan. The sight filled
Evan with dread. He sensed that somewhere among those
massive trunks and branches, which seemed capable of chal-
lenging the entrance not only of sunlight but of air itself, was
Abbie Guisbourne.

"Down, Evan," said Fielding. "Let's get on with it."

About two-thirds of the way down the tree, Evan ran into
an obstacle. He let go with his left arm in order to see what it
was. A black shiny face stared back at him.

"Jesus, Fran. You scared the daylights out of me. Move
over."

The puckish ape didn't budge.

"Okay," he signed. "Pass me by then." Evan maneuvered
himself to a thick branch and waited for her to pass him. She
followed him onto the branch and picked a leaf, which she
twirled beneath his face.

"Fran, not now. Down!"

"Evan," called David, "I don't think that branch can support both of you."

"Hug," signed Fran, bending forward.

"Fran," signed Evan, "this is hardly the time or place for this. Now move."

Evan's tone convinced Fran to climb back down the tree, and she descended gracefully. Evan followed her, certain at one point that she'd pinched him on the rear end, but David assured him it was merely a prick from an overhanging vine.

"All right," said Fielding, facing the interlaced vegetation. "Who goes first?"

"We'll take turns," said Ubalijoro, removing two scythelike tools, called pangas, from the satchel he carried. "M. Olgilvie and I will start. We'll trade off with each other in five-minute shifts."

"Why not let the gorillas go first?" said David.

"What?"

"A gorilla can burrow through that wall. They don't cut or trample vegetation like men do, but tunnel through it. Often the tunnels are as much as three feet off the ground."

"How do they do it?" asked Evan. "Don't they fall through?"

"Apparently not. It'll save a lot of time if we can just follow their path."

"How about it?" Evan asked Ubalijoro.

"All right," said the Burundian. "We'll give it a try. But if they can't do it, we go back to my way."

David led Winston over to the wall of foliage and broke through some of the vines, signaling the big gorilla to do the same. Winston pushed his way through the foliage almost effortlessly, his huge body disappearing into the undergrowth. Groaning shrubbery signaled his progress. He left a hole about two feet off the ground, as though he were suspended in air.

"After you," Fielding said to Evan with mock politeness.

Evan soon regretted being the first one to crawl after the gorilla. About two feet into the tunnel, he broke through the foliage and his knee bumped the ground. He tried to ease himself out of the dent he'd made, transferring his weight to his hands, but his arms, too, crashed through the undergrowth.

"Shit," he muttered. "How the hell does he do it?"

The journey was a painful one. Evan trailed the gorilla cautiously, breaking through every two feet or so, picking himself up, swearing, going on another two feet, falling, swearing, accruing assorted scratches and bruises during the slow progression.

The atmosphere in the tunnel was almost primeval, what Evan supposed the world resembled when it was blanketed by unruly vegetation—a world that witnessed the arrival of the first amphibians. A nettle stuck in Evan's side and he cursed, his patience growing thin.

Claustrophobia began to steal over him when, with the brilliancy of a blue electrical spark, light streamed in where Winston's bulky body had been. Evan tumbled to the ground, ripping his clothes on the bramble. Fielding spilled out next, in much better condition because of Evan's service as a human bulldozer.

"Thanks a lot for letting me go first," panted Evan, pulling strands of dried brush from his hair.

"Always a gentleman," replied Fielding, rubbing a scratch on his cheek.

They waited for the others to emerge before pressing onward. What time they'd gained by using Winston was quickly expended as they plunged into the next tract of land, a labyrinth of bamboo. Nurtured by heavy March rains, the bamboo had shot to eight feet in height. Its stalks grew close together as though shuttled by a weaver; pellucid leaves shimmered in the sunlight, bending and rolling like the crest of a wave. Where the bamboo had not grown, elephant grass flourished.

The trek was arduous. The thick stalks defied even the gorillas' strength. With Ubalijoro's pangas the men hacked their way through the bamboo, departing from a straight line of travel as they sought vulnerable spots. Dappled sunshine warmed their shoulders. Gradually, the bamboo became more passable, and they were able to plow a path with their bodies alone. As they passed through the translucent leaves, the bamboo fell back into place behind them like beaded strings over a doorway. A few deciduous trees encroached on the landscape, signaling to Evan that the group was nearing the end of what he had thought to be a valley, and was approaching the cavernous forest.

They were still in the fringes of the bamboo when David yelled. As Ubalijoro waited, Evan traced his way back to David, using the other members of the group as markers. Winston grunted as Evan passed him.

"What's the matter?" Evan asked when he reached David.

"Didn't you notice that we're missing someone?"

"Oh, God. Don't tell me Fran decided to play hide-and-go-seek?"

"No, not Fran." David pointed at the female ape, sitting just a few feet in front of him, partly hidden by elephant grass. "It's Joey. He was right in front of me, and now I can't find him."

"Swell."

"What'll we do?"

"Start calling for him," said Evan.

"But what if the FPL hears us?"

"Through that forest?" Evan gestured over his shoulder. "We're still too far away to be heard."

They spent the next few minutes calling for the gorilla. When Joey did not return, David suggested that they fan out and form a search party.

"All right," said Evan, "but not you. I want you here with Fran and Winston. Tell Ubalijoro to lead you out. Fielding will help me."

"I will, will I?" said the Englishman, appearing from behind a veil of bamboo. "Where're we going?"

"We lost Joey. You've got to help me find him."

"Damn," said Fielding. "I knew something like this would happen. Didn't I warn you against bringing these gorillas along?"

Evan ignored Fielding's comment and began wading through
the tall grass, pushing aside the leaves in a breaststroke manner. Disgruntled, Fielding handed Ubalijoro his rifle and
trailed after Evan. They'd gone no more than thirty yards
when Fielding tapped Evan on the shoulder.

"Stop a minute. Can you hear that?"

"What?" asked Evan.

"That rustle. It's coming from over there."

"Yeah. It sounds like something's pawing at the ground."

"Correct. And if gorillas are like chimps, they're partial to
little green bamboo shoots. I think we found our missing ape."

The two men walked softly. The bamboo and elephant grass
thinned out with their every step.

"There he is," whispered Fielding.

"Where?"

"Over there. That black fur behind those stalks."

"Good," said Evan. "I'll go grab him."

"Are you sure that's a good idea?"

"What do you mean?"

"It's not very intelligent to disturb any animal, let alone
a gorilla, when it's eating. It could be dangerous."

"What do you suggest we do?" asked Evan. "Hang around
here until he's had his fill?"

"Shhh," said Fielding. "Look, he's moving off again."

"Come on, we've got to keep him in sight."

Fielding and Evan hurried after the scurrying black form.
They broke through the last of the bamboo stalks into a grassy
area dotted with trees, full sunlight splashing their faces, and
came face to face with the object of their pursuit.

A leopard.

Leopards are widely distributed across Asia and Africa.
Similar in build to the jaguar, the only big cat native to the
American continent, the leopard has a yellow coat marked
with black rosettes. There is a melanistic, or darker, variety
of the cat, too. Often called a panther, it has a black coat.

The word "leopard" comes from the Greek word "leonto-pardos," or "lion pard." It was believed that the leopard was a hybrid, deriving its great strength from the lion and its agility—demonstrated by its ability to spring quickly on its prey—from the other big cats. In short, a dangerous adversary.

Most people are aware of this and react accordingly when confronted by a leopard.

"Oh, my God," said Fielding. "We're going to die."

"Don't move," warned Evan.

"Shit, why did I give my rifle to Ubalijoro while we went looking for that stupid ape?"

Had it been another situation, Evan might have reminded Fielding about his vow against killing animals. It didn't seem the right time. The leopard snarled, and the two men walked slowly backward.

"Up the tree," said Evan, indicating a gnarled tree behind them, garlands of green lichen hanging from its branches.

"I knew this expedition would turn out to be a disaster," hissed Fielding. "I never should have listened to you."

"Mic, get up the goddamn tree." Evan boosted the Englishman up with his shoulder, and scrambled up the slippery bark after him. The lichen left a slimy coat on his hands.

"Evan, you don't understand—"

"Talk later," said Evan, jabbing Fielding in the back while they groped their way toward a heavy limb. Evan sat down in the V of an offshooting branch. "Don't understand what?" he said, out of breath.

"That's a cat down there."

The leopard tentatively put its front paws on the tree trunk, its weight resting on powerful haunches.

"So?" asked Evan.

"Cats climb trees."

"Oh, Christ."

As Evan and Fielding shinned along the limb, the leopard made its final preparations to spring. The great cat rocked back and forth between ground and tree, its head bobbing, its hind legs searching for perfect footing. At the last second, it dropped back to the ground and sniffed the air.

A loud bark sounded from a few yards away. And then another, accompanied by a great thrashing. The cavalry had arrived, but in the guise of three very irate gorillas.

With the force of a runaway locomotive, Winston crashed through the bamboo stalks. Joey and Fran ran behind him. The great ape shook his head, and the rattling of his loose jaws produced a jarring sound. The leopard turned and fled. Winston stopped in his tracks and watched the leopard's retreat with pursed lips, his demeanor that of a victorious warrior.

David arrived and stood at the base of the tree while Evan and Fielding descended. "Good boy," he signed, patting Winston on the back. "Good, good boy."

"Thank God you showed up," said Evan, touching ground on rubbery legs.

"You can thank Joey," David replied. "He reappeared a couple of minutes ago and led us to you."

"Us?" asked Fielding. "Where's Ubalijoro and his man?"

"Right here, monsieur." The colonel stepped from behind a nearby tree, rifle in hand. "I was here all along."

"Well, shit, if you were there, why didn't you do something?"

"Our voices may not carry through the forest," said Ubalijoro, "but a rifle shot would. Be assured, if the leopard had not been scared off by your animals, I would have stepped in."

"It would have been nice to have known that earlier," said Fielding, relieving Ubalijoro of the extra rifle.

"It makes no difference now," said Ubalijoro. "Come. We've found the river."

As the Englishman and the two Africans ventured into the dark maw of the tall forest, Evan tentatively patted Winston's back.

"Thank you," he signed.

"He doesn't know what that means," said David, shepherding Joey and Fran toward the lofty woods. "We've never taught them the concept of 'thank you.' "

The big gorilla studied Evan's hands for a few seconds and, tossing a last glance in the direction of the leopard's exit, walked after David.

"Oh, I think he knows what it means, all right," said Evan, quietly. "He knows."

The third part of their foray was considerably easier. They entered a dense forest whose canopy towered high above the wooded floor. It was known as a gallery forest because splays of branches and leaves formed a dome over open aisles, or galleries. The dome blocked sunlight from the ground, thus inhibiting the thick undergrowth that earlier had slowed their march. They made good time, moving rapidly toward the river whose rushing sounds had betrayed its location to Ubalijoro.

As in the tunnel carved by Winston, the atmosphere in the forest was discomforting, but for a different reason. It was as if the area were shrouded by a permanent eclipse, that the moon had locked in place in front of the sun. The air was heavy with a musty odor of decay. Humidity covered them like a cloak.

David's leg cramped when he knelt to tie a shoelace, and Ubalijoro called a halt. The Burundian colonel and his lieutenant scouted the area while the others rested. Evan was glad for the respite. He hadn't fully recovered from the encounter with the leopard, and welcomed the opportunity to relax. He sank down against a stocky trunk. Fielding stood. David and the gorillas sat gratefully a few feet away.

From the canopy of the colossal forest, the group looked like aphids in a giant terrarium. Pendants of fragrant red flowers hung over their heads, one of the few spots of color in sight. From the flowers drooped an even more interesting product of the environment: fire ants. Two of the insects dropped onto Evan's neck, and made quick work of piercing his soft skin with their sharp mandibles.

Evan yelled and furiously slapped at his neck. Two more ants dropped from the tree, and he scrambled to the riverbank to pour water over the bites. The three apes watched his frenzied dance with mild curiosity. Fran copied Evan and stuck her hand in the flowing water. She dabbed her neck lightly as if the water were an exquisite and costly perfume. Evan plunged his entire upper torso into the icy stream.

"Evan, are you all right?" asked David. The young man's words were garbled to Evan's water-filled ears. "Evan?"

Evan surfaced, eyes blinking rapidly, hair plastered against his scalp. A leaf, stuck to his wet nose, dislodged when he wiped his hands across his face.

"What happened?" asked Fielding, handing Evan his handkerchief.

"Something bit me," Evan said, sitting back on his knees. "Man, my neck feels like a hundred burning needles are stuck in it."

"Ants," said Fielding, investigating the red lumps on Evan's neck. "They did quite a job."

At that moment, Ubalijoro and his lieutenant appeared through a gap in the trees.

"What's wrong?" demanded the colonel. "We heard you all the way where we were."

"Evan got bit on the neck," said David.

Ubalijoro turned down Evan's wet collar. "Fire ants," he said, disgustedly. "You almost gave away our location all because of a couple of fire-ant bites."

"Give me a break. They took me by sur—" Evan stopped. "Gave away our location? You mean you found the camp?"

"Yes, it's there, all right," said Ubalijoro's lieutenant. "A couple hundred meters down. There's a clearing in the forest and you can see it through the foliage. If you follow this stream all the way down, it leaves the forest and enters the clearing right where the camp is."

"Did you see anyone?" asked Fielding.

"No hostages," said Ubalijoro, "but quite a few FPL men.

Looks like some of them are preparing to leave camp. They've loaded a jeep. There's a guard standing outside the cottage nearest us. Must be where they're keeping the hostages."

"So what do we do now?" asked David, unconsciously cracking his knuckles.

"We cross over to the other side of this stream and get closer to the camp. I've spoken over the radio with my men, and they've secured a position twenty-five meters northeast of the camp, directly above the cottage. They're waiting for us to move down to the bottom of the clearing. Let's get going."

The group moved quickly down the riverbank in search of a shallow crossing area, speaking in whispers even though they were out of earshot of the FPL camp. They passed a clump of megaphynlum herbs, whose paperlike leaves Evan had seen folded in cones and used as cups. The earth receded sharply downhill, a sudden steepness to the rift escarpment leading to Lake Tanganyika.

"This'll do," said Ubalijoro, stopping. He cautioned Fielding, "Keep your rifle out of the water, above your head. We don't have the fancy waterproof ones like the Americans." The Burundian sloshed into the water, hands aloft.

"Okay, Joey," signed Evan, when Fielding waded into the slow current after Ubalijoro. "Follow the man."

The gorilla didn't move.

"Joey?" signed Evan. He looked at Winston and Fran, but they, too, were eyeing the water suspiciously.

"Evan, they don't like water," said David.

"What do you mean?"

"They're not going to cross."

"Deep," signed Joey.

"Deep?" said Evan. "That's not deep. That can't be more than two feet of water."

"Deep," repeated the ape.

"We've got a problem," said David.

"This is crazy," said Evan. "They don't have to go more than nine feet before they'll be out of it again."

Joey sat on the ground and chewed his lip with uncertainty.

A few yards away, Winston ran agitatedly back and forth along the riverbank, peering across the water.

"Hell," said Evan. "What's he doing?"

"I'm not sure," said David.

The big gorilla shifted his large frame from side to side, and then, with a mighty leap, propelled himself across the water. He landed in the middle of the stream, on a rock that was barely submerged.

"Did you see that?" said David.

"He must have been looking for a rock like that all this time," said Evan. "Who would have thought he could lift his weight that far?"

The gorilla raised his considerable bulk once more, and leaped to the other bank. Joey paced up and down fretfully, clearly wanting to follow the big ape, but uncertain of his ability. A reprimanding bark from Winston forced the issue, and the smaller gorilla threw himself in the direction of the submerged rock. His landing was less smooth than Winston's. He skidded on the rock, and nearly lost his balance. Water splashed his legs. A second effort sent him sprawling on the other side. That left Fran.

"Come on, Fran," signed Evan.

"Carry please," signed the ape.

"What?"

"Carry carry Fran water no please."

"Carry you? Not on your life."

Five minutes later, after all other cajoling had failed, Evan knelt down and the ape clambered onto his back piggyback style, a favorite hold of young gorillas at play. Evan walked carefully across the stream, giving great care to the placement of his feet. Luckily, the streambed was not slippery. Fran's bottom sagged at the midway point, and Evan almost fell while hoisting her farther up his back. The water swirled icily around his legs. After what seemed an eternity, they reached the opposite bank. Evan collapsed on the wet moss. Fran belched.

The group reassembled and, with Ubalijoro in the lead,

snaked down the bank in a noiseless single file. Concerned that Joey might meander off again, Evan kept a close eye on the young gorilla; thus he did not see the camp immediately. The five cottages, barely visible through the clump of trees that sheltered the travelers, were spread across the western end of the clearing. The largest cottage sat near the stream. Beyond the clearing, the forest resumed, thick and dark. To the east, Evan's left, the grassy earth dropped sharply, and over its ridge sparkled the blue rim of Lake Tanganyika. To the west, the forested hill they'd traversed blended with other like hills, all rising to a mountain range cloistered in powder-puff clouds. The old mining road leading out of the camp was obscured by one of the cottages.

As Evan and the others crouched low to the ground, a jeep loaded with four men left the camp. Evan's shoes squished as he shifted his weight from one knee to the other. His wet clothes were clammy against his skin, and a chill settled in his bones. Goosebumps ran along his arms; his teeth rattled.

"Nervous?" whispered Fielding.

"Just cold," said Evan, lying. He had not really felt the chill until he'd seen the men in the jeep. The FPL was no longer an overused abbreviation but a band of real men. He had seen them. What had begun as a wild fantasy—the rescue of Abbie Guisbourne and her students—now loomed as frightening reality.

The gorillas, tired from the long trek, lay on the ground. Joey reclined on his back with an arm thrown under his head for support. Fran was on her side, resting on a pile of leaves that she had gathered into a makeshift nest. Only Winston remained vigilant.

Evan crept toward Ubalijoro, but was momentarily side-tracked by a gaping hole in the foliage. He stopped to examine it. Branches had been snapped and broken twigs lay scattered on the ground as if a large animal had crashed through the greenery. The broken ends were still green; the destruction was recent. Footsteps were visible on the side of the foliage leading to the clearing, as well as along the riverbank. Evan presumed the track belonged to the FPL and moved closer to investigate. A sudden crescendo of splashing water redirected his thoughts.

He quickly turned. Ubalijoro's reactions were considerably faster. The Burundian's rifle was trained on Fielding even before the Englishman emerged from the stream on to the bank.

"I thought I heard something," said Fielding, embarrassed that he'd alarmed the group. "But it wasn't anything."

"You shouldn't have gone looking by yourself," said Ubalijoro, stonily. "You should have told me."

"It's no big deal."

"It could have been if it'd been one of them." Ubalijoro gestured toward the clearing. "You'd have a stump where your head used to be."

"I'm sorry."

"Sorry isn't good enough. Don't do it again."

Fielding's face flushed with anger. Evan, in hopes of preventing a blowup between the two men, stood up and blocked the path between the Englishman and the African. Ubalijoro resumed conferring with his men on the radio. Evan heard only snatches of the dialogue as he listened to Fielding gripe.

". . . the men who left in the jeep aren't coming back," crackled the radio. "They had a couple days' provisions and extra fuel . . . if we take the returned hostage's estimate that there were around two to three dozen of them . . . over the course of the last half hour we've seen five men go in and out the middle cottage . . ."

"Christ," said Fielding, "he should be glad I'm keeping my ears open. What if it *had* been one of those bastards?"

"All right," said Ubalijoro into the radio. "Tell Kalim we move immediately after the gorilla distraction. The arrangements you explained to me sound fine, but I want another group swinging out toward us in case we get in a spot . . ."

"Mic," said Evan, "he's just trying to do his job."

Ubalijoro clicked off the radio. "We'll be ready for the gorillas in a few minutes," he said, "so let's get in position.

objective was to remain alone with the FPL leader until the DAS attack commenced. The gunfire, with its clattering din, would add the final component to his plan and mask his escape.

It was nearly noon when the first shot sounded. Dalam rushed to the window of his cottage. While the FPL leader's back was turned, Mpinga withdrew his gun from the satchel he'd packed.

"We've been found," said Dalam, whirling around. "Alert Sandoa to—" He noticed the gun, and the resolve in Mpinga's eyes, and shook his head. "It won't work, you know. Without me, you'll be nothing."

"That's where you're wrong," said Mpinga, holding the gun steady. "The men are fed up with you. They'll flock to me."

"To you? You've never had what it takes, Mpinga," said Dalam, stepping forward. The exchange of gunfire outside grew brisker. "You don't have the guts or the creativity to lead. The men won't follow you. There's only one man in this camp outside of me they'd follow, and that's—"

Mpinga fired. Dalam's eyes, those mystical eyes, rolled up into his head. His body slumped to the floor, blood spreading across the front of his shirt.

Seconds later, Mpinga was out the door. The clearing was a crazy quilt of confusion as FPL men in various stages of dress fell to DAS bullets. Mpinga had shot Dalam before the FPL leader completed his sentence, yet it echoed in Mpinga's ears with the final word intact. He recognized the truth in his late leader's remark. He could not make his escape just yet.

Bunkeya was still alive.

As the DAS team streamed down the hillside, Ubalijoro and his lieutenant rushed the camp from below. It happened so quickly that Evan, who'd motioned the gorillas back to the forest only seconds before, feared that the apes might get hit in the crossfire. Without thinking it over, he left the protection of the trees to shepherd the three gorillas across the shrubby clearing.

"That bloody fool," said Fielding to David. "I'm the one who gets lectured on false heroics and he risks his life for a bunch of apes."

Crouched in the dark forest for so long, Evan was momentarily blinded by the barrage of sunlight. His claustrophobia abated, but was replaced by the greater fear of getting shot. He willed himself not to look up the incline where men were killing and being killed. Fran ran up to him.

"Back to the woods," he signed. "Quickly now."

He rounded up Joey and Winston, and exhorted them to pick up the pace. Joey fell behind.

"Joey," Evan signed, flinching at the sound of every rifle crack. "Hurry, hurry."

The gorilla's trot dropped to a slow ramble, then to a standstill. The edge of the forest, the gates of sanctuary, were ten yards away.

"Christ," said Evan. "What the hell is—"

Suddenly, Evan smelled the porridge. The wind, a northeasterly one, was blowing the smells of camp downhill. Dominant among them was a glorious scent of food. And food was, as Evan was about to learn the hard way, the ape's Achilles' heel.

"Fielding!" Evan cupped his hands over his mouth and called to the woods. "You got anything to eat on you?"

Fielding peered from the forest edge, exposing himself as much as he dared. "What?"

"Do you have any food?"

"Why?"

"Goddamn it, Mic, if you've got anything to eat on you, will you bring it out here!"

A bullet thudded into the ground near Evan's foot, and he jumped. Bodies of terrorists caught unaware by the initial DAS charge were scattered over the slope, blood oozing from their wounds, entrails spilling onto the ground. Ubalijoro and his lieutenant were on their stomachs, having thrown themselves there when the FPL who'd survived the first volley retaliated. Even as the DAS stormed the camp from above, one FPL terrorist determinedly stood his ground at the crest of the hill. It was his shot, aimed at Ubalijoro, that whizzed past Evan.

"Shit," said Fielding, ripping open a sandwich he'd packed for lunch, foie gras with thin slices of cucumber. He ran out into the clearing.

"Dangle it in front of Joey," shouted Evan.

Another bullet slammed into the ground. Fielding, sandwich in hand, ran to the ape with feet barely touching the earth, the jerky hops of a laboratory rat over an electrified grill. He feverishly waved the sandwich before Joey's nose.

"Look here," he said. "Food."

"Gimme," signed the ape.

"Okay, Mic," said Evan, running on ahead. "Start walking back to the trees. Fast."

Fielding walked rapidly backward, watching over his shoulder for obstacles in his path. A bullet pounded into a tuft of grass between him and the ape, obliterated it, and sent clumps of dirt flying around Fielding's ankles. He leaped to the side and nearly tripped over his own feet. The ape rushed after him with the hungry concentration of a greyhound chasing a mechanical rabbit.

"Just a little farther," shouted Evan. "You're almost here. That's it."

Fielding made the mistake of looking up. The rifle barrel of the lone FPL sniper on the hill crest was pointed directly at him. Fielding's feet became lead weights. His mind went blank.

In the next instant the rifleman's body jerked spasmodically; he fell to the ground and rolled down the steep incline. One of Ubalijoro's bullets had found its target. Fielding stumbled through the outlying foliage with Joey trailing after him. He dropped against the base of a tree, wheezing, the sandwich still clutched in his hand.

"Gimme sandwich gimme Joey food." The ape sat next to the winded Englishman, and tore a chunk of the crumbling sandwich from his grasp. Fielding was too dazed to protest. The ape swallowed the piece, licked his fingers, and signed: "No peanut butter jelly?"

Fielding stared uncomprehendingly at the ape.

"Damn," signed Joey, but like a gourmand offered Ofetra caviar when the Beluga has run out, he made do with the rest of the sandwich. "No peanut butter jelly," he repeated.

Mpinga's search for Bunkeya was no less difficult than Fielding's dash to the forest cover. He, too, used trees as shields and dodged ricocheting bullets, but no amount of gun-fire could deter him from completing his final act in the Iddan camp. He had covered most of the area: Only the hostages' cottage remained. Bunkeya had to be there. Mpinga readied his gun and bounded past the fallen guard to the small window in the door.

And was shocked by what he saw.

With Evan in the lead, Fielding, David, and the gorillas threaded their way uphill through the forest as per Ubalijoro's instructions. The foliage obscured their view of the camp, but a dialogue of artillery relayed the ongoing destruction. At a break in the foliage, Evan stopped and viewed the battle scene. Skirmishes dotted the landscape. At least one DAS man lay bleeding among the men of the FPL, flopping in pain like a fish out of water. Moans were audible during fractional pauses in the gunfire. Those who were beyond moaning lay in con-torted positions on the ground, mouths open, their screams preserved inside them like the tortured, frozen yells of men buried alive. The uninjured sprinted across the clearing in a jerky choreography.

Evan turned away, nauseated by what he saw. So this was what war was, a field of still, bloodied bodies lying in excrement. He continued up the riverbank until he'd drawn nearly parallel with the hostages' cottage. Once again, he positioned himself so that he could watch the combatants, no longer out of curiosity, but to await Ubalijoro's signal. The devastation struck him as unreal, as though he were watching the filming of a battle contrived for television. Or so it seemed until the terrorist directly in his line of vision exploded, blown apart by a gunshot.

For some reason, Evan had thought bullets made neat, circular holes. Round red spots. The man who fell to the ground did so in pieces, his chest and a good part of his right shoulder landing around him. He was one of those who did not moan.

A second man did have a round red spot on his chest, very neat, but his back, from which the bullet exited, was a massive, bloody hole in which a man's fist could fit. His cartilage splattered the ground. He had been hit with a blast from a different type of rifle, with a different, distinctive crack. The clearing was an international collective of weapons: Soviet AK 47s, American M16s, Japanese Armalites; Israeli, Belgian, and Chinese submachine guns. All killed with lightning speed.

In the time it took Evan's group to reach its new position, Ubalijoro's men had forced the remaining FPL members to take refuge in and behind the cottages. Gunfire became sporadic. The gorillas, closer now to the source of the noise, became agitated. Winston thumped the ground with his hands.

An explosion. Then another. The middle cottage burst into hurtling shards of wood and a great blue-gray cloud spewed overhead. Ubalijoro tossed away the grenade pin, and scrambled forward on his knees and elbows as smoke hovered in the air. He did not see the man darting around the corner of the far cottage. Evan did.

"Mic, quick," said Evan, tugging on Fielding's arm.

For a second, Fielding hesitated. Evan thought it was too late. Then the terrorist threatening Ubalijoro jackknifed, and a spurt of red gushed from his leg. Only later would Evan come to appreciate the kind of marksmanship required for that shot. Ubalijoro never knew who had saved his life, but an

FPL sniper did, and began pumping shots in Fielding's direction.

"We can't stay here," said Fielding. "We've got to move down."

"We won't be able to see Ubalijoro's signal," said Evan. "I'm going down now. Cover me."

Evan slipped out from under the cover of trees, and slid down the small incline to the cottage, digging his heels into the earth to keep from tumbling. He grabbed the doorknob but it was locked. Before he had time to glance in the window, a bullet pounded into the woodwork next to his elbow, splintering the framework. Evan dove headfirst to the ground, and nearly landed on top of the immobile body of one of the terrorists. The man was out cold. His arm dangled unnaturally from the middle of his forearm, exposing clean white bone, and he had vomited into the grass. Evan breathed through his mouth as he ransacked the body for a key. No luck.

Farther down the clearing lay another downed man. Scrambling on his stomach, Evan reached the man and hurriedly patted his clothes. His hands clasped a set of keys. As he withdrew the keys, the body moved. Evan felt a sudden stranglehold on his throat. The guard was still alive.

Evan fought furiously to pull the man's fingers from his throat, but was unable to get hold of the vulnerable little fingers. As he struggled, he lost his leverage, and the keys flew from his grasp. They shot into a narrow gap between the floor of the hostages' cottage, built on a pillar-supported foundation, and the sloping earth. Evan heard yelling, but did not understand what was being said. His thoughts, even as his larynx was in danger of being crushed, were on the occupants in the hut less than ten yards away.

David witnessed the assault, and turned to Fielding for assistance, but the Englishman was busy countering the attack by the FPL sniper. The young student was on his own. He was afraid to leave the gorillas, but saw no other course of action. To help Evan, he had to leave the woods.

And then he saw where Joey was. The gorilla had climbed a tree, and was idly sitting on one of its outermost branches. As luck would have it, he was directly over Evan and the wounded terrorist.

Without a second's delay, David picked up the heaviest rock he could find, grabbed Fran, and shoved her up the tree with it.

"Give the rock to Joey," he signed.

Fran scurried up the tree.

Evan punched the guard, but it didn't do any good. Though bleeding from the shoulder, the man had managed to roll a startled Evan onto his back and burrow his thumbs in Evan's windpipe. The pain Evan felt made the sting of the fire ants tame in comparison. He thrust his knee into the man's belly, but the kick lacked force and did little damage. As a last resort, Evan went for the man's eyes.

The next thing he knew, a large rock smashed into the ground alongside his leg.

"No, no, Joey," signed David. "Try again."

Loaded down with another rock, Fran returned to her perch next to Joey. She tapped her partially closed right fist, palm up, against her left fist, palm down.

"Rock," she signed once again, transferring the weight to the male gorilla's hands.

"Now, let it drop, Joey," signed David, hoping the gorilla's eyesight was good enough both to read his signs and to aim. "Hit the man's head. The head."

Joey dropped the rock.

"Catch," he signed, belatedly.

A pulse-thundering blackness closed in on Evan, and he dimly noted a limpness in his arms. Then, as suddenly as the attack commenced, it ended. The guard fell lifelessly on top of Evan. Evan rolled out from under him, gasping for air, and rubbed his throat as if to make sure it had not been torn off in the man's hands.

A large rock lay to one side of his attacker's body. Blood covered both it and the back of the guard's head.

"Evan," David shouted from the woods, "are you all right?"

Evan tried to answer but found that his vocal cords weren't working. Searing pain shot through his neck when he tightened his throat muscles. He waved his right arm in response.

"The keys flew under the cottage," David said.

Evan nodded and crawled back to the cottage. He ran an arm into the gap between the cottage and the ground, but was not able to reach the keys. Mindful of the continuing bursts of gunfire, he flattened himself out on his stomach and stretched his arm as far as it would go. No dice. He sat up and, with a sickening sensation in his stomach, saw a shadow waver to his left. He spun around, half expecting the explosive impact of a bullet fired at close range.

Winston grunted. The huge ape had trotted down the hill while David was instructing Joey and Fran, and was now standing by Evan's side like an enormous guardian angel. He scratched one long arm with the other, arms with a span of more than eight feet, a fact that auspiciously surfaced in Evan's memory. And with that trivia, a plan.

"Winston," Evan signed, excitedly, motioning the big ape out of the line of the dwindling gunfire. "See the keys? I need the keys. You get them. Here, like this."

Evan demonstrated to the gorilla how he should lie. When Winston tried to reach the keys, his stubby fingers fell inches short. Even the ape's prodigious arm span wasn't enough.

"Evan," called David. "Forget the keys. Have him break the door down."

"Right." Evan's voice issued out raspy and foreign-sounding. "I should have thought of that. Come here, big guy."

But Winston had other ideas. The big ape picked up a broken branch and, with a cunning dormant all these years, poked underneath the cottage. After five years of failed experiments with baseball bats and hanging bananas, Winston was finally demonstrating, in a minuscule evolution, the comprehensive use of a tool. The prize this time was infinitely more precious than a bunch of fruit: Abbie Guisbourne herself.

Evan stood perfectly still until he heard a clink. The gorilla hooked the key ring and, with astonishing patience, pulled the keys into the sunlight.

"Way to go, Winston," said Evan, taking the keys from the ape. He inserted the biggest key into the lock and swung open the door.

The room was empty.

One mile away, traveling a capricious curve cut into the earth by generations of flowing water, a scraggly group of individuals trudged through the dark gallery of trees leading downhill to Iddan. They were not outfitted properly for a tropical expedition—insects and stray branches brought welts to their bare arms and legs—nor did they carry the type of equipment required for forging through the undergrowth that gradually appeared as the canopy thinned. But they had one advantage over better-equipped explorers: desperation. And desperate people, as evidenced in times of war and natural catastrophe, are capable of superhuman feats.

Bunkeya led the way. Mpinga had erred when he thought he would find Bunkeya inside the hostages' cottage. The cottage had been empty for nearly two hours. Empty because Bunkeya, before the sun had even risen, had made up his mind to quit the FPL, and to take the hostages with him.

It hadn't been easy. At breakfast he'd had to communicate his plan to Abbie without arousing the guard's suspicion, and then devise a way to get the hostages out without being detected. Since the door to the cottage was the only exit, the escape route was limited. It all boiled down to timing. And luck.

It was ten o'clock when Abbie made her move, asking to go to the bathroom.

"All right," the guard said through the barred window. "Let me get someone to accompany you."

"Hell, I can't wait that long."

"It won't take—"

"That's all right, Gbenye," said Bunkeya, collecting the breakfast dishes from the cottage. "I can watch over the other hostages while you take Mlle. Guisbourne. They're just going back to sleep anyway."

The guard opened the door and let Abbie out. Bunkeya did not let the door close all the way. As Abbie and the guard tramped across the clearing, he scanned the campsite. It was devoid of activity. Most of the terrorists were in the middle cottage, discussing Engulu's reprieve.

"Are you ready in there?" Bunkeya whispered out the side of his mouth.

"Yes," said Juste, creeping next to Bunkeya. Chandra and Sara stood behind him.

"Remember," said Bunkeya, "you go one at a time. Just head straight for those trees and wait for us there. If anything goes wrong, you get down the river as fast as you can. Okay, who's first?"

"I am," said Juste.

"All right. You go on my signal." Bunkeya opened the door no wider than a foot, and stood to one side of it. "Go."

Juste slipped past Bunkeya and ran in a beeline for the forest, covering the fifteen yards in a few seconds. He hid himself safely behind an overlay of greenery.

"Next," said Bunkeya.

Sara pushed Chandra forward, signing last-minute instructions to the young deaf woman. Bunkeya surveyed the campsite once more, and sent the young woman hurrying up the incline. Sara moved to Bunkeya's elbow, ready to step forward, but he shoved her back.

From the middle hut, two young recruits strolled into the clearing. They smoked cigarettes. The curls of smoke rose lazily in the morning air.

"What's wrong?" asked Sara.

"There's someone in the yard," said Bunkeya, wiping sweat off his upper lip with his hand. Abbie and the guard would be returning at any moment. It was now or never. "We can't wait. Get ready," he cautioned the young woman. "Okay, go."

In her excitement, Sara paid no attention to the ground, and nearly stumbled over a large rock. The recruits blew a last string of smoke, and stamped their cigarette butts with their boots. Sara made it safely to the shelter of trees before the two men looked her way. Her hair comb, on the other hand, did not. It lay on the sloping earth, glittering in the sunlight where it had fallen just feet from the cottage, easily in view of the guard now returning with Abbie. Bunkeya closed the cottage door and gritted his teeth. Too late to do anything about it now.

Too late, at least, for him. When Abbie drew near the cottage, she shook her head rapidly back and forth, as one might do to dispel a crick in the neck. It seemed perfectly natural, as it did when she stooped to the ground, picked up the comb, and stuck it in her hair, all the while mumbling that she lost more combs that way. She straightened up and looked directly into the guard's eyes. Almost defiantly, thought Bunkeya. The guard noticed nothing. Bunkeya stepped forward.

"I'm sorry, Mademoiselle Guisbourne, you'll have to come with me. Dalam has asked to see you." To the guard he added, "Something about another picture. This could take a while. Don't expect her back soon."

The guard nodded and resumed his post. Bunkeya and Abbie walked toward Dalam's cottage, but doubled back and, when no one was looking, stole to where the others lay in wait. The reunion was a quick one. They set out immediately. At the most, they had until lunchtime before their absence was discovered. Bunkeya figured that, realistically, they could count on no more than one hour before the dearth of activity in the cottage alerted the guard to their absence.

Eleven o'clock found them at a fork in the stream, and

they opted for the right-hand branch. Juste's head wound was troubling him, and the group rested for a few minutes on the bank. Bunkeya's shirt, like those of the others, was wet with perspiration. The air was steamy and filled with wondrous sounds of unseen animal life.

As they rose to their feet, another sound joined the forest cacophony: the volley of gunfire. The five people by the stream listened intently.

"They came," said Abbie. "Someone finally came for us."

"Shouldn't we go back?" asked Sara.

"We can't," said Bunkeya.

"Don't you mean *you* can't?" asked Abbie.

"Can *you*?" demanded Bunkeya. "How do you know which side will be the victor?"

"I don't," she answered.

"Then," he replied, "you'll have to guess, won't you?"

"All that broken foliage," said Evan, "and those footprints leading to the stream. They were Abbie's."

Ubalijoro and his men had corralled the last of the FPL, and a contrapuntal quiet settled over the clearing. Fielding, David, and the gorillas joined Evan outside the empty cottage as the DAS squad carried out a methodical search of the campsite.

"You don't know that, Evan," said Fielding.

"They were fresh tracks. They couldn't have been there more than a few hours. And those broken branches, they were still green. They're the nearest part of the forest to this cottage. I tell you, somehow they escaped just before we came."

"Or were moved," said Ubalijoro, entering the conversation. He carried a captured rifle in addition to the one slung over his shoulder. "The number of FPL here is much less than Alex reported. We must have been spotted on our way here, and some of the FPL moved Mlle. Guisbourne and her students."

"But if we were spotted," said Evan, "why weren't they more prepared?" He swept his arm across the landscape of carnage.

"They were prepared," said Ubalijoro. "My men were just the superior fighters, that's all."

"Why did they let themselves be duped by our distraction if they knew we were coming?"

"There are breakfast dishes in the cottage," added David. "The leftover food's not even hard on them yet. They can't be far."

"Gentleman," said Ubalijoro, "we're not even supposed to be here in the first place. We came as a favor to you. And now on the basis of breakfast plates and footsteps on the riverbank, you want us to start a hunt through the forest?"

"We're wasting time," said Evan. "We still have a chance of finding them."

"No, Monsieur Olgilvie. I'm afraid the operation stops here. We have no idea where the hostages are now. You seem to forget that we're violating Zairian authority as it is. I took a risk with your scheme, but it didn't work. There's no point in making matters worse by traipsing around in these hills."

"But we know they're out there. We can't just leave them."

"I'm sorry. I've exceeded my authorization as it is. There's a point where even I have to pull back. The odds are too much against us."

The Burundian's argument was cut short by the shout of a DAS soldier. "Colonel Ubalijoro, come quick."

"What is it?"

"We just found Dalam. He's dead."

Ubalijoro jogged across the clearing and disappeared into the far cottage. Evan smacked his open hand against his fist.

"Evan, we did everything we could," said Fielding. "It was a good try."

"It's not enough. Mic, they're right out there. We can still reach them."

"Evan, you're not sure—"

"The footsteps were headed downstream. All I'm asking is that we follow them for a ways to see what turns up."

"We'd get lost. Besides, those gorillas can't travel much farther."

"Fielding, we've come all this way. We can't just give up now. We won't go far, I swear. David, what do you say?"

The young man ruffled the fur on Fran's neck. "I say it'll be a lot easier on the gorillas to walk a little more than to find out they won't be seeing Abbie."

Evan waited for the Englishman to respond.

"I wish I'd never left Muwali," said Fielding.

The three men and three gorillas plunged into the surrounding woods and formed a serried file by the riverbank. Their departure was not totally without witness. From his own position, farther upstream, Mpinga watched their movements with interest. Their purpose was clear: to find, in this maze of plant life, the path taken by Abbie Guisbourne.

Quite coincidentally, the same path taken by Bunkeya. Mpinga followed the strange collection of men and animals as they embarked on their search, taking care to keep out of sight.

Abbie's feet were caked with mud. She scraped the soles of her shoes against a rock, but in vain. The thick black muck did not budge. She tested the ground before her, lightly stepping on it with her right foot, and immediately sank up to her ankle in mud. Their path had become impassable. The stream had turned into a marsh.

"What now?" said Abbie.

"We go back to where the stream forked," said Bunkeya. "We chose the wrong branch."

"How do we know that the other stream won't get bogged down as well?" she asked, irritably. "I don't know, I'm beginning to think we might be better off taking our chances back at the camp. Juste's getting worse. I don't expect you to come with us. You've done enough already."

"Either way," said Bunkeya, "we've got to retrace our steps. Let's get going."

Fielding tied his handkerchief around his neck. It hung there like a sodden embodiment of their mood.

"Evan," said Mic, "don't you think we should turn back now? Ubalijoro's going to be furious."

Evan plodded on ahead. The gorillas trailed silently after him.

"Evan? I mean it, this is pointless. We don't even know if they came this way. Face it, we're off the track."

Evan stopped and rubbed the back of his sweaty neck. David sat on a nearby boulder.

"Damn," said Evan, kicking a branch out of the way. "We were so close."

"They'll show up safely somewhere. I know it," said Fielding. "We've knocked out the FPL's core. If they've still got Abbie and the others, they'll be forced to release them."

Evan stole one last glance downstream at the palisade of trees and tropical growth and, without a word, turned and began the climb back to the FPL camp.

"Come on, Winston," said David, tapping the big gorilla's back. Winston sniffed a brown sticklike object he'd plucked from the forest floor, then licked it. "Winston, I'll get you food later. Put that twig down."

The gorilla obediently placed the object on a rock illuminated by a solitary shaft of sunlight. The "twig" sparkled.

"Wait a minute," signed David, his curiosity aroused. "Winston, bring it here."

Winston retrieved the object and gave it to David. Though of a tortoiseshell hue that blended with the organic material covering the forest floor, the object was plastic. On one side, embossed in small letters, was a particularly familiar phrase: "Made in U.S.A."

"Evan," shouted David. "Look at this." He pressed Sara's comb into the older man's hand. Evan clasped the hair ornament in his fist.

"I think we just got put back on the track," he said, and headed downstream once more.

Behind the barricade of trees where Mpinga crouched, sunlight played upon his rifle casing. His damp shirt clung stubbornly to his back, and great rings of perspiration circled his armpits. Nearly an hour had passed since he'd begun following Evan's group.

When Evan resumed his downstream trek, Mpinga stepped out of his hiding place. He did not know why the American had stopped so suddenly, nor, conversely, why he started up again. A nonprofessional, this man. Mpinga questioned whether it was worth the effort to follow the men, and yet, no sooner did they round the bend than he set off after them.

For like a foxhound sprinting across a lush field of a Virginia estate, Mpinga had caught the scent. The pursuit could not end, he told himself, until Bunkeya's bloodied corpse lay at his feet.

"The gunfire stopped," said Abbie when they returned to the fork in the stream.

"Yes," said Bunkeya. "Some time ago. Have you made a decision?"

Abbie gazed in both directions of the stream, tracing the path of a single leaf carried along by the current. She squared her shoulders.

"Yes," she said. "We go with you."

Evan's group reached the fork in the stream just minutes after Bunkeya led the hostages down the left branch. Unfortunately, Evan, like Bunkeya before him, opted for the right branch. The others followed compliantly. All but one. Joey lingered behind, sniffing the air. And this time, it wasn't food that caught his interest.

*   *   *

Mpinga, too, had a choice to make at the point where the stream diverged. He could follow Evan down the right branch, and hope that Bunkeya had made the same decision. Or he could take the left branch, thereby covering both possible routes. With the latter scenario, if Bunkeya had borne left, he was Mpinga's; if he had borne right, he would fall into Evan's hands. But only temporarily.

Mpinga bore to the left.

"Joey, come back here," yelled David. "Where are you going?"

As Fielding and Evan waited impatiently a hundred yards down from where the stream split, David chased the headstrong ape.

"Joey," signed David, catching up with the gorilla. "Where are you going?"

"Abbie," signed Joey, quickly.

The ape's answer sent a chill through the young man.

"Joey," signed David, "what do you mean?"

The ape did not answer him in sign language. His excitement was answer enough.

"Mic. Evan. Come here, quick," shouted David. "I think Joey's found Abbie."

"Where?" panted Evan, running up the hill.

At that moment, Joey leaped into a nearby tree. With long arms extended, he swung hand over hand from branch to branch, propelling himself in a mode of transport called "brachiation" by anthropologists.

The travelers on the ground ran after his airborne form.

Mpinga's first reaction to sighting Bunkeya was to line up the tall African in his rifle sight. Before his finger squeezed the trigger, he rethought his course of action and dropped the rifle to his side. He had always killed anonymously. As with Dalam, here was still another man to whom Mpinga wanted his identity known. With furtive steps, he moved closer.

"—and it seems to be thinning out ahead," Bunkeya was saying. "It should be much easier going."

"Good," said Abbie. "Will we make it before night?"

"With luck we'll—" Bunkeya felt the sudden, unmistakable prod of a rifle barrel in his back.

"Drop the gun," said Mpinga. "Toss it to the ground."

Abbie and the students watched helplessly.

"Drop it," repeated Mpinga.

Bunkeya dropped the gun. Mpinga kicked it to one side.

"I thought you might have been taken," said Bunkeya, calmly, turning around.

"I had a head start. You see, I knew the rescuers were coming," said Mpinga, picking up the rifle and tucking it under his arm. "Come now, Bunkeya, you don't expect that you were the only one who noticed the careful placement of the hostages' hands in the photo? You may not like me, but do you think me stupid?"

Bunkeya's jaw went slack for a split second, just the response Mpinga had hoped to elicit.

"Of course," Mpinga continued, "I'm still puzzled why you let the picture go out like that. I'm not certain of your motives. At one point I thought you might be selling out to the government."

"Why didn't you stop the photo from going out yourself?" asked Bunkeya.

"I saw a way to turn it to my advantage. The failure of this kidnapping was not an altogether unpleasant prospect. Dalam couldn't afford another failure. I've been siphoning off men loyal to me for months now. This will convince others to follow me."

"And Dalam?"

"Unfortunately, our leader was felled by a stray bullet. He's quite dead."

"And you take over."

"Yes. As usual, Dalam took all the credit for the kidnapping idea, so in the men's eyes the disgrace is all his. I regroup with my forces and do things my way from now on. And get credit for them."

"So why aren't you with your men?" asked Bunkeya.

"I can't have my leadership undermined, and I'm afraid that as long as you're around, it will be. Do you recall my assessment of you? I advised you to get out before you were killed. A pity you didn't heed me in time."

Mpinga raised his rifle and aimed. The branches overhead shook violently. Mpinga looked up in time to see a black hairy form hurtling toward him. Joey landed on top of the African with the driving force of a battering ram, and knocked both of them to the ground. The gunshot veered off harmlessly into the woods, sending flurries of birds and small animals into frenzied flight. Abbie's eyes closed involuntarily at the sound, and when she opened them, Mpinga was writhing on the ground, a four-inch-long piece of muscle torn from his left leg.

"Joey!" cried Abbie in astonishment.

The red-topped ape bounded into Abbie's outstretched arms. Within seconds, Fran and Winston materialized in the treetops, and they, too, plunged earthward, vocalizing in loud grunts. Ten yards upstream, the rustle of leaves and snap of dry vegetation heralded the arrival of the gorillas' winded human companions.

As the two groups meshed in joyful reunion, Joey stood guard over the wounded Zairian. Mpinga made an obscene gesture at Joey, which the young gorilla, thinking it a new sign, did his best to reproduce. He flashed it back at Mpinga. The imitation was remarkably good.

In the time it took the ape to form the sign, Bunkeya slipped, unnoticed, into the green wood, and out of sight.

XIV

BUJUMBURA, Burundi (UPI)—In what could very well be the most bizarre story of the year, linguist Abbie Guisbourne and three other hostages held by terrorists near Iddan, Zaire, were rescued yesterday by a group of gorillas from the Burundi Primate Research Center. The Center, operated by Guisbourne, is an extension of Brice University.

Details are sketchy, but it is known that Mic Fielding, an anthropologist from Brice, led the attack on the terrorists, members of the Front Populaire de Libération, a group committed to the overthrow of Zairian President Mobutu Sese Seko. Accompanying Fielding were students from the Primate Center and three gorillas.

The gorillas, trained to communicate in sign language, were brought along to distract the terrorists, said Fielding.

The attack came on the heels of an investigation by a special division of the Burundian army around Iddan, a small village in eastern Zaire near Lake Tanganyika. The division was in Zaire at the request of the Mobutu government.

Fighting between the FPL and rescue forces apparently resulted in the death of one hostage, Tyler Hughes of Modesto, Calif., and several FPL terrorists, including leader Jambe Dalam. Another hostage, Alex Golding of Rye, N.Y., was released earlier.

The Front Populaire de Libération is believed to be an offshoot of the Paris-based Front National de Libération du Congo, or FNLC, led by Nathanial Mbumba, which was believed responsible for two invasions of Zaire's southern mining region, the Shaba province, in 1977 and 1978.

Guisbourne and her gorillas have returned to the Primate Research Center here in Burundi's capital, where she will continue her studies.

"Love you."

"I love you, too."

"Kiss me?"

"Sure."

He pulled her to him, and gently kissed her.

"Nice."

"Sure was. Now, will you get the hell off my lap, Fran?"

The ape in Evan's arms tugged playfully on his ear.

"She can't go yet," said Abbie from the corner of the trailer. "I want her to take Pig with her." She held up the newly diapered gorilla. "There, it's been a while but I haven't lost my touch."

Joey walked in the open door.

"What is this?" asked Evan. "Visitor's day?"

The gorilla wrapped himself around Abbie's legs. She bent down and cuddled his head.

"You know, they've been this way ever since I got back."

The screen door quivered, and Winston appeared in the doorway.

"Oh, good," said Evan, sitting on the edge of the bed, "we've got enough to get a good poker game going."

The gorilla studied the others in the room, bestowed an adoring look on Abbie, and threw himself contentedly at the foot of the bed, legs sticking straight out.

"Evan, I'll be right back," said Abbie. "I'm going to put Fran in her trailer."

She stuck out her hand and mussed Evan's hair as she walked by. Fran followed suit, but her fingers twined around a lock of hair, which she ripped out as she passed.

"Damn it," cursed Evan, massaging his scalp.

Joey followed the three females out the door, leaving Winston and Evan as the sole occupants of the room. The big ape raised himself off the ground and patted the bed. Convinced of its sturdiness, he climbed on top of it. The bed tilted under his weight like a sinking ship. He maneuvered himself close to Evan until the two were sitting side by side, Evan listing uncontrollably toward the gorilla.

Hesitantly, Winston threw his left arm around Evan's shoulders. Evan sat in nervous silence for a moment, wondering what had provoked this sudden burst of affection. Hell, he decided, if you can't understand them, join them. He threw an arm around the gorilla's torso. Winston grunted.

"Well, Winnie, my boy, we males got to stick together."

"You fine animal gorilla," signed Winston.

"That's man," Evan corrected.

"Gorilla," signed Winston, squeezing Evan's shoulder uncomfortably tight.

"What the hell. Gorilla, man. Not much difference." Evan softly patted Winston's formidable backside. "Hey, did you hear the one about the eight-hundred-pound man who goes into this bamboo patch? There are these two gorillas sitting there, see, and one gorilla says to the other, he says, 'Where does an eight-hundred-pound man sit?' And the other gorilla, he says, 'Anywhere he wants.' "

Winston beat his chest.